HER BEAUTIFUL BASTARD

SCANDALOUS BALLROOM ENCOUNTERS BOOK 6

VICTORIA VALE

PLAYLIST

Her Beautiful Bastard Playlist
Click to listen on Spotify
Goddess by Stanaj
Green Aphrodisiac by Corinne Bailey Rae
Love and Affection by Daley
Alone Together by Daley feat. Marsha Ambrosius
Hallucinations by dvsn
Until the Pain is Gone by Daley feat. Jill Scott
Hold on to Me by Kyle Dion
Suffer(Vince Staples & AndreaLo Remix) by Charlie Puth
Jealous by Labrinth
Fall Again by Glenn Lewis
Runnin' (Lose it All) by Naughty Boy feat. Beyonce
Can I Be Him by James Arthur
Down by Josiah Bell
Garden by Emeli Sande
Temple by Daley
Orion's Belt by Sabrina Claudio
Belong to You (Remix) by Sabrina Claudio feat. 6LACK

Indulge by JONES
Bloodstream by Stateless
Edge of Desire by John Mayer
Un-thinkable (I'm Ready) by Alicia Keys
Fire We Make by Alicia Keys feat. Maxwell
Burn Slow by Ro James
Easily by Bruno Major
I Just Died by Amerie
Best Love by Yuna
Bliss by alayna
Never Gonna Leave This Bed by Maroon 5
Rewrite the Stars by Zac Efron and Zendaya
If Our Love Is Wrong by Calum Scott
No Air by Jordin Sparks and Chris Brown
No One Else by Amel Larrieux
Nirvana by Sam Smith
Never Let Me Go by Florence + The Machine

LONDON, 1819

*L*ydia Darling pressed herself against the trunk of the tree she'd just climbed and closed her eyes. Perhaps, if she concentrated long enough and hard enough, she might disappear. Once she did, she could float away on the light spring breeze, carried back to Oakmoor, where she belonged. This trip to London and allowing her sister-in-law to sponsor her coming out had been a mistake. She did not belong here, among these people who spent all their time whispering over the slightest *faux pas* committed by their peers. What had the gentleman who'd shown up to Almack's wearing trousers instead of knee breeches been *thinking*? Didn't that married mother of two know she was far too long in the tooth to wear a *white* evening gown? And, oh, the unspeakably bad manners of those raised in the country . . .

She had stood on the other end of such scrutiny on several occasions since being brought out and had now become known as the girl who was 'not quite' like the other debutantes. She smiled too frequently and too freely; her laugh was not demure enough; her posture and carriage not as elegant as it could be. Her hair was blonde, but not quite that desirable shade like moonlight … no, it had too much a hint of brown, making it rather dull. Her figure was too rounded in places, keeping her from being a delicate porcelain doll like the girl who had been named this year's Incomparable.

Oh, no one seemed to dislike her, so much as they seemed to sense she was not one of them. Having lived her entire life in Norfolk, far removed from the bustle and glamor of London's West End, she had nothing in common with the women here. She proved too tone-deaf to play a proper pianoforte composition, found watercolors to be sleep-inducing, and while she enjoyed dancing could only claim to be adequate at best. She much preferred the freedom of the outdoors, of a long ride across sprawling green lands, target practice with a rifle, or running until her legs grew tired and her heart pounded so hard, she thought it might beat right out of her chest.

Thus far, her egregious breaches in propriety had included spilling lemonade on her hostess' gown at a luncheon, referring to an untitled woman as 'my lady', and a lady as 'Mrs.', tripping over the voluminous skirts of her court dress while making her curtsy, forgetting to wear a fichu with her day gown and exposing too much bosom, and laughing too loudly at a musicale. In short, she'd called far too much attention to herself … the *wrong* sort of attention. The London *ton* had inspected her and found her to be an oddity, wonderful to have about for entertainment, but not good enough for their sons or brothers to wed.

Not that the men avoided her. Actually, she'd heard it said that she was one of the most popular women to ask for a dance. A chap could enjoy her company without wondering whether she might angle for a marriage proposal. That she appreciated the same pursuits as many males was an added bonus—for them. They all relished talking to her about horses, and guns, and the like, but did not seem interested in marrying a woman who indulged in such things.

Lydia laughed aloud at herself, unable to believe her past foolishness. Just this time last year, she had been so excited to come to London. She'd dreamed of the glamor and beauty of it all, imagined herself dancing in the arms of dashing men, charming them with her wit and wholesome beauty. Perhaps not a diamond of the first water, she knew she was not without her own sort of allure. The young men of Norfolk had been sniffing about her skirts since she'd grown old enough to draw their attention. Perhaps she ought to go home and consider marrying one of them. She had thought she wanted a sophisticated man, one with a title and some sort of standing in society. However, after rubbing elbows with these sorts, she longed for the honesty of a country boy's smile, the warmth of a hand taking hers without the covering of gloves.

Opening her eyes, she heaved a sigh, turning her head to gaze over the low wall surrounding the townhome she'd escaped for a respite from the crush. The sun had set hours ago, but a cloudless sky and full moon illuminated the garden below her. The massive tree grew outside the wall, its large branches hanging over into the garden. She'd used the uneven bricks to climb and perch amongst the tree's limbs where she could see the night sky, and the narrow lanes between the houses.he'd used the uneven brick of the wall to climb and perch where she could see the night sky, as well as narrow lanes between homes.

Things were built so close together here; the buildings, the roads. How could people breathe? How did they live on top of each other?

A deep, masculine voice cut through her thoughts, drawing her gaze downward. The shadowy figure of a man moved along the lane below her. He was alone and seemed to be muttering unintelligibly to himself as he leaned against the wall below her, fumbling in the pocket of his coat. She supposed he must be a guest at the same ball she attended—his black evening kit offset by the white linen of his shirt and cravat.

A flare of orange sparked in his hands, a match being struck. He brought it close to his face, lighting what appeared to be a cheroot. She swiveled her body so that her legs hung over the limb on his side of the wall. Gripping the rough bark tight in her gloved hands, she leaned forward to get a better look at him.

Odd, this man lingering in an alley when he obviously belonged inside. There were men indulging in cigars and cards in a chamber off the ballroom, so it wasn't as if he needed to come out here to enjoy his cheroot. Perhaps he'd simply wished to cool off; the crush inside made the ballroom quite warm. Or, like her, he wished for a respite from it all—the people, the staring, the gossip, the censure.

Hair as black as the night sat touseled about his head in unruly disarray. A dark hue, she could see; perhaps black. He appeared quite sinister in all black, the shadows clinging to him as if he belonged here. Resting her chin in hand, she let one of her feet swing back and forth as her imagination ran away with her. Maybe he'd come out here to engage in a duel, and simply awaited his opponent. Or, he'd sneaked out for an amorous liaison with a lover. Such things were done in gardens at these events, even in Norfolk.

What if he wasn't a guest at all, but a highwayman, or a cutpurse in disguise in order to blend in? She could imagine him pilfering the snuffboxes and banknotes of London lords, coming and going as he pleased in the dark of night, his black evening clothes helping him melt away into the shadows.

She snorted, rolling her eyes and shaking her head at herself. Her brother, Michael, would tease her for being so dramatic and coming up with such a nonsensical story in her head.

A gasp caught in her throat when the man went still, then stiffened, turning left and right as if searching the darkness. Had he heard her?

She moved to throw her legs back over the tree limb and climb down her side of the wall. But she'd only managed to get one leg over when the slipper on her opposite foot fell loose. On its way down, it struck the man's shoulder, glancing off before hitting the ground with a soft thud.

"What the devil?" he muttered, crouching to pick up her slipper.

It only seemed to take him a moment to realize where the

offending shoe had come from. Straightening, he craned his neck, looking directly up and into her eyes. She gasped, audibly this time, though she could not seem to move. One would think she'd scramble down the wall and run back inside as fast as her legs could carry her, praying no one noticed her missing slipper. But, no. She could only sit there, straddling the tree limb, the skirts of her gown and petticoat riding up to her knees, one stockinged foot exposed for him to see.

"Well, well," he drawled, edging closer to the wall, his white teeth flashing in the dark when he smiled. "What have we here? A fallen angel, perhaps?"

A nervous sound emitted from her—a choked giggled. Oh, God. Now she was truly making a cake of herself. She *never* giggled.

"Just a mortified girl, I'm afraid," she replied. "I beg your pardon. My shoe slipped, and there wasn't time to warn you."

He shrugged one shoulder, holding up her lightweight slipper. "It is nothing to trouble yourself over. What sort of man would I be if I could not recover from falling footwear?"

Despite herself, her lips curved into a little smirk. She did like a man with a sense of humor. Her smile fled when he slid the shoe into his inner breast pocket, before taking hold of one of the uneven bricks, hoisting himself upward.

"What are you doing?" she asked, her voice raising an octave as panic flared in her chest.

He paused halfway up the wall, looking at her as if she'd gone mad.

"Why, returning your slipper, of course. I cannot allow you to go back in there without it. Whatever would the matrons say?"

Nothing that they don't already think about the uncultured country girl from Norfolk.

"Oh, do be careful!" she called out, as he continued up toward her.

Though, it would seem she'd had no need to warn him. He moved up the wall faster than she had, and with far more grace. One would think he did this sort of thing often.

In what seemed like no time at all, he was standing atop the wall, his height bringing his head nearly level with hers. Her mouth went dry when their gazes met, unprepared for the impact of his presence up close. His hair, as it turned out, was sable, not black. The moonlight made it gleam like polished wood, the strands now revealing themselves to be more artful in their disarray than careless, one perfect strand falling over his high forehead.

Her eyes widened as she studied him, her gaze tracing the arches of his eyebrows, the bridge of his nose, and lower, lower, to an arresting mouth. It was full and pouting, combining with his dark hair and eyebrows to make him appear like the hero of a romantic novel.

She had never seen a more perfect specimen of manhood in her entire life.

He was watching her back just as closely, those dark eyes of his traveling over her face, and then lower, over the slope of her neck and swell of her bosom displayed by the neckline of her ballgown.

"Just as I suspected," he murmured.

Even at a near whisper, the depth and resonance of his voice seemed to ripple through her, its vibrations shaking her to the core. Her skin broke out in gooseflesh, and she shivered, despite the warmth of the evening.

"What is as you suspected?" she asked, suddenly breathless.

He grinned, and those perfect, white teeth seemed to light up the night, proving even more beautiful up close.

"You," he replied. "I told myself before climbing this wall that you were just as lovely up close as you appeared to be from the ground. As I suspected, I was right."

She laughed, the sound too high, too shrill. It covered her anxiety over having a man who looked like this one scaling walls and spouting such nonsense at her.

That only made his smile widen as he braced his arms on the tree limb she straddled.

"Now that I've risked my neck to return this to you, I must know why you are sitting in a tree, instead of being partnered on the dance floor inside," he said while reaching into his coat.

He came out with her slipper, and for a long moment, she could not form words. Her stare was focused on his large hands, one of them cradling her shoe, the other reaching out for her foot. He wore no gloves. She stiffened when he touched her, his naked fingers making contact with her stockinged ankle. He had long, graceful fingers with thick veins running along the backs and disappearing into his shirt cuffs.

He took his time replacing her shoe, easing the slipper over her toes, his fingers squeezing her ankle and skimming upward an inch by the time the back had come over her heel. A shudder rocked her at even so slight a touch, and she mourned it when he'd dropped his hands, going back to lean against the tree limb.

Remembering that he'd asked her a question, she cleared her throat. "I wished for a bit of fresh air."

He inclined his head at her, his probing stare far too astute. "When one wishes to take air, one simply steps out onto the terrace. Climbing a tree in a darkened corner of the garden indicates a desire to escape."

This man was impertinent. More than that, he was too familiar. He had no business saying such things to her and probing into her reasons for being out here. However, she remained well aware of how she appeared—skirts raised, sitting in a tree like some ill-bred strumpet. What he must think of her.

Yet, as she met his gaze once more, she saw nothing more than genuine curiosity in the depths. She'd met so many disingenuous people since coming to London that she hardly knew what to do when confronted with someone who presented themselves without pretense.

However, instead of answering him, she became seized with the desire to ask a question of her own. "Would you happen to be escaping also?"

Raising one eyebrow at her, he pursed those perfect lips. She'd always envied people who could do that—lift only one of their eyebrows. And, of course, he looked downright gorgeous with such an expression on his face.

"The lady evades my question," he teased.

Folding her arms over her chest, she shrugged. "It is only that you are also quite far from the terrace, where it would have been perfectly acceptable for you to indulge in your cheroot. Or, you might have enjoyed it in the company of the other men in the card room. Yet, you are here, far removed just like me."

His expression became neutral once more as he tipped his head up, studying the moonlit sky. "You've found me out, angel. I am, in fact, escaping. Or rather, hiding. Would you like to know why?"

She nodded quickly, leaning forward a bit in anticipation of his answer. Why she should care was beyond her. She only knew that she wanted him to say that he was like her—that he was out here for the same reasons she'd left the ballroom and climbed this tree.

"It is simple, really," he said, his gaze still turned upward. "I do not belong in there, with those people."

Since he wasn't looking at her, she allowed herself to study him more thoroughly. He fit his evening clothes quite well, his broad shoulders and chest tapering into a narrow waist and slim hips, his legs comprised of long, lean cords of muscle. Well-formed, and she'd be willing to bet he wasn't wearing an ounce of padding or shaping underneath to achieve the effect. He was handsome, seemed charming and witty, and looked like any other young bachelor of the *ton.*

"You certainly appear to fit in," she managed, hoping it would coax him to reveal more.

He chuckled, the short little sound rough with sarcasm. "I am not certain whether to take that as a compliment or an insult. Yes, angel … I look like the well-bred, blue-blooded men in there, but there is one essential difference."

She leaned even closer, so close now that she could smell his shaving soap and whatever balm had been applied to his hair. Her eyelids drooped, and the urge to bury her face in his neck and take a deep inhale overwhelmed her.

"I am a bastard," he declared, his voice remaining even and flat, as if they were discussing the weather.

Her eyes went wide, for she had never known a person to openly admit such a thing. Sure, baseborn children were common, even in Norfolk, but such things were not generally discussed. No person of dubious parentage that she'd ever known would ever openly declare themselves as such.

"My father was a viscount," he went on. "He ensured I was raised alongside those titled snobs in there, that I was taught to emulate them, and move about society like them. But, there is not a person in that room who would hesitate to put me in my place on a whim. So, little angel, that is why I do not belong in that ballroom."

Inclining her head, she wrinkled her brow, trying to untangle the mystery of this man who spoke so freely to a stranger about the circumstances of his birth. He did not know her, yet seemed surprisingly content to stand here on the edge of a wall, speaking to her of how he did not belong.

"Why would they invite you, then?" she asked. "Why would you come?"

He seemed to mull that over for a moment before responding. "I suppose they invite me because I make a titillating guest. They can boast having me in their midst, scandalizing their staunch neighbors with my sullying presence. It might also have something to do with the fact that I'm wealthier than half the men in that room, despite having no title. As for why I come ... I suppose it amuses me to do so. Half the room avoids me, while the other half engages me for the simple aim of being able to say they've done so."

She shook her head, bemused. "I will never understand this world."

His head turned suddenly, his gaze pinning her to the spot. "Then you are a bastard, just like me."

She flinched, rearing back as if he'd struck her. "I-I most certainly am not! My parents were wed and bore two other children before me."

Uncertain why his assumption should upset her so, she turned her head to break the connection of their locked gazes. Aside from being impertinent, this man was quite shameless.

As if to further prove this, he reached out and touched her face.

His fingers came against her jaw, gentle but firm, his thumb pressing her chin.

Her lips parted, a little huff of surprise emitting from between them as she was forced to look at him again. He did not smile this time, only studied her with a solemn expression.

"I did not mean that you are baseborn," he amended. "I simply meant that you clearly aren't one of them. You are too … something."

She frowned, uncertain whether he was insulting her or complimenting her. "Too *something*?"

He nodded, still holding her face, his gaze moving as if he catalogued the various details of her aspect. "Too warm. Too loud and sunny and witty. Too real."

Her breath hitched, and her belly quivered as she realized that he had just whispered everything that was supposedly wrong with her in the eyes of the *ton* while making them sound like the attributes of a goddess.

"So, you see," he continued, his thumbnail skimming the edge of her lower lip for a brief moment before he dropped his hand. "In that sense, you are like me. An outsider. We are all bastards in their eyes."

It was true, she realized. Just like him, she seemed to have become a *thing* for them to amuse themselves with. Good enough to garner invitations due to her family connection to a marquis, but too green, too much the wide-eyed country girl to fit in with their porcelain dolls.

"You should go back inside," he said abruptly.

Despite his warning, he was pulling himself up onto the limb to sit across from her, mimicking her posture and straddling the thick branch, legs dangling.

"Why?" she asked, still too shocked by him to do anything other than sit there.

He was too … *something*. Just as he'd accused her of being. Too handsome, too charming, too utterly irreverent and incorrigible.

She liked it very much.

"Because to be found in the company of a man like me could ruin you," he told her.

She scoffed. "I hardly care about anything like that. Besides, it isn't as if any of the men in that room will ever offer for me."

He shifted closer to her—so close now their knees touched. He was hot beneath his clothes, the warmth of his skin searing her through the layers of his knee breeches and her stockings. She was more aware than ever of her bared legs, her skirts revealing more of her than she'd ever displayed in front of a man who was not one of her brothers.

"If it is any consolation, the loss is entirely theirs," he remarked.

Not for the first time, she found herself taken aback by his words. "You are exceedingly bold."

"Yes. A man in my position can afford to be."

She wondered if he meant because of his wealth, or because being a bastard without a title meant he was freer than most to say and do what he pleased.

"Is it not better for people to speak honestly and without artifice?" he challenged. "For instance, I should make you aware that I have every intention of kissing you, angel."

Instead of the maidenly outrage that should overtake her at such a bold claim, Lydia experienced a heady rush of blood straight to her belly. Heat suffused her face and neck as her gaze dropped to his mouth. She'd been kissed a handful of times, and not once had any of the young men announced their intentions before the fact. She hardly knew what to make of it.

"Is that so?" she managed, trying to force nonchalance into her voice.

"Very much so," he confirmed. "In fact, I require it as payment for rescuing your shoe."

"You believe returning my own property to me merits a kiss?" she asked, now more amused by his brazenness than shocked.

Turning his head, he glanced over the wall, down at the spot he'd just been standing in. "It's quite a ways down, is it not? The velocity of your shoe dropping might have done me serious bodily harm. I could have fallen during my climb and broken my neck. Going back down will prove more of a challenge than ascending. So, yes, angel, I do believe my heroism to be deserving of a kiss."

Raising her chin, she extended one of her hands to him and smirked. It was ridiculous to carry on this way, especially since this was just the sort of situation Michael and her sister-in-law had warned her against before the start of the Season. But, she could not seem to help it. His teasing made her want to tease him back, to laugh with him and forget about having to eventually return inside.

"Very well, then, sir," she quipped. "Please, accept the offer of my hand for your kiss. I give it freely as my thanks for your daring feat of courage."

For a moment, she thought he meant to refuse her hand, but then, he was grasping her wrist, lowering his eyes to her satin glove. She sat and watched, motionless, as he began tugging it loose at her fingers, then pulled it away completely. The material slid over her skin like a caress, making her shudder in response. He laid the garment over his thigh, then pulled her arm taut, palm up.

His dark head dipped, his grip on her light enough that she could escape, but firm enough that she understood he did not wish to let go. He would if she demanded it—she understood that without having to be told. For all the times she'd been warned to guard her virtue, Lydia somehow knew this man would not be a serious threat to it.

Warm breath whispered against the inside of her wrist, making her pulse race in a wild gallop. She wondered if he could feel it as his lips brushed the place where the delicate blue veins pumped her lifeblood. He didn't quite kiss her, seeming content to skim his lips over that sensitive spot, inhaling slow and deep as he breathed in her scent. He exhaled in a rush, his lips moving over the heel of her hand, then pressing against the center of her palm.

She was trembling now, equal parts terror and anticipation making it difficult to draw breath. No one had ever kissed her this way, making her feel as if she'd been set aflame … and his mouth had barely touched her.

"Ah, angel," he whispered, turning her hand over to kiss the back, his lips searching out her knuckles, moving over her fingers. "I'd climb this wall a hundred times more for the same honor."

She opened her mouth to reply, but her words broke off on a gasp when he opened his mouth, enveloping her little finger into the depths. His lips closed around the digit, his tongue laving it with excruciating slowness as he sucked his way up from the knuckle to the tip. A little sound emitted from the back of her throat in response, and it seemed to trigger something in him, some answering reaction. His eyes snapped up to meet hers, and he swiftly released her hand before reaching out to wrap an arm around her.

His hand spanned the small of her back, urging her closer—so close, she was nearly in his lap, straddling *him* instead of the tree limb. If she'd thought his kiss upon her wrist had awakened her, it was child's play compared to this. The sensation of sitting astride his strong thighs, his body hard yet soft and warm beneath her, the muscles of his chest humming against her palms with barely contained power … it was too much, yet not enough all at once.

Her sister-in-law, Amelia, had taken her out of earshot of her mother and explained to her quite a few things about male and female relations using frank and direct speech. The mysteries of what went on in the bedchamber were no longer unknown to her, so she fully understood what the hardened flesh pressing against her mons through the fabric of her gown meant on behalf of her mysterious gentleman. Yet, even knowing how close she hovered on the brink of ruin could not stop this. Every instinct within Lydia urged her to stay, not run.

"You should tell me to stop now," he whispered, his voice hoarse and thick, all the playfulness it had previously held gone. "You should slap my face, and push me away, and run, angel. It is your final chance."

His eyes had gone heavy-lidded, and the expanse of his chest heaved beneath her hands, as if he struggled to breathe just as she did. Her gaze fixated on his mouth, which had made her feel so good with just a brush against her wrist and a kiss on the palm. How much more could he electrify her by putting those lips on hers, tasting her, letting her taste him?

There was only one way she could be sure.

"Don't," she whispered, sinking more fully against him, her body melting into his. "Please, don't stop."

He issued a rough groan, both his hands clutching her back as he swooped in to comply. His lips found hers, urgent, but gentle, capturing and releasing her mouth with short, sweet, nibbling kisses that left her feeling drugged. Her head spun, the sensation of dizziness forcing her to grip the lapels of his coat. She was panting against his mouth, her ardor a match for his as they learned each other, turning their heads to attempt different angles, nibbling, tasting, searching.

Then, his arms went tight around her at the exact moment he slipped his tongue into her mouth. She moaned at the first real taste of him, in reaction to the feel of his velvety tongue tickling hers. The sound was completely wanton and unlike her, but he seemed to like it, matching it with an answering growl. Her back arched, and the world overhead tilted and whirled.

Dear God, she was *swooning*.

It was ridiculous, the entire thing. She'd found herself in a scene straight out of a dream, in which moonlight was the only light, and a man with perfect lips knew just how to kiss her, just what to say to make her melt. She should put a stop to this, push him away and climb down the tree, rush back into the house.

But, God, he tasted wonderful, like tobacco and brandy, and his body fit so perfectly against hers, and this all felt so right.

"Angel," he murmured between kisses, his breath tickling her cheek. "You will climb down this tree right this instant and put me behind you. Run, go back inside."

Even as he commanded her to leave, he was still kissing her—her cheek, her jaw, her chin, her throat. She tipped her head back to let him taste more of her, drunk from the heady feeling of being worshiped by a stranger.

"W-why?" she stammered.

"Because, soon, I will not be able to stop," he whispered, pressing his lips to her ear. "I will want to snatch up your gown, tear open my breeches, and find my way inside you. And I can promise I will not let the fact that we are in a tree impede me."

She shuddered at what his words promised, and realized she wanted it, all of it. She wanted his hands beneath her gown, touching her intimately. She wanted to know what it was like to have a man inside of her—*this* man.

But, with a ragged sigh, he ceased his kissing and cupped her face in both hands, leaning back to look her in the eye.

"Now, angel," he admonished. "Go, now. You … you were perfect. Incredible, in fact. But this cannot go on, or we will both come to regret it."

She frowned, wondering at his sudden reticence when he had been so forward at first. Perhaps he was lying about how much he'd enjoyed the kiss and wanted to let her down gently. Her back stiffened, and she moved to pull away from him, but he merely tightened his hold, his thumbs caressing her cheeks.

"It isn't you, angel, it's me," he reassured her. "I am not meant for one such as you. Do you understand? A sweet little thing like you … you should run as far and fast away from me as you can get."

She smiled, though it was shaky, her stomach twisting as she realized that this was ending before it had even begun. "I cannot imagine that is true. You seem so perfect."

He shook his head, returning her smile. "I am not the man for you, little angel. But know that I wish I could be. Do you believe that? Even though I do not know you, and you do not know me. Do you believe that I wish I could be the sort of man to court you and win you?"

She nodded emphatically, believing that with all her heart. "Will you at least tell me your name? Mine is—"

His first finger came down over her lips, cutting her off before she could utter it. "It is better this way. I will think of you as Angel, and you can think of me however you wish."

I wish I could think of you as mine.

Lydia pushed the thought down, not wanting to examine it too closely just now. Perhaps later, when she was alone and no one could see her pining after a man she'd just met.

"Go," he urged once more. "I will sit up here and watch until you disappear inside. I want you safe."

Biting her lower lip, she sighed, shoulders sagging. "All right. Will I ever see you again?"

His solemn eyes made her heart ache just before he looked away from her. "I doubt it very much, angel. But, this is how it must be."

She wanted to ask him why—why things had to be this way, why they could not come to know one another, and perhaps even fall in love. Loving him would be so easy, and she felt certain he was a good man. His parentage meant nothing to her, though she had a feeling he would not relish hearing that from her just now.

So, Lydia did the only thing she could. She moved to climb off the limb, accepting his assistance. Then, under his watchful eye, she descended the way she'd come, finding her foot and handholds in the jagged brick and making her way to the ground.

Once there, she took one final look at her mysterious gentleman, the moon framing him just so, the breeze rustling his mussed curls. She could not see his eyes from here, but she felt them on her, watching and waiting for her to do what he'd said.

With shaking hands, she turned her back to him and made her way down the path leading to the house. As the noise and candlelight of the ball drew her back toward the open doors of the terrace, she realized with a sinking feeling in her gut that he had been right.

Less than an hour in his company, and she was absolutely ruined.

CHAPTER 1

*L*ydia clenched and unclenched her gloved hands as she walked down the lane leading to the sprawling Buckton Manor. Her palms had begun to sweat, and she could not decide if it might be due to the stifling warmth of the afternoon, or the nervousness making her gut twist and her pulse race. Perhaps some combination of the two.

Pressing a hand against her roiling belly, she took a few deep breaths and raised her chin a notch. There was nothing to be nervous about. She had been invited here to interview for the position of governess, had been fortunate enough to find herself in the running for said position because of her acquaintance with the neighboring family.

While she had been assured that she could continue relying on the hospitality of her dear friends, the Egglestons, she had made up her mind that she could impose upon them no longer. She had made the decision four years ago to make her own way in the world, and that choice had not failed her yet. Certainly, her life had not turned out the way she'd thought it would as a young girl filled with notions of romantic whimsy. Yet, she had survived this long on her own and would continue to do so.

Her brother would insist she return home to Oakmoor, and her mother would agree. But, she no longer felt as if she belonged there—truly, hadn't felt as if she belonged anywhere for quite some time. While she loved her family dearly and missed them terribly, she could not go back there. Because, if she did, they would see how much she had changed, and perhaps wish to know why. Then she'd be forced to reveal the reason she'd vowed to never return to London after her first Season, or why she could never marry. It was not something she wished to endure, and quite frankly, did not even like thinking of such things herself.

So, it would be this, then.

As she approached the smooth, stone steps leading up to the large double doors of Buckton, Lydia reminded herself that the position was all but hers. With several sterling references, as well as the letter of introduction from the Egglestons, she was being fed this position on a silver platter. All she had to do was make it through the interview.

After ascending the steps, she made use of the massive, brass door-knocker. It did not take long for one of the doors to open, and for an austere butler to fill the gap.

"Good afternoon," she said when he simply stared at her, unblinking. "I am Miss Lydia Darling, here to meet with Mr. Welby."

The man's blank expression shifted to display polite interest, and he held the door open wider, stepping back to allow her entrance. "Ah, yes. You are here to interview for the governess position."

"That is correct," she confirmed, sweeping into the vestibule and turning to face the man as he closed the door.

"I shall see you directly to his office," the butler offered. "But first, may I take your things?"

Untying the ribbons of her bonnet, she carefully lifted it off her head and handed it to the man, but opted to keep her pale yellow spencer on over its matching walking gown. She did remove her gloves and gave him those, as well, then smoothed a hand over her chignon.

After handing her effects off to a silent footman, the butler gestured toward a corridor that led deeper into the house. "Right this way, Miss."

She followed him, taking a cursory glance at her surroundings. She had certainly been in more opulent homes, and Buckton was not even half the size of Oakmoor, but she found it no less impressive. Expensive wallpaper, painted ceilings, elegant wainscoting, thick, Aubusson rugs, and tasteful wall art, all portraying wealth and status. The Clayton family, who owned Buckton, gained their wealth primarily from the cherry orchard stretching out from the back of the manor for miles upon miles. However, Katherine Eggleston had told her that Mr. Sinclair Clayton was known to have a head for investments, many of his ventures turning up impressive profits. This country home was one of many owned by the Claytons, their vast holdings also including a seaside cottage in Brighton and a lavish townhome in London.

So similar to the other families she had served over the years, though she did hope they might prove different in one very important way. It was her hope that they would keep her on for more than a paltry few years. It had been difficult, moving from post to post for some reason or another. Her first family had disposed of her after their sons grew too old for a governess, needing a more appropriate tutor. Her second family had replaced her with a friend of a relation who had been in dire straits and, apparently, needed the room and board and funds more than Lydia did. Her third family had only employed her for a few short months before the lady of the house had deemed her far too 'attractive' to continue working for them—citing the wandering eye of her eldest boy, though Lydia suspected the woman was more afraid for her husband than her son.

She would find a home and a long-lasting position with a family if it killed her. Thus far, the Claytons seemed like her best prospect.

The butler came to a stop at a door halfway down the corridor and knocked. A male voice bid them to enter, and the servant led her inside. The small space boasted shelves upon shelves of what appeared to be ledgers for the keeping of household accounts. A large desk took up most of the available space, covered in papers and open books, as well as several quills and an inkwell. Two immense windows allowed in plenty of light and offered a picturesque view of the orchard, as well as the house grounds and woods in the distance.

A man dressed in the typical austere attire of an upper servant stood from behind the messy desk, a wide smile stretching across his face. Not overly handsome, but not plain, either, he possessed short blond hair and twinkling blue eyes, the lines around them indicating he smiled often. Lydia found it easy to smile back as he rounded the desk and came toward her with one hand extended.

"Miss Darling, I presume," he said in a light, pleasant voice.

"Mr. Welby," she replied, placing her hand in his. "I do hope I am not too early for our appointment."

He shook her hand, his grip firm but gentle. "No, not at all. Please, make yourself comfortable."

Mr. Welby nodded to the butler, communicating silently. The butler inclined his head and backed from the room, leaving the door open and disappearing back down the corridor.

Lydia took one of the two chairs facing the desk and sat, folding her hands in her lap. "Thank you for meeting with me. I take it the position of governess has not yet been filled?"

Lowering himself into the chair, he began rearranging his desk—stopping the inkwell, then shuffling a handful of documents. "Not yet, and I must admit that we have become quite desperate at this point."

Thank God.

She would hate to be the only desperate person in such an arrangement. If the Claytons were hard up for a governess, then she'd arrived at just the right time.

"Do not worry," he added. "I will take you to meet with Lady Clayton in a moment, as the decision to hire you will be hers, in the end. However, as Mr. Clayton's steward here at Buckton, it is my duty to vet all the potential household staff and conduct the preliminary interview."

Reaching into the pocket of her gown, she came out with the sealed letters she'd brought with her, reaching out over the desk to hand them to Mr. Welby.

"My references," she declared once he glanced up and noticed what she presented. "Three families who can vouch for my education and experience."

He accepted the sealed letters, but did not bother to open them, placing the missives on his desk. Leaning back in his seat, he inclined his head at her.

"The letter from Mrs. Eggleston was good enough for me, if you do not mind me saying so," he told her. "Though, Mr. Clayton and Lady Clayton may wish to read them. I understand that you have served as a governess for four years."

"Yes," she said with a little nod. "Unfortunately, my first families outgrew me. It is my hope to find a more longstanding arrangement."

"I would imagine that is not the only reason you might have been let go from your former households," he said, startling her with his bluntness.

Her eyes widened, and she sat up straighter, her mouth going dry. "I beg your pardon?"

Clearing his throat, Mr. Welby leaned forward, bracing his arms on the desk and folding his hands together. "Forgive me, I only meant that a young, attractive woman such as yourself must suffer the envy of her employers from time to time. Many a governess has found herself sacked for the simple reason that she is lovely enough to attract the notice of the men of the house."

Her face flushed, and she lowered her gaze to her hands. However, Mr. Welby's voice remained light and filled with good humor when he spoke again.

"Allow me to put you at ease, Miss Darling. You shall hardly have such a problem here. There are no adult male relations living at Buckton. Mr. Clayton divides his time between various estates, and because this place runs itself efficiently without his constant management, he does not spend much time here. As well, he is a man above reproach, a man you needn't fear making untoward advances on your person. Also, Lady Clayton … well, you shall have to meet her for yourself. But, I daresay you will understand right away why you needn't worry about petty jealousy when it comes to her. We need a governess, Miss Darling, and as you seem to be the most qualified for the position, may I be so bold as to welcome you to the household?"

Lydia lifted her gaze to find him smiling at her again, his eyes twinkling merrily. He was handsome in an unassuming way, and she found him charming. The steward at her last home had been an insufferable snob, so this would be a pleasant change.

"Already?" she asked, still slightly taken aback.

Mr. Welby shrugged one shoulder. "If I have not missed my guess —and I am almost never wrong about such things—Lady Clayton will like you. I expect you'll be offered the position on the spot. If you are ready, I will take you to her now."

Lydia nodded eagerly, relieved that things were going so well thus far. She had known that the letter of introduction from Katherine would help ease the way, but had not expected to be so warmly welcomed, or to be assured of her new position in the household so soon.

"I would like that, thank you, Mr. Welby," she said.

He stood, and she followed suit, and before long, they were exiting the small office. As she walked along beside him, she stifled a giggle at the oddness of her circumstances compared to four years ago. As a debutante, it would never have done to be found alone with a strange man. Now freed from such strictures, no one seemed to think it strange that a butler would leave her alone in a room with the steward, and she preferred things this way. The rules and morals of the

London *ton* were ridiculous at best, and hypocritical at worst. She was grateful she no longer had to abide by them.

They came to the front hall again, but this time, Welby took her toward a steep staircase leading to the next level of the house. She noted more of the opulence marking this as the home of people of means, but mostly focused upon the meeting at hand. While Mr. Welby seemed to like her, the lady of the house would have the final say. What if she found Lydia too young, or decided that she'd worked too short a time for her previous employers?

All she wanted was a chance to start over, and this opportunity was the best she'd come across. She needed this position.

Mr. Welby paused before a set of double doors painted white, with ornate knobs affixed to them. "Wait here. I will ensure she's ready to receive you."

Lydia nodded her agreement and watched as he knocked and waited for a response. A thin, lyrical voice bid him to enter, and he opened the door, stepping inside and leaving her in the hall. Their muffled conversation came at her through the door, and a moment later, Mr. Welby reappeared.

"Lady Clayton will see you now," he announced. "Best of luck, Miss Darling."

"Thank you. Mr. Welby."

He stood back, watching her, and she supposed he waited for her to go inside before he took his leave. She slipped into the room and pulled the door shut behind her, taking one last look at the kind steward before she did. He gave her an encouraging nod just before disappearing from sight.

Stepping farther into the room, Lydia was swallowed by a place that seemed as if it came from a dream. Decorated in nothing but white, the space gleamed with the light of the afternoon sun shining through half a dozen floor-to-ceiling windows. Pristine white couches and chairs littered the space while white rugs and silver-fili-greed wallpaper made the room glow like the moon. Sheer curtains allowed in plenty of light, and the polished silver sconces and other fixtures made her feel as if she stood inside a diamond.

And in the center of it all, reclining on a chaise longue, was the most stunning woman Lydia had ever laid eyes upon.

Lady Clayton lay draped in a pale pink dressing gown, the bottom of a white garment peeking out from beneath its hem. Dainty feet sported matching slippers, with ribbons tied around slender ankles and adorned with flirtatious bows.

As Lydia approached and soaked Lady Clayton in, she noted a waif-thin frame that bordered on emaciated, though it did not rob the woman of her beauty. In fact, it seemed to enhance it. Everything about her was delicate and graceful, from the tiny feet to the long, slender hands scrawling something in a little leather-bound book. White-blonde hair hung loose over her shoulders in a tumble of near-perfect waves. It framed a sharp, angular face that looked as if it had been sculpted from pale, white marble—aristocratic nose, thin but shapely lips, prominent cheekbones. The limpid blue eyes that peered up at Lydia from beneath a fan of pale blonde eyelashes should have looked overlarge in the slender face, but instead appeared as perfect as the rest of her.

Now she grasped the purpose of the room's décor. It seemed a calculated decision, one meant to enhance and call attention to the angelic beauty of its occupant.

As Mr. Welby had predicted, Lydia understood why her own attractiveness would pose no problem in this household. What man in his right mind would give her a second glance with the ethereal Lady Clayton ruling over Buckton like some sort of goddess?

For a moment, the woman met her gaze with those pale blue eyes, and a foreign sensation trickled down Lydia's spine. Despite their limpid beauty, those eyes were razor sharp at their edges, cold and glittering like hard chips of ice. In that moment of silent staring between them, she felt like some hapless doe stalked by a predator. As if at any moment, the woman might lunge across the space between them and rip her to shreds.

But then, the lady blinked before offering her a little smile, and Lydia wondered if she had not imagined the entire thing.

"Good afternoon, my lady," she managed, once she had recovered from the shock of laying eyes on such a ravishing creature. "I am Miss Lydia Darling."

The woman let the book fall into her lap, turning slightly to set her pen on a nearby side table. "It is lovely to meet you. I am Lady Drucilla Clayton."

As Lydia neared, Lady Clayton gestured toward a nearby armchair. She followed the unspoken command and sat, trying not to stare at her too overtly. Yet, the signs of sickness she had missed upon first entering the room made themselves apparent close up. A slight redness around the eyes, a light flush to the cheeks, and an unmistakable sheen to her pupils marked Lady Clayton as quite ill.

The lady retrieved a lace-trimmed handkerchief from the pocket of her dressing gown and held it over her nose and mouth as she began to cough. The hacking lasted for a while, leaving Lydia concerned and feeling quite guilty for her previous thoughts. Brows furrowed, she searched the room, standing when she found a tea service nearby along with a china cup in a saucer that looked as if it had already been used.

She did not ask for permission, reaching out to pour tea and lace it with sugar while the unfortunate Lady Clayton went on coughing into her handkerchief. Finding a bowl of wedged lemons beside the service, she took one and squeezed its juice into the cup, recalling that lemon had always soothed her sore throat whenever she had a cold.

By the time she approached the ailing woman with the cup and saucer, Lady Clayton had gone silent, resting her head against the arm of the chaise with a sigh. She accepted the offering of tea, with a tight smile.

"Thank you," she said in the soft, lyrical voice, which was now strained from her coughing fit. "What a sweet thing you are."

Lydia took her seat once more. "Think nothing of it."

"Do forgive me," Lady Clayton murmured between sips of tea. "I am never quite certain when such fits will befall me. It seems to have passed now, so we can begin. You came highly recommended by our neighbors, the Egglestons."

Lydia nodded. "Yes. Mrs. Eggleston is a dear friend of my family. They've graciously taken me in while I seek a new position, and I am grateful to them for leading me to you."

Lady Clayton glanced up from her teacup, her delicate brows pinching together. "Darling … Darling … I know that name. Would you happen to be a relation of Lady Amelia Darling, sister to the marquis of … oh, something or other."

"Ashton," Lydia supplied. "And yes, Amelia is my sister-in-law. She wed my eldest brother some time ago."

Five years, she recalled suddenly. Michael and Amelia had been wed for five years—since just before her first Season.

"Ah, yes," Lady Clayton replied with a weak smile. "Such a lovely lady, your sister-in-law. We are not well-acquainted, but I always found her to be a singularly charming sort of person."

Thinking of the woman who had stolen her brother's heart while wearing breeches and acting without propriety, she could not help a little chuckle. "That she is, my lady."

Sitting up a bit straighter, Lady Clayton took another sip of tea. "Mrs. Eggleston says you have served three families before arriving here in Hertfordshire, and that you are well-educated."

"Yes, my lady," she confirmed. "I am qualified to instruct your children in Reading, Writing, and Arithmetic, as well as Art, History, Geography, and the French language. I regret to inform you that I am only passable at best on the pianoforte, but do command a bit of talent with watercolors and charcoal."

Lady Clayton nodded. "That will do, I am certain. There is only one child here; my son, Henry, and he is four years of age. So, instruction in the pianoforte will be unnecessary."

Lydia stifled a sigh of relief to know she would not need to teach anyone anything related to music. Her brother often teased her over her horrible playing and wobbly singing voice. She'd been born practically tone deaf, and had long come to terms with that fact.

"I think you will find Henry to be an exceptionally bright child," Lady Clayton said, a bit of warmth creeping into her voice at the mention of her son. "At this age, he's become a bit much for his poor nurse to handle on her own, so his father and I believe he is ready for a bit more structure."

"Yes, he is at the perfect age for instruction," Lydia agreed. "And it is my belief that a child's lessons should be tailored to his own abilities rather than how many years he is. Henry, being a bright boy, might take well to lessons other governesses are teaching to children six or seven years of age."

A soft smirk curved the corner of the woman's mouth, and Lydia could not tell if Lady Clayton were pleased or amused.

"Well said, Miss Darling. I believe Henry will like you. Mr. Clayton will be pleased with you, as well, though you should not expect to interact with him much, as he is hardly ever in residence."

Lydia experienced a niggling of pity for the woman, whose husband ought to be on hand when she was obviously so ill. It was no wonder she needed the help of a governess. She hardly seemed strong enough to aid the nurse in keeping the child occupied.

"I do believe I would enjoy serving your family, my lady," she said honestly. "Little boys are my favorite pupils, if I may be honest. While some governesses find them challenging, I enjoy their natural precociousness."

Lady Clayton raised her eyebrows. "You sound like a woman who was raised with many men underfoot."

Lydia laughed. "Two elder brothers. How did you know?"

The woman giggled, but the sound was scratchy from her coughing fit. "Your forbearance for the male sex. You will need it when it comes to Henry. A sweet boy, but a bit of a trickster. He's chased off two governesses already with harmless pranks."

Her lips quivered as she held back another laugh. "My eldest brother, Michael, delights in tormenting me, even after he has grown old enough to have outgrown such things. It delights me to torment him right back."

Lady Clayton smiled again, setting her cup and saucer aside. "It would seem you are the perfect woman for the job. Consider yourself hired, Miss Darling."

Despite having already been assured by Mr. Welby that the job was all but hers, relief flooded her in a rush. Lady Clayton had been intimidating at first, but she supposed she ought to have trusted the steward's word.

"Thank you, Lady Clayton," she said, the tension in her spine melting a bit. "I appreciate your confidence in me. I am certain Henry and I will get on well together."

Lady Clayton nodded her agreement. "Quite so. I would like you to begin as soon as possible. We can send for your things today, and have you settled into your living quarters this evening, if that suits you."

If she were any happier, she might weep. "Thank you, my lady. That would be fine."

It was more than fine … it was perfect. As she rose to her feet, Lady Clayton sat up a bit straighter, though did not attempt to stand.

"Please see Mr. Welby on your way out," the lady said. "He will ensure you are settled in and ready to begin tomorrow morning. He will also introduce you to Henry."

She executed a swift curtsy. "That sounds wonderful. Thank you, again."

Lydia turned to quit the room, a wide smile stretching across her face. Her fears over how she would get on for the next few years eased, the knot in her belly loosening. It was true that she might only be here until Henry grew too old for a governess, and with no other Clayton children in sight, she might then be let go. Still, it was better than returning home and admitting defeat. Besides, she could always hope that one of Mr. Clayton's sporadic visits home produced another child.

Thinking of the poor woman upstairs, she cringed. Perhaps not.

Whatever the case, Lydia looked forward to even a few years of peace and stability. It was not the life of grand passion or romance she'd once wanted for herself, but those had been the dreams of a young, inexperienced girl. This was her reality, and while her family might insist she deserved more, Lydia would be content.

She would be content, and leave her dreams where they belonged—deep in the corners of her mind.

CHAPTER 2

The first fortnight of Lydia's new post went so well, she often felt the urge to pinch herself to ensure she wasn't living in some sort of dream. After being hired on the spot by Lady Clayton, she had been sent back to Mr. Welby, who had taken her around to introduce her to the staff. Many of them were polite but standoffish—a phenomenon she'd come to expect in any home she worked in. As a governess, she was not quite a servant, but not family, either. It put her in a unique sphere, one only occupied by herself, Mr. Welby, and other servants such as Mr. Clayton's valet (who traveled with him), Lady Clayton's personal maid, and little Henry's nanny, the widowed Mrs. Beecham.

After meeting much of the household staff, Mr. Welby had then showed her to her living quarters on the third floor. The room she'd been given proved larger than any she'd ever occupied. She'd stood in the doorway, open-mouthed, stunned into silence while soaking it in. Bright and airy, it had been decorated in cheery shades of yellow and white. The furnishings were plain and efficient—a simple bed with a matching side table, an armoire, a damask-upholstered sofa facing the hearth, and a table with two matching chairs set near a large window.

Said window overlooked the orchard, allowing her a view of the cherry trees growing for acres upon acres and the picturesque countryside in the distance.

It was not so different from her chamber back home at Oakmoor, with only the plainer furnishings distinguishing it. The wood paneling and bright yellow and powder-blue striped wallpaper made it seem more like a room for a distinguished guest, not a mere governess. And while she came from a family that was wealthy in its own right, Lydia had grown accustomed to her new place in the world. She was well aware that this was above and beyond what she should have expected.

Turning back to face Mr. Welby, she had shaken her head. "This is far more than is necessary."

The man's lips had curved into an amused grin. "You should see the nanny's room. In fact, all the rooms at Buckton are thus appointed. I've seen the servants' quarters upstairs and can attest, even they are nicer than what you'd normally find. Mr. Clayton's doing, that. And because Lady Clayton possesses a knack for decorating, it amuses her to furnish and renovate various rooms through the manor. Compared to some of the other chambers, this one is downright plain."

She'd moved to the center of the room, turning in a slow circle to soak it all in. "It is a lovely room. I suppose I must endure the hardship of living in it."

The steward had chuckled at her joke, motioning back out into the hall. "When your things are delivered, they will be placed here for you to unpack. Shall I show you the rest?"

Lydia had followed him down the corridor, where he'd pointed out a water closet, a drawing room, and the place that would become her domain for as long as she worked at Buckton—the schoolroom. She'd found it perfect for her needs, with a desk for herself and a smaller one for Henry. Upon it had sat a brand new slate, ready for his use. Shelves against one wall held books on a variety of subjects, all of them new and in pristine condition.

Mr. Welby had watched from the doorway, chuckling as she'd selected one of the volumes and opened it, inhaling deeply the scent of its pages. She'd flushed at being caught, and had tried to appear nonchalant.

"There is something about the smell of new pages," she'd explained.

He'd nodded. "I understand entirely, Miss Darling."

Replacing the book, she'd allowed him to guide her to the nursery, where they had found Henry and his nanny, Mrs. Beecham. The boy was introduced to her briefly before the nanny ushered him off for his afternoon nap, though the meeting had gone swimmingly. She'd found Henry a charming, handsome lad with a golden head of hair a few shades darker than his mother's, and blue eyes that twinkled with mischief and good humor. The smirk he'd given her while shaking her hand had reminded her of her elder brother.

She knew that look well, and had thought to expect a prank of some sort on her first day teaching him. The thought had made her smile. One of the things she missed most about living at Oakmoor was repaying Michael for some lark or another, and having someone to continue the tradition with at Buckton would make her feel much more at home.

From there, she'd been taken to the dining room, where Mr. Welby invited her to take lunch with him and a handful of other upper servants. They did not eat in the room off the back of the kitchen where the lower servants dined—one more thing separating them, she supposed. The fare at Buckton proved beyond decent, yet another mark in its favor.

After the meal, Mr. Welby had taken her through the rest of the house, pointing out a small library, a lovely solarium with doors that opened onto a terrace overlooking the cherry grove, and several drawing rooms. From there, he'd returned her to her chamber, where her trunks had been delivered and sat waiting for her to unpack. She had taken the rest of that afternoon making herself at home in the spacious, sunny bedroom. She'd filled the armoire with her most modest and efficient garments—taking care to fold and tuck away her men's togs, which she liked to wear while riding or romping outdoors. Her sister-in-law had made her aware of the benefits of donning breeches, and Lydia often found she preferred them over gowns.

Then, she'd arranged all her toilette items on the washstand, draped her dressing gown over the back of a plush armchair that sat near the bed, and settled the miniature, framed portraits of her family on the bedside table. Sitting on the edge of the bed, she'd stared at the likeness of her brothers, mother, sisters-in-law, and nieces and nephews. The family had grown by leaps and bounds during her time away, with Archie and Hesper adding a fourth child to their brood, and Michael siring a daughter and a son on Amelia within two years. It made her glad to see them so happy; yet, it was also difficult to see—watching them all grow and change, so in love with each other and so blissfully content. All it did was remind her of the one glimmer of passion, desire, and happiness she'd had with another person … a fleeting moment that had changed her forever.

After her kiss with the mysterious stranger, she'd been unable to muster even an ounce of interest in another man—resulting in a miserable Season. She'd looked for him everywhere, kept an ear out for the sound of his voice, searched the face of every stranger of the male sex she'd encountered for those dark, velvety eyes. Despair had set in then, as she'd realized he had stayed true to his word that they would never see one another again. Because she had not known his name, it had been impossible to ask about him. It had occurred to her to describe him to Amelia and ask if she might be acquainted with him, but had decided against it.

What was she to say?

Oh, dear sister, I believe I've fallen in love with a stranger who kissed me while sitting in a tree in a garden at a ball. He has the most beautiful dark brown hair and eyes to match, the most perfect lips I've ever seen, and a voice that could turn a woman's knees to jelly. He also happens to be the bastard son of a viscount. Could you kindly help me discover his identity?

Snorting at herself, she had flopped back onto her neatly made bed.

"Pitiful," she'd muttered aloud.

For all she knew, the man had been fabricated by her desperate, lonely mind. Perhaps he did not exist at all. How foolish she'd been to imagine herself in love with a phantom.

Yet, bringing the tips of her fingers over her lips, she had remembered his kiss so clearly, even after four long years. He had certainly *felt* real. Closing her eyes, she had imagined the thrilling moment he had pulled her against him, fitting that perfect mouth of his over hers. Lydia's pulse had raced as she'd recalled the taste of him, his scent flooding her senses, his strong hands touching her, holding her as if loath to let her go.

A light fluttering between her thighs had made her whimper, and she'd squeezed her legs together, trying to stifle it.

What good would come from remembering and allowing herself to long for him yet again? She had resolved to move forward with her life, finding fulfillment by engaging her mind, by shunning closeness with anyone. While she could not pretend she'd been particularly happy, she could say that she was content, that she'd been safe away from eyes that examined her too closely … from her family, who despite their best intentions, would never understand what she'd gone through.

Thus resolved, she'd left the bed and quit the room altogether, determined to make the best of this new opportunity. The rest of her time before dinner had been spent exploring the house, taking her time in the rooms Mr. Welby had already shown her, then venturing outdoors to lose herself in the beauty of Buckton's grounds. She'd wandered so far and for so long that exhaustion had claimed her shortly after dinner, prompting her to turn in early.

Beginning that next day, Lydia had fallen into the comfort of a familiar routine. Each morning, she took breakfast in the dining room with the upper servants before going to the nursery to collect Henry from his nanny. She began by assessing the boy to determine what he already knew, and found him as bright as his mother had claimed. He could recognize all of his letters and write a few with a neat hand. He excelled at recognizing his numbers, and had duly impressed her with how high he could count. He could also introduce himself in French and had memorized a handful of phrases with an expertise many adults she knew did not possess. She'd decided to begin by teaching him to write his letters and numbers—something he took to with an ease that hardly surprised her.

As she'd suspected, they got on well together, the prank Henry had pulled on her setting the tone for their relationship on the very first day. When she had gone to sit in the chair behind her desk, her eyes had widened at the feel of something mushy and wet soaking her left buttock through the layers of her gown, petticoat, and chemise. Custard, if she hadn't missed her guess based on its consistency.

Lydia hadn't so much as batted an eyelash, nor had she taken Henry to task for the custard in her chair. In fact, she had simply launched into the first day's lesson, keeping a straight face and level voice the entire time. The boy had gone from snickering behind one hand, to staring at her in confusion, to sulking over his slate while forming his letter 'A'. She'd struggled not to laugh when he had glanced up at her every few seconds as if to determine whether she'd noticed that she sat in a puddle of pudding.

She'd managed to keep her composure, right up until the moment had come to approach his desk to check his work—when she'd stood, she had pressed her hand into the mess on her chair and taken it with her behind her back. Still pretending nothing was amiss, she'd braced one hand on the back of his seat and leaned over to view his work, praising him for his penmanship and reminding him to attempt to keep his lines straight. Then, she'd patted the top of his head and murmured 'well done,' walking away after leaving a healthy serving of the custard in his hair.

They'd shared a laugh over it, and spent the following days playing pranks on one another between lessons. Not difficult to feel affection for a boy who reminded her so much of her own brothers, and who applied himself so readily to instruction. Even after such a short time at Buckton, she had already decided that this family, this home, was her favorite. Even if she rarely saw Lady Clayton—who spent most of her time shut away in the ethereal white drawing room, where she received her many callers. While she still seemed quite ill, she also proved popular, entertaining a steady stream of visitors each day from the comfort of her preferred chaise. Henry would be sent for in the evenings to spend time with his Mama, after which he'd be returned to his nanny to prepare for bed.

Everything was going smoothly, even if her days had grown a bit predictable, monotonous, even. It was the life she'd chosen, one she had grown accustomed to. And for the nonce, she could allow herself to feel a sense of security, as Mr. Welby assured her that Lady Clayton was pleased with her work, and that Mr. Clayton would be, as well.

So accustomed to her routine had she grown, that the day a third person stepped into the schoolroom, Lydia *felt* it. The air in the room seemed to vibrate with the intruder's presence, and she knew before she'd even turned around that this was not Mrs. Beecham, Mr. Welby, or even Lady Clayton.

She'd been standing with her back to Henry, scrawling a few short words for him to begin learning to read and spell on the slate board nailed to the wall, when she'd realized they were not alone. Lydia had known even before Henry did … even before she'd registered the sound of the boy's chair scraping back from the desk and his hurried footsteps over the floorboards.

"Papa!" the boy cried.

With a little smile, she set her chalk aside, then wiped her hands on the apron she'd tied around her waist over her morning gown—a practice she'd learned to adopt after having been governess to little boys. Their grubby hands never failed to make a ruin of her gowns. It would seem their instruction was finished for the day. Henry sounded so happy to see his father, Lydia would never dream of forcing him back into that chair.

She swept a hand over her hair to ensure it hadn't been mussed too badly, and took a deep breath, preparing to meet her employer. Yet, when he spoke, she found herself rooted to the spot.

"Well, hello there!" Mr. Clayton exclaimed with a chuckle. "Is it possible you've grown this much in my absence? You appear to have shot up an entire foot since I last saw you!"

Henry laughed and said something in response, but Lydia could barely register it. She could only stand there while that deep, resonant voice vibrated through her, that belly-warming laugh suffusing her with heat from the inside out. Her palms became damp, and she clung to her apron to try to still their shaking. Her ribs seemed to constrict, robbing her of breath, making her heart hammer wildly in her chest, her mouth going dry.

No … it could not be him. She was hearing things, her imagination running away with her. Her mother had chastised her often for being prone to flights of fancy, and this proved just another instance of her mind running off to places that did not exist in reality.

But then, he spoke again, and she felt certain—absolutely certain— that she had heard things correctly.

"You must be the new governess," he said to her back. "Welby tells me nothing but good things."

Her spine stiffened as she steeled herself to turn and face him, to put a face she already knew to the voice that seemed to echo through her very soul with a haunting reverberation. That voice had disturbed her nights, robbed her of sleep, sent her pulse aflutter with longing … and now, it was here, in this room, in this house, wrapping itself around her like a warm blanket.

Swallowing past the lump in her throat, she turned, her eyes going wide as her gaze fell upon him for the first time in four years.

Her mystery gentleman … her heart's most acute but ridiculous desire … the bane of her existence for all the havoc his memory had wreaked on her life.

Time had changed him very little. The perfection of his bone structure, the line of his jaw, the straight ridge of his nose. His eyes were as dark and fathomless as ever, even the light of the sun streaming through the schoolroom windows not enough to lighten the rich hue. His hair sat in tousled waves about his head, that one lock falling over his forehead, same as it had the night they'd met. Her stare lowered to his mouth at the memory of their kiss. His lips parted slightly, and hers followed suit, a sharp inhale flooding her senses with his scent, mingled with that of horse, leather, and the outdoors.

He spoke again, drawing her eyes back up to meet his. It was low, nearly imperceptible, but she heard him clearly when the one word fell from his lips … an incredulous question mingled with a sigh of … relief?

"Angel?"

Sinclair Clayton had never felt happier to be home. Despite owning a handful of estates ranging from opulent to modest scattered across England, he had always preferred Buckton over the rest of them. It was a testament to his hard work, to the numerous obstacles he'd overcome in order to call this place his own. He knew every part of it —every cherry tree and blade of grass, every hillock, every creek and well-worn path. He had left the house mostly as it had been left to him, as he'd fallen in love with the place on first sight.

As he'd arrived back in Hertfordshire after four weeks' absence, he had relaxed in the saddle, a soft smile curving his mouth. No, life here was not perfect; it was where his wife preferred to reside, after all. However, it was also where his son lived, and he'd missed Henry so much, as he always did when matters of business took him away from Buckton. It was where he felt most at peace, the one place where he did not have to bear the scorn or curiosity that inevitably followed someone finding out he was the bastard son of the late Lord Clayton.

He made haste to the stables, leaving behind the coach and driver bearing his belongings. Sinclair had never been able to abide staying in a cloistered carriage for long periods of time, preferring the open air of the outdoors and sitting astride his own horse. It got him to the stables quickly, where he dismounted and handed the reins off to a groom before making his way toward the house at a trot. After his long ride, he was in need of a hot bath, clean clothing, and a meal, but he would greet his family first.

He grinned at the thought of appearing in Drucilla's sitting room wearing dusty boots, no cravat, and his most worn, comfortable frock coat. She valued appearances as much as any other well-bred woman born to privilege, and nothing irked her more than him tramping about their perfectly decorated home in a state of dishabille.

He took the front steps two at a time, a wide smile breaking out over his face. He had so few joys in life, so he would take much pleasure from standing close enough for her to catch wind of the scent of horse and the outdoors clinging to him.

The front doors swung open, and he found Amberly, the butler, awaiting him with a smile. "Welcome home, Mr. Clayton."

"Thank you, Amberly," he replied, pausing to clap the man on the shoulder.

Drucilla often accused him of being too familiar with the help, but he'd never seen the sense of putting on airs when everyone in Hertfordshire knew who he was and where he'd come from. Who was he to look down on people who must work for a living, when he himself knew what it was like to be in their position? In many ways, he identified with them—how it felt to be looked down upon, perceived as 'less than.' Thinking of his servants as family instead of people to be ill-treated was another one of those things that made Buckton feel like his true home.

"Shall I send for a bath and a meal?" the butler offered.

"Just the meal for now," he replied, removing his gloves and handing them off to an approaching footman, along with his hat. "Have it sent to my chambers. The bath can wait until after I've greeted Drucilla and Henry."

Combing his fingers through his undoubtedly mussed hair, he watched Amberly bustle off to do his bidding. Just before he set off for the staircase, he found his steward, Charles Welby, striding toward him, an ever-present smile on his face.

"Sinclair," he said, offering a hand. "Welcome home. I saw you coming up the lane from my window. How was Essex?"

"Quite the same as it was last time I was there, if you must know," he jibed.

The other man laughed, falling in step with him as he approached the stairs. "I suppose you will want to get settled in before we discuss estate matters, but I thought it prudent to inform you that Lady Clayton has found a new governess."

He paused on the landing, turning to face Charles with raised eyebrows. "Is that so? How long as said governess been in residence?"

"A fortnight, and the little beastie hasn't chased her off yet," Charles quipped. "I had high hopes for this one, and it seems I was right to place my faith in her. I conducted the preliminary interview, and strongly advised Lady Clayton to hire her before introducing them. She must have been impressed with Miss Darling, because the young lady was hired on the spot."

"Darling?" he said with a little shake of his head. "What a name."

Charles smiled at that. "Miss Lydia Darling ... the surname is fitting, actually. You will see what I mean when you meet her. She and Henry have gotten on well together thus far, and Lady Clayton seems pleased with reports of his progress even after so short a time."

He nodded his approval. "Very well. They are in the schoolroom, I suppose?"

"They are," the other man confirmed.

"Good. I will go up to them in a moment. I take it Dru is in the usual place."

"Of course," Charles replied.

"Tell me, do I smell like a horse?" he asked, leaning close.

Charles inhaled and then shrugged one shoulder. "Most definitely."

"Ah, so you are saying that I should *not* go into Drucilla's drawing room just now, looking and smelling the way I do?"

Charles' lips twitched, and he cast a quick glance at the closed door. "I wouldn't advise it."

"Excellent," he murmured before throwing the door open without preamble.

He strode into the room, making a beeline to where she lay draped on her favorite chaise. His gaze flitted over her in cursory inspection, and he experienced not an ounce of the affection he'd once had for her. In truth, she made him cold, and had for quite some time. It was quite baffling how the pale, delicate beauty that had so enraptured him in his youth now disgusted him. Perhaps it was because he could see through her façade far better than anyone—knew the venom pumping through those delicate blue veins showing on the inside of her white, nearly translucent wrist.

She lay draped in one of her many dressing gowns, along with slippers sporting blue gems on the toes. Always a fashion plate, even when lying-in.

"Hello, my darling wife," he muttered drolly, leaning down to kiss the top of her head for no other reason than it amused him the way she reared away, scrunching her nose.

"Honestly, Sinclair," she snapped, waving her hand through the air before her face as she glared at him. "One would think you'd at least have the grace to bathe before coming in here. You know how sensitive I am to smells … and you look like hell."

With a mocking grin, he dropped to one knee before her, remaining as close as possible. He was aware that his scent was not *that* offensive, but his wife was prone to dramatics.

"My dearest Dru, are you not happy to see me? I came straight to you, as my heart could stand the strain of separation no longer."

Pulling a lace-edged handkerchief from the pocket of her dressing gown, she sneezed into it. With a sniffle, she glowered at him again.

"The whores you sully your prick with might think you amusing, but I do not," she grumbled.

"No one would know what a whore finds amusing more than you," he fired back, his tone biting and clipped.

She looked away from him, turning her gaze to some point across the room, her jaw growing tight. His hand curled into a fist as he rose, his gut churning with the familiar turmoil that never ceased to come over him in her presence. He *hated* who he was when they were together ... hated the sort of man he'd become since marrying her.

"There is a new governess," she said, her voice edged in frigid scorn.

She saved all her warmth and love for Henry, and for that, at least, he was grateful. They might despise one another, but their mutual love for their son was one thing that offered them common ground. It was why when he'd first suggested Henry might be ready for a governess, Drucilla had agreed and undertaken the hiring herself.

"So Charles tells me," he replied.

"I do not like how familiar you are with them, as if they are equal to us," she groused. "*Mr. Welby* is a servant and should not be allowed to traipse about this house using your Christian name. Whatever should the neighbors think if they catch wind of such things?"

He shrugged. "I am not one of *us*, as you have seen fit to remind me so many times in the past. As long as he does not address you in a way that you do not like, I do not see how what he calls me is any of your affair."

She sighed, the little huff carrying every ounce of her vexation. Good. He'd hate to be the only one.

"Miss Darling is a more than adequate governess, if you care to know," she went on, as if she'd never brought up the subject of his familiarity with Charles. "Henry seems to like her and has not yet chased her off with his pranks."

His lips twitched at that. "This Miss Darling has mettle, then. Good. She will need it if she will survive Henry."

She seemed ready to offer a response, when a coughing fit seized her. Covering her mouth with the bit of cotton and lace, she coughed for near a minute, her slender body trembling from the force of it. He furrowed his brow, studying her more closely than he had upon entering the room.

Dark smudges marred the skin beneath her eyes, and her cheeks had flushed red from her exertions. She had gotten thinner since he'd left Buckton and was practically swimming in her dressing gown.

"Have you sent for Doctor Tunstall?" he asked.

She waved him off dismissively. "It is only a cold."

"The last 'cold' turned out to be pneumonia," he reminded her. "The cold before that lasted for weeks, and you could barely talk for coughing so much."

"I am fine, Sinclair."

He came close again, reaching out to touch her forehead. He'd expected her to be feverish, but she was clammy instead, her brow damp.

She slapped his hand away. "Do not touch me."

Holding his hands up defensively, he sighed. "I only wanted to determine whether you were feverish. Do you remember when you used to actually enjoy my touch?"

Her nostrils flared as she glared at him, her lovely mouth pulling into a sneer. "That was before I knew how the touch of a real man could feel."

His teeth ground together as he fought to keep from lambasting her with every insult swimming about in his mind. She knew how to sink her daggers deep, in the places that would hurt him most. A talent she had only honed more and more the longer they were wed.

He should have gotten used to this by now—her constant rejection and contempt. He'd told himself several times that he did not care, that he hated her, wanted no part of her. But deep down, a shred of him still clung to the memory of the girl he'd fallen in love with, the one he'd built his entire life around only to have her destroy him.

"I'm sending for Tunstall," he ground out, turning his back to her. "I will not let it be said that I let you languish until death while you lay ailing. Prepare yourself to be examined when he arrives."

Without waiting for her to respond, he stormed into the hall, slamming the door behind him. It never failed—Drucilla always found some way to paint him as a villain. If he pretended not to notice she was ill, she would moan and complain that he never paid her heed.

When he tried to care for her, even in such a small way, she shunned him.

Why do I bother?

It was a question he'd never been able to answer, a problem he could not seem to solve. Even hating her as he did, the responsibility of seeing to her welfare, of taking care of her, hung over his head. He'd promised her father, after all, and Lord Stratton *had* cared about Sinclair, even if his daughter did not. He'd promised to love, cherish, and protect her on their wedding day … and while he no longer loved her and found it difficult to cherish a woman with as much warmth as an icicle, he could still protect her, if nothing else. He provided well—even she could not complain that he was lacking in that regard.

Taking the stairs up to the third floor, he put Drucilla out of his mind. He'd send for the doctor and stay out of her way whenever he could—which was exactly how they both preferred things whenever he was in residence. He would stay for as long as he was able, craving the time spent with his son. Inevitably, one of his other estates would demand his attention, and he would be forced to depart. However, he was home for now, and he intended to enjoy it—which meant not allowing his wife to get under his skin.

Reaching the third floor, he quickly found the schoolroom and reached for the door. At the sound of a woman's voice on the other side, he paused. While he could trust Drucilla to see to Henry's best interest if nothing else, he still wanted to see for himself that this governess was worth her salt. He slowly turned the knob and opened the door a crack, peering into the room. He found Henry seated at his little desk, head bent over his slate. Farther into the room, he spotted Miss Lydia Darling, standing before the slate board he'd had Charles send for from London, chalk in hand.

From this distance and from behind, she seemed like any other governess. Modest attire, the strings of an apron tied into a neat bow at the small of her back. His eyebrows rose at the evidence of a lush, curved form making itself apparent beneath her prim, sprigged muslin frock. Hair the color of spun gold was twisted into a plain chignon at her nape, a stray strand caressing the back of a slender neck. Thank God his son was only four years of age; otherwise, the sight Sinclair now took in would prove enough to distract Henry from his studies.

He read what she scrawled on the blackboard and nodded in approval. Here for only a fortnight, and she already seemed to be coaxing Henry into learning to read and spell.

Straightening, he decided to stop acting the voyeur and make his presence known. He entered the room, the sound of his footsteps alerting Henry to his presence. Sinclair felt as if his heart had been gripped in a vise as the boy glanced over his shoulder, his eyes widening in surprise.

"Papa!" Henry cried, leaping up from his chair and rushing across the small space that separated them.

His eyes stung as the boy threw himself into his arms, and he closed his eyes for a moment while he embraced his son and took in his scent. When he opened his eyes again and looked down into the boy's face, he experienced the same visceral devotion that had overwhelmed him when he'd held him as a babe. With golden hair a few shades darker than Drucilla's, his eyes were the same shade of blue as hers, though warmer, more open. While Henry had inherited his mother's looks, he'd gotten none of her undesirable traits—none of her petulance or scorn, none of her artifice. Sinclair had not thought anything could make him love Buckton more, but his son's presence here proved him wrong time and time again.

"Well, hello there!" he said with a laugh as Henry clung to him, fighting against being set back on his feet. "Is it possible you've grown this much in my absence? You appear to have shot up an entire foot since I last saw you!"

The boy laughed and reluctantly allowed himself to be put down. "Mama had to send for the tailor to fit me for new clothes—the old ones did not fit any longer."

Sinclair observed the smart new attire Henry wore and recognized his wife's taste for the finer things. He never understood why she insisted on spending so much to outfit their son as if he were a grown man, when the boy would inevitably find his way into a puddle of mud.

"You look quite the gentleman," he said aloud, smoothing a wayward lock of hair back from the boy's forehead. "Are you being a good pupil for your new governess? Charles tells me she is good."

Henry nodded emphatically. "Oh, yes, Papa. Miss Darling is ever so nice … she even plays pranks!"

He smirked at that, understanding the importance of this to his son. The boy liked nothing better than to get the best of someone. It was nice to know that this governess would not be chased off as easily as the others.

"I should go introduce myself," he said, leaving Henry lingering near the desk and coming farther into the schoolroom.

The governess had put her chalk aside, but still had her back to him. He noticed her smoothing her hair; she seemed to take a moment to compose herself. He felt terrible about imposing on her during their lessons, but had wanted to meet the woman who had taken on the education of his son.

"You must be the new governess," he said, trying to keep his tone light and put her at ease. "Welby tells me nothing but good things."

Tension gripped her, making itself apparent in the way she squared her shoulders and straightened her back before turning to face him. He wondered if Drucilla had told her something unflattering about him. He certainly would not put it past her.

She seemed hesitant to face him, to speak or move or even breathe. Yet, she did move, turning to present him with the rest of her.

What he found stole the air from his lungs.

A pair of vibrant, cornflower-blue eyes met his, ringed with long, spiky lashes the perfect shade of gold. They went wide at the sight of him, recognition flickering in the depths. His own gaze began to wander, tracing over the lines and planes of a heart-shaped face, taking inventory of all the things that called to mind an evening in a dark garden, hidden away from the world and the *ton*. A night that had changed him profoundly, in a way that only he could see or feel. This face ... he could never have forgotten such a face. The wisps of perfectly shaped eyebrows over those enchanting eyes, the softness of cheeks that had flushed when he'd put his lips to her wrist, the shape of a mouth made for kissing, the tiny cleft in her chin that lent character to a face that might otherwise have been thought unassuming. But, if anyone thought her plain, they simply were not paying attention. Beauty was written into every one of her features, with sensual allure embedded in the lush curves of a body made for sin. Even that prim little gown and apron couldn't hide her from him—the breasts he'd remembered being pressed against his chest, the softness of a waist that wasn't overly thin, the flare of hips that could fill his hands and cradle him with softness and warmth.

No, he wasn't seeing things. It was her, after all this time, here, standing in front of him.

He could hardly find the presence of mind to consider the ramifications of this, not when the breath he'd been holding came out on a sigh of relief. He felt as if he'd been waiting for her for every day of the four years that had separated them ... and now, here she stood.

Despite now knowing her name, he couldn't help the word that fell from his lips; a word he hadn't uttered aloud to anyone since the night he'd given it to her.

"Angel?"

CHAPTER 3

For a long moment, Lydia was incapable of speech. She could only stand there, eyes wide, mouth hanging open as she soaked him in. Her stranger in the flesh, his presence a heady reminder that she hadn't dreamt their encounter four years ago—solidifying her memories of him with his scent, his nearness, the impact of his allure. Her dark, beautiful mystery … but no, not a mystery anymore, not a stranger. He was Mr. Sinclair Clayton, the father of her pupil. The *husband* of her mistress, Lady Clayton.

The shock of it doused her like the splash of frigid water thrown in her face, and she shook her head, breaking the haze that had fallen over her at the sight of him. He, however, seemed to be lost in that place, his gaze roaming over her as if memorizing every inch, his hand coming up as if to touch her face.

She recoiled with a gasp, backpedaling just in time to avoid his touch. Her cheek burned as if his fingertips had made contact, the painful realization that she wanted them to rippling out from the center of her chest. Of course he could not touch her—he could never touch her again. He was her employer, and she a governess hired to join the ranks of the servants who cared for his family.

God … the man she'd spent four years fantasizing about and longing for had a *family*. He had a wife, and a son, and had obviously moved on from their encounter in that garden.

Clearing his throat, he seemed to remember himself, coming back to the present as abruptly as she had. Inclining his head at her, he gave her a little smile. It was forced, holding none of the seductive promise she remembered from that night in London.

"Sinclair Clayton, at your service," he said, his voice a bit strained, the warmth she'd heard when he had addressed Henry gone.

She executed a swift curtsy, lowering her eyes so she did not have to look into the velvety brown depths of his. "Miss Lydia Darling. It is good to meet you, my lord."

A little sound escaped him—a derisive snort. "Mr. Clayton will do. Becoming wealthy and marrying the daughter of a marquis were not quite enough to endow me with the title of Lord."

Her face flamed hot, and a mass of horrified embarrassment dropped heavy in her gut. She'd known that, had been taught the difference in the various ranks and how to address them. She was also well aware that the circumstances of this man's birth meant he would never be called 'lord' despite his father being a viscount.

His sudden reappearance had muddled her mind, and now, she was making a complete fool of herself.

"Yes, of course," she managed. "Mr. Clayton."

Silence stretched between them for what felt like an eternity. She felt him looking at her again, felt the stroke of his eyes to the far reaches of her body.

"Henry tells me he has enjoyed having you as his governess thus far," he said suddenly, the words coming out rushed, as if he'd just plucked them out of thin air.

Her gaze settled on the boy, peering at her from around his father's leg—a safer place for her to set her eyes. "Yes, we are getting on quite well. Henry is a bright child, as I am certain you already know. He takes to numbers especially well."

Sinclair beamed down at his son, the pride and love he felt toward the lad on full display. "That is good to hear. I do apologize for imposing on you in the middle of your lesson, but I have been away for weeks and could not wait to see Henry."

Still avoiding his gaze, she forced a tense smile. "Of course, Mr. Clayton. I am certain he missed you sorely. In fact, I was just thinking that I should release him for the day, so he can spend time with you."

Henry bounced on the balls of his feet, a wide smile lighting up his little face. "Oh, Papa, can I? Can I, please?"

This time when Sinclair smiled, turning the full force of that warm expression on his son, Lydia's chest tightened, the air stolen from her lungs. She'd forgotten how beautiful it was ... how beautiful *he* was.

"Now, now," he chided. "I'm certain Miss Darling has an entire afternoon worth of lessons planned for you. We shall not let her hard work go to waste, shall we?"

"But, I insist," she blurted, suddenly overwhelmed with the need to quit the room, to get away from Sinclair so she could pull herself together. "His lessons can wait one day, and I hardly think I need worry that he will suffer for it."

He was looking at her again, and this time, she couldn't resist lifting her eyes to meet his gaze. His pensive stare bored into her, seeming to try to unravel her, to peer inside her soul. A shiver raced down her spine, but she maintained her composure—back erect, chin slightly raised, hands folded.

He put an arm around Henry. "Very well, but only for today. Tomorrow, you are to return to your studies and apply yourself. Yes?"

Henry nodded. "Yes, Papa."

Taking that to mean she could leave, Lydia turned away from the pair and swiftly began untying her apron strings, draping it over the back of the chair behind her desk.

"Enjoy your day of respite, Miss Darling," Sinclair called out as she hurried passed him.

That stopped her in her tracks, and she paused, staring up at him for a moment before nodding, her face warming under his unguarded perusal.

"Thank you, Mr. Clayton."

She fled, breaking into a run once she reached the corridor. Her breath raced as she gathered her skirts and dashed toward her bedroom just down the hall. The pressure in her chest had become unbearable, and she needed to closet herself away and find the space to grapple with her tangled emotions, to accept what had just happened.

Throwing open the door, she stumbled over the threshold, barely making it inside before she crumbled. The panel slammed behind her just before her knees gave way and she sank to the carpet, her chest heaving as she struggled to breathe.

This could not be happening. She could not have found the perfect position in the perfect household, only for it to turn out that the father of her charge was the man who'd touched her soul with a kiss. She had fought her foolish heart for so long, reminding herself over and over that she would never see him again. After he had disappeared like some sort of phantom, she had been determined to forget him, to try to carve out a quiet life of her own removed from the sorts of things that would make her long for a man she could never have.

How was she to get on now? How could she work for this family, encountering him daily, knowing he lived under the same roof as her? How could she watch him interact with the son he'd made with another woman? God, what would it feel like to watch him show Lady Clayton affection, give her those devastating smiles of his?

It was ridiculous to feel betrayed knowing he had gotten married and sired a child—ridiculous to feel as if he'd ripped her heart out and swallowed it whole. Yet, that was exactly the emotion that overcame her as the first tear fell, streaking off the edge of her jaw and wetting the bodice of her gown.

She had spent years pining for him, missing him, thinking about him and imagining that he thought of her, too. Lydia had wanted to be a part of his life, a part of his world, a part of *him*. Coming face to face with him today, she realized now that there could be no room for her. And why should there be? He had everything a man could ask for …

Lydia couldn't possibly mean anything to him when measured against all of that.

Lowering her head and drawing her knees up to her chest, she buried her face against her skirts as the first sob tore from her chest.

A few hours later, a composed Lydia left her chambers on a summons from Mr. Welby. She had spent the afternoon shut away, trying to get her tumultuous emotions under control. After a good, long cry, she had bathed her hands and face with cool water from the washstand, then sat in one of the chairs near the window, gazing numbly out at the scenery.

However, it had been difficult to put Sinclair Clayton out of her mind, when he and his son eventually came into view. The two had set out for a ride together, Henry nestled in the saddle in front of his father, who kept him safe with an arm around his waist, his other hand maintaining a tight hold on the reins. The large stallion they sat carried them away from the house, its inky black tail and matching mane fluttering in the breeze.

Her heart had throbbed, the pain of it dulled now that she had cried what felt like every tear her body could produce. She had accepted that the man of her dreams belonged to someone else. And why wouldn't he? He was handsome, wealthy, and charming. What woman wouldn't want him? Even his low birth wouldn't have been a deterrent if Lady Clayton had desired him badly enough.

Wrinkling her brow, she watched father and son ride, growing smaller in the distance as the horse picked up speed once clear of the cherry groves and in an open field.

A sudden realization niggled at the back of her mind, demanding closer inspection. Turning away from the window, she paced across the room, thinking over what little she knew of her new employers. Henry was four years old … yet, she and Sinclair had met *four* years ago. She gasped, a hand coming over her mouth as she realized that he had to have been married the night they'd met. Not just married, either. Lady Clayton would have been pregnant or just given birth to Henry.

Closing her eyes with a pained sigh, she clenched her hands into fists at her sides. She'd had no right to feel betrayed, to be hurt by discovering her employer was actually the man she'd shared that special night with so long ago. She'd had no right, because, in truth, Lady Clayton was the one who had been betrayed. Her husband had traipsed off to London, leaving her lying in—either pregnant or with a newborn child—while he spent his time carousing at balls and kissing unknowing debutantes in darkened gardens.

Bitter bile rose up in the back of her throat as memories of that night rushed back to her mind … the subtle hints at Sinclair's status as a married man.

Will I see you again?

I doubt it very much, angel … but, this is the way it must be.

Of course it had to be that way when he was married. Why would he want to see her again when he was wed to Lady Drucilla Clayton, perhaps the most beautiful woman Lydia had ever seen? She'd been a temporary distraction, an amusing little plaything for him to enjoy for a short moment before discarding.

Do you believe that I wish I could be the sort of man to court you and win you?"

She had. She'd believed him so ardently that she had manufactured an entire future for them in her mind. Lydia had imagined it so many times—Sinclair appearing at one of the parties in London, spying her from across the room. He'd smile, relieved to see her, regretting that they'd parted ways that night. He'd ask her to dance and tell her his name … he'd call upon her at Ashton House, where she'd taken up residence for the Season. He'd woo her with honeyed words, sweet kisses, and secret caresses. Then, one day, he would declare his love for her and ask her to be his wife. She'd imagined their wedding night while touching herself, stroking her body to climax … thought over how many children they might have and what their names would be.

"Idiot," she spat, shaking her head, appalled at herself for such naiveté.

No matter. He had made a fool out of her once; he would not do so again. She was here to educate Henry. Mr. Clayton, who she'd been told was rarely in residence at Buckton, would not ruin this for her—the final chance she had at securing and keeping a long-term position.

As she neared Mr. Welby's office, she fixed her face into a genial mask, hoping it adequately concealed her anger and despair. She had splashed her face with cold water several times more before leaving her chamber, and it had helped with the redness of her cheeks caused by weeping. When she lingered in the open doorway of the steward, she presented the bland façade of an unassuming governess.

The man glanced up from his work when she cleared her throat. A genuine smile brightened his features, and he stood, motioning for her to come inside.

"Miss Darling," Welby said, his voice as warm and welcoming as the day they'd met. "I trust you are enjoying your day off."

Forcing a smile, she sank into one of the chairs facing his desk, folding her hands in her lap. "I am, thank you. You wished to see me?"

He sat again, leaning back in his chair with the casual air of a man comfortable in his surroundings, as much a part of Buckton as the cherry trees and fine furniture.

"Yes," he replied. "Mr. Clayton has asked me to inform you that your wages are to be increased."

Outwardly, she showed no reaction to Welby's words. However, her insides whirled in a chaotic storm of emotions. Confusion, first and foremost, anger quickly coming on is heels and overwhelming it all. Lydia's stomach churned as she thought over all the reasons Mr. Clayton might wish to increase her pay. Silence, perhaps?

Her tone was more clipped than she intended when she replied. "I see. I was led to believe that Lady Clayton would be handling the matter of Henry's education as well as my employment here. I was quite content with the two-hundred-fifty pounds per annum she so generously offered. It is far more than I was paid at my previous posts."

Welby's eyebrows knit together, and he inclined his head, studying her as if trying to puzzle out her sudden shift in demeanor. "While that is certainly true, Mr. Clayton has the final say in all financial matters—including the payment of Buckton's staff. He is quite generous with pay for all his servants and employees. When apprised of your salary, he informed me that he wished the amount doubled to five hundred pounds per annum."

Lydia fumbled for words as Mr. Welby's reply sank in, jarring her quite effectively. "*Five hundred?* Mr. Welby, the amount is absurd! No governess I've ever known can command such a sum."

The steward smiled at that, his blue eyes twinkling with amusement. "Perhaps not, but then, those governesses never worked at Buckton."

"I cannot accept that," she argued, her hands clenching together in her lap, fingers aching from how hard she gripped. "It is too much."

It was too much for a governess to command. But what if Mr. Clayton had something else in mind? What if he thought paying her so much money entitled him to demand other things from her—indecent things? Her face reddened with equal parts embarrassment and rage. What would the rest of the household think of her should word of her obscene salary become known?

"Mr. Clayton has demanded it, and as steward, it is my job to distribute pay to the household staff," he informed her. "You will be paid five hundred pounds per annum for as long as you are employed here, unless Mr. Clayton says otherwise."

Pinching her lips together, she fought the urge to declare that Mr. Clayton could go to the devil. She did not think the steward would think so highly of her if she allowed that to slip.

"I understand," she said after getting her wayward tongue under control. "Is that all?"

Mr. Welby nodded. "Of course. Enjoy the rest of your day, Miss Darling."

Relieved to be dismissed, she rose and gave the man a little nod. "I will. Thank you, Mr. Welby."

His only reply was another one of those genial smiles, so she turned to leave, clenching her shaking hands around the skirt of her gown. Her skin still felt hot, too tightly stretched over her flesh, so she made a beeline for the front doors. She burst out onto the front steps, squinting against the late afternoon sun. It wasn't proper for her to be out in the open without a hat and shawl or spencer, and she supposed that ought to make her concerned over what her employers might think should they catch her being so indecorous.

Yet, she could not bring herself to care, holding up her skirts as she descended the front steps, setting off in no direction in particular. It was her day to do with as she pleased, and just now, she needed the soft breeze and the warmth of the sun on her face. Going back inside where she might encounter Mr. Clayton was out of the question.

As she drew farther away from the house, Lydia began to turn over her current dilemma in her mind, examining it from all angles. Abandoning her post within a fortnight of accepting the job was not an option. She could not afford the blow to her reputation as a governess. She would be seen as unreliable, inadequate, someone who should not be taken seriously. Besides, she had no desire to leave, not when she and Henry got along so well.

The small problem of Mr. Clayton was easily remedied. At the first opportunity, she would simply inform him that she was not a whore who could be bought, and she had no intention of telling anyone what had happened between them in that garden, so he had no need to purchase her silence. She was here to take on the education of his son, nothing more. He would be made to understand that, and Lydia would go on with her life, doing her best to pretend he did not exist. With any luck, the man would leave on business or some other pretense, freeing her from the vexation of his presence.

By the time she had reached the stables, she felt better about the entire thing, her mind slightly eased. A nice walk or ride always helped her to clear her head and manage her thoughts, this time proving no exception. She smiled at the scent of hay and horse that came at her from the wooden structure, the smells reminding her of home. Oakmoor boasted massive stables, with large paddocks built around them, where the family's horses were brought out for exercise and training.

She missed Apollo, the palomino quarter horse Michael and Amelia had purchased as a gift for her eighteenth birthday. The last time she'd visited home, she had taken him for long, bracing rides across the estate, reveling in the feel of the beast between her legs and the whip of wind through her unbound hair. That visit felt so far behind her, a lifetime of hurt and loneliness stretching between herself and the girl who had loved to ride so recklessly. In truth, that girl now seemed like a different person than who she'd become, someone she no longer knew.

So lost in thought was she, as she paced toward the open doors of the stable, hoping to simply take a look at the animals inside, that she did not hear the rumble of his voice until it was too late. She came up short just within the building, breath catching at the sound of those deep, warm tones echoing through the space and filling it until there was room for little else.

Lydia spied him on the far end of the stable, crouched on one knee and affectionately petting a massive bloodhound while a second beast lay on the ground just beside him. The one he petted panted and snorted, the little sounds holding the excitement of a dog thrilled at the return of its master. Its tail whipped back and forth through the air, declaring for all the world its joy.

"Who's a good boy?" Sinclair murmured, using both hands to chafe the dog's short coat, a broad grin pulling back his mouth to expose his teeth. "Yes, I missed you, too, Barkley."

Her belly quivered at the picture he made, a far cry from the man she'd met in London, yet still so similar. The easy grace in his movements was still present, as well as the devastating good looks. Only, now, those looks seemed far more dangerous, less refined out of a black evening kit and without the presence of moonlight. Hair unruly from riding, jaw covered in days' worth of stubble, and his clothing … the worn breeches, soft boots, and coat with no benefit of waistcoat or cravat gave him an athletic air, showcasing the sinew of strong thighs and powerful shoulders.

She snorted derisively at herself, annoyed that the sight of him could make her lose hold of her senses so quickly. He had proved to be a cad, a lecher, an adulterer. What more did she need to relinquish her girlish fantasies where he was concerned?

Seeming to have heard the rough sound she'd made, Sinclair turned his head, glancing up at her. His smile melted away, replaced with an intense inspection that put her on edge. Her every muscle tensed, her limbs tingling with the urge to flee; yet, she remained rooted to the spot, unable to move, even while knowing she should run without looking back.

"Lydia," he murmured, his deep voice carrying across the space between them.

The impact of her Christian name on his tongue made her head spin. She had underestimated the effect it would have to hear him say it.

"Miss Darling, if you please," she snapped, folding her hands in front of her to stop their trembling.

Clearing his throat, he rose, still absently scratching the head of the hound, who went to its haunches and stared lovingly up at him. "I apologize. We are not so formal here at Buckton. I refer to my employees by their first names and invite them to call me Sinclair. However, if you prefer Miss Darling, I will certainly respect that."

Inclining her head, she pursed her lips. "I do, thank you."

He nodded, staring at her in silence. She did not like the way his dark gaze slid over her, taking her in from head to toe with slow deliberation. His glance did not feel lascivious from this distance, but rather a curious perusal, a steady calculation. Just now, she cursed herself for not going back inside for a bonnet, for a shawl, for anything that would act as a barrier between her and his eyes.

"Actually, I am glad we encountered one another," she added, deciding that now was as good a time as any to set him straight on a few matters. "I wished to speak with you regarding my salary."

Wrinkling his brow, Sinclair started toward her, those lean cords of muscle stretching and bunching beneath his clothes. She found herself about to retreat and fought against it, not wanting him to know how much the prospect of his nearness affected her. She idly wondered where the stable grooms might be, as they were utterly alone at the moment; a circumstance she had not considered when deciding to remain.

"I asked Charles—er, Mr. Welby—to inform you that your wages have been increased," he said, pausing just before her, hands folded behind his back. "Did he not tell you?"

"He did," she replied. "That is why I wished to speak with you. Mr. Clayton, the amount is too high. No governess earns so much in a year."

He raised his eyebrows. "You are qualified to teach my son French and Geography aside from the usual subjects of Reading, Writing, and Arithmetic. Your references were all sterling, your previous employers insisting that you are worth your salt. As well, I distinctly recall meeting a genteel lady at that ball four years ago, which means you are a woman of breeding. Are all these things not true?"

She blinked before answering, slightly taken aback. "Y-you read my references?"

"I did. I want Henry to have every advantage this world can offer him, and that includes a good education. I do not mind paying what I feel you to be worth in order to provide that."

Yet again, he had shocked her. It was the last thing she had expected to hear. However, she never thought she'd come face to face with him again after four years to find him married with a child. That thought bolstered her, bringing back the ire that had fizzled at the sight of him.

"I suppose you will not expect anything else from me for such a grand salary?" she prodded, folding her arms over her chest.

Confusion that seemed genuine flashed in his eyes, a few tiny lines appearing between his eyebrows as he took in her defensive posture. "Anything else?"

That he would play coy only infuriated her further.

"You are not to take my acceptance of this new salary to mean that I am open to arrangements of any other sort between us," she spat, having reached the edge of her patience, nerves frayed beyond repair. "Nor should you feel you need to part with so much money in order to gain my silence. I am embarrassed enough about what occurred between us four years ago without needing to compound it by telling your wife."

His eyes went wide, her meaning finally sinking in. Shaking his head, he took a step toward her, hands outstretched as if to touch her. She felt that touch, even though it did not land. Her shoulders practically burned from the intent of those reaching hands as she took a swift step backward, leveling a warning glare at him.

Holding his hands up in a placating gesture, he shook his head again. "Lydia—"

"*Miss Darling!*"

"Miss Darling," he said quickly. "I believe you have the wrong idea concerning my intentions. I meant what I said, and believe you are worth every cent of the five hundred pounds per annum I intend to pay you. I expect nothing else from you but that my son receives the best education possible."

Her throat began to burn from the words simmering there, the expletives she wanted to hurl at him. The tears she'd been holding back stung her eyes, threatening to emerge once more. But she would not give him the satisfaction. She would not allow him to see how much this hurt—learning of the family he'd had here at Buckton on the night he'd made her feel like the most desired woman in the world.

The feeling became acidic, boiling in her gut and scorching her throat, her tongue, her lips ... she could no longer hold them in.

"You would have me believe that, even after you—a married man—attempted to seduce me in that garden?" she demanded, the accusation flying out before she could stop it. "You dare present yourself to me as being above reproach after your duplicity? Do you think me daft? Do you think I—a governess with my *qualifications*—am incapable of simple math? That I cannot clearly comprehend that Henry had to have been a newborn on the night we met? Did you think I would not puzzle out that the man who kissed me, who said all those flowery things to me, was *married*?"

His expression quickly melted into one of horror, and he was coming toward her again, reaching out to touch her. This time, his hands landed, his fingers lightly wrapping around her upper arms. For a moment, she was shocked into stillness, the heat of his touch and the impact of his scent swirling up her nostrils overwhelming all the instincts telling her to push him away.

"It was not what you are making it out to be," he insisted, his piercing stare unwavering, holding her captive. "That night, I was … It is complicated. My entire life is complicated. It has been since I was born. But with you, in that moment, everything felt easy. It felt right."

She shook her head, fighting the sensation his words caused deep in her chest, battling the hope, the desperation. "Don't."

"I think about it often," he continued, as if he hadn't heard her. "Constantly, in fact."

"Mr. Clayton."

"I think about *you* so often, it is laughable," he rushed on. "What sort of besotted fool can't stop pining after a woman he met *once* four years ago?'

"*Mr. Clayton!*" she bellowed, shrugging out of his hold and moving far away enough that she could no longer smell him, or feel the impact of his proximity. "Enough! Your words mean nothing. We both know that you withheld the truth from me. You tricked me into … I would have never … I will not lie with another woman's husband!"

"I am not asking you to," he stated, his voice quavering a bit on the last words. "Lydia, please—"

"For the last time, it is Miss Darling!" she snapped. "And there is nothing for you to say to me, unless I have somehow missed my guess.

Were you, or were you not, wed to Lady Clayton on the night we met?"

He clenched his jaw, tearing his gaze from her and setting it on one of the stalls and the nickering horse inside. For a moment, she thought he would not answer, a muscle in his jaw flexing and loosening in spasms, as if he ground his teeth.

"Yes," he managed after a moment of tense silence.

She had known, but hearing him admit it struck her like a fist to the gut. She placed a hand over her belly, taking a deep breath as she absorbed the pain.

"Then there is nothing left for you to say," she declared, doing her best to pretend as if this revelation meant nothing to her. "I believe I have made myself clear, Mr. Clayton. I am here to act as Henry's governess. Nothing more."

"Of course," he ground out, each syllable strained, as if he held himself in check.

"Unless it pertains to my pupil, you are not to speak to me or attempt to engage me in private again," she added.

She was pushing her luck, speaking to her employer this way, but it felt so good after the shock she'd suffered today—her due after so many years of missing him, longing for him, only to find he was a charlatan.

"As you wish," he said with a little nod.

She gave a curt nod of her own, then spun on her heel and left the stable as fast as her legs would carry her. Lydia felt his gaze on her, following her all the way to the house. It took every ounce of her will to keep from looking back.

CHAPTER 4

Sinclair left the bathtub, his water having long grown cold while he sat brooding, gaze fixated on the setting sun through his bedroom window. The day's events after his long journey from Essex had drained him, and he wanted nothing more than to dry off and climb into his bed. There, he might yank the bedclothes over his head and burrow deep, shutting out the world as exhaustion pulled him into oblivion.

However, such actions would not stop the constant drifting of his mind back to the woman who had lingered on the edges of his thoughts for four long years. Even hours after their tumultuous conversation in the stable, he was hard-pressed to forget the way those large, blue eyes had stared so accusingly at him, or the way her mouth had curved in derision at the sight of him. The weight of her words, and the pain he'd heard in each one, had stayed with him, pressing down with crushing force.

Were you, or were you not, wed to Lady Clayton on the night we met?

The question had damned him, as all he could do when it was hurled at him was tell the truth. Yes, he had been married to Drucilla on the night he'd met Lydia. Yes, he had left Buckton for London shortly after Henry's birth, where he'd buried himself in the revelry of the Season in order to avoid coming home to confront things he'd rather not face.

However, he had been unable to put into words how finding Lydia in that darkened corner of a London garden had been like a soft breeze cutting through stale, stifling humidity. He couldn't have explained how kissing her, touching her, holding her for so short a time had so profoundly affected him.

Even if he had been able to say those things with Lydia looking at him, tears and disappointment brimming in her eyes, he doubted she would have believed him. And why should she? Examining their night together from her perspective, he measured it against the moment she had turned to find him standing before her in the schoolroom—in a home where he lived with his wife and son.

Pausing in the middle of drying off, he closed his eyes and heaved a pained sigh. God, what she must think of him.

He had thought leaving her in that garden without a look back, without telling her his name, was the hardest thing he'd ever done in his life. But he had done it knowing that he could never give her what she needed, what she deserved. He had walked away, hoping that she would remember him as fondly as he would her.

Sinclair had never given any thought to how it might feel to see her again and have her learn the secret he had kept from her, the reason he hadn't told her his name or any of the other facts she might have thought to be pertinent. And, perhaps they were important now, but then, they hadn't seemed to matter. He had not wanted to be Drucilla's husband, or Mr. Clayton, wealthy bastard son of a viscount. He had only wanted to be the man Lydia looked at with wonder and desire in her eyes. He had wanted to be the man who banished the sadness he'd seen all over her face—the rejection she carried after months of being made to feel like an outcast by the London *ton*. With her, for less than an hour, he had felt as if he belonged somewhere. It hadn't mattered that that 'somewhere' had been in a tree bough with a beautiful stranger. It had felt right to him, and even after all this time, it still did.

He thought of it often; mostly at night when his son or the business of the day did not occupy his foremost thoughts. Sinclair would often lie in his cold bed alone and fantasize about being able to meet her as a bachelor, free and unattached. The possibilities were endless then, the numerous ways he could court, woo, and win her playing out in his mind so many times in so many different ways.

As he pulled on his dressing gown, belting it at the waist while crossing to the door separating his chamber from Drucilla's, he attempted to bring his thoughts back to the present. There was nothing to be done about it. He could not travel back in time and do things differently with Lydia—perhaps telling her he had a wife, neglecting to kiss her or take any of the other liberties with her that he had. And, truthfully, if he could go back and do it all again, he was not certain that he would change anything. It had been one of the brightest spots of the last ten years of his life, second only to becoming a father.

Because he could not change the past, he could only look forward and hope that some way to make amends would present itself. He had done a poor job of explaining himself in the stable, still reeling from the impact of her sudden presence in his life. With more time to clear his head, he would think of some way to tell her the truth. He could only hope she would listen, and even if she did not forgive him for hurting her, perhaps she might understand.

It would be difficult, occupying the same home as her, going about life at Buckton knowing she was under the same roof as his shrew of a wife. However, letting her go was out of the question. If a woman with Lydia's prospects had fallen to life as a governess, there must be some reason. He did not think she would have applied for work as a governess without cause, and he would not be the reason she went hungry or without a place to live.

That decided, he knocked upon the door, waiting to be allowed admittance. A travesty, that he'd been made to feel like an intruder on the threshold of his own wife's bedchamber; yet, here he stood, waiting to be allowed inside.

The door opened a few inches, and he was confronted by Alice, Drucilla's lady's maid.

"Have they finished?" he asked, casting a glance past the woman. He caught sight of Drucilla perched on the edge of her bed, righting her clothing while Doctor Tunstall went about replacing his instruments in his leather bag.

"Yes, Mr. Clayton," the maid replied, stepping back and opening the door wider to admit him. "The doctor was just about to send for you."

"Very good," he declared, sweeping into the room. "You may go, Alice. Her Ladyship will ring for you if she has a need."

Alice inclined her head at him, giving a swift curtsy. They always did that—bow or curtsy to him, even though he was not a man of rank. He often wondered if it had anything to do with their salaries, which were more than others in their position might earn in other households. Or, perhaps it was his way of treating them as family that gave them such respect for him. Whatever the case, he never wanted to take that for granted.

He gave Alice a little smile. "Thank you."

She smiled back, then turned to quit the bedroom, quietly slipping out as Sinclair moved farther into the chamber, approaching the bed.

"Doctor," he said, as the physician closed his bag and straightened, turning to face him. "Thank you for coming on such short notice. When I returned to Buckton and noticed Lady Clayton's cough, I became concerned it might be pneumonia again."

Drucilla allowed Sinclair to help her into bed, lying back against the pillows while he pulled the bedclothes up to cover her. She only allowed it because the eyes of the physician watched them. As always, she portrayed the perfect picture of a demure wife, submitting to his attentions. Quite a skilled actress, his wife, her performances fooling everyone into thinking her devoted to him. Only Sinclair and the servants of Buckton Manor knew better.

"It is not pneumonia this time," Doctor Tunstall declared, coming forward to meet him near Drucilla's bed. "However, she is showing signs of croup, which I find to be just as concerning. I have instructed Her Ladyship to remain abed until the prolonged coughing fits have passed. She is not to exert herself unnecessarily."

Sinclair cast a glance at his wife, the pity he used to feel whenever she became ill distinctly absent. All he could conjure now was annoyance, knowing that he'd been right to insist upon calling the doctor while she argued she suffered from a simple cold. It was almost as if she *liked* being ill, reveling in the attention that it earned her.

"I will see to it that she is kept abed," he told the doctor. "Am I to assume her diet should be the same as last time? Broth and tea?"

Tunstall nodded. "She might try bread as she gets stronger … if her stomach will allow it. As well, I've left another bottle of the draught I provided during her last bout with croup. It should help ease the cough a bit. Keep her bedroom shuttered, warm and dry. I predict she will be on the mend within a fortnight."

Sinclair looked at the glass bottle resting on Drucilla's bedside table. She claimed to hate the taste of the potion, but he always noticed a marked improvement in her cough if she ingested it often enough.

"Thank you, Doctor," he replied. "We've been through this before, so I believe we shall get along just fine. See Mr. Welby on your way out, and he will ensure you receive a little something for your trouble."

Tunstall's eyes glittered at the prospect, despite already commanding a fair salary to be at the beck and call of many well-to-do families in Hertfordshire. Still, Sinclair did not mind parting with a bottle of his best Burgundy or a few choice cigars to keep the man amenable. With how often Drucilla fell ill, he was forced to call upon Tunstall more than any other family in the county.

"I pray you recover quickly, my lady," Tunstall said, giving a little bow to Drucilla before going to gather his bag. "I will return to look in on you soon."

"Thank you, Doctor," Drucilla replied, her voice light and sweet, a perfect imitation of the young girl Sinclair had fallen in love with when he'd been but a boy.

God, had it been so long? Long enough for everything to change, he realized as he rounded the bed to retrieve the coughing draught. As the door closed behind Tunstall, he lowered himself onto the edge of the bed, close enough that his hip fit against the curve of her waist.

She stiffened, her breath going still and quiet as she narrowed suspicious eyes on him. Sinclair pretended not to notice, unstopping the bottle and pouring a healthy amount of the draught onto a spoon that had been left resting on the bedside table.

"Come, Dru," he urged. "You heard Doctor Tunstall."

Scowling, she turned her head, lips pinched at the corners. "I hate that foul-tasting poison."

He sighed, in no mood for her petulant behavior. "This *poison* will ease your cough so that you can sleep. If you are not coughing all night, I do not have to hear you hacking through the door, and *I* might get a decent night's sleep, as well."

Sitting upright, she parted her lips, allowing him to spoon the bitter-smelling liquid into her mouth. She grunted as she swallowed, a cringe of distaste hardly robbing her of her ethereal beauty. Sinclair remained where he sat, studying her pensively while he stopped the bottle and set it, along with the spoon, back on her bedside table.

The first time he'd ever laid eyes on Lady Drucilla Stratton, he had only been four and ten years of age. She'd been the most beautiful creature he'd ever seen, even then, the first blush of womanhood already overtaking the girlishness of her perfect features. He'd thought her an angel, some untouchable thing that could never be his. But then, she'd begun casting sidelong glances in his direction whenever he'd come to Buckton Manor with her elder brother. She'd looked at him with interest and desire, and Sinclair had hoped with the madness of youth that she could become his. He'd fought for her, earned her with blood, sweat, and tears over the course of several years. He had thought that winning her would be the end of his hardship, a prize rightfully earned.

How naive he had been. Marriage to Drucilla had only been the beginning of a life filled with emptiness and regret. It had, quite possibly, been the gravest mistake of his life.

"You may go now," she snapped when he did not speak for a long moment. "No one is here, so you do not need to pretend you care whether I live or die."

In the past, her venomous words might have gotten a rise out of him. Now, he could only roll his eyes over her dramatics.

"Are you certain you wish me to leave?" he countered. "Without me, you have no audience whose pity you might play upon. You will be without your visitors for a fortnight … one would think you would revel in my presence."

She snorted, arranging herself more comfortably amongst the pillows. "I would rather share my bed with a viper."

"It is only natural for you to prefer entertaining one of your own species," he fired back almost without thinking.

Regret did not settle in until after he'd realized what he had said, and by then, it was too late to take it back. It was always too late. Yet again, he found himself despising the man she'd turned him into. He had not always been so brooding, so angry or sarcastic. It seemed that with each passing year, his worst qualities rose to the surface, and he had no real notion who he was any longer.

"I do care, Dru," he said, his voice low as he averted his gaze across the room. Looking at her hurt too much, the reminder that she wasn't the girl he'd fallen in love with anymore always the most acute. "For Henry's sake, most of all. I hardly wish for him to have to endure the death of his mother. I know all too well how painful that can be."

She did not reply for a moment, and he began to think she would not. She likely did not believe him—perhaps thought that he wished for her to die so that he did not have to live with her any longer. In truth, he could not settle on one emotion in particular. Perhaps death would free them both, but it would also trap him in a life with a boy who mourned his lost mother. Another part of him, the young boy who still loved the memory of who he'd thought Drucilla was, only wanted the passion of his youth back. It was a heady, torrential mixture, one that sat in his belly with all the weight of a boulder.

"Henry seems happy with his new governess," Drucilla said finally, landing on the one topic that did not inevitably hurtle them toward yet another row. "I think this one will last."

"Yes," he agreed. "I met with Miss Darling this morning. She seems well-qualified. So much so that I increased her salary."

He went on avoiding looking at Drucilla, who—for all her faults—knew him better than anyone. It was an uncanny ability of hers, ferreting out someone's secrets with nothing more than a glance, figuring out what made a person tick.

"They are not all like you, you know," she said. "Some of them are aware of their place, and do not have the audacity to think they can ever be anything more than what they are."

He snorted, shaking his head. "I had a bit of help working up the audacity to think myself above the manner of my birth, did I not?"

Silence stretched between them again, stifling and heavy. When had him being a bastard begun to matter to Drucilla? Perhaps after the allure of being with someone unsuitable, someone beneath her, had lost its thrill.

"Miss Darling is different," Drucilla went on. "Her brother married the sister of a marquis, and the Darlings own quite a bit of land in Norfolk."

He raised his eyebrows at that, his curiosity piqued by this revelation. It became even odder now, finding Lydia here after all this time. She'd been at a ball in the home of a member of the *ton*, and now, he knew that her presence had been due to family connections. With such wealth and a familial tie to a marquis, what had driven her to seek work as a governess? Perhaps the Darlings had fallen onto hard times. Or, maybe…

"She might have fallen from grace or some such thing," Drucilla said, echoing his own thoughts. "Not uncommon for a genteel woman to seek employment after becoming ineligible for marriage. Whatever the case, I suppose we ought to be grateful she is here."

Sinclair could not find the words to respond, not when his head had begun to spin with so many thoughts tumbling over and about one another. What could have happened to send Lydia running to Hertfordshire? What—or who—was she hiding from? Had some young buck taken advantage of her during her first Season and deflowered her, sending her back to her family a fallen woman? He thought of the young lady he had held and kissed in the garden four years ago. She had been an innocent, sweet and pure, untouched. The thought of any other man tasting her lips made him feel ill. Wondering if she'd been hurt, forced to spread her legs for someone who cared not whether she refused, made his blood boil, his hands clenching into fists in his lap.

"Sin?"

Drucilla's questioning voice drew him out of his reverie. He blinked, giving his head a little shake to clear it. He found his wife watching him with her eyebrows drawn together, gaze sharp and assessing as always.

Damn it all to Hell. The last thing he needed was for her to discover that he'd carried a torch for their governess for the past four years. He didn't even want to consider what she might do to exploit such information.

"I am exhausted," he declared, rising quickly to his feet. "The ride from Essex was long. Good night, Dru."

"Good night," she replied to his back.

He was halfway to the door, his mind having already flown across the house to where he knew Lydia slept, one floor below them. Worry for her twisted in his gut, along with a need to help make things right if he could. For reasons he did not understand, he felt responsible for her, as if he might have had some hand in her fate. That he was paying her several times more than a governess might be worth was not enough. He had to know what had happened to her, and he also needed her to understand the truth of their first meeting. He needed to find a way to express to her what he'd failed to that afternoon in the stable.

After he stripped off his dressing gown and fell into bed, sleep eluded him despite his exhaustion. As she always did when he was alone in his bed, Lydia overwhelmed his thoughts, leaving room for little else.

The next morning, Sinclair entered the dining room to find it already occupied. As he did every morning, Charles Welby sat enjoying coffee and biscuits before starting his day's work. Sinclair often teased the steward by asking if he might not have coffee at his own home. Charles would merely laugh and tell him that the quality of it was better here. And because he enjoyed talking over the upcoming day of work with his friend before the morning truly begun, Sinclair had instructed the cook to make sure the coffee and biscuits were available each morning.

Seated across from Charles was Lydia, her head lowered over a plate filled with offerings from the sideboard. He paused in the doorway for a moment, stunned into stillness at the sight of her. It was going to take some getting used to—entering various rooms of his home and finding her there. In the years that had passed since their first meeting, he'd often daydreamed about having her at Buckton. Wondering how she would look with the morning sun shining on her through the floor-to-ceiling windows lining one wall of the dining room couldn't have prepared him for this. Her golden hair gleamed like wheat, the soft yet simple chignon and loose strands at her temples creating a picture both alluring and demure. She wore a rather plain day gown of cream in a simple design—a far cry from the finery she'd worn on the night they had met, yet she was all the more compelling because of it.

He soaked in everything: the slope of her neck, the line of her jaw, even the parting of her lips as she raised her cup to drink tea. He smirked at the sight of her plate, filled more substantially than that of any lady he'd ever seen. A country girl, he remembered, she would be used to meat and eggs each morning as opposed to simple toast and tea. He supposed it must be responsible for the lush frame pressing at the confines of her gown, the soft curves that had filled his hands when he'd held her. Difficult to avoid comparing her to Drucilla, who had always possessed a long, downright willowy frame.

"Good morning, Sin," Charles called out.

Lydia stiffened, her teacup held halfway to her lips at the mention of his name. Now that he'd been found out, he could not go on staring at her from the doorway. So, he entered the room, hands clasped behind his back.

"Good morning, Charles," he replied, trying to keep his tone light and his eyes off Lydia. "Miss Darling."

She paused in cutting into a slice of ham, casting a swift glance up at him. "Mr. Clayton."

The clipped tone with which her voice cradled his name stung like a razor across his skin. When thinking of their brief moments together, their kiss, he'd always wondered how much better the experience could have been with her whispering his name. Just the thought of her whimpering or moaning his name, the sound slipping out between mewls of ecstasy as he kissed his way down her body, made his blood run hot.

"Miss Darling was just telling me that she discovered a shortened bed sheet upon retiring last evening," Charles said with a little chuckle.

"Henry," he muttered.

While he stood at the sideboard, filling a clean plate to his satisfaction, a footman quickly filled the cup at his place at the head of the table. The scent of coffee made his mouth water from across the room, and by the time he arrived at his place, it had been laced with milk and nothing else, just the way he preferred.

"Thank you, John," he said to the footman, who gave him a little nod before going back to his corner of the room.

"And how have you decided to repay him, Miss Darling?" Charles asked between bites.

Lydia's lips twitched with amusement. "I once played this trick on my brother, Michael … stuffing a handkerchief into the toe of his left shoe, so that when he tried to put it on, it no longer fit."

"And the right one does!" Charles exclaimed, roaring with laughter as he leaned back in his chair. "Very clever, Miss Darling. Do you not agree, Sin?"

He took his first sip of coffee and hummed with approval. It was perfect.

"Yes, quite," he agreed, daring another look at Lydia. "It would seem Henry has met his match."

She actively avoided looking at him as she went on eating. "Life with two elder brothers has prepared me for all contingencies."

"Still," he pressed, buttering a slice of toast. "If he makes too much a nuisance of himself, do inform me. I do not want him chasing you off."

She waved a dismissive hand. "Oh, I do believe I can manage. Besides, it is all in good fun. None of his pranks have been harmful."

Her perspective on his son's predilections was refreshing, to say the least. There had been two governesses before her, and neither had found Henry very amusing. It was nice to know that Lydia would be able to give as good as she got with the lad.

The dining room fell into silence as Charles polished off his coffee while Lydia and Sinclair went on eating. Tension thrummed between him and the governess with such stunning force, he wondered if Charles could feel it. Her movements had become stiff, her back erect, her shoulders tense as she ate. He was unable to keep from stealing glances at Lydia whenever he could, though she seemed determined not to look at him.

"Well, I suppose I'd better get to work if I wish to earn those biscuits," Charles quipped, wiping his mouth with his napkin and then rising from his chair. "Sin, I will be ready to go over those ledgers whenever you are."

Sinclair nodded in response, mouth full of coddled eggs. Charles bid Lydia good morning, then disappeared through the open dining room door.

His absence seemed to suck the last of the fresh air from the room. Sinclair was suffocating, his every breath and movement stifled by the tension clogging the atmosphere. He turned to glance at the footman, who remained in his corner, watching like a hawk in case someone required more coffee or tea.

While Lydia had been adamant that he not try to accost her alone again, he did not want to leave things the way they'd ended the day before. As well, the mention of her family had him even more curious about her past and her reasons for seeking employment. He could not satisfy said curiosity with a footman lurking about, listening in.

"That will be all, John," he said.

The servant obeyed, giving him the opening he needed.

"Miss Darling," he ventured, setting his now empty cup in its saucer.

Still avoiding looking at him, Lydia lifted her napkin off her lap, then used it to wipe her mouth before laying it beside her plate. "I do believe I have finished. Mrs. Beecham ought to be waiting in the schoolroom with Henry now."

He spoke before she could stand, hands braced on the arms of her chair. "This will only take a moment. Please, stay."

While his words might be a request, he had used a tone that bordered on a command. To his surprise, she relented, folding her hands on the table before her and inclining her head at him.

"Yes, Mr. Clayton?"

"I was speaking with Lady Clayton last night, and she happened to mention that you have a family in Norfolk," he began, plucking his words out of thin air and hoping he would not offend her.

To her credit, she maintained her bland expression as well as her even tone. "Yes. My mother, brothers, sisters-in-law, and nieces and nephews reside in Norfolk."

He nodded. "I simply wanted to say, should you ever wish to go to visit them, we would be happy to provide transportation. A coach could be prepared, a driver and footman sent along with you. In a few months, Christmas will be upon us, and Charles always takes that time to visit his own family. I … well, I realize that living with a family you do not know well can be difficult during such times. The offer will stand, should you ever wish to take advantage of it. As well, should you desire to send correspondence to them, simply deliver it to Charles' office. He will ensure it reaches them through the post."

At last, she looked at him, her eyes a bit wide, something like astonishment glimmering in the depths. Had he shocked her? Perhaps she'd never had an employer offer her such a kindness before.

Her expression softened, causing the tight knot of anxiety in his gut to ease.

"That is very generous, Mr. Clayton. I have been meaning to write them and inform them of my new position. I will have a letter to give to Mr. Welby tomorrow morning."

"Very good."

He should have been satisfied with that, but the mention of her family had opened a door. He might not have another opportunity like this one.

"Might I ask …" He cleared his throat, now unable to maintain her gaze as he prepared to delve into her personal life. "That is … the young lady I met four years ago was … I would never have thought to find her applying to work as a governess."

She made a little sound, and when he glanced up in response, he found her smothering her shock with a mask of annoyance.

"That is hardly any of your business."

Her brusqueness did not put him off. If anything, it only made him want to pry further. He had obviously struck a nerve.

"Perhaps not. However, any servant of Buckton can tell you that I take a personal interest in the people who work for me. You are no exception. It simply puzzles me that someone who might have made an advantageous marriage has found herself here. If something happened … if there might be anything I can do to help—"

"There is nothing for you to do," she interjected, laying her teacup in its saucer with a bit more force than was necessary. "As you can guess, I did not make a match my first Season. I decided not to pursue a second as I found the process to be tedious. And instead of becoming a burden upon my relations, I decided to strike out and make a life for myself. I enjoy teaching young children, and am quite fulfilled by my work."

For a moment, he grappled with words. He wanted to tell her that he doubted she could ever be a burden upon anyone. He wanted to tell her that the men who had refused to offer for her were bloody fools, and that if he were free, he would have claimed her as his own the night they'd met.

However, she already thought of him as a lecher who had attempted to prey on her despite being married. He couldn't stand for her opinion of him to sink any lower.

"I see," he said. "Thank you for enlightening me, Miss Darling. Please know that we treat our staff like family here at Buckton. So, if there is anything you need … anything at all … please inform Charles, and he will consult me about seeing it done. We want you to feel at home here."

Pushing her chair back from the table, she rose. "That is kind of you, Mr. Clayton. I will bear it in mind. I should go now. Henry will be wondering where I've been."

"Of course. I hope you have a pleasant day … and that your prank has frustrated Henry to no end."

As he watched her breeze toward the door, he could not help but notice the twitching of her lips, as if she held back a smile. She paused in the doorway, swiveling in an instant to look at him. He flinched at being caught staring after her, but could not look away once those eyes of hers met his. They were like a clear summer sky—cloudless and bright blue.

"The men of London," she said, her voice low. "They liked me very much. Many of them told me so. But, as a man might like another man—one he indulges in card games and cigars with, one he hunts and rides with. I was not … I wasn't the sort of woman any of them wished to marry. That is why I did not make a match. After the Season, I decided there was no use trying again. None of those men desired to wed me, and I did not desire to shape myself into something I wasn't to snare a husband."

Her face flushed after she'd finished, and he realized that the words had come to her mouth unbidden. That she'd confided in him, even without wanting to, touched a part of him he'd thought long dead. He smiled at the realization that there were parts of him Drucilla had not yet destroyed, parts that weren't beyond salvaging.

"Those men were fools," he replied. "If any of them knew what it was like to marry one of those perfect porcelain dolls, those ladies with pristine manners and flawless bloodlines, well … they would long for a different sort of marriage. One where a man might talk to his wife as if she were his best friend, instead of talking to her as if she were a stranger. They would have flocked to you in droves, giving everything they had to win and keep you. You would have become the standard by which all other debutantes are measured."

He clamped his lips shut too late, his mouth having run away with him. Just as it had on the night he'd climbed that wall and sat on a tree limb beside her. Just looking at her brought something out in him, something that he could not seem to stifle.

Her lips parted, but no words were forthcoming. Her brow furrowed as she seemed to try to think up a response.

At last, she settled upon a simple "thank you." Then, she turned to leave, hurrying through the open dining room door, her footsteps fading down the corridor.

CHAPTER 5

For several days following Mr. Clayton's arrival at Buckton Manor, Lydia went through her routine in a bit of a fog. It felt as if her body moved around on its own, working from memory, while her mind wandered about, removed from the rest of her.

To the eyes of Henry and the other occupants of the manor, she probably seemed like her usual self. Quiet, unassuming, strict when her pupil required it. She rose each morning, took breakfast in the dining room with Mr. Welby and Sinclair—remaining silent while the two chatted about matters of the estate—then spent her day in the schoolroom with Henry. Her evenings were her own, but even then, she could not seem to find contentment in her usual hobbies. None of her books appealed, and the bit of needlepoint she'd been working on failed to keep her interest. She often stared listlessly through her window, mind racing as Sinclair's words echoed through her mind.

If any of them knew what it was like to marry one of those perfect porcelain dolls ... they would long for a different sort of marriage ... You would have become the standard by which all other debutantes are measured.

While she wanted to believe his words were no more than the empty flatteries of a rake, something within her had latched onto them. Yet, in the time since he'd been home, Lydia had not heard a single note of laughter coming from the floor above hers, where the suite of the master and his lady were situated. In fact, Sinclair seemed to spend most of his time outdoors or in his study while Lady Clayton lay abed nursing croup.

The last time Lydia had visited Oakmoor, her sister-in-law, Hesper, had come down with a cold. Her brother, Archie, had spent every waking moment at her bedside, feeding her broth and helping her to take sips of tea. That sort of devotion seemed to be a mainstay of Oakmoor, where her parents had filled the manor with love and laughter. Her brothers and their wives carried on in the tradition.

When comparing her experiences back home to the atmosphere here at Buckton, she could not help but wonder what had happened between Sinclair and his wife. Lady Clayton had insinuated that her husband rarely inhabited Buckton. Lydia had assumed he traveled to his various estates on matters of business, but perhaps there were other reasons—some explanation why he did not wish to live under the same roof as his wife.

None of this should matter to her. She'd come here to teach Henry, and things were going well. Sinclair even maintained his distance, just as she'd asked him to. Understanding the complexities of the Claytons' marriage would not aid her in her duties. Yet, she could not seem to stop thinking of it, along with the impassioned words Sinclair had spoken to her over breakfast.

On the fourth day following Sinclair's return, Lydia ended her lessons with Henry an hour earlier than usual. He seemed restless after three days of constant rain, and itched to go outside now that the sun had begun to shine. Standing at the schoolroom window and gazing out at the immaculate landscape, she decided a bit of time out of doors might do her some good, as well. Rushing to her room to retrieve a shawl, she then exchanged her slippers for sturdy boots as the grass might still be a bit wet after all the rain.

With Henry in the care of his nanny for the rest of the evening, she would attempt to finally free her mind of destructive thoughts. Taking the path toward the wooded area ringing the house grounds, she hoped to lose herself in the tangle of trees and underbrush for a few hours. It might even make her feel as if she were getting a taste of home.

Halfway down the path, she encountered a man coming from the opposite direction, a wide-brimmed hat shading his face from the sun. Squinting in the absence of her own headwear, she made out the slender form of Mr. Welby. He smiled as he drew near.

"Miss Darling," he said, his tone as warm as ever. "I suppose lessons have concluded for the day?"

"Yes," she replied, finding it easy to return the man's smile. "I was just taking a walk before dinner."

"The weather is certainly perfect for it. I've just come from enjoying a walk of my own. I will not keep you—"

"Actually," she said, before he could take his leave of her. "If it isn't too much of an imposition, I was wondering if you might tell me more about Buckton. I confess to being wildly curious about the place."

His eyes crinkled at the corners when he smiled again, something he seemed to do often. "Of course it is not an imposition. My duties are completed for the day, and I have nothing left to do but return home, where I live alone. Walking and talking with a lovely young woman … well, that appeals to me far more."

Coming from anyone else, his flattery might have sounded hollow. Yet, Mr. Welby oozed sincerity and openness in a way that made him easy to talk to. They'd worked up a rapport during her short time at Buckton, and it was nice to feel as if she had a friend here.

He gestured back in the direction he'd come, so she fell into step with him along the path through the trees. For a short while, they simply walked, the silence comfortable instead of strained. Buckton's steward struck Lydia as being the sort of man who brought comfort with him wherever he went. Never had she felt uneasy while alone with him.

"So," he said once they'd been swallowed by the thick woods ringing the main grounds of the estate. "What would you like to know about Buckton? As I am certain you gathered when you arrived, we grow cherries here."

Thinking of the endless rows upon rows of cherry trees she saw daily through her bedroom window, she laughed. "Yes, I rather thought that might the point of all those trees. How does the estate manage? Are there no tenants?"

He shook his head. "No tenants or farms here, though Sinclair does own a few smaller estates with tenant farms attached to them. However, Buckton is his largest holding, as well as his most profitable."

She raised her eyebrows. "I had not realized that cherries were so popular … or that they could afford a man such a lifestyle."

Mr. Welby shrugged. "Sinclair also has a head for investments—has a keen instinct for business, as well. Buckton would never have flourished as it did if not for him."

At Lydia's confused expression, the steward smiled.

"Perhaps I ought to start over. You see, it is impossible to speak of Buckton as it is now without tying it directly to Sinclair. He's the son of Viscount Clayton, if you did not know."

Remembering the night she'd met Sinclair, and recalling the frank way he had informed her that he was baseborn, she supposed he would not mind Mr. Welby so casually speaking of his parentage.

"Yes, I was aware," she replied.

"His mother was an actress who died when Sinclair was ten years of age. The viscount had provided well for them before her death, and it was said that he was quite besotted with her. Perhaps that was what compelled him to take Sinclair in and claim him, much to the viscountess' dismay. The woman was not thrilled to be forced to endure his presence alongside her own children—three boys and a girl. But the viscount adored him, probably more than his own heir, because of the affection he'd had for Sin's mother."

Her gaze wandered to the trees surrounding them as she tried to imagine Sinclair as a child. It was difficult to imagine him without the mournful, dark eyes or brooding facial expression, lips pushed into a slight pout.

"It could not have been easy for him," she remarked. "Being thrust into an entirely new world, amongst people he did not know. He must have missed his mother terribly."

"I am certain he did. However, being in the Clayton home offered him certain advantages. He was found to be a clever lad and sent to school, where he swiftly caught up to his peers. When he visited home on holiday, the viscount would take him into his study and teach him everything there was to know about money, investments, business. He had an inheritance set aside for Sinclair and wanted him to possess all the tools he would need to grow the seed, to stand head and shoulders with any other gentleman of society. He was being groomed into someone who could command influence, so that his birth would not have to matter in the right circles."

"How wonderful for him."

Despite being angry with Sinclair, and as confused as ever concerning his intentions toward her, she knew that life as a bastard could have been far worse for him. At least, he could take comfort in a father who had claimed him and given him the best of everything life had to offer.

"It was," Welby replied. "At school, he formed connections, which was how he became acquainted with Lord Milton Stratton—elder brother of the woman who would go on to become his wife, Lady Drucilla."

Her ears began to tingle, her spine straightening as they paused on the path, coming to an opening in the trees. She could hardly pay attention to the gently sloping hills stretching on for miles ahead of them, or the outcropping of buildings in the distance. Not when her palms had broken out into a sweat at the mention of Lady Clayton.

Now, he was coming closer to the information Lydia craved for reasons she would rather not examine too closely.

"Sinclair and Milton became fast friends," Mr. Welby went on, hands braced on his hips as he stood taking in the countryside, eyes narrowed against the glare of the setting sun. "And because the atmosphere at home could often be strained, Sinclair opted to spend some of his holidays off from school here at Buckton with the Stratton family. Here, he found Milton's parents, who were warm and accepting of Sinclair, even knowing he had been born on the wrong side of the blanket. He found a sort of home away from home, and a closeness with Milton he did not have with his own brothers. And, of course, he found Lady Drucilla."

She glanced at Welby from the corner of her eye, finding his mouth tightening at the corners at the mention of his employer's wife. It was a phenomenon she'd noticed amongst the other servants, as well. They were always respectful, of course, but there was a fondness they seemed to express for Sinclair that was markedly absent when it came to his wife.

"He was enamored with her from the start," Welby stated. "Even knowing he stood no chance with her. His education and inheritance notwithstanding, she was the daughter of an earl, and he the bastard offspring of an actress. That did not stop him from charming her at every turn, something that seems to come natural to a man like him."

Her face grew warm at the memory of him climbing the garden wall to return her slipper, slyly angling for a kiss, then tipping her world off its axis with the simple touch of his mouth against her own. How well she understood Mr. Welby's words.

"And she loved him?" she prodded, unable to help that her breath caught after she'd asked the question—then, she could not breathe until it had been answered, uncertain why it should matter.

Welby turned to meet her gaze, his brow drawing down over his clear, blue eyes. "You know ... I like to think perhaps she did. For his sake, I *hope* she did. But it would be easy to assume that she liked the forbidden nature of it all, wanting something she thought her father might be opposed to. Lady Clayton was as beautiful then as she is now, and she knew it—*everyone* knew it. Every young buck from Hertfordshire to Scotland wanted her, and she loved flaunting Sinclair, walking on his arm in full view of anyone who would spread the gossip. It made them clamor for her, trip over themselves to impress her enough to turn her head from a bastard."

Thinking of the delicate, sickly woman lying abed inside the manor, Lydia had a difficult time conjuring the picture of such a spiteful young woman. But then, she remembered the hard icicle edge of those eyes, the inexplicable feeling she'd gotten while being trapped in that gaze—the moment of doubt in which she had wondered whether the lady might be more than she seemed.

Welby was a close friend and obviously a confidant of Sinclair's. He must know more about Lady Clayton than Lydia did, so she could not argue.

"Did her father oppose the relationship?" she asked, leaning a bit closer. This story grew more intriguing by the second.

"No, to everyone's surprise," Welby said with a little chuckle. "In fact, the earl doted on Sinclair and saw in him all the qualities that Lord Clayton did. He took a personal interest in Sinclair and did everything he could to bolster the business acumen he had already gained from his own father. He treated Milton and Sinclair like equals, molding them, even going so far as to endow them both with a large sum of money upon their completion of university—a loan, he called it. The young men were to invest the money, increase it, and then keep the profits after paying the earl back his loan. Sinclair tripled his investment in a matter of a few years and paid the earl back with interest. It was then that the earl invited him to come to Buckton to work for him ... as a steward."

Lydia's mouth fell open, her mind reeling as all that Mr. Welby had just revealed sank in. It was the sort of story people told over tea in London drawing rooms, the kind that caused a man's reputation to precede him. How had she never known of Sinclair before encountering him at that ball? It seemed that someone who had made so much of himself from such humble beginnings ought to be legendary, spoken of far and wide—even as far as Norfolk.

"My God," she murmured, for lack of anything better to say.

"Quite a surprise to Sinclair, as well, but he gladly took the position," Welby replied. "His father's health had begun to fail, and his stepmother made it clear that he would not be welcome there once the viscount had died. He needed to make his own way in the world, and despite having the money to try his luck in London, he chose Buckton. Partly out of loyalty to the earl, but mostly because of Lady Drucilla. He loved her and had expressed an interest in wedding her. So, the earl struck up a deal with Sinclair."

Mr. Welby's hand gestured toward all the land stretching on for what seemed like an eternity, nothing but green rolling hills and neat little buildings.

"All of this could be his if he could double Buckton's productivity and profits as its steward. And if he could earn it, he could have Lady Drucilla's hand in marriage—provided she wanted him, of course."

Her eyes widened. "Did Milton not take exception to such a deal?"

Mr. Welby scoffed. "He stood to inherit an earldom, which came with several smaller titles and two massive estates that would earn him more than he could ever spend in a lifetime. Buckton was nothing to him when measured against that. He had no interest in the business of growing and selling cherries. Because this property was one the earl had acquired on his own and was not entailed or attached to his title, it could be bequeathed as he saw fit ... and he saw fit that Sinclair should become its owner."

"Fascinating," she said with a blink and a swift shake of her head. To say that Sinclair's story impressed her would be an understatement. "As he is now the master of Buckton, I assume he met the earl's requirements?"

"He met and exceeded them," Welby replied with a wide smile, the admiration he felt toward Sinclair apparent in his tone. "You see, while Buckton turned a steady profit, there was the problem of waste which caused them to bleed funds year after year."

"How so?" she asked, truly curious to know.

Her life as the daughter and sister of a gentleman farmer had taught her much about how an estate like this ran, though she knew more about wheat and sheep, Oakmoor's primary sources of income.

"Cherries ripen in the summer and must be picked at just the right time," he replied. "And once they've been plucked, they must be carted away and sold before they spoil. Every cherry that goes sour before it can be sold is another penny lost. Sinclair determined that in order to squeeze every cent out of each summer's crop of cherries, Buckton could not only be an orchard. It must be a place where goods made from those cherries were produced. Thus, all these buildings you see before you."

Lydia gazed out at the cottages shown to their picturesque advantage against the transforming colors of the sky. "It is genius."

Welby nodded. "It is. Sinclair oversaw the erection of these buildings himself—places where the cherries could not only be washed and prepared for carting to neighboring counties, but also where they could be turned into jellies and marmalades, sauces and such to be used in the kitchens of every fashionable home from here to the edges of England. There's even a chandler's house, just there ... where cherries are processed for use in sweet-smelling candles. They're all the rage in London."

She smiled, a feeling she could not deny welling in her chest. Pride. She was *proud* of Sinclair for the things he had accomplished. He had not allowed the fact that he'd been born a bastard to stop him from reaching out to take what he wanted. It was no wonder the servants admired him so.

"Profits increased after the first summer harvest with Sinclair as steward," Welby told her. "His new strategies had another pleasant effect—giving many of Hertfordshire's residents the opportunity to gain summer employment. There are many women who come from all over the county to assist in the harvesting process, as well as the jam and candle-making. Those who work on farms which yield spring or fall crops are able to come here and earn additional wages for a few weeks' work. It has made him a well-loved figure here."

I am finding it would be difficult for anyone to hate him.

The thought came unbidden to her mind, yet it held fast and would not dissipate. She wanted to continue being angry with him for his duplicity, but she found that more difficult the more she learned about him.

"I suppose he then earned the right to claim Lady Drucilla's hand," she said.

Welby sighed. "That he did, within one year instead of two. Shall we?"

She took his arm once more and allowed him to lead her back toward the house. The sun had nearly disappeared, and dinner would be served soon.

"They were wed a few short months before the earl suffered an apoplexy," he continued as they walked. "It was a difficult time for Sinclair … his own father had died not long before then. He lost them both almost at once, and the grief of it … by then, we'd become friends, and he'd begun speaking of hiring me to take his place as steward. I was there to witness much of the hardship he endured, trying to carry on when both the men who had fathered him in their own ways were taken from him."

Her throat tightened, and the undeniable prick of sympathy stung her from somewhere deep inside. "How awful for him. I am certain Lady Clayton and her brother were a comfort to him."

"For a time," Welby hedged, his tone growing strained. "Milton— now the earl, could only stay for so long before his new duties drew him away. He resides primarily in London, serving in the House of Lords and managing his estates from there. In time, Sinclair found solace in his work, in caring for and growing his wealth. In the decade since then, he has procured three additional estates and increased his wealth several times over with wise investments. He has elevated himself from being the mere bastard of a viscount to being a formidable man in his own right, demanding respect."

They had come back into view of the house now, the path winding toward the looming structure in the distance. Yellow light bathed the lane from its windows, creating an inviting picture.

"You must admire him," she observed, turning to glance at her companion. "You speak highly of him."

"He is my dearest friend," Welby said with a sheepish smile. "Seems odd to befriend a man I work for, but Sinclair does not treat me as if I am beneath him. He might tell you himself that he sees no difference between us other than the privileges he's been afforded. So, he endeavors to treat people as equals, from the lowest scullion to the educated governess."

She smiled at that, thinking of the exorbitant salary she'd been offered. Now that she knew more about Sinclair, his increasing her wages did not seem like the salacious move she had named it. In fact, she now felt ashamed of herself for even suggesting it.

Lydia wanted to ask more questions, her curiosity over The Claytons' burning her up inside. However, they were ascending the front steps now, and night had fallen. Besides, she did not want to risk upsetting the man by prying into things that were not her affair. What did it matter if Sinclair and his wife were estranged? Lady Clayton was still his wife, and Lydia no more than a governess in his household. That was all she could ever be.

Turning to face her once they'd reached the front door, Welby smiled at her. "It has been a pleasure, Miss Darling."

She smiled back at him as easily as ever, in no hurry to return inside, even though Amberly lingered in the open door, watching and waiting for her to come back into the house.

"The pleasure was all mine, Mr. Welby," she replied. "Thank you for accompanying me on my walk."

Taking her hand, he lifted it to his lips. "Please, you must call me Charles."

For a moment, she could not respond, shock rippling through her as he kissed her knuckles. It was quick, warm, and chaste; yet, it took a moment for Lydia to respond. He'd caught her unawares, the kiss seeming to come from out of nowhere. But, as she met his gaze, she saw it … the unmistakable gleam of attraction, admiration. Her face flushed.

"Very well … Charles. Then you must call me Lydia."

"Lydia," he murmured, his voice deepening a bit, caressing her name.

She could not help but notice that it did not affect her half as much as when Sinclair had said her Christian name. Shaking her head, she tried to send the thought flying from her mind. What a ridiculous thing to dwell on at a time like this!

"I shall see you again on Monday," he declared, reluctantly letting go of her hand.

Recalling that tomorrow was Sunday, and that they would both be free from their duties, she nodded. "Yes, Monday. Good evening, Mr. Wel—Charles!"

His smile widened, and he tipped his hat to her before turning to trot down the front steps. "Good evening to you, Lydia."

She waited until he had disappeared in the direction of the stable before turning to go inside.

"Good evening, Miss Darling," Amberly said to her with a jovial grin. "Enjoy your walk?"

"I did, thank you."

"Very good. Dinner is being served, so you returned just in time."

"Splendid," she said, a hand coming over her rumbling stomach. "Thank you, Amberly."

The man gave her a little bow, as if she were a grand lady instead of a governess, then winked at her. She waved, then went off toward the dining room. Her heart leapt into her throat as she neared the open door of the dining room. Some evenings, Charles remained for dinner, providing a much-needed barrier between herself and Sinclair, the only other occupant of the room. Henry often ate in his chambers with his nurse while Lady Clayton still remained abed, recovering from her illness.

However, this evening, it would seem she would eat alone. She found the dining room empty, save for the footmen standing like sentinels in separate corners. There were no courses served here at Buckton for so few diners. Instead, various dishes were left on the table between the chairs flanking the one at the head of the table, and those who came to eat could serve themselves at will.

She sat in the chair to the left of where Sinclair might sit if he were here, unable to decide whether she was relieved or disappointed at having to eat alone. Without either man here to fill the room with the deep tones of their voices, the space seemed far more cavernous, almost cold. She ate quickly, not relishing so much time spent alone at a table large enough to seat twenty. Once she had finished, shunning another measure of wine being offered by the nearest footman, she glanced over at Sinclair's place setting. On her way to the dining room, she'd spotted the open door of his study, candlelight spilling over the landing. Perhaps he toiled over his work late into the night and had not realized he'd missed dinner.

Her brother did it often, and some well-meaning servant typically took the time to deliver a meal to his study so that he could be sustained through a late night's work. Oftentimes, she'd seen her sister-in-law taking his tray herself, ensuring her husband did not go hungry.

Had anyone seen to it that Sinclair did not go hungry in his own home? Did anyone care enough to make sure he took an evening meal?

Clearing her throat, she stood and turned to the nearest footman. "Excuse me. Would you happen to know whether a tray has been sent to Mr. Clayton's study? It is rather late."

The footman blinked, seeming taken aback for a moment before answering. She was acutely aware that she overstepped her bounds here, and the footman recognized this as well. However, she hoped the unconventional relationship between Sinclair and all his servants would offer her a bit of leeway here.

To her relief, the footman did not call her out on it.

"I do not believe so, Miss."

Nodding decisively, she took up an empty plate and began filling it, taking care to select a bit of every dish, uncertain which might be his favorites. Then, before she could allow herself to think over her actions too much, she quit the room, making a beeline for Sinclair's study.

CHAPTER 6

Sinclair glanced up from his correspondence to find a figure shrouded in shadow standing in the doorway. His hand tightened around the paper, the sound of its rustling mingling with the crackle of the fire in the hearth. His gut began to churn, even before he saw her face, for he knew it must be *her*. The form slowly coming into view as it peeled away from the darkness of the corridor was too feminine to be anyone else's, though not so slight that he mistook it for his wife's. Besides, Drucilla never disturbed him here. No, it could only be her.

Lydia.

He released a breath at the sight of her, the flames' light catching on the golden strands of her hair and setting them aglow while flaunting the angles and planes of her face. He had no idea why she was here, but he wanted her to stay. He wanted her to sink into one of the chairs opposite his desk, curl those dainty little feet beneath her, and stay. Forever.

The heady rush of blood that thought sent through his body went straight to his head, making him feel quite out of sorts. Clearing his throat, he attempted to pull himself together, resisting every impulse demanding he go to her, pull her into his arms, kiss her, strip her bare, and take her down to the rug before the fire. He did not think any such desires had ever struck him with a force this swift, not even when he'd imagined himself in love with Drucilla. Her beauty had inspired devotion and admiration from a distance, like some untouchable, intangible thing. Lydia's inspired a need to worship up close, to fall to his knees and pay her supplication with his lips, not stopping until he'd tasted every inch of her skin.

"Miss Darling," he managed, his throat still a bit tight at the arousal wreaking havoc on his body. "To what do I owe the pleasure?"

She raised one hand, drawing his attention to the plate she held, laden with veal, fish, mashed turnips, stewed peas, and bread. "You missed dinner. Charles has gone for the evening, and I thought … well, I supposed you must be hungry."

Dual emotions warred in him as he realized two things at once. She had thought of him and had gone out of her way to bring him dinner. She had also referred to his steward by his first name. For a moment, he could not decide whether to be elated that she'd think of him at all, or enraged that she and Charles had become so familiar while she kept *him* at a distance.

He decided to focus upon his delight that she'd come to him with a full dinner plate—and that she had thought to include a slice of pound cake for dessert. It seemed preferable over wallowing in envy he had no right to feel.

"That was kind of you," he said, rising and setting his letter aside.

He rounded the desk, meeting her as she came forward to offer him the plate. Their hands touched briefly as he accepted her offering, but he focused on taking the cloth napkin she extended with her other hand, a knife and fork wrapped inside them.

"Think nothing of it," she said as he moved back to his desk, using his elbow to shove aside stacks of envelopes and his inkwell to make room for his dinner.

He hadn't even realized how hungry he'd been, or how many hours had passed since he'd taken the afternoon meal. Most evenings, when he found himself working so late, he'd be left up to his own devices, slinking off to the kitchen in the late hours to scrounge bread and cheese before retiring. Sometimes, if Charles noticed him burying himself in work, he would prod him to go to the dining room to eat. This evening, he'd been too busy distracting himself from thoughts of Lydia that he'd neglected to notice the time.

"I try not to make this a habit—working so late into the night," he muttered, for lack of anything else to say. He did not want her to go, and she did not seem inclined to, standing where he'd left her, holding a shawl around her body, gaze flitting about his study with curiosity.

Those eyes of hers landed back on him, trailing over his attire. He supposed he must look a tad indecent, having opted for mere half-dress today as his duties had not taken him out of doors. He wore a brocade dressing gown over a shirt and trousers, his stockinged feet slid into comfortable slippers. He'd worn a cravat throughout the day, but had shed it hours ago, opening the top button of his shirt.

He felt the weight of her gaze fall to his exposed throat, locking there and holding for far too long. For so long that he began to fantasize about grasping her hair in his fist, guiding her lips toward the exposed patch of skin until she kissed and nibbled at the point of his pounding pulse. A shudder ripped through him.

"Would you care for a nightcap?" he offered, gesturing toward the sideboard where Amberly kept the crystal decanters full of a variety of spirits. "That is … if you are not in a hurry to get off to bed."

It had been the wrong thing to say … because now, all he could think about was her going up to her room and taking off her prim gown by candlelight, the muslin falling away to leave her in her stays, chemise, and petticoat. He imagined standing behind her, pulling at the stays to loosen the undergarment, gazing over her shoulder to watch as the full globes of her breasts were freed. His fingers itched as he imagined tossing the corset aside, then using his hands to rub the wrinkles it had caused out of her chemise, as well as her skin. Kissing her collarbone while pulling her chemise off one shoulder, pulling the pins from her hair and making it fall down her back.

Christ, he was losing his grip on sanity. Thankfully, she spoke and snapped him out of it.

"Whisky would be lovely, if you have any."

His eyebrows shot toward his hairline, shock parting his lips. "Whisky?"

"Yes, of course. And, please, do not do me the insult of offering sherry instead—I detest the stuff. My brother introduced me to whisky years ago, and it is my favorite."

God, this woman. He had never known anyone like her. No lady of his acquaintance would admit to enjoying a stiff whisky. Drucilla would turn her nose up at the stuff, declaring it unladylike. He wondered what other unladylike predilections Lydia might be hiding.

"You are in luck," he told her, going to the sideboard and selecting her requested drink. "I happen to have a very fine whisky, fit for any connoisseur."

He quickly poured three fingers into two clean tumblers, then stoppered the decanter before turning to offer her one. She accepted took a moment to swirl the liquid in her glass, sniffing it and issuing an appreciative hum. He paused with his own tumbler halfway to his lips, unable to help watching as she took her first sip. She shocked him yet again, tasting the whisky like someone used to its sting, barely even wincing when she swallowed. Raising her eyes to look at him, she nodded as if in confirmation of the liquor's quality.

"It is quite good," she said.

"I am glad you like it," he replied, turning to go back to his desk and the dinner rapidly going cold. "Please, sit. I'd like the company."

She obliged him, still holding her shawl over her chest with one hand and her glass in the other as she took one of the two plush armchairs facing his desk. He sipped his own whisky, enjoying the warmth of it going down before reaching for the utensils wrapped in his napkin.

He began eating, the hunger easing more and more with each bite. Across from him, she sat staring into the hearth, the tumbler held between both hands in her lap. So intent was he in studying her that he forgot to eat for what felt like all of two minutes.

Sinclair grimaced at the realization that he would only go on staring at her, slack-jawed, instead of eating, if he did not do something to fill the silence. Clearing his throat, he lowered his gaze to his plate.

"How do you occupy yourself once you've quit the schoolroom for the day?" he asked, keeping his tone light.

Their past few conversations had been heavy and loaded with the unspoken. This time, he would endeavor to avoid such.

"Most evenings, I indulge in reading, writing letters, or needlepoint," she replied.

The low tone of her voice mingled with the crackling fire to create a sort of intimacy. Despite the door hanging wide open across the room, he felt as if they were cut off from everything else—from Drucilla and the rest of the house, from the world.

"If the weather allows it, I like to walk for exercise," she continued. "Tonight, the weather was so fair, I indulged in a little exploration of the grounds. I was fortunate enough to encounter Charles, who gave me a bit of a tour and told me more about the cherry groves."

His insides twisted as his friend's first name fell from Lydia's lips for the second time. He did not like the way it made him feel to know how familiar they'd become. It made his food taste like ash.

"I see," he remarked, glancing up at her between bites. "And what do you think of my precious Buckton?"

She met his gaze, giving him a little smile. That slight motion of her lips struck him like a fist, temporarily winding him.

"I will admit to being quite impressed," she replied. "He told me Buckton's history—your hard work in turning it around, specifically. It was quite the intriguing story."

He inclined his head and studied her more closely, wondering just what Charles had told her. Sinclair knew he could trust his friend not to divulge too much, which meant she must only be privy to the means by which he'd acquired the estate through Drucilla's father.

Those memories proved bittersweet when he allowed himself to dwell on them. He'd loved Lord Stratton as much as he had his own father, the two lords having shaped him into the man he had grown into—one who boasted more successes than failures, a great deal of wealth and land. The disadvantage of his birth had meant nothing with the two of them guiding him, molding him, elevating him above his bastardy.

"The old earl was good to me," he stated. "I was fortunate to learn from him, to be given the opportunity to apply what he'd taught me to Buckton and help it flourish."

She shook her head, slouching in the chair a bit so that she sat more comfortably. "I think you do yourself a disservice by crediting the men who raised you up. They were certainly instrumental, but no other man could have achieved what you have. You're a singular oddity, Mr. Clayton … an anomaly of the best sort. It is inspiring."

Now, instead of being deprived of air, he overflowed with it, his chest swelling until he felt it would explode. A grin stretched across his face before he could stifle it. He must look like quite the idiot, smiling as if she'd just pulled the sun out of the sky and presented it to him. It was a heady feeling, earning this sort of respect from her when he'd done nothing to deserve it.

"Thank you," he said, attempting to rein in his joyous expression. "I've been more fortunate than most men in my position. I take none of it for granted."

"No," she murmured, lowering her gaze to her tumbler, breaking his gaze. "I would imagine you do not."

Silence fell over them once again, as tense and loaded as ever. There were a hundred things he wished to say to her, none of which felt appropriate. So, he bit the words back and returned to his dinner.

This time, it was Lydia who broke the silence.

"How fares Lady Clayton?"

He swallowed a bit of mutton, his teeth grinding at the mention of his wife. It was bad enough that her phantom presence invaded this space between them, a constant reminder of why he could never have what he truly wanted with Lydia.

"Well enough," he remarked, setting his fork down and reaching for his tumbler. Drucilla drove him to drink even when she was not in the same room with him. "I suspect she will be back to her usual self soon enough. This is not the first time such illness has befallen her, and it will not be the last."

At her puzzled expression, he took another sip of whisky and continued.

"For as long as I have known her, Drucilla has been prone to these spells. A weakness of the lungs, the physicians say. Some strange disease that makes her disposed to croup, pneumonia, and other such things. A common cold is enough to lay her up for weeks at a time."

Lydia's eyes went wide with concern. "How awful for her."

In the past, he'd been inclined to agree with such a sentiment. It had been part of what had drawn him to Drucilla—a seemingly fragile woman, displaying such beauty and strength even when illness laid her low. He'd doted on her, cared for her, remaining as close to her side as propriety had allowed in those days before their marriage when she'd become ill. She'd seemed to revel in his attentiveness, relying upon him when she grew weak. Over time, however, as her scorn for him had grown, she'd begun shunning his attention. Now, she would hardly countenance his presence in her sickroom.

"Yes," he said. "It is difficult for Henry, as well. He worries for his mother."

"And do you worry for your wife?".

As quickly as the words came out, she gasped, shaking her head as if wishing she hadn't spoken at all.

"Forgive me. I should not have—"

"It's all right," he interjected with a dismissive wave of his hand. "The truth is … no. I do not worry about Drucilla when she is ill. Honestly, her disease has been a part of our lives for so long. I have seen this before, lived through it often. Drucilla is far too … strong-willed to allow herself to be laid low by croup."

Lydia nodded, though she studied him as if wondering if there might not be more to it than that. Of course, there was more; but how could he explain? How could he speak of the way his marriage had decayed so badly he could hardly stand the sight of the woman he'd married? How could he tell her *why* he'd come to feel this way?

"You know quite a bit about my family," he said, hoping a change of subject would ease the tension thrumming between them, vibrating like a plucked cello string. "But I hardly know anything about yours. Tell me something, Miss Darling … something about your life in Norfolk."

With a sigh, she leaned against the back of her chair, her gaze growing wistful. "There is not much to tell.My father was a gentleman farmer, and my elder brother is one after him. I grew up at Oakmoor, in Norfolk, as you know. My life was like that of any other country girl. I had my parents, my elder brothers, Michael and Archie. As time went on, my father died—from pneumonia, of all things. It is odd, living in Oakmoor without his presence. He always seemed so strong to me. A large man who could not be broken by anything."

"I am very sorry to hear about your father," he said, his heart breaking at the forlorn picture she presented, a young girl who obviously missed her papa. "I understand all too well how it feels to lose that strong presence. It is something one never quite recovers from, isn't it?"

Her eyes took on a glassy sheen, as if she might cry. "No. I do not imagine I could ever fully recover. But, Michael fills his shoes nicely. He is like my father in so many ways; hardworking, loving, dedicated. He has turned Oakmoor into a warm place to live, despite its size and the demands of the estate. The manor is quite massive, but seems to overflow with people. There are Michael and Amelia, and their two children. Archie and his wife Hesper live there, as well, with all four of their brood. My mother is in residence, a doting grandmama."

Sinclair smiled at the image her words conjured. It was the sort of thing he'd wanted at Buckton—the warmth of a growing family, the halls echoing with the laughter of children. His heart sank at the reminder that he would never have what he so craved.

"I imagine she is very proud," he replied. "A grandmama with so many little ones to lavish with love."

Lydia giggled. "She spoils the little beasts rotten, that is for certain."

He stared at her for a moment, a burning question sitting on the tip of his tongue.

Why did you leave?

Seeming to pluck the unspoken question out of thin air, she answered as if he'd asked aloud.

"My sister-in-law, Amelia … she is the sister of a marquis. A powerful man with many connections. When she wed Michael, it was thought that she might be able to help me make an advantageous match in London. It was what I'd always wanted, you know. I was young and naive … I did not understand that the things I *truly* wanted would not be mine just because I managed to capture the attention of a man with a title and lands. But I wanted it—the glamor of a London Season, the balls and parties, the attention. I wanted a dream that could never be real."

He wanted to assure her that it could be real, that the right man had to be out there, somewhere, languishing in loneliness for wanting a woman just like her. But, how could he do that when his own dreams had come crumbling down around him within a few short years of marrying Drucilla—when he had striven so ardently to have everything he'd ever wanted, only to find that none of it was what he'd truly desired?

"After that one Season, life at Oakmoor did not feel the same," she went on when he did not speak. "I felt like a stranger in my own home … an intruder among those two perfect couples and their beautiful children. Because I would never marry, never have the things they had, it felt like torment to keep subjecting myself to life there. So, I left. I struck out to find a family who would hire me as a governess. It was the only occupation I possessed the skills for, and it neatly removed me from the home I'd come to feel like a prisoner in. I suppose you must think me daft. I know that my friends and family do."

He shook his head, leaning forward and resting his chin in one hand. "No. I understand entirely. I know exactly how it feels not to belong anywhere. You might be able to blend in where you are required to … you might even be able to convince others that you belong there. But only you know the truth. Only you can feel the restlessness of needing something that cannot be found."

This time, the quiet that followed his words was comforting, a moment of connection with someone who could understand better than anyone else how he felt. Just as he'd known on the night they'd met, Sinclair could see how alike they were—how their standing amongst society as outcasts of sorts tied them together. As close as he was with Charles, even he could not understand how Sinclair was a part of high society, but only as far as his wealth could take him. And even then, the stain of his birth followed him, marking him for all the world to judge. Only Lydia understood. For the first time in years, he felt just a little less alone.

"The hour has grown quite late," he remarked, as he noted the darkness outside his windows and the nearly spent fire in the hearth.

"Oh!" she exclaimed, setting her empty tumbler aside. "Heavens. I hadn't realized … I should go."

He rose at the same time she did, his entire body tensing, a dull ache blossoming in his chest at the thought of her going away from him, leaving him alone in the cavernous study once again. A room that usually offered him solace in solitude now felt cold, hollow.

"It is late, and the corridors are darkened," he insisted. "Let me see you upstairs."

Even in such meager lighting, he saw her discomfiture. She bit her lip, her eyelashes fluttering downward as she glanced at her feet.

"I would not want to inconvenience you …"

"It is no trouble," he pressed, already rounding the desk toward her. "I must pass your floor of the house to get to my own. It is on my way."

She ceased protesting when he took her hand and placed it in the crook of his arm. That light touch seared him through the layers of his dressing gown and shirt, through his skin and muscle, imprinting itself as deep as the bone. He could not bring himself to put distance between them, when he felt as if he'd been starving for her for four long years … when he hadn't experienced a woman's touch in so long. She stiffened slightly, but did not refuse him, keeping her grasp on his arm light as he took up a taper and began leading her from the room.

Sure enough, the servants had turned in for the night, leaving the hallways dark and empty. No one ever expected a soul to prowl the house this late save him, and he always lit his own way with a taper or a lamp. The little circle of yellow light guided the path upstairs, which they took in silence. With the thick blanket of night wrapped around them, he could not help but be aware of her in every way—her scent, the soft curves of the body just inches from his own, even the way loose tendrils of golden hair fell past her chin, caressing her neck.

They reached her chambers far too quickly. She opened the door to the room Drucilla had chosen for her—a spacious chamber done up in cheery shades of yellow and powder blue. He'd known the room would suit her, and realized just how true that was as she stepped inside, his candle working with the moonlight streaming through her open curtains to illuminate her and creating quite a charming sight. Lydia amongst white lace and sunny yellow wallpaper. It was just like he'd imagined.

Turning to face him, she smiled, though this time it seemed strained. "Thank you for seeing me up, Mr. Clayton."

Sinclair, he railed inwardly. *Just one time, angel … say my name.*

He bit the inside of his cheek, the sudden sting chasing the words off the edge of his tongue. It would be reckless to utter them, to destroy the fragile camaraderie they'd only just found.

"You are most welcome, Miss Darling. Rest well."

Reaching for the door, she began swinging it closed. "You, too."

He maintained her gaze until he couldn't any longer, the door clicking closed with an echo that struck him to the soul. Releasing a rushed breath, he reached up and braced a hand against the panel and closed his eyes. It was torment, standing on this side of the door, with something he'd wanted for so long just on the other side. But he could not have it, touch it, taste it. He could not use it to find relief from the strain of a life that wore upon him more with each passing day.

With another sigh, he forced himself to lower his hand, to turn away and seek out his own bed. All the way to his chamber, the worst imaginable thought crossed his mind. That Buckton should have been the place where Lydia could belong, where she might find the same sort of contentment he'd discovered for himself. Yet, on its heels came the reminder that while Buckton was his, he could not give it to her. He'd already built it up as a shrine to a woman who neither wanted nor appreciated it. A woman he'd offered his heart to, only to have her crush it in her fist.

In truth, nothing was his to give to Lydia … and that thought brought on a sorrow the likes of which he'd never known. It made each of his steps heavy as he climbed the stairs, his heart sinking into his gut and staying there. It made his empty chamber and cold bed hurt far more than it ever had.

CHAPTER 7

Another sennight passed Lydia by, during which life at Buckton became far less strained. It was as if her evening conversation with Sinclair over whisky had changed everything. While there was still so much she had yet to learn about him—or the family she served—they seemed to have reached an understanding of sorts. Whatever had driven Sinclair to kiss her that night at the ball, it had not been as nefarious as she'd first supposed.

That much became clear the more that was revealed about him. He'd appeared forlorn in his study alone, so late into the night, and she'd begun to realize that such loneliness ruled his days, as well. He closeted himself away in his study with Charles, before the two would ride or walk out over the estate to attend to matters in preparation for the cherry harvest. He spent time with Henry whenever his work allowed it, and those seemed the only moments he appeared truly happy. Lydia would watch from afar as father and son rode together toward the woods or ran about between the house and stables, the hounds chasing them in circles, barking happily.

She no longer avoided him, and even engaged in small talk over the meals they shared in the dining room with Charles. And if she noticed him watching her intently, his gaze wandering to places that set her face on fire, then she pretended not to notice. No good could come from allowing herself to be flattered, to let her attraction to him make her forget her place. She threw herself into her work, finding contentment in Henry's quick grasp of any subject she put to him.

However, on a sunny Tuesday afternoon, she found him restless. As she approached his desk to inspect the haphazardly written words he'd scrawled on his slate, she sighed. The fair weather had held up, with today being one of the warmest and brightest in weeks. The poor lad would much rather be outside, and Lydia could not find it in her heart to reprimand him for woolgathering. *She* would much rather be outside herself.

"Well done, Henry," she declared, bracing a gentle hand on his shoulder.

He turned to glance up at her, then down at his tablet and back out of the window once more. "Thank you, Miss Darling."

Her lips curved in amusement at his clear suffering. She'd be a horrid governess indeed if she subjected him to any more of this when the sunny sky and rolling hills so obviously called to him.

"I think that is enough of writing for today," she declared. "In fact, I do believe it is time we leave the schoolroom altogether."

Henry frowned, watching as she began untying the strings of her apron. "But, it is not yet noon."

"I know. But, it is too fine a day to remain cloistered indoors. Perhaps we might go for a walk and practice our French? We will seek out objects and name them in *Français. Oui?*"

The boy's eyes grew wide, and he looked so enamored with her in that moment, her heart gave a little pang. She was becoming quite fond of Henry, and it only had a little to do with the fact that she was also hopelessly enamored with his father. Henry also reminded her so much of Michael, and that seemed to ease a bit of her homesickness.

"Oh, thank you, Miss Darling!" he blurted, jumping from his seat and rushing forward to wrap his arms around her legs. "I would like that ever so much."

With a smile, she ruffled his golden hair, its shade a richer, darker hue than his mother's near-silver. "Very good. Off to Mrs. Beecham … inform her you are to be dressed for the outdoors. I shall come collect you from the nursery once I am ready."

With a nod, he released her and dashed off to the door. She watched him go, then neatly hung her apron on a nail beside her slate board. After setting her desk to rights, she then went to Henry's desk and took a moment to clean his slate. He would be so happy with her over this, she could look forward to at least a day or two without one of his pranks. That made her chuckle as she left the schoolroom, quickly ducking into her chamber for a hat. She left off a shawl or any other covering as the day was far too warm, and she wished to feel the sun on her skin. The brim of her hat would suffice to keep her cool as the summer afternoon grew hotter.

She found Henry waiting anxiously for her, in a pair of old trousers with leather braces over his shirt, his eyes glittering with excitement. Taking his hand, she urged him to slow down once they'd reached the stairs, his excitement enough to send them both tumbling if he wasn't careful.

Once outside, she released his hand and let him run, watching as he hopped down each of the front steps, landing in the grass with an excited 'whoop'. She followed, skirts held in her hands as she trotted to catch up.

"Come now, Henry," she called out, urging him back to her before he could dash off across the lawn. "Tell me … what is this? *En Français, s'il vous plait.*"

She pointed down at the grass, and he promptly responded.

"*Herbe.*"

"*Très bien,*" she replied. "And its color?"

"*Verte.*"

"Well done," she said, leading him down the path.

They continued on that way for several minutes, pausing on the path as she pointed out a flower, the sky, the clouds, the trees. She helped him with words he did not remember, correcting his accent when necessary.

As they neared the line of trees leading into the wooded area surrounding the house grounds, the sound of barking drew their gaze toward the east, where they found both hound and master coming toward them over the grass.

Lydia's pulse fluttered at the sight of Sinclair in riding attire, snug breeches clinging to his sinewy thighs, dusty brown boots flaunting well-formed calves. He'd forgone a coat due to the heat, his shirt-sleeves cuffed at the elbow to display his forearms. She found herself unable to look away from the exposed skin, the dark hairs lightly sprinkled over it, prominent veins showing along lean cords of muscle.

"Well, good morning," he called out as he grew near, the hound yipping excitedly as Henry rushed forward to greet him.

"Good morning, Mr. Clayton."

"Barkley!" the boy exclaimed, reaching out to pet the dog.

Tearing her gaze away from Sinclair, she focused upon her pupil. "Ah-ah. *Français!*"

Frowning, he gazed up at her, the sun forcing him to squint. "How do you say 'Barkley' in French?"

She smirked. "The French word for 'dog' will do, Henry."

The boy wrinkled his brow, seeming to try to remember the word she had taught him. Before Lydia could remind him, Sinclair spoke up.

"The word is *chien*, son," he offered. "*Le chien est marron.*"

Henry swiveled his gaze from his father back to Lydia. "What did he say?"

"The dog is brown," she translated before turning back to Sinclair, eyebrows raised. "Well done, Mr. Clayton. You speak with a good accent."

"*Je vous remercie*," he replied with a little bow and a smile. "You are too kind. I am a bit rusty, but I do remember most common phrases. What brings the two of you outdoors?"

"The fine weather," she replied. "We were both growing a bit rest-less cooped up indoors, so I decided we could just as easily practice our French while taking a walk."

"Papa, are you going hunting?" Henry asked, drawing Lydia's attention to the rifle Sinclair held braced over one shoulder, as well as the pouch of what she assumed must be ammunition slung across his body on a string.

"Just a bit of target practice," he replied. "I sent Charles into Ware on an errand for me, and have nothing to do to occupy myself until he returns."

Henry bounced on the balls of his feet. "May I come, Papa? Please?"

Lydia felt an undeniable yank upon her heartstrings at the stern look Sinclair attempted, but at which he failed horribly.

"Now, Henry … what sort of papa would I be if I pulled you away from your studies?"

She could see that he wanted to indulge his son, and she could hardly resist the pleading look her pupil cast at her. "An hour away from his lessons will hardly disrupt our day."

Lydia did not add that she thought it would do Henry some good to spend the time with his father, who would soon be inundated with overseeing the summer harvest. That felt more important to her than ensuring the boy practiced his French.

"Very well," Sinclair relented. "But only if you study twice as hard tomorrow to make up for it."

"Oh, I will," Henry replied gravely.

"Miss Darling, would you care to join us?" Sinclair offered, glancing at her as he took hold of Henry's hand.

She shouldn't. Going back inside to prepare for the rest of Henry's afternoon lessons seemed more appropriate than trailing after them. But, she was not yet ready to cloister herself away indoors, or bury herself in her work as she'd done this past week. In truth, she was not ready to be out of Sinclair's presence.

"I would like that, thank you," she replied.

The smile he gave her in response flooded her insides with warmth and made her belly quiver. This was dangerous; yet, she could not stop herself from falling in on Henry's opposite side, walking along with father and son in the direction of the stables. Allowing herself to spend time with Sinclair in any capacity unrelated to her job put her in a position she'd been trying to avoid since she'd discovered his identity. Nevertheless, here she was, desperate for even a few moments near him, close enough to hear his voice, to soak him in. She was truly pitiful.

They passed the stable, Barkley on their heels as they crossed a clearing toward two trees. Between them, a line had been tied, holding several silver implements that Lydia recognized as spoons when they drew closer.

"Your targets?" she quipped as they came to a stop at an ideal distance for rifle practice.

He raised an eyebrow at her and smirked. "The best targets to be found. They do not obliterate when struck, and cannot be killed."

Back home at Oakmoor, her brother had erected a wooden practice device for his wife, who indulged in target practice often. Brown paper drawn with targets were nailed to the wooden boards, which absorbed the impact of Amelia's gunfire. The spoons, Lydia could see, would offer more of a challenge.

"Sit, Barkley," Sinclair commanded without giving the hound a glance.

The dog responded to the authority in his voice and promptly sank onto his haunches, tongue lolling out of his open mouth. Lydia stood back and watched as Sinclair loaded the rifle, his hands swift and deft as if he did this often. She watched with interest as he urged Henry to stand back before lifting the rifle, pulling back the hammer, and taking aim. He had good form, his body angled just so, grip firm but relaxed, the butt of the weapon pressed against one shoulder. A light squeeze of the trigger produced the familiar sound of gunfire, and the bullet was sent careening through the air toward the string of spoons hanging between the trees. Her lips parted into a stunned smile as his shot hit true, striking one of the spoons with a 'ping', sending it spinning on its string.

Henry released a little sound of surprise, then began jumping up and down. "Again, again!"

She fought down the urge to mimic him, wanting to see the impressive display once more. Sinclair obliged them, taking a moment to reload before treating them to a repeat performance. He fired off five rounds back to back, striking true three times, but missing two. Henry cheered, his eyes bright and wide as he looked on. When he begged to take a turn, Sinclair obliged his son—something Lydia began to see he did often. There did not seem to be a thing Henry could ask for that his father would not give.

What must it be like to be lavished with such devotion from him? Had he once been this indulgent with Lady Clayton? If so, how could the woman not wish to spend her every waking moment basking in his attention? Had she any idea what she had in Sinclair?

Biting her lip, she tried to reel in her wandering thoughts, which had begun taking her into forbidden territory. Coveting her mistress' husband was surely a sin and would likely only result in more misery. She must not allow herself to entertain such thoughts.

Oh, but it became harder by the minute, as she watched Sinclair go down on one knee, positioning the boy in front of him. Father patiently showed son how to hold the rifle, ensuring the butt was braced against his own shoulder so that its recoil was absorbed by him. In a low, firm voice, he murmured instructions to Henry—how to pull back the hammer, how to curl his finger around the trigger. He was patient with the boy, gentle yet firm. Watching them together reminded her of her own father, who had exhibited those same qualities.

The two spent some time practicing, Sinclair pausing between shots to instruct Henry before reloading and letting him try again. The boy missed more spoons than he struck, but Lydia found herself impressed with the ease with which he handled such a large weapon. She supposed Sinclair's confidence emboldened him.

After a moment, Henry turned to gaze at her. "Now you, Miss Darling!"

Sinclair rose from his place on the ground and grinned. "I am not certain if Miss Darling would want—"

"Actually, I'd love to," she interjected, stepping forward and holding out one hand for the rifle. "I haven't practiced in ages, but I used to be a crack shot."

Sinclair started, obviously taken aback. His gaze traveled over her, taking in her hat, her demure clothing … her femaleness. He seemed dubious, which should have insulted her. Instead, it amused her, made her itch to wipe that doubtful expression off his face.

"Is that so?" he said, his tone light and teasing as he loaded the rifle before handing it over. "I am intrigued."

Turning to face the targets, she raised the rifle to her shoulder, surprised at how easily her hands returned to embracing the weapon. It was as if she'd never stopped practicing. A little smirk pulled at her lips as she adjusted her stance, closing one eye in order to aim at the spoon of her choosing. She felt Sinclair's gaze on her, Henry's awe at the sight of her handling the weapon as well as his father.

She took a slow breath, then exhaled, pulling the trigger with an ease born of experience. Across the yard, her bullet struck the spoon with a resounding *clink*, sending the utensil spinning on its twine.

"I say," Sinclair blurted, the shock in his voice quite satisfying. "Bloody good shot, Miss Darling!"

With a little smile, she lowered the rifle and turned to face him. "Shocked?"

He chuckled, reaching into his pouch to retrieve another bullet to offer her. "Yes, but I realize now that I should not be. Why *wouldn't* you be able to shoot a spoon at twenty yards with a rifle?"

She could not resist answering his grin with one of her own, the familiar quiver in her middle striking again. She could have stood there for hours just basking in that smile of his.

Clearing her throat, she tore her eyes away from him and focused upon the task at hand. Just then, she was thankful for the distraction of the rifle as she reloaded the weapon and prepared to take aim once more. It offered a diversion from the man who was rapidly stealing all her focus. Bad enough she could hardly stop thinking of him when they were not together; now, she could not even stand in his presence without the urge to drink him in with her eyes, gorge herself on the sight of him.

They spent another hour taking turns with the rifle, Henry drumming up a bit of competition between her and Sinclair by keeping a tally of who struck the most spoons. By the time they left to return to the house, Sinclair's ammunition pouch had gone empty, and Lydia had bested him with twelve spoons to his eleven.

"You are quite good," Sinclair remarked as they took their time walking toward the manor.

Ahead of them, Henry ran with Barkley, circling back every few minutes, then venturing further ahead.

"Better than good, actually," he added. "I gather one of your brothers taught you how to shoot."

She scoffed. "Archie is an abominable shot, and Michael would never have thought to teach a girl. No, it was my sister-in-law, Amelia, who taught me. When she wed Michael and came to Oakmoor, we became fast friends. One of the first things she ever taught me was how to shoot. I'm quite fair with a pistol, as well."

Sinclair shook his head with another little smirk. "I can only imagine. You, Miss Darling, are full of surprises."

She'd just opened her mouth to reply when Henry's surprised shout from farther up the path drew her attention to the house. The boy dashed toward the front steps, at the top of which his mother stood. Lydia stumbled over her own two feet, quickly righting herself at the sight of Lady Clayton, out of bed and impeccably dressed. White muslin draped her willowy frame in soft frills, and her elegant chignon accentuated a slender neck and the angle of a perfectly formed jaw. She was a vision framed by the house's front pillars as she opened her arms to the boy rushing up the stairs toward her.

Lydia's stomach twisted, her heart picking up a rapid cadence. The unmistakable sensation of guilt suffused her as she glanced at Sinclair from the corner of her eye.

But, why? She had nothing to feel guilty for. The time spent with Sinclair and Henry had been perfectly innocent, a pleasant diversion for the boy. So, why did returning from behind the stable with Lady Clayton's husband and son make her feel as if she'd been caught doing something she oughtn't?

Sinclair's jaw tightened, his eyes seeming to darken as if storm clouds passed over them at the sight of his wife. By the time they reached the front steps, Henry had begun to chatter excitedly to his mother, filling her in on everything she had missed while abed.

"Good afternoon, Miss Darling," Lady Clayton said in her soft, lyrical voice as they drew near. "I went to the schoolroom expecting to find the two of you there … yet, here you are."

Lydia folded her hands before her to still their shaking, her mouth suddenly dry as she attempted to form words. "Henry was a bit restless, my lady, so I thought a bit of fresh air might do him good. We practiced our French while taking a walk, then encountered Mr. Clayton at target practice. I supposed a short respite would do him more good than harm, so we joined to watch."

The lady smiled at her, but the expression never quite reached her eyes. The blue orbs were similar to Henry's, but colder, lighter in color. They created quite an ethereal effect with her pale hair and luminescent skin.

"A fine idea," Lady Clayton replied. "I was just about to send for tea. Perhaps you and Henry would like to join me? We can take the time to discuss all that you are teaching my son."

No, she wanted to insist. *No, I cannot sit at tea with you, risking that you will be able to take one look at me and see that I have inappropriate feelings toward your husband.*

However, she could hardly refuse or offer such an excuse, so she was left with no choice but to smile and agree. "That sounds lovely. I'd be happy to."

"Tea!" Henry exclaimed, clinging to his mother's skirts. "May I have sugar in mine?"

Lady Clayton cast her son an affectionate glance. "Just a bit, Henry. I wouldn't want you to become overstimulated. Sinclair, will you join us?"

Lydia dared another glance at Sinclair, who shook his head, avoiding his wife's stare. "No, thank you. Charles will return from Ware soon, and we will have affairs to attend. Though I am glad to see you are feeling better."

"It is good to be out of bed," she replied.

Neither of them sounded as pleased as they claimed, stiff formality coloring every word of their exchange. Lydia could hardly fathom such a strained relationship between husband and wife, nor the effect Lady Clayton's presence seemed to have had on Sinclair. All the warmth had melted away from him, leaving a cold, hard man she hardly recognized in his place.

Before she could think on the matter any more, Sinclair was gone, calling out "Barkley, come!" as he set out toward the stable with long strides. Which left Lydia with no choice but to join her mistress and pupil in going inside. She did not quite understand why she felt as if she approached the executioner's block instead of a simple drawing room for tea.

CHAPTER 8

At first, Lydia realized she must have fretted over nothing. For an entire hour, she and Lady Clayton sat and shared tea, and it was lovely. There was a tiered serving platter of various cakes and biscuits, which Henry helped himself to with gusto, filling a small plate with a towering pile of delicacies. Lydia had been too nervous to eat and left her biscuit untouched on her plate, though she did sip at her tea while answering the other woman's questions concerning Henry's lessons and behavior.

She assured Lady Clayton that the boy acquitted himself well in the schoolroom, and aside from the occasional prank—which Lydia repaid in kind each time—proved the perfect pupil. She informed her mistress of his progress in reading and writing, as well as their splendid beginning with French. Lady Clayton offered to send for a collection of maps, as well as a globe so that they could begin Geography, a prospect that made Lydia happy. A new subject to immerse Henry in would offer a fresh challenge, something else to keep her from pining after the boy's father.

The afternoon passed splendidly, giving her an opportunity to observe the lady with her son. Just like Sinclair, Lady Clayton was obviously fond of Henry, indulging him with tea and as many cakes as he wanted … though she did seem disdainful of the old clothes Henry had worn for their romp outdoors. She spent more time than Lydia thought necessary smoothing the boy's tousled hair and attempting to keep him clean while seated in her pristine, white and silver drawing room. Henry bore it all with the sort of impatient squirming characteristic of a boy his age, but reveled in his mother's hugs and kisses once his face had been wiped clean of jam.

After a while, the lady dismissed her son into the charge of his nurse, declaring he needed a nap after such an eventful afternoon. When Lydia rose to follow, wondering what she would do with her afternoon now, Lady Clayton shook her head and motioned for her to be seated once more.

"Miss Darling, stay a while longer, if you please."

The tone was light and as sweet as the bowl of sugar cubes resting between them on a low table. However, Lydia discerned the clear command in the words and could do nothing but sink back into her chair. The ease with which the previous hour had passed seemed to flee in an instant, a sudden tension coiling between herself and her employer.

"More tea?" Lady Clayton offered, already helping herself using the porcelain pot resting on a polished silver tray.

"No, thank you," she replied, too overwrought now for tea.

Her stomach began to churn, her palms growing damp for reasons she did not understand. Why did being alone with Lady Clayton make her so anxious? The woman could not know what had happened on the night Lydia had met Sinclair, could she? What if she did? Lydia felt as if she might faint as she imagined being confronted with the incident and losing her position. The thought of never being able to see Henry or Sinclair again made her want to weep.

"I apologize for being a bit absent during your first weeks at Buckton," Lady Clayton continued after dropping a sugar cube into her teacup and following it with a drop of milk. Her spoon clinked against the side as she stirred, her eyes fixed upon Lydia over the rim.

"You can hardly be blamed for falling ill," Lydia replied. "I am glad to know you are feeling better."

"I am certain my husband informed you that it happens frequently. These illnesses."

"H-he did," she ventured carefully, uncertain where this could be leading. She would say as little as possible to keep from incriminating herself and allow Lady Clayton to lead.

"Nevertheless, I do endeavor to give Henry as much of my attention as I am able, and when I do not fear infecting him with whatever malady I might be suffering from at the moment," Lady Clayton continued. "It is a relief, I must say, to have a reliable governess who might fill a bit of the void left when I am unable to tend to Henry myself."

Lydia forced a smile, sitting up a bit straighter in her chair. "It is no trouble at all, my lady. Henry is a joy to teach. He speaks highly of you, you know. He is quite fond of his mama."

The lady smiled at that, the expression downright angelic. The realization, yet again, that this must be the loveliest woman she had ever seen struck Lydia like a physical blow, making her all-too aware of her own flaws. Of the freckles marring her cheeks, the roundness of her hips that always showed through her gowns no matter how they were tailored, the plainness of her features in comparison to the angel sitting across from her.

"Henry is fond of you, as well," Lady Clayton replied. "So, apparently, is my husband."

Lydia was grateful she had not accepted the offer of more tea, as the sudden shift in the conversation would surely have caused her to choke. Furrowing her brow, she looked at her mistress and hoped she did not look as guilty as she felt.

"I beg your pardon?" she managed.

Lady Clayton simpered, raising one perfect, blonde eyebrow. "Oh, come now, Miss Darling. We are both worldly women, are we not? Surely, we may speak frankly with one another. While I have languished in my sickbed, my husband has lingered at Buckton for far longer than usual. I think we both understand why."

Her mouth fell open, then snapped closed, gaping once again as she struggled for words, certain she must appear like a fish out of water. "I … that is … Mr. Welby mentioned that the summer harvest would be soon. And I … well, I am certain that Mr. Clayton has also missed Henry. The two have spent much of their time together."

Lady Clayton made a little noise—a disdainful huff that set Lydia's teeth on edge.

"That might be so, but Sinclair's presence is hardly needed for the harvest when Mr. Welby practically runs Buckton. I suppose the arrival of a pretty new governess has piqued his renewed interest in the place."

Lydia's face flushed hot, her jaw clenching as she thought of Sinclair's loneliness, his seclusion in the study each night, the story Charles had told her of all he'd done to secure Buckton and made it flourish. The woman's words did not fit the picture the two men had painted for her, and the words to defend Sinclair lingered on the tip of her tongue. However, instead of using them, she decided to defend herself. After all, she could be out of a job if this woman believed Lydia had designs on her husband.

"My lady, I can assure you that I am here for one purpose, and that is to teach Henry," she said carefully. "I find both you and Mr. Clayton to be kind employers, and I enjoy living at Buckton. In my years as a governess, I have never acted in an unseemly fashion, and do not intend to now."

"Oh, I believe you," Lady Clayton said between sips of tea, her gaze too knowing by half. "You seem a good sort, Miss Darling … intelligent and far too sensible for your head to be turned by someone like my husband. I simply thought to warn you."

Lydia frowned, once again taken aback. "Warn me? Whatever for?"

"Do you think you are the first to catch his eye?" Lady Clayton countered. "My husband is a man of … healthy appetites. He has made it clear to me on more than one occasion that he prefers the beds of others over mine."

Lydia gasped, one hand coming up over her open mouth, but Lady Clayton went on.

"I can see I've shocked you, and I apologize for that. However, you are of an advanced age and are no simpering miss. Matters of marriage should hardly be shocking to you. A man must satisfy himself some way, mustn't he? And my husband is never here long enough to do so with me. It is no secret that he … well, he seems fond of a certain type. Blondes are his favorite."

For a moment, Lydia could only sit there, her face burning as if she'd been slapped. Her mind reeled as she remembered first meeting Sinclair, then encountering him again at Buckton. Their every interaction flitted through her mind, and she tried to remember his words, his actions, tried to decipher the intent behind them.

Her eyes began to sting as she wondered how many other young debutantes he had kissed, how many fair-haired women had stood in as a convenient replacement for Sinclair's wife. She could not deny the ring of truth in Lady Clayton's words. She'd been told by household staff that he never remained at Buckton for long. She'd heard chambermaids whispering about how the master and mistress of the house never shared one another's beds. She had seen the evidence of their estrangement with her own eyes.

Sinclair had spoken of their kiss as some sort of singular event, a moment of weakness for a lonely man. But, what if that wasn't the case at all? Her head began to spin as she tried to untangle her thoughts, to make sense of the things she knew and fill in the gaps of what she did not know.

Lady Clayton moved until she sat perched on the edge of the sofa, reaching over the table to rest one of her hands atop Lydia's, which were folded in her lap. The other woman's pale blue eyes glittered with something that made Lydia's blood run cold, a complete contradiction to the warmth and pity in her voice.

"Do not feel badly, my dear," the lady crooned. "It is hardly your fault, and I regret that you've been put in such a position. But do not worry. Sinclair grows bored quite easily … this I know from experience. He will soon turn his interest elsewhere, and I am sure you will be relieved."

This woman was quite the skilled actress, displaying sympathy and camaraderie on the surface while the underlying threat in her voice was made quite clear. Lydia had been put in her place and reminded that her position here could be temporary, that she could be cut loose for encouraging Mr. Clayton's wandering eye. She did not need to be told these things to be able to clearly puzzle them out.

"I think we understand each other," Lady Clayton added when Lydia remained silent.

Nodding, Lydia attempted to force herself to move, to speak, to extricate herself from this situation so she could retreat to her bedchamber in peace. So she could escape this woman and her husband and the complications of their lives, at least for the rest of the day.

"Yes, my lady," she whispered, her voice hoarse from the emotion she fought to keep at bay.

"Good," Lady Clayton replied, removing her hand from Lydia's and settling herself comfortably upon her sofa once more.

Clearing her throat, Lydia kept her eyes lowered, working to take deep, even breaths. "May I go now, my lady?"

She hated being put in this position, resented being forced to make a graceful exit after having been verbally threatened and put on edge. Yet, her position required it, demanded it, even.

"Of course," Lady Clayton answered with a dismissive wave of her hand. "You may have the rest of the day to yourself. After Henry awakens from his nap, I intend to take him out in the carriage to visit a neighbor of ours."

She rose swiftly, dipping into as good a curtsy as she could manage. "Thank you, my lady."

Swiveling toward the door, she forced herself to walk slowly and not run, tear the door off the hinges and go barreling down the corridor. She must keep herself together until she could find some place to be alone. The piercing eyes of Lady Clayton followed her, stabbing her through the back and impaling her heart, which Lydia felt might never stop aching. Her head continued to whirl, her thoughts so convoluted, she did not know what to think, what to believe.

Her wish to be left alone would not be granted, for at the exact moment that she approached the stairs, she found Sinclair coming up from below, one hand scraping through his wind-tousled hair. She faltered, her heart stuttering to a near stop before picking up a rapid drumbeat, pounding against her ribs. Her hand came up to the spot just beneath her breast, and she could feel the organ hammering with relentless insistence, her veins tingling from a heady rush of blood.

Sinclair paused, one foot on the stairs, another on the landing, his brow furrowing as he took her in from head to toe. He observed her stricken expression, her posture, seeming to understand almost immediately that something was amiss. His gaze darted to the door of the drawing room, which still hung lightly ajar, and understanding seemed to dawn, alighting in his widening eyes. His jaw grew slack, and he surged toward her, arms outstretched as if to reach for her. She moved away from him, smothering a strangled cry as she narrowly escaped being taken into his arms.

"Lydia," he whispered, shaking his head slowly. "Whatever she said—"

"Don't!" she hissed, trying to keep her voice low lest they be heard through the door.

She whirled away from him and moved toward the stairs as swiftly as she dared. One hand gripped the railing while the other gathered her skirts to keep her from tripping over them. Her slippers fell silently on the steps, his boots thudding lightly on the carpet as he gave chase. Her heart jumped into her throat and stayed there, choking off her breath until her chest began to burn.

They reached the third floor, and she broke into a run, making a mad dash for her bedchamber door. It was just ahead ... if she could only outrun him. However, that proved impossible with his long strides helping him to catch up with her easily. He took her arm and spun her around, pressing her back against the wall.

"Lydia," he said, more firmly this time, both hands holding tight to her upper arms. "What did she say to you? Tell me right now, so that I might—"

"There is nothing to be done," she interjected, attempting to twist out of his hold and failing.

He was too strong, too determined, and she was so, so weak, wanting to be in his arms, even after the things his wife had just accused him off.

"There is if she upset you," he insisted. "Drucilla detests me, and I've come to accept that. But I will not allow her to treat you poorly."

"And you will treat me so much better?" she countered, trying once again to shrug his hands off her shoulders.

He parted his lips to reply, but quickly snapped them shut as the sound of two feminine voices coming up the nearby servants' stairwell rang out at them. His eyes grew wide as he glanced over his shoulder at the opening of the staircase, just a few steps away from them.

Before Lydia knew what was happening, he had snatched open the nearest door and propelled them inside a dark space. She gasped as she found herself pushed against something both hard and soft while Sinclair's body caged her in, blotting out the meager light coming from the corridor. The door clicked shut behind them, just as the maids who had been on the stairs burst into the passage, their voices muffled through the door, but still far too close.

Her every nerve ending came alive, the surface of her skin prickling as Sinclair's masculine body fit against hers, pressing her against what she realized were shelves stocked with clean linen. He'd pushed her into the nearest closet to keep from being discovered with her. It had been a close call; the maids coming up that stairwell just as he'd stood a stone's throw from her bedroom door, holding her as if … as if …

Her face grew hot as she realized they'd almost been caught in a compromising position. It did not matter that Henry's chambers were just down this corridor, or that the schoolroom stood nearby, as well. Without the boy's presence, the two of them had no business skulking about in empty corridors alone.

"Shh," Sinclair whispered, his breath tickling her ear as he adjusted his stance, legs parting a bit until his feet were planted just on the outside of hers, his arms braced against the shelves and caging her between them.

She sucked in a sharp breath, and with it, inhaled his scent, mingled with that of the open air outdoors. Even in her anger, she could not cease responding to him, becoming all too aware of the hard ridges of his body mashed against hers, his chest against her breasts, his thighs sturdy against hers, his breath tickling the loose hairs at her temple.

When the voices of the maids continued, still sounding far too close for comfort, he muttered an oath under his breath.

"They are dusting, I think," he whispered, his voice at once soft and deep in her ear. "We will have to wait them out."

Damn it all, this was the worst possible situation Lydia could have found herself in. How could she look Lady Clayton in the eye after having been trapped in a closet with the woman's husband, her nipples pebbling against his chest and her thighs clenching in reaction to his proximity? And that most male part of him … God, it was thickening, hardening, pressing against her body with an insistence that could not be ignored. His breaths grew harsher, his inhales deeper, as if he took in her scent, as if being so close affected him the same way it did her.

Closing her eyes, she swallowed past the sensation in her throat making her feel as if she were being strangled. Slowing her breaths, she tried to relax until the maids had finished their work. It had to only have been minutes that they stood there in silence before the maids' voices grew thinner, and then the corridor beyond grew silent altogether. Yet, it felt like hours.

The moment she felt it might be safe, she pressed her hands

against his chest and pushed, attempting to put some distance between them. "They are gone … let me out."

He wrestled with her, taking her wrists in a firm but gentle grip, trapping them between their bodies. "Not until you speak to me. Tell me what was said in that room."

She squirmed and writhed, but soon realized this only made matters worse, creating a friction between their bodies that made her nipples stiffen even more and liquid heat pool between her legs. Biting her lip, she went still and closed her eyes once more, wrestling her impulses under control. As it was, she wanted nothing more than to surrender to the need, the torrent of desire ripping through her; the urge to kiss him, let him have his way with her inside this cramped closet. If the stiff organ attempting to batter its way through the layers of their clothes were any indication, he'd take whatever she offered. That thought only made her angry again as she recalled Lady Clayton's claims of his preference for blondes.

"I will not be your next conquest," she spat, still keeping her voice low in case someone else happened by. "I do not know or understand what sort of marriage you and Lady Clayton have, but I will not be party to cuckolding an innocent woman in her own home!"

For a long moment, Sinclair was silent, his gaze searching her out in the dark. Her eyes had adjusted a bit, so she could see his shadowy outline, as well as the flash of his teeth when he chuckled.

"Innocent," he muttered with a shake of his head. "There's a word I have not heard applied to Drucilla in quite some time."

"It could hardly be applied to you," she argued. "Though it is none of my affair if you wish to go about tupping every blonde that crosses your path. Just know that I do not intend to be next, so you may turn your attention elsewhere, if that is what you are after."

Sinclair heaved a heavy sigh, his hands tightening a bit on her wrists. "Is that what she told you? That I am a rake who goes about sticking my prick in every blonde in England other than her?"

"It's true, is it not?" she accused glaring at his outline in the dark.

"Everyone in this house claims you rarely visit, the maids gossip that you keep to separate beds, and then there was the night we met—"

"The first and only time in my ten years of marriage to Drucilla that I've touched another woman," he declared.

A shocked gasp burned in her throat, but she could not release it, could hardly breathe as his words sank in. Could that be true? No ... it made no sense. A man as virile as Sinclair could not go for years living like a monk. No man she'd ever known had such willpower. Why else would whores and mistresses be able to make a living sating such desires, with bachelors and married men alike?

"For six years, I went about thinking my marriage was like any other," he went on, releasing her wrists, but making no attempt to let her out of the closet. "For six years, I was faithful to Dru, and I believed she returned the courtesy. Even when her affections for me began to dwindle ... even when we bickered and argued more than we made love ... even when I began to see that she no longer loved me, may never have loved me at all."

She slowly deflated, her anger melting away to be replaced by the same pity she'd experienced when finding him alone in his study late at night. It was the same heart-wrenching empathy that had led her to bring him dinner, to offer him her company for a short time.

"What changed?" she asked, searching for his eyes, regretting that she could not see into the dark depths.

"I met you," he murmured, his lips skimming her forehead, angling toward one of her eyebrows.

She sighed when his lips pressed down in a fleeting kiss. "Mr. Clayton—"

"I hadn't touched her in months the night we met," he whispered against her temple, kissing her again there. "And I haven't touched a woman since ... not until right now."

Her breath hitched, then began racing as if she'd been running, her heart once again threatening to beat right out of her chest. "Mr. Clayton ..."

His hands came to her waist, his fingers sinking into flesh she found to be entirely too soft, but that he touched with such reverence, urgency radiating from the tips of his fingers and into her skin.

"I have wanted," he continued. "I have yearned and been tempted. There have been many opportunities for me to commit adultery, to sate my needs. But a part of me—the part that loved the angelic-looking girl with the powerful father—would not let me. I did not care that she'd stopped giving me her devotion … a part of me would not let me stop giving her mine."

"What changed?" she asked again, wanting to know, *needing* to know.

"I discovered a real angel," he replied, and this time, his mouth was right against the corner of hers, less than an inch away from gracing her with a kiss. "And I realized that I'd never known what true devotion looked like, what purity and goodness were. I didn't know *you*, Lydia. Finding you that night, seeing in you all the things I had been missing … it made me hate myself for building my entire life around an illusion. It made me angry that I married Dru when I did, when I should have waited."

She trembled as his hands came around to her back, his fingers spread, spanning her shoulders, pulling her closer, so close that not a breath of space existed between them.

"Waited for what?" she whispered, her lips parting just as his soft sigh skimmed across her lips.

"For you," he murmured just before fitting his mouth over hers for the first time in four long years.

She hadn't realized how badly she'd wanted it, how starved she'd been for it, until the moment their lips met, coming together in a melding of breaths and flesh. Her memory of their first kiss had been a poor substitute played out in her mind so many times that it had started to lose its sharpness. It felt so distant that it had become like some sort of dream. But this … this was real and raw, and in such sharp focus that she could do nothing but sink into it, drown in him, and in perfect bliss.

His lips were soft yet firm, just like she remembered, moving over hers gently at first, and then with a building urgency that took her breath away. His tongue skimmed her lower lip, his hands tightening at her back, holding her against him, pressing her breasts against his chest. She opened her mouth to him, tilting her head back to accept his invading tongue and meet it with her own. Hot flesh touched hot flesh, and they moaned together, Sinclair's sound deep and guttural, hers high and breathy. His taste flooded her palate, the slight hint of brandy mingling with that of oranges.

He pulled away for a moment, tearing a shrill cry of regret from deep in her chest. She reached out for him, clutching the lapels of his coat and drawing him back in, now desperate for more of what she'd gone without for four years. Her senses had been dulled all this time, she realized as he came back to her with a low groan, his teeth nipping at her lower lip before he slipped his tongue back inside, consuming her with a desperation she felt to her core. She had forgotten what it was to feel, to live, to revel in primal sensation. She was akin to some storybook princess, awakened by a kiss, brought alive by a touch … arching into him as something long dead sparked back to life in her.

He shifted one of his legs between hers and pressed against her, his hold lifting her feet from the floor and straddling her over his thigh. She gasped into his mouth, shudders wracking her in response to that hard limb pressed right up against her mound. A rapid pulsation began there, her hips moving of their own accord to grind her pelvis against him, seeking out pressure, friction, closeness. Even pressed so tightly against her and his tongue thrusting into her mouth, he wasn't close enough, deep enough.

He palmed her buttocks, squeezing, kneading, pulling her against him so that she could feel the strength of his erection, hard as flint now.

"Lydia," he moaned against her mouth. "You're just like I remember you. So sweet, so perfect, so responsive."

She whimpered in response when his lips strayed to her chin, her throat, the patch of skin just below her collarbone and above her bodice.

"I've dreamed of you, angel," he rasped against her ear, nibbling the lobe, teasing the edge with his tongue. "I've lain in my bed alone and stroked my cock to thoughts of you and only you … under me, on top of me, naked and spread for me. Tell me I was not alone. Tell me you wanted me, that you thought of me, too."

"I … I …"

He bit her shoulder, and she cried out, swiftly clenching her teeth to silence herself. If they kept this up, they would be discovered, for certain.

"Say it, Lydia," he demanded, his hands skimming her thighs, squeezing, exploring, his lips roaming to kiss whatever exposed skin he could find. "Tell me."

"I … I thought of you," she whispered.

"Yes," he groaned. "Tell me more."

"I dreamed about you," she told him, the darkness emboldening her, making it easy to say such things. "So many nights, I woke up sweating and shivering, tears in my eyes because a mere dream could never satisfy me."

He sighed, lazily nibbling on her neck, his tongue flicking out at her pulse now and then. "What did I do to you in those dreams? Did I kiss you … touch you … undress you?"

"Yes," she moaned, her hands traveling up and into his hair, holding him against her, neck arching in an offering. "You did."

"Where?" he urged, dipping his head to nuzzle her breast through her gown. "Where did I kiss you and touch you?"

She shivered when he teased her nipple, the little bud now an aching point. "Everywhere."

"God, yes," he growled. "It's what I dreamed of, too. So many nights. I want that … I want it all … I want *you*."

She stood a few seconds away from surrendering, from telling him he could do whatever he wanted with her, fulfill every one of his debased fantasies. But guilt drove her to put her hands to his chest and push, to turn her head just as he'd been about to claim her lips again. Every part of her ached, the slick channel between her thighs most of all, her clit swollen and throbbing, her breasts painfully tight. However, thinking of the young boy taking his nap down the corridor, of his innocence and love for his parents, made her feel like the most wretched sort of person.

"We cannot," she replied. "What would Henry think if he knew that his father and his governess were … had …"

"He is a child," Sinclair argued, though she heard the doubt in his voice. "There are things involved in this that he could never understand."

"Yes," she agreed. "He is a child. All he knows is that you and Lady Clayton are his entire world … that *you* are the man he wants to be when he has grown up. I cannot have a hand in destroying that, in destroying a family."

Despite not being able to see his face, she heard the torment in his voice when he responded. "We aren't a family, Dru and I. We never have been. Even Henry's birth could not change that."

"Perhaps not. But you are the family he knows. I am sorry, but … my conscience will not allow me to act on my feelings."

"But there are feelings," he urged. "I haven't been imagining this … this *thing* between us?"

She shook her head, unable to lie to him after what had just occurred. "No, you have not imagined it. I feel it, too."

Releasing another pained sigh, he shifted closer, his forehead resting against hers, his hand cupping her jaw. "You are right. I am sorry for putting you in this position. Do you believe me when I tell you that I am not what Drucilla has painted me out to be? I do not go about looking for women to coax into my bed."

"I want to believe you," she replied honestly. "But … there is so much history here, between you and your wife. These matters are none of my concern."

"What you think of me is *my* concern. I am not a perfect man, Lydia. I might not even be a good man. But I have always endeavored to be honest with the people in my life, and you … I have only ever been honest with you."

The conviction with which he spoke, in such stark contrast to his wife's icy tone and underlying threats, made her want to side with him. She'd seen for herself his loneliness, his sadness. Yet, even if she did believe him, what then? What could she have with him aside from a few secret moments, hasty tumbles, and a broken heart when this had all ended?

"I think that you are a better man than you realize," she offered, the only consolation she could give. "But we must resist this. We cannot do something we might come to regret."

He released her, his hands falling to his sides and his body moving away from her as far as the closet would allow. "You are right, of course. I cannot promise that my feelings will ever go away, but I can endeavor to behave like a gentleman in your presence. This will not happen again."

Raising her chin, she feigned a confidence she did not quite feel. "Then I shall endeavor to do the same. We … we can get through this."

Even as she said it, the words rang false. She felt as if she might die just from being in his arms again. Now, she must shove this encounter into the back of her mind, where she might pull it out to examine along with their first kiss whenever she was alone in her bed. However, remembering was all she could ever do. To act on her feelings for him would be a sin she might never be able to come back from.

"Yes, we can," he agreed, sounding as unsure as she did. "I will go out first. Wait a few moments before you leave this closet in case someone else happens down the corridor."

"Of course," she agreed.

Without another word, he was gone, quickly disappearing through the door, leaving her alone in the dark. Wrapping her arms around herself, Lydia fought not to weep as she realized how cold she felt without his closeness.

CHAPTER 9

"I think I should like to throw a house party," Drucilla declared one morning over breakfast.

Sinclair paused in the middle of slathering his toast with butter and glanced up at his wife. Now recovered from croup, she graced the dining room with her presence each morning for breakfast and each evening for dinner. In the days following her emergence from her bedchamber, he'd come to revile her presence more than ever—if for no other reason than she seemed to snuff out every bit of the friendly camaraderie he, Lydia, and Charles shared when it was only the three of them. Now, they ate in silence, the only sound in the room that of utensils clinking against china.

Odd that she should choose to break the silence this way.

"A house party?" he repeated. "With the harvest beginning this week?"

She rolled her eyes, spoon poised to crack the shell of a boiled egg. "The harvest itself will take no longer than a fortnight, which is how long it will take me to plan the affair. Just a short party ... three or four days, I think. It will be fun. We have not had guests to Buckton in quite some time. As well, it is hunting season, and I know many of our neighbors envy you the game to be found here."

Sinclair resumed buttering his toast, keeping his gaze on his plate and away from the woman seated on his other side. Lydia remained silent throughout the exchange, though he was aware of her every movement. He seemed cognizant of her always, her scent drifting up his nostrils, her warmth radiating at him like some tangible force. Yet, whenever in Drucilla's presence, he fought the urge to drink her in with his eyes or speak to her more than was necessary.

He still had no idea what exactly had been said between them over tea. However, he knew his wife well enough to know that if Drucilla had intentionally attempted to hurt Lydia with words, it was because she knew something. Perhaps nothing about the night they'd met. No, it would be enough for Drucilla to suspect that he had a *tendre* for their governess—that he cared about her at all. It was all his wife would need in order to bare her fangs and lash out like the snake she was.

Perhaps the right thing to do would be to let Lydia go with a sterling reference. Maybe he could even help her secure a position with another family in Hertfordshire. He certainly had enough connections. However, just the thought of sending her away, of not being able to see her each day or lay his head upon his pillow each night knowing she occupied the same home as him ... no, he could not do it. Even without being able to have her in all the ways he wanted, he needed her close. He wanted whatever parts of her he could possess— even if they were only the sight of her, her scent when she walked past, her voice floating down the corridor.

"Besides," Drucilla continued when he did not respond. "I did not suppose you would be in attendance. You never bother to remain at Buckton longer than necessary. I had assumed you would be on your way back to Essex, or London, or wherever else it is you run off to so you may escape me."

At his side, Charles choked on a sip of tea, coughing and sputtering as he reached for his napkin. Sinclair clenched his jaw, his eyes narrowing as he gazed up at his wife. She merely gave him a decorous smile, deceptive sweetness thinly veiling the animosity radiating from her.

"Actually," he ground out, his fingers curling around his fork as he battled the urge to throttle her. "I had thought to remain a bit longer. My affairs are quite in order at the other estates, and I'd like all the time I can get with Henry before I'm obligated to depart again. So, I am sorry to disappoint you, but you'll have to tolerate my presence for at least another month or more."

Drucilla's smile widened, a cat-like motion of lips and a flashing of teeth akin to a predator about to devour its prey. "For Henry."

Her gaze flickered to Lydia, and she chuckled.

"But, of course. I had quite forgotten how *eager* you've been to spend time with our son. It will be lovely to have you for the party."

His nostrils flared, and the urge to strangle her became more acute than ever. Across from him, Lydia had gone red, her eyes lowered and her hands folded in her lap under the table. Most of her food remained untouched, and for some reason, that angered him most of all. One thing he'd learned about Lydia was that she possessed a hearty appetite. That she was not eating disturbed him.

"I must get to the schoolroom now," she declared, slowly rising from her chair without meeting anyone's gaze.

"Of course," Drucilla declared before anyone else could reply. "Have a pleasant morning, Miss Darling."

Lydia gave a silent curtsy, then quit the room. Sinclair set his own fork down and leaned back in his chair, his own appetite obliterated, the conversation having left a bitter taste in his mouth. Not surprisingly, his wife went on eating as if nothing were amiss, her own taste for food stronger than ever now that she'd gotten over her illness.

Wiping his mouth with his napkin, he stood, nodding at Charles to indicate it was time to begin their day's work.

"Plan your house party," he said to Drucilla. "But, do try not to beggar me in the process. If you would keep the expense reasonable, I would be grateful."

"But, of course," she replied. "I thank you for your generosity, dearest husband."

Sinclair did not have it in him to spar with her as he usually did, so he simply pinched his lips together and left the room. As usual, she'd begun to wear on him, and predictably, the desire to leave Buckton to get away from her began to rear its ugly head. Only, this time, that desire warred with the need to stay, because Buckton was now the place where Lydia resided … the place where he could glance around a corner at any moment and find her there, all golden hair, big blue eyes, and lush lips.

"I suppose we've a bit of incentive to get the harvest done in time," Charles quipped from his side as they walked toward their connected studies.

Sinclair, who abhorred opening his home to a dozen or more people he barely tolerated, snorted disdainfully. "On the contrary. If not for the fact that the cherries might spoil, I'd insist we draw the harvest out for as long as possible."

His friend laughed at that, which helped to lift his spirits a bit. He decided that this house party might not be a terrible idea. If it would distract his wife, all the better. That meant she would not be underfoot to irritate him, or terrorize Lydia.

That decided, he turned to Charles with a grin "What do you say we shun work for a few hours in favor of a ride?"

He was too restless at the moment, and a short time spent out of doors would do him more good than harm.

Charles' expression melted into one of relief. "I say that sounds like a fantastic idea."

In the fortnight that followed Drucilla's announcement of the house party, Buckton became a flurry of activity. While Sinclair and Charles oversaw the cherry harvest, his wife set the household staff to work with preparations for their arriving guests. Invitations were sent out, meals planned, activities decided upon, with Sinclair only being consulted about which days he might wish to take the men out hunting.

As the event drew nearer, guest chambers were prepared—linens laundered, rooms aired out, coal gathered for hearths, additional servants hired in from Ware in order to ensure the needs of each guest was met. New drapes were ordered for the largest drawing room, where Drucilla would do the bulk of her entertaining. The best silver and china were prepared, and a *modiste* had been sent for to fit his wife with new clothing for each day of the affair—for it would never do for her to be seen in garments she'd worn in public on other occasions.

Meanwhile, Sinclair immersed himself in what must surely be the busiest time of the year for Buckton. Those who had been hired on to assist with the harvest came at dawn each morning. He and Charles rolled up their sleeves to help, climbing the wooden ladders to fill woven baskets with cherries, which were then packaged into crates and loaded onto wagons—some to be washed and transported to various places, others to be processed into jam, candles, and other such things right here at Buckton. The house grounds bustled with wagons coming and going from their destinations, he and Charles riding back and forth between the groves and the various buildings to ensure everything went smoothly.

They worked from sunup to sundown, which kept him away from the house in the hours Henry and Lydia might be about. He spied them at times, out for walks, or even through the open windows of the schoolroom. However, there were no more late evenings in his study with whisky and conversation, no more stolen moments in closets, or even small talk over breakfast. It might have been for the best, as his self-control where she was concerned would only grow weaker. Maintaining his distance was torture, but standing close enough to touch her and being forced to resist would be even more so.

By the night preceding the house party, his weariness had sunk bone deep, and he wanted nothing more than to crawl into his bed and sleep. By midday tomorrow, twenty guests would descend upon them, and Sinclair would be forced to appear at Drucilla's side to greet them. While a few days of respite after the grueling harvest would be welcomed, he did not look forward having to pretend as if he did not loathe the woman he had married for the benefit of people he hardly ever saw. It would entertain Henry, at least. He would be excited for the moments when Drucilla sent for him, as it always amused her to flaunt their son before company, to dazzle everyone with how handsome and bright he was. Perhaps he would even bring Henry along for the hunt. The boy had seemed to enjoy learning to fire a rifle.

Tired as he was, when he stood on the front steps of the manor and gazed out at the setting sun, he could not find it in himself to go inside. Instead, he wanted to enjoy being outdoors without dozens of people underfoot, and cherries greeting him at every turn. While the fruit was his livelihood and had helped him amass much of his fortune, this time of year, Sinclair grew sick to death of cherries and quite often felt as if the sight of one might make him wretch. So, when he set off for his walk, he went in the opposite direction of the groves, deciding to head toward the rolling hills stretching away from the house instead. Hands in the pockets of his trousers, he stared at the horizon, studying the mottle of orange and pink, a thick curtain of navy blue beginning to fall over the world. Overhead, stars had begun to appear, small and distant.

He wandered for some time—until the house had become a tiny speck in the distance—and even then, exhaustion nagged him. He ignored it, restlessness plaguing him and chasing away the fatigue. He knew that if he went to his bed now, he would only toss and turn, unable to find any sort of peace.

After a while, he spotted another lone figure not far ahead, perfectly outlined by the vibrant sunset, the soft breezing pulling at the ends of a shawl.

"Lydia," he murmured, recognizing her even from such a distance.

His hands clenched, then opened, his legs propelling him along faster. Suddenly, getting to her felt more important than anything else. Even if just to look at her, breathe her in, hear her voice.

As he drew nearer, his long stride taking him over the uneven ground, he noticed the way twilight reflected off her hair, the way loosened wisps caressed her face and neck, the way she walked—her steps sure and purposeful, with a grace all her own.

Noticing his approach, she stopped, allowing him to catch her up.

"Good evening," he said once he had reached her. "I did not realize your walks took you so far from the manor."

Shrugging, she accepted his offered arm and fell in step with him as he continued walking. He did not question that she allowed the intimacy. Perhaps their distance from the house made her comfortable being close to him. Or, like him, she had craved the contact. It was a foolish hope, but knowing she'd thought of him as often as he had her all these years made him wonder if, even now, she missed him as much as he did her when they were apart.

"Not always," she replied. "But I received a letter from home and wished to walk while reading. It was filled with so much news from Oakmoor that by the time I'd finished it, I realized I had wandered quite far."

He smiled, clearly detecting the warmth in her voice at the mention of her family. "All is well in Norfolk, I hope?"

Her teeth flashed white in the dark when she smiled. "Yes, actually. Michael writes that Amelia is with child again. Their brood will overtake Oakmoor before long."

His gut twisted, his heart plummeting even as he realized how excited she must be to have yet another niece or nephew to love. Yet, he could not help the twinge of agony that resounded through him at the thought of a manor home such as his overrun with children. It was what he had wanted, one of the many reasons he had worked so hard to secure Buckton for himself and Drucilla. It was supposed to have been the place they would grow old together, fill with children. His progeny would return often, and perhaps even some of them might choose to remain, adding grandchildren to the household.

Buckton filled with running feet and laughter … it would have been the manifestation of his every dream. Yet, it would never be his, and hearing that some other man—some man he did not know, but envied—seemed to be living it, made him want to weep.

He studied Lydia from the corner of his eye and wondered if she felt the same way, if she'd wanted a family of her own but now found herself helping to raise another woman's child. His gaze slid down her body, to the front of her gown lying flat against her belly. What he wouldn't give to be the one to give her the children she might have wanted, to watch her grow. As wonderful a governess as she made, he knew she could be an even better mother.

"Your mother must be elated," he said once he'd found words again.

"Oh, certainly," she replied. "Michael says she has never been happier, being so surrounded by little ones. She is in the midst of planning a celebration for my nephew's seventh birthday in a few weeks."

Sinclair inclined his head. "It sounds as if life at Oakmoor is never dull."

"Certainly not. We Darlings love any excuse to plan a party. With such a growing family, it seems there is always something to make a fuss over."

"You must miss it."

She sighed, the sound so soft, he wondered if Lydia even realized she had made it.

"I do … not that I have not enjoyed my time at Buckton. I truly have. Henry has been the best pupil I've had the privilege of instructing. His pranks certainly keep my days lively."

That got another laugh out of him. "Care to tell me about his latest stunt?"

"Oh, it was quite brilliant, really," she said with a little giggle. "I came into my chamber a few nights past and opened the drapes to allow in a little moonlight. It was then I saw the shadow of a great bat against the window, flapping about … it scared me half to death!"

Sinclair's lips quivered as he tried not to laugh at her expense. "It was not a bat, obviously."

"Only a bit of paper he'd cut out and affixed to a few twigs," she replied between laughs. "He'd tied it to a string outside the window. In the dark, with the breeze blowing just so, it appeared quite real. Bloody brilliant of him. I'll have to think of something especially diabolical to repay him."

The two exchanged glances and erupted into laughter again, the sound carrying out over the grounds as they began drawing nearer to the house. He could see it against the horizon, outlined by moonlight, and his heart sank. Slowing his steps, he hoped to create more time with her out of Drucilla's reach, outside of the walls of a house that reminded him of all the reasons Lydia couldn't be his.

"I had hoped to see you before tomorrow," she said after a moment. "I realize that your days have been quite busy, so you may not be aware that Lady Clayton decided Henry should have a respite from his studies during the house party."

He nodded. "I was not informed, but I can understand why. With so much activity in the house, he is bound to be distracted."

"Yes, that is what Lady Clayton said," she replied. "However, you should also know that she has invited me to take part in the festivities. Charles and I both, actually."

That did give Sinclair pause. He came to a stop, forcing her to halt along with him, their arms still linked. He released her, turning so he could look down into her eyes.

"You are not obligated to attend," he stated, his mind reeling as he tried to determine what Drucilla could be about ... what she thought to accomplish by inviting the governess and steward to her house party. He suffered no delusion that it had been done out of the kindness of her heart.

Lydia shook her head. "I want to. Besides ... nothing could be more boring than hiding away in my room while you get to have all the fun."

He could not help but smile at that as he heard what she said, as well as what she did not say. Drucilla could not intimidate her. She had done nothing wrong and had no reason to hide. Despite being slightly on edge without knowing exactly what his wife might be up to, Sinclair found he would enjoy the party all the more with Lydia about.

"Perhaps you will join the men on the hunt," he quipped. "I know a few who could learn quite a bit from observing you with a rifle."

She snorted. "Yes, that will certainly be entertaining."

He raised an eyebrow at her. "I believe you underestimate the effect the sight of a woman holding a weapon can have upon a man. It could only be heightened if you were to don men's attire."

Biting her lip, she edged closer to him, her eyes glittering like those of a young girl about to disclose a secret. He found himself leaning in, holding his breath to hear whatever it was she might say.

"Back home at Oakmoor, I wore them all the time," she whispered, her voice low as if she worried someone might overhear.

When he breathed again, it came out on a rough wheeze, his chest burning and his gut clenching at the thought of her wearing snug breeches. With the lush flare of her hips and the sturdy legs he'd glimpsed that night in London, he could not imagine a more enticing sight.

"Is that so?" he managed, barely able to think past the throb in his groin caused by his wandering mind. "How … interesting."

"Oh, yes," she continued, oblivious to the effect she'd had on him. "I found breeches to be quite the most comfortable thing I'd ever worn. My sister-in-law, Amelia, is the one who introduced me to wearing them. She is known in London for her preference for men's clothing, you know. I suppose being the sister of a marquis afforded her the freedom to do as she pleased. Well, that and a sixty-thousand-pound dowry."

"This sister-in-law sounds like a horrible influence," he joked.

"Oh, she is the absolute worst," Lydia said, though her voice was too heavy with affection for Sinclair to mistake her words as anything other than ones of love. "She is the one who taught me to shoot, as well. If you think I am good, you should watch her. In truth, she was the first person ..."

She fell silent, clamping her lips shut as if she'd thought better of whatever she had been about to say.

Taking another step toward her, he reached up and cupped her face. He did not think anything of it until his fingers made contact with her skin, and by then, it was too late. He was touching her again—something he knew he ought not do; yet, it felt too good to stop, her skin like satin against his palm.

"The first person who what, Lydia?" he prodded, having a feeling that what she'd been about to say was important. He needed to hear it.

Her chest heaved as she stared up at him, her eyes wide as she seemed to struggle with herself for a moment. As if wondering whether she could trust him with her words, her thoughts, her secrets.

"The first person who made me realize that it was all right for me to be who I am without shame," she murmured. "My mother ... she is a wonderful woman. But she does not understand a girl who cannot play the pianoforte, or who would rather run about outdoors than spend her time composing letters or managing a household. I spent so much of my life learning all the things that would make me an acceptable young lady—a marriageable one. But, then Amelia comes along, and she is unlike any other woman I've ever met. She shoots, rides astride, and wears breeches. She speaks her mind, and people love her for it, even when they hate her. I suppose she was the first person I'd ever encountered who made me feel as if it was all right for me to be unlike the other ladies. That it was enough for me to simply be me."

He caressed her cheek with his thumb, counting the freckles adorning her face, observing the way the moonlight made prisms of darker blue come alive in her irises.

"If it means anything, I would never want you to be anyone other than you," he remarked with a little smile. "The girl I met in that garden ... she was like a breath of fresh air after so much London fog. She was too ..."

"Something," she finished for him with a smile of her own. "Too something."

"Exactly," he replied, his thumb still stroking, wandering over her face, smoothing a cheekbone, the arch of an eyebrow … then back down the slope of her face and toward her lips.

Instead of drawing away, she tilted her head back in a silent offering, her lips parting. Her breath raced against his thumb as he gently traced the curves of her upper lip, then the edge of her lower one.

Her eyelashes fluttered, and in that moment, Sinclair knew he could have had her lips. He could have kissed her, drawn her close. In the dark, removed from the house, he might have had more than a kiss. He'd never wanted anything more in his life, his body on edge, his mind overrun with all the possibilities.

Yet, her words from the linen closet came back to him now, and guilt assailed him so powerfully, he was forced to unhand her and take a step away.

He would never forgive himself if he caused her to do something she would regret. She had made herself clear on the matter of avoiding temptation.

She blinked, a frown marring her features as she seemed to come back to her senses.

Clearing his throat, he gestured toward the house once more. "Shall we?"

Her gaze grew shuttered as she gathered her shawl tighter around her body. Her only response was a swift nod.

He did not offer his arm again; to touch her right now would prove a grievous error. He was so on edge, one touch from her would hurl him into a pit of insanity. He would forget all his good intentions and kiss her, keep kissing her until she acquiesced to his every salacious desire.

They walked side by side, until they'd come close enough to the manor that the yellow light spilling from inside illuminated them both. He paused, just outside that circle of light, gazing up at the house.

"You ought to go in ahead of me," he said. "In case …"

He did not need to explain why, even though they hadn't actually done anything wrong. The touch of his hand to her face hadn't been nearly as intimate as their heated kiss in the linen closet. Still, he felt the weight of it in his belly, yet one more encounter he would remember with fondness and longing.

"Of course." With a cursory glance back at him, she added, "Good night, Mr. Clayton."

"Good night … Miss Darling," he replied, watching as she made her way swiftly up the front steps.

CHAPTER 10

"Have they arrived yet?"

Lydia glanced down at Henry, who tugged on her skirts for the third time. Reaching down to smooth the persistent cowlick rising up from the center of his head, she smiled.

"Not yet, but soon. Your mama said they would arrive at midday, and it is nearly two in the afternoon now. Patience, Henry."

Despite being able to see through the window of the upstairs drawing room himself, he had persisted in asking her every few minutes whether or not the guests had arrived. She supposed Henry thought her capable of seeing farther. Alas, the tree-lined lane stretching away from the front of Buckton Manor remained as empty now as it had five minutes ago.

"I'm hungry," the boy whined. "I wish they would arrive so we might have tea."

Lydia pressed a hand against her belly, inwardly agreeing with the boy. She was starving, though she felt certain the twisting in her gut had as much to do with the prospect of coming face to face with Sinclair again as with hunger. She had lain awake for hours after returning indoors the previous evening, thinking over their

149

encounter several times. That moment in which he'd touched her face had been less than a minute; yet, it had seemed to last for an eternity, those strong, dexterous fingers of his tracing the lines of her visage, paying tribute to every feature, pausing over her flaws as if they appeared her greatest attributes in his eyes.

Had any woman ever felt so desired, so cherished, from nothing more than the simple touch of a hand? She'd felt as if she might fall to her knees when he'd taken that hand away, leaving the places he'd just touched cold. Then, almost as soon as he'd spoken, breaking the spell, she had remembered. She had no right to feel that way when he touched her.

One would think she'd be nervous over the impending house party and her sudden position, thrust back into society in a sense. However, as she'd dressed this morning, selecting one of her best morning gowns, she had found herself looking forward to it. Most of the guests were unlikely to be those she would have encountered in London. Residents of Hertfordshire who were accustomed to country life, they would have much in common with her. Lady Clayton was likely to be the highest ranking woman in attendance, so Lydia had no reason to worry over excess scrutiny or committing some sort of faux pas.

Which left only one worry. She must conduct herself in a way that did not draw attention to her feelings for Sinclair. A task made more difficult the longer she resided at Buckton. She felt as if her longing for him radiated from her eyes, rang out in her voice every time she spoke, made itself apparent in her every movement.

Taking a deep breath, she smoothed her hands over her skirts, her fingers skimming over the blue flowers embroidered on the white muslin. There was nothing to worry about. The party would be a fun diversion, and perhaps even help to take her mind off her troubles.

Taking another deep breath, she glanced down at Henry, who had begun bouncing up and down as an outlet for his restlessness. Crossing to the corner of the room, where she had stashed a basket of toys for just this purpose, she pulled out a spinning top and offered it to him. With a huff, he accepted it, though rather grudgingly.

However, after a few minutes crouched on the floor, he'd forgotten about his hunger or watching for the guests, attempting to keep the little toy spinning across the rug.

Lydia went back to keeping watch, though they would not descend to join the others until they'd been sent for. Thankfully, there were tin soldiers, a skipping rope, and a toy train inside the basket. If her luck held out, Henry could be kept occupied until then.

Half an hour—and one skipping rope—later, she caught sight of the first conveyance coming down the lane, laden with the trunks and various belongings of its occupants. She called Henry to the window, and together, they watched the arrivals, a stream of carriages that came one after the other, opening to reveal the arrivals.

Henry made a fuss over the horses while Lydia inspected people approaching the manor's front steps. She spied a few pairs that appeared to be married couples, as well as a handful of matrons along with their young daughters. One carriage opened to reveal a group of four young bucks—eligible bachelors for the young misses, no doubt. A nice blend of people to comprise a good house party, she decided; even numbers of males to females, and people of various ages. Her mother would have planned it much the same way.

The house became awash in activity, voices and pounding feet upon the stairs echoing down corridors as servants came and went, situating guests' belongings in their chambers. Henry became impatient in truth then, anxious to be allowed to join the party and to sate his hunger. Thankfully, they were not made to wait for long. Relief washed over her when the drawing room door opened to reveal Charles. He'd left off his typical austere black today, donning a dove grey morning coat, his waistcoat a brocade navy blue. The colors made his eyes appear brighter, and she found the attire suited him.

"Good afternoon," he said with his ever-present smile. "Don't you look especially handsome today, Master Henry. You might actually be able to fool your parents' guests into thinking you a good, well-behaved little boy."

Henry had been dressed in a tailored suit complete with waistcoat and short pants, his shoes polished, and a little linen cravat giving him a dapper air. His mother had dressed him herself and declared that he was to endeavor not to wrinkle or stain his attire. So far, he had managed it, though Lydia did not think his shirt or cravat would survive tea time.

"Uncle Charles!" Henry exclaimed, throwing himself at the man and wrapping slender arms around his legs. "Is it time to go downstairs now?"

Charles attempted to smooth the boy's cowlick just as Lydia had done, to no avail. The wild lock made its way back up into the air, adding a charming aspect to his getup. He could not have looked more adorable if he'd tried.

"Indeed it is, my good sir," Charles said with a chuckle. "However, you must remember your manners. A gentleman must offer a lady his arm and escort her. Watch … see how it is done."

Leaving Henry lingering near the door, he came toward her, his eyes bright and sparkling with interest while he took her in from head to toe. His perusal made her mouth go dry as she recognized the signs of attraction in his manner. It caught her quite off guard when he extended a hand in a silent request for hers, then placed a kiss against her knuckles when she acquiesced.

"Miss Darling," he murmured. "I do not think I've ever seen you looking so lovely. I shall be the envy of every man in that drawing room when I am privileged to walk in with you on my arm."

Lydia's mouth dropped open, but she quickly shut it and swallowed, fumbling for composure. She'd known Charles liked her, but the way he was looking at her just now went beyond appreciation for her attire. He was gazing upon her much the way Sinclair often did.

"Thank you," she managed after a moment. "You look quite dapper, as well. You've arrived just in time. Henry has been on pins and needles all morning."

"As have we all," Charles remarked, offering her his bent arm. "Shall we?"

She placed her hand in the crook of his arm and allowed him to lead her toward the door where Henry awaited. Taking the boy's hand, Charles winked down at him, then led them from the room. Together, they navigated the corridor toward the stairs, doing their best to steer clear of the footmen toting trunks and portmanteaus through the open doors of various guest chambers.

As they descended, the soft hum of voices rang out at them, which prompted Henry to quicken his steps and hurry them along. With a chuckle, Charles gave the boy's hand a tug and urged him to slow down.

"The cakes aren't going anywhere," he teased.

A moment later, they arrived in the blue drawing room, a massive space which was actually two salons made one by the opening of a set of doors. Done in shades of blue and gold, it was obviously meant for entertaining large numbers of guests, as well as flaunting the wealth of the Clayton family. Chippendale and Hepplewhite furniture was arranged just so, allowing those who sat full view of those who milled about on foot, talking and indulging in refreshment. Several tea services had been set up around the room, along with tiered serving platters of cakes, biscuits, and delicate finger sandwiches. Footmen stood unobtrusively along the wall, their livery helping them to blend in with the blue and gold patterned wallpaper, only making themselves known when a guest seemed to be in need of something.

The guests milled about in pairs, as well as threesomes and foursomes, their voices held to socially acceptable levels as they chattered about their journeys to Buckton and indulged in other manners of small talk. A few eyes strayed to them as they came farther into the room. However, the attention of the majority of the guests seemed centered upon Lady Clayton, who sat in their midst holding court.

She'd placed herself on a settee arranged in full view of the entire room, her white skirts spread decorously around her. White muslin draped in lace covered her from bosom to feet, her neckline a bit more daring than was typical for a morning gown. As if to enhance the effect, a silver and pearl brooch had been pinned between her breasts, drawing the eye straight to the slight swell of her décolletage.

The lightest hand had been used with cosmetics upon her face—so light, one might think the pink flush on her cheeks and dark ring around her pale blue eyes to be natural. The rouge applied to her lips was just enough to make her mouth noticeably pink. Her hair had been styled in artful dishabille, soft waves disturbed only by a white silk bandeau, a white muslin flower pinned near one ear. She was a vision, at her most vibrant when surrounded by so many people.

Lydia could see how Sinclair had fallen under her spell … how he'd fallen so deeply in love with her without truly knowing her. She was magnetic, and truly at her best when lavished with such attention. It appeared half the men in the room were besotted with her, the women both envious and admiring.

As the lady noticed their approach, she stood and smiled, the expression as artful and controlled as the rest of her appearance.

"Ah, here they are," she exclaimed, opening her arms and rounding the low table holding yet another tea service and platters of food. "Come, come, allow me to introduce you to everyone."

She took Henry from Charles and proudly presented the boy to those gathered around.

"I do not know if you've all had the chance to meet my son," she said, holding the boy close against her side. "Henry, say hello to everyone."

Henry lifted his chin and squared his shoulders in a way Lydia knew he'd been taught. "I am Henry Lewis Ulrick Clayton, and I am very pleased to meet you all."

This produced raptures from several women, and a few chuckles from the men. Some came forward to shake his hand, which the boy accomplished with so much grave concentration, while one lady approached to pinch his cheek and fuss over him.

Then, Lady Clayton indicated Lydia and Charles. "Mr. Welby is the steward of Buckton, and Miss Darling is Henry's governess. They will be joining us, of course."

Lydia detected a few murmurs of what a benevolent mistress she must be to allow members of her staff to enjoy the house party.

Others murmured polite greetings, and within moments, everything returned to the way it had been before their arrival. Lady Clayton took Henry onto the settee at her side, treating him to tea and a plate filled with the delicacies he liked best. Freed from her duties as Henry's nursemaid for the day, Lydia gestured toward a cluster of unused chairs near a sideboard laden with refreshments.

"Shall we sit?" she asked Charles.

Her companion nodded. "Of course. I am famished, aren't you?"

"Positively starved," she said with a smirk. "We can remedy that right now."

They went undisturbed for a few minutes as they helped themselves from the sideboard before occupying two armchairs flanking a small end table the perfect size for resting their cups and plates upon. While she sipped tea and nibbled a scone, Lydia allowed herself to study the occupants of the room more closely. She did not recognize any of the guests, nor did she see Sinclair among them.

"Where is Mr. Clayton?" she asked.

"There was a matter in Ware he had to attend to this morning," Charles answered. "He should return shortly, I imagine. He will not hurry back out of excitement, of course. He abhors affairs like these."

She murmured something in response, her attention suddenly stolen by a man standing behind Lady Clayton's settee. He was gazing down on Lady Clayton, his hands resting on the back of the chair as she gazed up at him over her shoulder. The two exchanged smiles, their glances trading silent secrets. Lydia's fingers tightened around her teacup as she observed the exchange, her teeth clenching when the man's hand came down upon the lady's shoulder. The touch was far too familiar, his thumb stroking slow circles near her neck, where her pulse might thrum.

"That would be the Viscount Wortham," Charles stated, seeming to notice the direction of her gaze.

Blinking and tearing herself away from the pair, she looked to Charles, whose expression had gone grim.

"A friend of Lady Clayton's?" she asked.

A muscle ticked in Charles' cheek, and if she weren't mistaken, his lips curled in something like disdain. She'd never seen him wearing anything other than a smile, this sudden change in demeanor puzzling her.

"Of a sort," he ground out. "I did not know he had been invited, so I know Sinclair didn't, either. He will not like it."

Glancing back at the viscount, Lydia watched as he conversed with a smiling Henry, chuckling at something the boy said. She furrowed her brow, something strikingly familiar about the man eluding her. Taking stock of his appearance—the golden hair, high forehead, and aristocratic features—Lydia tried to place what made her feel such a strong sense of déjà vu.

Then, the man glanced up and in her direction. Having caught her staring, he inclined his head and gazed right back at her. After a moment, his lips parted in a smile, the motion heavy with unspoken innuendo. He grinned like a viper, and she half expected a forked tongue to appear between his teeth. It sent a shiver down her spine, reminding her too much of the sorts of men she'd been warned to avoid before her London Season. Everything about him was off-putting, despite his classical handsomeness. Yet, she found herself unable to look away, and in an instant, the reason why overwhelmed her, forcing a gasp from deep in her chest.

She could not look away because she realized just then what it was about the man that struck her as so familiar. It was subtle—the line of his nose, the shape of his mouth, the light cleft in his chin. Each and every one of those features had been etched, in a smaller, more inno-cent way, onto Henry's face.

Sinclair hovered in the doorway of the blue drawing room, hands clenched so tight, he was surprised the bite of his nails into his palms did not draw blood. Admittedly, he had not paid much attention to Drucilla's efforts in planning this house party, not only because he didn't care much for the details, but also because the harvest had consumed so much of his time. So, he had been caught off guard to return home after his morning trip to Ware to find Lord Miles Wortham amongst the guests milling about his drawing room.

He stood stone-still, his blood roaring, the rushing cadence of it pounding through him blotting out all other sound. His jaw clenched until he grew surprised his teeth did not shatter. If his spine were drawn any straighter, it might snap. It took every ounce of his discipline to keep from charging into the room, upending every one of the serving platters, crashing the china against the walls, and roaring like the beast he felt growing within. He fantasized about staining the rugs with that man's blood before wrapping his hands around Drucilla's throat and squeezing until her lips turned blue.

She dared to bring this man into their home … dared to flaunt him before Sinclair and their guests. Drucilla had always been bold, and she'd proved time and time again how vindictive she could be, but he would never have thought she possessed so much gall. And she knew he could do nothing about it with so many people in the room, several of which he conducted business with on a regular basis. The cunning little witch had him over a barrel at the moment, and she knew it.

He realized just how much she knew it when she glanced up and noticed him standing there, giving him a smile that made flames of rage roar in his belly.

"Oh, Sinclair, darling!" she called out, sending every eye in the room skittering toward him. "I am so pleased you've returned home. You are just in time for tea."

He unclenched his hands and unwound his jaw, forcing himself to appear at ease in front of his guests. "I am glad to see everyone has arrived. Welcome, all. My wife seems happy with my late arrival, though we all know that most of you care not a whit whether I am here when Dru is entertaining."

Laughter rippled through the room, easing a bit of the strain thrumming through the air between himself and his wife. The only people in the room who did not smile or laugh were Charles and Lydia. The latter sat staring at him with a mournful expression pulling at the corners of her mouth and marring her forehead. Their gazes locked, and something heavy dropped into his gut, cold and twisting like a bundle of writhing snakes. The pity in her eyes washed over him, much like the look she'd given him when he had revealed his baseborn origins to her. And he realized without having to ask what had put such an expression on her face.

She *knew*.

For some reason, that knowledge disturbed him more than anything else. It was one thing for her to have thought him a lecher at first, and perhaps a man of low moral standards. Perhaps she'd thought him a boor at times for his treatment of Drucilla, though living at Buckton, she also seemed to understand that it wasn't ever unwarranted. But for her to also know what a fool his wife had made of him, for her to see the evidence of it and then pity him for it … it was more than he could bear.

He tore his gaze away, unable to look at her just now, his emotions too turbulent, his nerves rubbed raw. Around him, conversation resumed, as well as the clink of cups, saucers, and spoons. Forcing himself to move, he made his way through the room, wearing as good a smile as he could manage while he was greeted by one guest after another. After a few moments, he found it easier to don the mask he'd worn for so long, the one he displayed in order to hide the truth of his misery from the world. He had done it for so long that it came like second nature for him to smile and laugh and talk about tomorrow's planned hunt when he stood a stone's throw away from his wife and the man who had cuckolded him years ago … who might even find his way into Drucilla's room later to do it to him again.

That thought lingered in the back of his mind throughout the entire day. Even after tea had ended, after which many of the guests adjourned to different areas of the house to amuse themselves. A few of the women played at cards in one salon while others conversed in a quiet corner, and the men retreated outdoors with him for a tour of the grounds.

Even when they all dispersed to dress for dinner, he maintained his composure, his outward façade of aloofness. Yet, he did not forget the picture of Wortham standing behind that settee, hand on Drucilla's shoulder, smiling down at his son. He did not forget the perfect picture of the three of them, handsome and beautiful and blond. He did not forget the anger he'd felt upon noticing just how much Henry resembled Wortham, wondering if he would be more a likeness of the viscount than Drucilla as he grew older, thinking about the sort of gossip that would inspire ... how it would hurt the boy if he ever knew.

It put him on edge during dinner, where he sat sulking while everyone enjoyed the five-course meal Drucilla had planned. It drove him to drink more wine than he usually did, and once the men had broken away from the women for spirits and cigars, he went straight for the brandy bottle. While the other men made use of the chamber pots and fell into the sort of conversation they could not indulge in with women present, Sinclair retreated to a corner of the room and lit a cigar, hoping to hide behind a cloud of smoke.

No such luck.

Wortham seemed to be everywhere at once, as he had been all day —always within Sinclair's line of sight during the tea, the tour, the dinner party where he had flirted shamelessly with Drucilla in full view of the entire gathering. These things would not have ordinarily irked him. He never cared what Drucilla did, not after she'd killed the last shred of his affection for her. Yet, it all seemed to hurt so freshly with Lydia looking on, seated farther down the table in a lovely, demure green silk gown, her pitying gaze flitting to him every few minutes, her mouth turned down. He adored her for caring, for being saddened on his behalf ... but oh, how impotent it made him feel, to be forced to endure this, to have her look at him as if he were some wounded animal.

And so, when Wortham loped toward him from across the room, brandy tumbler in hand, smug smile fixed on his infuriating face, Sinclair had had just about enough. He stood on the edge of his control and forbearance. He could no longer hold his tongue.

Keeping his gaze on the other men in the room and discerning most stood out of earshot, he then turned a glare onto the viscount, who had helped himself to a cigar from the humidor.

"I say, Clayton," the man remarked after taking his first puff from the cigar, sending fragrant smoke billowing around them. "The party is off to a good start."

"So it is," he ground out, fighting to keep his tone level. "Though, I suppose you ought to reserve your judgment until after you've availed yourself to *all* that Drucilla's hospitality has to offer."

Wortham frowned, cigar in hand. "Come now, Clayton. It has been so long—"

"Not long enough for me to have forgotten how you befriended me, then proceeded to help yourself to my wife," he snapped.

Wortham sighed. "You judge me too harshly. Drucilla led me to believe—"

"Speak again, and I will put that cigar out in your eye," he interjected, swiveling toward the viscount and taking a step closer and lowering his voice. "I do not care what she led you to believe, or what you thought, or what either of you wanted. What's done is done, but Henry is *my* son. You might have dipped your prick into his mother's cunt, but that does not make you his father. *I* have claimed him, raised him, loved him."

"Of course you have," Wortham replied, despite Sinclair's warning. "No one is disputing that he is yours, Sin."

"Don't call me that!" he spat, his voice rising and drawing the attention of a few of the other men.

Gritting his teeth, he swallowed the bile building in the back of his throat, his fingers clenching so hard around the cigar, he was surprised it did not snap in half. The other men went back to talking once they seemed to decide nothing of any interest was happening.

"I love her," Wortham whispered.

"So did I," Sinclair retorted, lowering his voice one more. "So does everyone. Do you think you are special because you managed to impregnate her? You're an even greater fool than I thought."

Downing what remained of his brandy, he slammed the glass onto a nearby side table.

"Help yourself to Drucilla all you wish ... I have not cared for quite some time what man she's giving her cunt to on any given week," he ground out. "But if I find you anywhere near my son ..."

He met the other man's gaze, ensuring Wortham could see what he did not say. The viscount, apparently, deciphered the message. He simply nodded, lips pinched, gaze shuttered. With a curt nod of his own, Sinclair quit the room, not bothering to offer any explanations to his other guests. This late in the day, no one could fault him for leaving, especially when they were all accustomed to keeping country hours.

At some juncture, the men might rejoin the women in the neighboring salon for charades or cards or some other such thing, but he could not think of that. He could not look forward to being in the room with so many people again when he felt turned inside out, wrung dry, and exposed. He felt as if all the world could see him for a fool, a cuckold, a bastard who had dared to reach for a place in society that did not belong to him. With every slight he suffered, every embarrassment or bit of scorn, he was made to feel more and more like that boy who'd been brought to live with his father's wealthy family after his mother's death. He felt out of place, as if he wore someone else's skin.

Yet, there was no escape. This was his life now, and while he'd had no control over his upbringing, this particular circumstance—his loneliness, his loveless marriage—were traps of his own making. *He* had built Drucilla up as some paragon of love and grace in his mind. *He* had spent years earning his way into her life and, he'd thought, into her heart. *He* had deluded himself into thinking she loved him back. And now, he must endure this, as there was not much else he could do short of murdering Drucilla and burying her body behind the cherry groves. Bad enough he was a bastard; there was no need to compound that by also becoming a killer.

He barreled down the corridor and toward the stairs, desperate for solitude lest he do something he might come to regret. He could not have his neighbors spreading gossip about his quick temper or irrational behavior—for to them, it *would* seem irrational, him erupting into a fit of rage, destroying everything he got his hands on before physically ejecting the viscount from his home and then wringing his wife's neck. Oh, they would say, they'd always known Sinclair Clayton was barbaric. He was, after all, a bastard. Who would expect anything less?

He would pull himself together. He would emerge from his chambers in the morning ready to face them all, his pretense of detachment once again in place.

CHAPTER 11

The first day of the house party passed Lydia in a blur, so much so that she would be hard-pressed to remember a single detail should anyone ask. She could not think past the stunning moment she had gazed upon Lord Wortham and recognized him as Henry's true sire. Most people looking at Henry for the first time would think he favored his mother ... which he did, on the surface. The light blond hair, the pale blue eyes ... both seemed taken straight from Lady Clayton and gifted to her son. There were other things marking him as her child—his hands, the shape of his eyebrows, the way he laughed.

Yet, with the viscount's stunning presence for comparison, it was difficult to ignore the signs. Anyone paying even the slightest bit of attention would be able to see that Sinclair had not fathered the boy, and even those oblivious to that fact must be able to see the way the man interacted with Lady Clayton, displaying far too little discretion and far too much familiarity.

Lydia's belly had churned as she'd sat beside Charles during tea. Despite the steward's best efforts at drawing her into conversation, she had become unresponsive, unable to do anything other than sit and watch Sinclair attempt to interact with his guests. In the time she'd known him, she had come to recognize the signs that something was bothering him—the little lines between his eyebrows, the tightness at the corners of his lush mouth, the turbulence in those dark eyes. Perhaps he had not expected the viscount. Lydia could only imagine the upset such a surprise had caused him.

Her entire day had been filled with such thoughts, her mind turning over the things she'd already known and fitting them together with this new information. On the night she'd met Sinclair, Drucilla should have been pregnant with Henry, or lying in after having just birthed him. Had Sinclair known, even then, that another man had sired his child? Was that what had driven him to kiss her, charm her, woo her? Had it only been a part of the tit-for-tat that seemed to rule his existence with Drucilla?

No, that could not be it. She might not understand all that had happened, but she believed Sinclair's feelings for her, whatever they might be, were real. They were as real as her own, which only made this all the more difficult. All she wanted to do was go to him, lay his head in her lap and comfort him, take on his burden as her own. She wanted to do something, anything, to take away the pain. The man suffered right before their eyes, and his guests, his wife, could only sit about smiling and laughing over dinner while wearing their finery, ignoring his despondent expression and the massive quantities of wine he'd drunk.

By the time dinner ended and the women all gathered in one of the smaller salons to give the men their time alone with brandy and cigars, Lydia had been worn thin. Her constant worry exhausted her, and being in the same room with Lady Clayton only made her angry. She could not understand why anyone who'd been given Sinclair's heart would throw it away so callously. It was the one thing Lydia wanted; yet, his wife had destroyed it without a care. The urge to shake the woman overwhelmed her.

As Lady Clayton sat preening for her captive audience, sharing the details of the design for the new gown she wore, Lydia found she'd had enough. She could not endure another moment in the company of her employer without doing or saying something that might cause her to lose her position.

So, she had excused herself, feigning a headache and leaving the room after several women wished her well and bid her good night. Lady Clayton had ignored her, and for that, Lydia was glad. She had trudged to her room and fallen into bed fully clothed, not even bothering to unpin her hair. The emotional exhaustion of the day had dragged her into unconsciousness within minutes, and she awoke the next morning no better off. Her head pounded, and her chest still ached from the squeeze of so many conflicting emotions.

Yet, knowing she would be expected downstairs, she rose and peeled off her gown, taking a moment to freshen up at the washstand before donning a simple morning dress of lavender muslin.

When she arrived in the dining room, she found it filled with guests, Sinclair seated at the head of the table and Drucilla at the other end. She chattered and smiled, her focus upon the people sitting closest to her. Meanwhile, Sinclair seemed to pointedly ignore her, his deep voice lowered to a murmur as he conversed with a man seated to his left. From the looks of things, their conversation must involve business of some sort, their attention fixated upon whatever they discussed.

Lydia discovered Charles seated near the middle of the table, an empty seat left between him and a woman she'd been introduced to the previous day. Abigail, she believed the girl's name was—a young, unmarried chit not long out of the schoolroom. She gave Lydia a bright smile as she sat and immediately engaged her.

Between Abigail and Charles, she was able to lose herself in pleasant conversation over breakfast. As she ate, she noticed the men had dressed in hunting attire, and supposed that this morning would find them out for the anticipated hunt. Envy had her wishing she attended this event back at Oakmoor, where no one would think anything of her and Amelia joining the hunting party in breeches and boots, rifles slung over their shoulders. She fought not to sigh at the thought of spending her day inside with the women, writing letters or reading or doing some useless activity meant to pass the time while the men had all the fun.

As if he'd read her thoughts, Charles turned to her then. "I do wish you were accompanying us on the hunt this morning, Miss Darling. Sinclair tells me you are a crack shot."

At her side, Abigail gasped. "Truly, Miss Darling? You hunt?"

She smiled at the younger woman and nodded. "It has been an age since I indulged in an actual hunt, but yes. My sister-in-law is quite the rifleman. When I took an interest in learning, she was gracious enough to teach me. Whenever I am privileged to visit home, my brothers invite me to join them on their hunts."

"How intriguing you are, Miss Darling!" Abigail exclaimed, staring at Lydia with wide curious eyes.

"I'll say," called out one of the men seated across from them—Mr. Grenville, a gentleman farmer from a neighboring county. "Why on Earth would you not join us, then?"

Lydia's face flushed as the man's query brought even more attention to her, many other men adding their agreement. Of course she should join them, they insisted. It would be a ripping good time for them to be treated to a show of her skill. Naturally, she realized that most of them thought they humored her. It was always this way whenever she revealed her interests. The men would indulge her, right up until she showed them she was as good as, or better, than most of them. At which point, they became quite fond of her ... but, only as a dear friend, of course. What man did not wish to befriend a woman who liked whisky, billiards, and shooting rifles? She might as well be a man as far as they were concerned.

"I think that is a fine idea," Charles chimed in, his eyes crinkling at the corners as he gave her one of his charming smiles. "Won't you join us, Lydia?"

Glancing about the table, she found just about every eye on her now, including Sinclair's and Lady Clayton's. Her mistress looked as if she wished to speak against it, to insist that Lydia remain behind with the women. As Lydia's employer, she would have every right. Yet, Sinclair spoke first, putting to rest any objection his wife might have made.

"You are welcome, if it is your wish to be a part of the hunt, Miss Darling," he declared, before turning back to the man he'd been speaking with earlier.

Lydia was quite taken aback by his dismissal, as well as the ghost of a glance he had given her. He spoke as if he cared not at all whether she took part in the hunt. It stung, but she also knew why he did this. He could not risk allowing anyone to see what went on between them. Not that anything of any substance had happened. Nothing that others might not see as innocent or at least within their own moral boundaries. They had never been intimate beyond a few kisses and whispered words. Nevertheless, she felt the weight of each encounter, every word spoken between them, and each one felt momentous to her. Standing under the moonlight with his hand upon her face had been one of the most significant moments of her life, and yet, no one could ever know.

Her heart sank, but she put on a brave face, offering Charles and the others an agreeable smile. "I would love to join you."

Breakfast continued, with Lydia now forced to entertain the curiosity of those who wished to know more about her interests. Several of the women became even more curious once they were informed that she was sister-in-law to the sister of the Marquis of Ashton—a notorious figure in London whose eccentricities were whispered about far and wide. Lydia did not think she'd ever been so popular at any party.

Once the meal had concluded, Lady Clayton urged all the women to join her in her favored white and silver salon, where they would await the return of the men.

"Miss Darling, I would urge you to be cautious during the hunt," Lady Clayton said to her. "But knowing your ... background, I daresay you shall fare just fine with the men, so I shall not worry for you at all. Do enjoy yourself."

Lydia felt the lash of those words, even as wrapped up in sweet honey as they sounded. She glared at the other woman's back as she exited the room, leading the others with her. Yet, she maintained her composure, as always. It was no greater a slight than any she'd suffered while in London, and truly, she would rather be outdoors with the men than cloistered inside, anyway.

She declared her intentions to meet the hunting party outdoors once she'd had a moment to change, and Sinclair assured her they would wait. Lydia rushed upstairs as quickly as she dared, a smile pulling at her lips as she thought of being able to hunt again. It had been so long, and despite the circumstances, she found herself more excited about this than she'd been about anything in quite some time.

Rushing into her room, she went to her armoire, rifling about until she found the clothing she'd hidden away toward the back of the cabinet. The worn buff breeches and brown waistcoat had been tailored to fit her, and once paired with a brown coat—also made to fit her—and matching boots, proved to be her favorite attire for romping out of doors. Back home at Oakmoor, she owned several other ensembles such as this, but these were the only men's items she had brought with her to Hertfordshire, and in truth, had never thought to wear them outside her chamber.

Becoming downright giddy as she replaced her muslin and lace with the buckskin and leather, she could not get back downstairs fast enough, taking the stairs two at a time. Once she reached the front steps, she found the men waiting for her as promised, rifles slung over shoulders, hounds held on leashes. The dogs barked and bounded about as far as their leads would allow, excited to begin the hunt. Sinclair stood at the forefront, Barkley yapping excitedly, leaping up to rest his paws on his master's chest.

The men all seemed to turn to notice her at once, expressions of amusement, shock, and open interest widening their eyes. Sinclair turned his head at the exact moment she began descending the stairs, his jaw going slack as his gaze traveled over her from head to toe before he looked up into her eyes. His irises simmered like hot coals, his nostrils flaring and his face conveying a hundred words that his mouth could not say. She faltered on the bottom step, locked in his stare, her pulse racing as she tried to imagine what she must look like through his eyes. The coat fell to her hips, but did little to conceal how the breeches clung to her form.

She'd never felt anything but free in these clothes, comfortable. With his gaze on her that way, they took on an entirely new allure for her—making her feel more sensual, more womanly than she'd ever felt in any gown.

He had been staring at her for far too long without speaking, though no one else seemed to notice. A few of the men had begun to applaud while others laughed and made comments about how 'fetching' she looked in men's clothing. She grinned and took a little bow, which amused them all the more and kept them from seeing the way Sinclair's fist tightened around Barkley's lead, his jaw clenching as he stood there listening to them shower her with compliments. Raising her eyebrows at him, she cleared her throat.

"I'm ready."

"Wonderful, we're all here," he replied, finally snapping out of it with a shake of his head. "Shall we go?"

The handlers of the restless hounds were all-too happy to oblige, following Sinclair toward the woods. Along the perimeter of the trees, servants waited for the hunt to begin, so that they could come behind the hunters to collect their kills and take them to be skinned and cleaned.

Charles approached her, a second rifle extended in silent offering. She accepted it, murmuring her thanks as he also offered her a pouch of ammunition, which she slung across her body.

"As always, you shock me, Lydia," he remarked as they walked, following the others through the trees and deeper into the thickly wooded area surrounding the house grounds.

She issued a little huff of laughter. "I do hope I have not caused you to think badly of me."

He glanced at her from the corner of his eye, his gaze slipping down to the breeches allowing the world to see just how plump her hips and thighs were. Becoming accustomed to having these parts of her body so prominently displayed had taken some growing used to, and now, she hardly noticed unless someone made a point of looking. However, she found the same appreciation for her figure in Charles' eyes that she had noticed in Sinclair's.

"On the contrary," he replied, meeting her gaze once more. "The more you shock me, the more I find I admire you."

She looked away swiftly, unable to maintain his gaze while the back of her neck burned hot in reaction to his words. Not the first time he'd said something of the sort to her; yet, she could not become excited over it. Here was a man she could admire, respect … even come to care for if she allowed herself. He made a good life for himself as a steward, and he was quite possibly the kindest man she'd ever met aside from her brothers. In fact, Michael and Archie would probably get on well with Charles, and she could almost see the three of them lounging about Oakmoor, talking about horses and rifles over whisky.

So, why, then, did her heart plummet into her gut at the thought of him there instead of Sinclair? Why did her mind shrink away from the thought of opening herself up to the possibility of any sort of romance with Charles, who clearly saw her as more than a mere friend? Why couldn't she stop thinking of the way Sinclair's hand had caressed her face under the moonlight and how badly she'd wanted his kiss then?

What the devil was wrong with her? Sinclair could never truly be hers. After she had given up on marriage, meeting Charles might be the best thing that could have ever happened to her. Where was her joy that here, finally, was a man other than Sinclair who took an interest in her—the true Lydia who enjoyed unconventional pursuits and did not fit in with the London misses?

"You flatter me," she simply murmured, realizing he would expect a response. "I simply find it refreshing to be myself and enjoy the things that make me happy. I cannot do that if I worry over appearances and conventions."

If anything, these words proved the exact wrong ones to say. They only seemed to make that gleam in Charles' eyes brighter when he smiled at her again.

"Indeed," he said. "Wise words from an exceptional woman."

Thankfully, she was saved from replying when the howling of the dogs ahead of them indicated prey had been found. She and Charles hastened to join the others, and the hunt was on.

For hours, they tracked hares, pheasant, and foxes through the woods, even encountering a buck, which Sinclair felled with a magnificent shot. The party split into two groups after a time, then three, and before long, Lydia found herself alone with Charles, the two of them having fallen behind the leader of their pack and the hounds guiding them along.

Their pace had begun to slow, and she supposed that soon enough, the decision would be made to return to the house. Glancing about, she found no one near, did not even hear any of the others' voices. Only the distant barks and howls of the hounds rang out at them through the trees.

"I hope you do not find me too forward," Charles said, breaking the silence.

Frowning, she turned to glance at him. "What do you mean?"

He shrugged with a sheepish smile. "Only that I do not wish for you to misconstrue my compliments toward you. I would not want you to gain the wrong impression."

She sucked in a sharp breath. His word struck curiosity and fear in her with equal measure. Feigning confidence she did not feel, she laughed and waved him off.

"Oh, do not be silly! Of course I would not allow a few compliments to lead me to believe you are interested in me."

His hand came gently around her upper arm, drawing her up short. As she was forced to a stop, turning to face him, he grasped her other arm, holding her far closer than could be appropriate. There was no way to misconstrue this.

"Of course I am interested," he murmured, his eyelids lowering, the warmth in his voice leaving no doubt as to his meaning. "I simply meant that I would not want you to think my interest is of a salacious nature. I like you, Lydia. I find you charming and lovely, and quite frankly, I'm perplexed as to how you've managed to go unwed for so long."

It should have been insulting. However, she'd heard the sentiment before. Everyone 'liked' her. No one could understand why she remained a spinster governess. It had stopped being an insult, and was now simply a fact.

"Charles, I am flattered," she managed, once she found her voice.

"I'd much rather hear that you return the sentiment," he replied, his words holding an unspoken question, his gaze searching as he looked into her eyes.

She forced a smile, very much aware of the fact that he was still touching her. His hands were strong, large, firm on her arms, but still gentle enough that she could escape him if she wished. At the moment, she was not certain what she wanted. On one hand, she could not stop thinking of Sinclair, and how she'd rather feel his touch than Charles'. However, she could not forget her position and Sinclair's marriage. This man liked her, could come to love her ... and if the way he was looking at her was any indication, he wanted her. What could be the harm in testing herself—letting herself see if she could feel anything for him beyond friendship?

"I ... I like you, as well," she stammered, maintaining his gaze, willing herself to do this. She had to do this for herself, for her own sake. Going about life pining after a married man was no way to live.

He smiled at that, leaning in closer—so close, their bodies touched, pressing together from chest to hip. The man had a pleasing form, slender but wiry, much like Sinclair. Yet, even such close proximity did not spark half as much desire in her as she felt when Sinclair stood this close. Hell, she felt more for Sinclair when he was clear on the other side of the room.

His breath whispered against her cheek, and his lips found her there, gently, questioningly. She lifted her head in response, granting her permission, holding perfectly still and awaiting the kiss. His lips moved, hovered over hers, close enough that she could almost feel them. She parted her own and waited, holding her breath.

The kiss never came.

Footsteps crunched over the foliage on the ground, warning them of someone else's arrival. Lydia gasped, backpedaling from Charles far too late. Someone appeared from between two trees before his hands had fallen away from her, and as she turned to find Sinclair entering the clearing, her stomach twisted violently until she felt she might be sick.

Sinclair stood watching the pair standing in the little copse of trees, far removed from the hunting party. When the rest of the group had come together, only for him to discover Charles and Lydia were not among them, he had urged the others to return to the house without him, then set out after them himself. He was not certain what he expected to find. That they'd gotten a bit lost, perhaps. Instead, he'd walked into the clearing to discover Lydia in the arms of his closest friend, her head tipped up invitingly, waiting for a kiss.

He'd been forced to admit to himself that they made quite a sight—golden heads, young, handsome and beautiful, a matched set. And taking notice of that only made matters worse. He felt fit to kill as he approached, ensuring to make as much noise as possible as he pulled Barkley along, boots crunching over the twigs and leaves in his path.

The two moved swiftly away from each other, the shame bringing redness to Lydia's face satisfying him in a way he knew he had no right to feel. That did not keep him from being glad he'd stopped the kiss before it could happen, that Lydia now looked as if she wished the ground would open up and swallow her. It did not prevent him from wanting to tackle his friend to the ground and beat him into the dirt, perhaps wrap Barkley's lead around his throat and squeeze until he ceased to draw breath.

"There you are," he snapped, coming near enough that he could clearly see Charles' irritation over having been interrupted. "We grew worried when we all came together on the path and did not see you."

His tone held a heavy measure of accusation, which seemed to draw Lydia's attention. She looked up at him with wide eyes.

"We are fine," she said, her voice a bit hoarse.

From desire, he wondered? Desire for his friend? Had Charles affected her when he'd touched her, drawn her into his arms? Tension seized his neck and spine, and he felt as if the vein in his forehead might burst at any moment.

"We simply wandered from the others a bit," she added.

"Yes, well, we are all going back inside for tea," he said, swiveling his gaze toward Charles and narrowing his eyes. "I would like a word with Miss Darling, and Barkley has gotten a bit restless. If you would not mind returning him to the kennel ..."

His request was really a disguised order, and Charles knew it. He stood rooted to the spot for a long while, staring at Sinclair with equal parts disbelief and annoyance dancing in his eyes. Sinclair met the other man's challenge without speaking, daring him to object. Using his power as the master here should have made him feel like a cad. Instead, it only made him grateful when Charles sighed and came forward to take the hound's lead.

"Of course."

As he accepted the lead, he cast Sinclair a 'look.' One that told him they would speak of this later ... not as employer and steward, but as friends. Sinclair did not care, so long as the man took his leave before he was forced to do him bodily harm.

"I am certain you know the way," he said as Charles brushed past him, Barkley in tow. "You know these lands well."

Charles stiffened, but did not reply, simply continuing on until he disappeared through the trees. Sinclair waited until he could no longer hear the sounds of the other man's footsteps, his gaze falling onto Lydia. She met his stare without speaking, hands balled into fists at her sides, chest heaving as if she had run a long distance and now struggled to draw breath.

The rushing of his blood did not let up. On the contrary, he found that every drop of it now seemed to make its way toward his groin, pooling with liquid heat. The sight of her, face flushed, lips parted, hair slightly mussed from the exertions of the day … all of it was enough to stoke his desire as well as his fury. Charles had been about to kiss her, and she had seemed willing enough. If Sinclair had not happened upon them, she would have allowed it. A muscle in his jaw ticked, his teeth grinding together.

"Well?" she prodded when he simply stood there, observing her without speaking. "You wished to have a word with me?"

Inclining his head, he took one step toward her, then another, closing the space between them. She stiffened, but did not flee, standing her ground to await his approach.

"I take it you and Charles are enjoying the house party," he stated, his words coming out far harsher than he intended. He could not seem to help himself, this beast inside of him roaring and growling at the thought of anyone else touching her.

She flinched as if he'd struck her, brow furrowing. "And just what is that supposed to mean?"

He was so close now, he could see her lower lip trembling, detect the thump of her pulse in the hollow of her collarbone.

"It should come as no surprise that the two of you should develop a *tendre*," he remarked, ignoring her question. "After all, many a romance has begun during a house party. In fact, I'm certain it is often the aim of these affairs to match eligible bachelors with unwed chits."

"Mr. Clayton—"

He took another step, the press of his body against Lydia's silencing her. Her voice broke off on a gasp, and she shuddered, though she did nothing to put any distance between them. Sinclair's entire being seemed to vibrate as if he were an instrument, a plucked string rippling through his body on a long, low note. His cock stirred, his desire rising to mingle with his anger in a tangle so heady, he could not tell one from the other.

"Has he confessed his love for you yet?" he spat, aware he acted the fool, but somehow unable to stop. "It's a bit early, but Charles always was the sentimental sort. How long do you suppose he will wait before proposing?"

She made a derisive sound in the back of her throat, turning her head to avoid his gaze. "Do not be ridiculous. I have no idea what's gotten into you, but what occurs between Charles and me is none of your affair."

Her words struck true, piercing him right through the chest with all the savage effect of a dagger. She was right, damn her, but he would never admit it … could not allow himself to remember just how little claim he had to her.

Reaching up to cup her face, he forced her to look at him, his grip light on her chin. His other arm came around her waist, molding her up against his body, keeping her there.

"Isn't it?" he murmured, lowering his head so that his lips brushed her forehead. "Tell me you want him, Lydia. Tell me you want Charles, and I will let the matter drop. Say it."

He kissed his way down the bridge of her nose, then nuzzled it with his own, his lips whispering over hers. She whimpered, sagging in his arms, her eyelids fluttering as she seemed to fight against the sensations.

"I … I …"

"Did you want him to kiss you?" he asked, voice hoarse from the strain of needing to ask but not wanting to know the answer. "Did you want more than a kiss?"

"I wanted …"

He slid his hand back into her hair, fingers closing around her chignon so he could tip her head back, opening her to him, exposing her throat, parting her lips. Another sound emitted from her, this one breathy and helpless, sending even more heat surging straight between his legs.

"I wanted to be kissed," she murmured, her voice low and throaty, her eyes glassy as if she were half-drunk with need. "I thought if I kissed him, perhaps it might feel good. I thought, if I liked it, that would be enough."

His stomach twisted itself up even more, his hold on her tightening both in her hair and on her waist, until she whimpered and squirmed. Even still, he did not let go, refused to let go unless she told him to. She was melting into him, her limbs slack, her body pliant and becoming one with his. They could only be closer if he were inside of her, and the thought dragged a groan from him, desperate and tortured.

"What, Lydia?" he urged. "Enough for what?"

"Enough to make me stop wanting you," she whispered.

The moment the last word had fallen from her lips, he was on her, his mouth seeking hers hungrily. Her moan was muffled by his kiss, an answering sound burning his throat as he kissed her with a wild abandon he'd never thought himself capable of. He nipped at her, biting her lower lip, stroking it with his tongue, then delving inside, consuming her, sating the persistent craving for her taste. She answered in kind, bringing her hands up to clutch the lapels of his coat as she raised up on tiptoe to fit her body against his.

He gave in to the urge to touch her, letting his hands wander down her back, cupping the soft, round buttocks left accessible by the downright indecent breeches clinging to her frame. He could feel every bit of her through them, her luscious arse, the womanly mound between her legs, her supple thighs. It only infuriated him more, knowing that Charles might have been doing this right now if he hadn't come along —helping himself to the bounty of Lydia's body, tasting her, plundering what Sinclair coveted every waking hour of every day.

"Tell me you want me," he commanded, hands tight on her hips as he lifted her clear off the ground.

With a sigh, she wrapped her legs around his waist, clinging to him as he sank to the ground with her, going to his knees with her on his lap.

"I want you," she whispered, letting her head fall back as he kissed her chin, her throat, every inch of skin he could access.

"Only me," he demanded.

"Only you," she relented, squirming in his lap, giving him delicious friction and pressure where he needed it most. "Always you."

He practically purred in response, the possessive, jealous beast inside him satisfied with that, pacified by knowing he alone owned her desires. Cupping her arse with both hands, he ground her against him, urging her on as her hips rocked at the rhythm he created, leaving her shuddering and biting her lip to contain little groans of pleasure.

"Say my name, angel," he demanded, desperate to hear it falling from her lips, tinged with passion. "Even if it's only this once … I have longed to hear it since the night we met."

She arched her back, clinging to his neck and riding him, rutting against him in a mindless fit of need. He could feel the heat of her through the layers of his breeches and hers, registered the tension in her body, like a spring pulled taut.

"*Sinclair*," she whispered, his name coming out of her mouth on a breathless sigh.

He closed his eyes and absorbed the sound, letting its impact resound through him, sinking into his skin and rippling out to the tips of his fingers and toes. It would haunt every night after this, echoing through his memories and keeping him warm as he slept alone, reviving his dashed hopes.

"Lydia," he answered, one hand finding its way between them, smoothing down over the buttons of her waistcoat … then lower, lower to the fastening of her breeches.

She made a little sound of shock as he loosened one button, then another, and another, opening the garment to access her body. Yet, she did not stop him, allowing him to slip his hand into the opening and find her bare skin. This time, her gasp came out strangled, as if she'd tried to keep it trapped between her lips and had failed. He moaned at the feel of her, his knuckles brushing ever so lightly over the plane of her lower belly, tracking a slow path even lower … until he encountered the downy curls shielding her mons.

"Sinclair?" she whispered, the word now holding a question, a plea.

"Shh," he urged, nibbling the shell of her ear, then kissing her neck. "I need to touch you … just this once … let me …"

She nodded, burying her face against his neck as he reached deeper into her breeches, seeking her cunt. He would never have thought touching her could feel more pleasing, more intensely erotic. Yet, this action of opening men's clothing and finding her feminine body underneath … it was more wildly thrilling than anything he'd ever experienced.

Her breath raced against his neck as he found the seam of her mons, tracing it with his middle finger, exploring the secret flesh hidden within. She was already soaking wet, coating the tip of his finger in her juices, the evidence of her need making his mouth water.

"God, you're so wet," he whispered, circling around her opening, a passage so tight, it had to be unexplored. "Has anyone ever touched you this way?"

"N-no," she groaned, her hips moving against his hand instinctively, as if her body knew what to do even if she'd never been so intimate with anyone. "I've only ever touched myself there."

He made a rough sound against her shoulder, squeezing his eyes shut and fighting for composure. The thought of her touching herself had nearly undone him.

"I want to taste you," he said, sliding his finger upward, seeking out the center of her pleasure. "I want this wetness all over my lips, your legs spread for me so I can devour you."

He found her clit and pressed against it. Despite his light touch, she bucked against him, nearly rearing up out of his lap in reaction.

"I'd put my tongue right here," he told her, slowly circling his finger over the little nub. "I'd lick and suck you until you screamed and begged me to stop. But I wouldn't stop, Lydia. Once I got a taste of you, I don't think I could ever stop."

She fisted the front of his coat, holding fast as he stroked her rhythmically, slowly at first, then faster, until the sounds she made told him all he needed to know. She was close, on the precipice of climax.

"Oh, but I'd have to stop," he murmured between kisses along the column of her neck. "Because after I'd tasted my fill of you, I'd want more … I'd want this tight little quim wrapped around me. I'd want to be so deep inside you that would never find my way out."

She trembled, the little shocks that jolted her emanating from her body to his fingers, responding to him as if she'd been made to be touched by him and only him.

"I'd take my time with you," he rasped, his own need making it difficult to breathe, let alone speak. "I would sink into you, stroking inside you with my cock while you lay under me, hands clenching the sheets."

"Sinclair," she moaned, stiffening in his arms, the tension in her body reaching its breaking point, her culmination so near.

"You'd whisper my name just like that," he went on, still steadily stroking her, increasing pressure, pushing her toward her end. "With every stroke of my cock inside you, you'd say my name, each utterance speaking of your pleasure in a way no other words could."

He pressed his thumb to her clit and sought out her passage with his first finger, her wetness allowing him to ease inside. She cried out, burying her face against the fabric of his coat as she came apart in his hands, shaking and quivering as her inner channel began pulsing and shuddering around his finger.

He used one arm to hold her tight, still steadily teasing her, riding out her orgasm to the finish, refusing to let up until she'd gone silent and still.

Lydia slumped against him, her breath sawing in and out while he held her, softly kissing the top of her head and whispering to her— senseless words that could never mean anything outside this moment.

Words that he could never follow through on, promises he could never keep.

After a while, he urged her to sit up so they could begin untangling from one another. Drawing his hand from inside her breeches, he found his fingers still slick with her essence. Unable to resist the impulse, he raised those fingers to his lips and sucked them into his mouth, cleaning them of her and indulging in her taste at the same time. His cock leapt, seeking shelter inside her, impeded by the layers of their clothing. He closed his eyes and stifled a groan, now forced to beat back the urge to lay her down on the ground and finish what he had begun.

"We have tarried too long," he said, urging her to her feet and following, his legs tingling with a rushing of blood. "If we do not return soon, someone might come looking for us."

Lydia stared at him, lips stained red from the pressure of his, eyelids heavy over unfocused eyes. She seemed to be in a daze, the afterglow of her climax still consuming her mind, heart, and soul. He smoothed his hands over her hair, quickly tucking stray strands behind her ears, then adjusting the collar of her shirt. After ensuring the tails had been properly tucked in and she looked as decent as he could manage, he cupped her face in his palms. Dipping his head to kiss her, he took his time, despite the urgency of the moment. He claimed her lips gently, slowly, making it last just a bit longer, loath to return to the house and the life in it that made no room for her. He wondered if she could taste the essence of herself that he'd just lapped off his fingers. Imagining that she could only made his erection all the more painful.

"Lydia, we have to go now," he urged, even as he smoothed his thumb over her lips and contemplated kissing her again.

"We ... I ... we should not have done that," she murmured, lowering her eyes.

He nodded. "I know. But I cannot find it in me to feel sorry for it ... or anything I've ever done when it comes to you."

Her eyes snapped up, and their gazes met. In her stare, he found a turbulent mixture of wonder, desire, regret, and turmoil. He felt every one of those things deep in the pit of his gut.

"I do not know what happens now," she said.

He sighed, pressing his forehead against hers and closing his eyes. "Neither do I. I just know … the way I feel …"

She took his hand and pressed it to her breast, her heart beating a rapid cadence against his palm. "I know. I feel it, too."

"I do not want you to think I only want you physically," he declared, opening his eyes to meet her gaze once more. "I would never want you to believe that I think to make you my mistress or my lover, or anything so common. You mean so much more to me than that."

She nodded. "Sometimes, I think becoming your mistress or your lover might be the most shameful thing I could ever allow myself to be. Then, other times, I wonder if being anything to you at all is better than being nothing."

"You could never be nothing to me," he replied, lifting her chin and giving her another swift, short kiss. "Even if you never allow me to touch you again, you'd always own a part of me. The part of me no one else has ever touched … not even Drucilla."

At the mention of his wife's name, she took a step away, her gaze growing shuttered once again. The phantom presence of his wife between them, even this far from the house, could never be outrun, it seemed.

Silently, he offered her his hand, wanting the closeness with her, the contact of her skin on his until they came into view of the manor. She accepted it, and together, they began the long walk back.

CHAPTER 12

The rest of the house party seemed to drag past Sinclair with excruciating slowness, his constant awareness of Lydia making it increasingly difficult to act naturally. Drucilla kept their guests occupied nearly every hour of every day, and most times, the men remained in the company of the women—to encourage romance between the unwed, obviously.

For three days, Lydia remained almost constantly within his line of sight. He heard her laughter as she sat across the room playing cards with a group of other guests. He saw her seated just down the table each night at dinner, her gowns not as opulent as those of the other ladies; yet, she outshone them all in his eyes. Drucilla with her pale, untouchable beauty could never compare.

He could smell Lydia every time she walked past him, her fragrance seeming to invade his senses and remain there long after she had gone. His attempts at keeping his eyes off her often failed, though he could not bring himself to care if anyone noticed. That might happen to be because his wife and Lord Wortham drew quite a bit of attention to themselves. He wouldn't be surprised if everyone left this party gossiping about the mistress of Buckton, who had no care for propriety and flirted shamelessly with the viscount while her husband stood but a stone's throw away.

In the past, he might have grown angry over it. He would have cared about Drucilla embarrassing him, would have been hurt at her disregard for his feelings. Now, he couldn't care less if she opened her legs for Wortham. Hell, she could invite every man at this party into her chambers, and he still would not care. Not when Lydia overtook his every waking thought—as well as most of his sleeping ones.

The night after their encounter in the woods, he had awakened in a cold sweat after dreams of her had worked him to fever pitch. He had stumbled to the washstand, panting for breath as he'd palmed his cock and stroked himself to the memory of touching her, tasting her, watching her fall apart in his arms. His release had nearly doubled him over, the force of it wringing him dry. Even then, his urgency had remained as strong as ever, until he'd had to literally talk himself out of running downstairs to her bedroom and tearing her door off its hinges so that he could finish what they'd begun that afternoon.

He could hardly find it in himself to care that he approached his room each night to the sounds of Drucilla's giggling and another man's low, rumbling voice from beneath the crack in her door. Not when he could hardly sleep for wanting and needing Lydia in a way he'd never wanted or needed anyone else.

Now, on this final night of the party, he found himself pondering her words on the day of the hunt.

I do not know what happens now.

Neither did he, though it was clear they could not go on like this. This pull between them would only continue to grow stronger. He could not deny himself when she was near, and her defenses were clearly slipping, as well.

But, what could they do? As long as he was wed to Drucilla, Lydia could never be anything other than his mistress. And what sort of life was that for a genteel lady who had been raised and groomed for far better? He thought of her hidden away in some cottage he would visit whenever he could escape his duties, the children she would bear in shame.

Bastards.

His throat constricted at the thought of any child of his being condemned the way he had been, shunned in certain circles, carrying a mark of disgrace upon them for the rest of their lives. He thought of Henry, who would grow to see his father as a scoundrel who'd created a family separate from his own, siring children he would never think of as his true siblings.

He could never do any of it. Hurt his son that way, or reduce Lydia to the status of mere mistress. He could never acquit himself the way his father had, creating impossible situations for everyone involved.

Turning away from the looking glass with a sigh, Sinclair realized the only thing he could do was send her away. Yet, that prospect hurt him most of all. It made his stomach twist and his heart throb as if a fist gripped it tight. It was the right thing to do, yet putting Lydia out of his reach felt wrong. It felt like the end of him.

A soft knock upon the door drew him out of his reverie.

"Enter," he called out, wondering who it could be. His valet had left him, and Drucilla dressed in the neighboring room and had no reason to come to his.

He was surprised when Charles appeared, wearing black evening attire, his face set in a grim expression. The two had not spoken much since the incident in the woods. An unusual occurrence, as Sinclair was used to speaking with his friend daily. In any other situation, Charles would have been the one he unburdened himself to over Lydia. However, the knowledge that his friend also had a *tendre* for her made that impossible.

"I had hoped to find you alone," the steward said as he closed the door behind him. "We have not had a chance to talk since the hunt."

Coming toward the center of the room, Sinclair folded his arms over his chest. "Very well. Is there something on your mind?"

He knew exactly what Charles wanted, but would not broach the subject of Lydia first.

Leaning against the door, his friend observed him pensively for a moment before speaking. "If you wanted her for yourself, the least you could have done was tell me."

Well. That had not taken long. Though, Sinclair realized he should not be surprised. Charles had never been one to hedge around the subject at hand.

"What was I supposed to say, Charles?"

"You might try honesty. A simple 'I'm in love with the governess' would have done."

"What would it have changed?" he argued.

"I might not have made any sort of advances upon her, for a start."

Running a hand through his hair, Sinclair let out a little huff of frustration. "And why not, exactly? You are unattached, and so is Lydia. I …"

"You what?" Charles asked. "Love her? Want her?"

"Yes!" he exclaimed, his voice raising to fill the room. "Yes, I want her! Yes, I love her! But what good is any of that while I'm married to Drucilla?"

Charles gave him a pitying glance, coming farther into the room. "I have been your friend for a long time, Sin. I've watched you love Drucilla and try to give her the world. I have also watched her shun you, spurn you, and make a fool of you in return. I watched you grieve after she gave birth to another man's child, then pull yourself together and take that boy as your own. I do not know a more honorable man than you."

"Then why do I feel like such a cad?" Sinclair asked with a shake of his head. "Why do I feel as if I am ruining Lydia by loving her? She should be with someone who can give her the things I cannot. She should be with a man like you."

Sighing, Charles pinched the bridge of his nose. "In another situation, I might agree with you. I admire Lydia, but it became clear to me after truly observing the two of you these past days that she loves you as you love her. And maybe … maybe it is all right for the two of you to take what happiness you can find."

Sinclair's mouth fell open as he eyed his friend in disbelief. "Are you suggesting that we indulge in an affair?"

"I am not suggesting anything," Charles hedged, raising his eyebrows. "I am simply saying that you've suffered long enough, and perhaps, so has she. I am saying that a situation like this one is never completely right or wrong, black or white. If it were, you would never have been conceived."

Sinclair thought about that for a moment. He thought of his parents, of his father who had declared his love for his mother openly and often. It was why he'd given Sinclair everything he'd been able to; it was why he'd been claimed and raised alongside his siblings. He had once hated his father for siring him on the wrong side of the blanket, for subjecting him to life as a bastard. But his mother had always told Sinclair that he'd been the joy of her life and thought that perhaps, in a way, he'd been a gift to her. Perhaps, for her short time on Earth, his mother had found a bit of happiness with his father, and with him, as well.

"She deserves better," he argued feebly.

Charles smiled, bracing a hand on Sinclair's shoulder. "I do not know a better man than you."

He smiled back, but it was weak, strained. His mind still whirled dizzily, every possibility, every choice swimming back and forth before him, each one with its advantages and pitfalls.

"For the sake of our friendship, I will not pursue her any longer," Charles added.

Sinclair shook his head. "I cannot ask that of you."

"It is for my own sake as well as yours," his friend quipped. "If I'd actually managed to kiss her, I believe you might have killed me."

That got a laugh out of him, and as they approached the door to leave for the final dinner of the party, Sinclair felt a little less burdened. It was not right nor fair for him to be glad Charles would not pursue Lydia. Yet, he was glad all the same.

As they entered the corridor, they found Drucilla coming through the door of her chamber dressed, as always, in pure white. This particular evening gown had been etched with silver thread along the bodice and hem, a silver bandeau enhancing her white-blonde curls. Ropes of pearls decorated her neck, while more of the white stones adorned her ears. A white and silver embroidered shawl with a delicate fringe hung from one shoulder, draping over the crook of her opposite arm.

"My lady," Charles said, pausing to bow to her. "You look lovely this evening."

Drucilla gave him a tight smile. "Thank you, Mr. Welby."

At the rough, tortured sound of her voice, Sinclair frowned, taking a closer look at her. She was paler than usual, her eyes a bit red-rimmed. Producing one of her lace-trimmed handkerchiefs, she coughed into it for a few seconds, shoulders trembling.

"Dru, are you all right?" he asked. "You look a bit pale."

As always, she shunned his concern, even after she'd spent the past several nights with another man in her bed while her husband slept in the next room. Even after she'd forced him to occupy the same space as the man who had cuckolded him.

"It is just another cold," she insisted. "The cough isn't nearly as strong as it was during that bout of croup."

He looked her over, certain she was falling ill yet again. He'd come to know the early signs, such as her glassy eyes and overly-rosy cheeks. Yet, he only offered her his arm—the obligation of escorting her downstairs not going away just because he loathed her.

"As you say," he relented, deciding he would send for Doctor Tunstall first thing in the morning. He had a feeling she had overtaxed herself planning and executing this house party when she ought to have been resting.

They descended the stairs, and soon found themselves among the guests milling about in the drawing room. From there, everything went as usual. Sinclair affixed a mask of polite boredom and tried his best not to look at Lydia, who was modest but lovely in the same green gown she'd worn to dinner on the first night. Her only embellishment were the flowers she'd fashioned into a little cluster and pinned to her bodice. They adorned her better than any rope of pearls or string of string diamonds could have.

The night began without a hitch. After drinks in the drawing room, there was dinner, which the cook had turned out with resplendent flair, having saved his best dishes for last. After the sumptuous meal, they returned to the large drawing room, where someone declared there should be music and dancing, which prompted one of the young ladies to take a seat at the pianoforte and begin to play. Furniture was moved, a few rugs rolled back, and then the dancing began. Those who did not wish to dance sat to watch.

Drucilla ordered champagne brought in, and while the footmen served their guests, he found himself obligated to lead her in the first dance. Always the dutiful husband, always attending to appearances and helping to squelch gossip, he took her in his arms in the midst of the others who had joined them in the center of the room. Her movements were sluggish and slow, lacking the crisp grace of a dancer as accomplished as her. He compensated for her to keep from embarrassing them both, then deposited her into a chair near the piano.

"Rest, Dru," he muttered in her ear before leaving her.

She surprised him by remaining seated for most of the songs, though she *did* muster the strength to dance with Wortham before taking her chair once again. The sounds of her coughing rang out through the drawing room periodically, making it impossible for Sinclair to ignore her for long. Yet, every time he glanced her way, she talked with her guests, smiling, hands moving, face animated. If her eyes looked far too glassy or her cheeks far too flushed ... well, she had made it clear that was none of his concern.

The party had reached a crescendo of merriment when everything turned sour in an instant.

Sinclair happened to approach the sideboard to help himself to a tumbler of whisky when he overheard a group of men talking about the one subject guaranteed to snare his full attention.

Lydia.

"A lovely thing," one of the men was saying. "Far too pretty to work as a governess."

"Not that you could ever do anything about it, William," another said. "Being leg-shackled already, and all."

Sinclair joined them, silently sipping his whisky and following their gazes to where Lydia stood in the midst of the other dancers, letting Charles lead her through a country reel. He could not help but notice that she danced just as he'd known she would—boisterously, with a smile on her face. She drew every eye in the room to her, joy emanating from her like a beacon. She made every man in the room want to dance with her, Sinclair included.

"Must be distracting with such a lovely bit of skirt about all the time, eh, Clayton?"

Sinclair blinked, tearing his gaze away from Lydia and Charles and glaring at the man who'd asked the inane question. Some acquaintance of Drucilla's … he could not even remember the idiot's name.

"I beg your pardon?"

Mr. Grenville slapped him on the shoulder with a chuckle. "Come, now, Clayton. There is no need to play coy around us. Many a man has succumbed to such temptation … especially when it is so readily available."

"You are mistaken," he snapped, the rigidity of his tone leaving no room for argument. "Miss Darling is Henry's governess and does a splendid job of it. That is all. I certainly do not make a habit of bedding my household staff, and if you had any sense at all, you would not, either."

His hands shook as he raised his tumbler to his lips, the whisky doing nothing to soothe his frazzled nerves. Did they know? Had someone seen them together in the woods? Or had they merely been able to see what Charles had observed?

No, he told himself. It was all conjecture on their parts; it had to be.

"Don't be foolish," argued the first man, the one whose name Sinclair still could not recall. "With Lady Clayton for a wife, a man would be hard-pressed to find his head turned, even by so pretty a lady as Miss Darling."

Chuckles and murmurs of agreement rippled through the group, and Sinclair relaxed a bit.

Until Lord Wortham's voice cut through the laughter, setting his teeth on edge once again.

"Well then, Sin … if you aren't going to help yourself to the girl, then I just might."

Sinclair's teeth ground together, his empty hand curling into a fist at his side. "What was that?"

Wortham, fool that he was, merely smiled. "Well, as you stated, you have no claim on her, and her other admirers seem to be leg-shackled. Which leaves only me. Mother has been after me for some time to settle down. A lady such as Miss Darling would do nicely, indeed."

Sinclair's hand tightened around his tumbler, shaking as fury swept through him, hot and fast. Just the thought of Wortham anywhere near Lydia made him want to smash the glass against the man's face.

"Miss Darling is far too good a woman to be corrupted by your sort," he ground out.

The other men took this as a jest and began to roar with laughter, drawing the attention of several in the room. Wortham, however, clenched his jaw and met Sinclair's challenge head-on.

"Is that so?" he replied. "Perhaps I will put that to the test. You might find yourself on the hunt for a new governess should I have my way, Clayton."

More laughter, but Sinclair found nothing amusing about any of it. Despite knowing Lydia wanted only him—she'd said as much herself —he thought of Wortham pursuing her in earnest, and his blood ran cold. He'd charmed Drucilla right out from under Sinclair, was known for his ability to have any woman in his company simpering and blushing within seconds of meeting him. Could Lydia be swayed by him, as well?

His grip on the tumbler clenched even tighter. "Have you not had your way enough with my wife? Now, you must try pilfering my governess, as well?"

He'd spoken the words low, yet silence fell over those gathered around them. Apparently, Wortham wasn't the only one who'd heard. Sinclair took a step toward him, not caring who saw or who heard. He'd reached the end of his forbearance for this man who had once been his friend, but had revealed himself to be a wolf in sheep's clothing.

Wortham's eyes darted about, his mouth pinching at the corners. "Have you gone mad?"

"No, but you must have," Sinclair retorted. "If you think I will stand here and listen to you speak that way about a woman under my care, then you are in for a rude awakening."

Wortham frowned, leaning close and lowering his voice so no one else could hear. "What is this about, truly, Sin? Are you bedding the little governess, and now grow afraid that a real man will come along and take *her* from you, too?"

Sinclair's hold on the tumbler clenched until the glass cracked, and before he could stop himself, he'd taken a swing, crashing it against the side of Wortham's head. Screams and cries of alarm rang out through the drawing room, the music coming to an abrupt stop as Wortham went down on one knee, hand over his bleeding temple. Whisky mingled with blood trickled down the man's face, slivers of glass sprinkled over the carpet. Sinclair barely registered the sting of his palm from cracked glass.

"Ah, goddamn it!" Wortham bellowed, glaring up at him. "What the devil is wrong with you?"

What remained of Sinclair's control melted away, the years' worth of rage and pain he'd kept compressed in his middle unfurling all at once. It was spilling out of him in a rush he could not control.

This, he realized as he stooped to grasp Wortham's lapels and haul him to his feet, had been inevitable.

"You," he rasped, his upper lip curling with derision as he looked

Wortham in the eye. "*You* are what is wrong with me, and you have been for quite some time."

Keeping hold of his lapel with one hand, Sinclair drew back his opposite fist and let it fly. It met Wortham's nose with a satisfying crunch, a spray of blood warming his hand and splattering his cravat. The man crumpled, and Sinclair went down on top of him, unable to stop now that he'd drawn blood. He had fantasized about this for so long … killing with his bare hands the man who had cuckolded him.

He blotted out the sounds of the cries of his guests, the shouts of the other men urging him to stop. As he went down on top of Wortham, he put his weight behind another swing, this one crashing into one perfectly sculpted cheekbone. He knelt over the man, battering him with his fists, his chest burning from all the fury sawing in and out of his lungs in enraged pants, the fire in his gut roaring hotter and hotter with each blow.

"Sinclair! Sinclair, stop that this instant!"

He faintly registered Drucilla's voice, her exclamations coming at him between hoarse coughing fits. A hand closed around his arm, but he shrugged it off, going back to the man whose comeuppance had been five long years in the making.

"Sinclair!" Drucilla wailed, pausing to cough and hack before screeching at him again. "Stop! You will kill him!"

Good. Sinclair wanted to kill him. He wanted to destroy the man who'd had a hand in tearing his world, his life, to shreds. And when he was done, he wanted to kill the second person responsible. He wanted to wrap his hands around her lily white throat and squeeze until she ceased to draw breath.

Fury drove him, all rational thought melting away in the wake of the emotions he'd held at bay for so long. He was unsure how long he went on pummeling Wortham, but he was eventually jerked away, a strong grip hauling him swiftly across the room. He twisted and writhed in the hold, roaring and spewing epithets, demanding to be let go so that he could continue taking his frustrations out on

Wortham. The world around him seemed to have faded away, and he stood in a place where only he and the objects of his torment existed.

Until Lydia appeared before him, her face twisted in a mask of horror and concern, one hand reaching out toward him. Calm suffused him the instant her hand cupped his face, going slack in the arms of the man he soon realized was Charles. His friend held him down, arms like tight bands around his chest while Lydia knelt in front of him, eyes filled with tears.

"That's it," she whispered, so low Sinclair felt certain only he and Charles could hear. "Come back to me. It is over now. You have to come back."

Shoulders heaving from the force of his ragged breath, Sinclair blinked glassy eyes and glanced around the room. He'd been oblivious to the destruction he'd caused in his fit of rage, but the sight of it shamed him now—an overturned table and shattered vase, the twinkling shards of the tumbler he'd broken over Wortham's head, the man himself lying in a heap a few feet away. Drucilla knelt at his side, sobbing and coughing at the same time, her voice tortured as she wailed for her beaten lover. The man groaned and turned his face into her skirts, staining the white crimson. All the while, their horrified guests looked on in stunned silence, too shocked by what they'd just witnessed to even whisper about it among themselves.

"Oh, Miles ... my poor, poor love," Drucilla sobbed. "What has he done to you?"

Sinclair sneered, disgusted by the pair of them, his ire reemerging so swiftly, he could barely contain it. But then, Lydia's hand stroked his face, and she edged closer, her body acting as a barrier between him and his wife fretting over a man who'd just been on the business end of his fist.

"It does not matter," she murmured, her hand soft on his cheek, her voice like a soothing balm flooding his insides. "They cannot hurt you anymore. You won't let them. It is over."

Forcing a swallow through his constricted throat, he shrugged to be free of Charles' hold. "Let go."

"Only if you promise me that you are done," Charles declared, his grasp never letting up for a second. "Promise me, Sin."

"I said, let go," he snapped. "I will not kill the bastard … this time."

Charles reluctantly released him, and Lydia stood to offer him a hand up. Even once he'd gotten to his feet, she held fast, her fingers tight around his, her eyes searching his face. He hated that she'd witnessed his loss of control, but could not pretend to regret what he had done. He had allowed Miles and Drucilla to make a fool of him for too long. There had been something freeing about finally giving the other man a taste of the pain that had been inflicted upon him, however temporarily.

He turned to find a handful of footmen hovering nearby, brows wrinkled and eyes darting as they seemed to wonder what they should do in such a situation.

"Have Lord Wortham's carriage brought 'round and toss him inside," he ordered. "I want him off my property within the next ten minutes."

"Right away, Mr. Clayton," one of them replied before rushing off.

The other two promptly knelt to lift Wortham's limp body and carry him away. Drucilla rose to her feet and followed, murmuring mindless words of comfort to her lover, promising to come and nurse him herself. Sinclair was half-tempted to order her thrown into the carriage with Wortham.

His wife whirled on him once Wortham had been carted from the room, face reddened, eyes wide and wild. "You-you idiot! You son of a bitch! You … you …"

"Bastard?" he offered with a dry scoff.

"*Bastard!*" she spat with every ounce of venom he knew her to possess. "You've ruined absolutely everything! I wish I had never laid eyes upon you! You are a lowly, baseborn commoner, and I wish your father had left you in the gutter where you belong!"

He stared at her in silence for a long moment, acutely aware of the low murmurs and gasps traveling through the party. The gazes falling upon him now were sympathetic ones, pitying and assessing.

Before he could respond, she lapsed into another coughing fit, doubling over as the powerful spasms wracking her body seemed to rob her of strength. Despite what she'd put him through tonight, and through the entire length of this house party, he would not stand there and watch her suffer.

"Come, Dru," he snapped, reaching out to take her arm. "You must retire to bed while I send for Doctor Tunstall."

She reared away from him, upper lip curling back in disgust. "Do not touch me! I cannot abide the feel of your filthy hands on me."

Sighing, he shook his head. "Dru, cease this. We've made enough of a spectacle of ourselves for the night, don't you think? You need to get into bed."

"I told you, it is only a cold," she protested, right before being seized by another coughing fit. "Stop pretending … as if you give a bloody damn … about me."

This time, the coughing did not stop, seeming to go on and on while Sinclair crouched to try helping her to her feet again. She sagged, forcing him to put an arm around her to keep her from falling. Her face fell against his chest as she began coughing again, her slight body so violently seized by the hacking that he was surprised she did not shatter into a thousand pieces.

More gasps rippled through the room as her head tipped back to reveal the bright stains she'd left against his white shirtfront, more of the same marring her lips and chin.

Blood.

CHAPTER 13

$\mathcal{L}$ydia stood near the window of her bedroom, staring listlessly out at the moonlit night. She shivered, despite the warm fire she'd just stoked in the hearth and the shawl draped across her shoulders over her nightgown.

Hours had passed since the shocking incident in the drawing room, and she was still reeling. Her gaze grew unfocused, her mind returning to the moment Hell had broken loose among the guests, gasps and cries of alarm warning her of the brawl taking place on the other side of the room. Things had been going so well, despite the tension thrumming between herself and Sinclair. It had been difficult, trying to act naturally after what had occurred between them in the woods. Especially when she felt as if the truth of those stolen moments had been written across her face for the world to see.

Yet, the final evening of the party had been jovial, with a wonderful dinner, and dancing afterward. It had been years since anyone had asked her to dance, and despite the turmoil still simmering in her belly regarding Sinclair, she'd been enjoying herself. She had been partnered for each song of the impromptu ball, smiling and chatting with Charles, who was all polite friendliness after their near-kiss a few days before.

She was not certain what had been done or said to set Sinclair off that way, but one moment she'd been dancing and having a lovely time; the next, she'd stood by watching in numb shock as he pummeled Lord Wortham half to death. Thankfully, Charles had known what to do.

"Help me calm him," he'd said, taking her arm and propelling her toward the mêlée. "He will listen to you."

She hadn't been certain about that, very much aware of the reasons for Sinclair's anger. Yet, he had shocked her by calming almost instantly once she'd gotten close enough to touch and speak with him.

It had all happened so fast—the fight and the resulting fallout, then Lady Clayton's collapse. From there, she'd been all but forgotten as Sinclair had swept his wife off her feet and bellowed for Charles to send for the doctor. There had been a flurry of movement, guests dashing about, offering a cold compress for the lady's head, exclaiming over the copious amount of blood she had just coughed up all over Sinclair's shirt. Lydia had found herself the center of attention then, the remaining guests watching her with a scrutiny that made her anxious to hide, to escape their probing eyes and their eventual sly questions and innuendo. So, she'd murmured "excuse me," then had fled, swiftly making for her own chambers.

And here she had remained in the hours that followed, the sounds of footsteps and voices from overhead as anxious and frenzied as the beating of her heart.

What would happen now? She felt certain that the little display downstairs had let the party guests in on quite a few of the Clayton family secrets. Anyone who had wondered but been uncertain about the affair between Lady Clayton and Lord Wortham would now have their suspicions confirmed, which could only lead to more scrutiny toward Henry. And she had felt the eyes upon her as she'd knelt to help calm Sinclair, feeling the way their assessing stares had watched her as she'd touched him with such tenderness and familiarity. There would be gossip about her, too, about the tart of a governess who had seduced her pupil's father. If Lady Clayton decided to toss her out on her ear—a distinct possibility—she might never find work again.

Sighing, she drew her shawl tighter around herself and leaned forward, resting her forehead against the windowpane. So much had happened in such a short time, she hardly knew how to fathom it all. She only knew that her heart ached from wanting to do something for Sinclair, to soothe the turmoil and pain that seemed ever present in his eyes, turning those warm dark orbs into pools of despair. He'd truly lived a life of loneliness, even in the midst of all the wealth he had accumulated, even with a wife and son … he had always been completely, utterly alone. It made her want to be everything that no one else had ever been to him, even if that meant compromising her morals, tossing aside propriety and rational thought. It frightened her to no end.

A soft knock warned her seconds before the door creaked open. She turned to find Sinclair standing on the threshold, the meager light from a lamp he held illuminating him with a yellow glow.

He had cleaned up and changed out of his evening attire, his hair brushed back from his face, appearing slightly damp from being washed, a brocade dressing gown belted at his waist over trousers and a clean shirt. As he entered the chamber and closed the door behind him, her gaze fell to the hand holding the lamp, and she gasped at the sight of his tortured knuckles. She rushed to him without thinking, taking the lamp and holding it up, inspecting his knuckles. They were tender and swollen, a red ring glowing angrily around the purple stains.

Gazing up, she found him watching her closely. Maintaining his stare, she lifted the hand to her lips and brushed them over the bruises. She heard his sharp intake of breath and kissed him again, pressing her mouth to him more firmly, kissing each knuckle before turning his hand over and holding his cheek to her palm.

He released a long, low sigh as he pressed his lips to her forehead. "Lydia."

She closed her eyes, stroking her cheek against the inside of his hand, holding fast to his wrist, keeping him close. "Sinclair."

"I came as soon as I could," he said, cupping her cheek, his thumb stroking her skin with absent movements. "I wanted to come to you right away, but—"

"I understand," she interjected. "How is Lady Clayton?"

He scowled. "Doctor Tunstall is with her now. He has offered to watch over her through the night. This does not feel like the other times she fell ill. It is far worse."

Despite the things the woman had done, Lydia hadn't been able to help the sting of pity she'd experienced watching Lady Clayton collapse. She could not imagine becoming so ill so swiftly, nor the sort of pain that must accompany the coughing up of blood.

"I would rather not speak of it just now," he declared when she didn't answer. "I had hoped we could talk about what happened this evening."

Taking his hand once more, she drew him farther into the room, toward the little table where she sat to compose her letters. She motioned for him to take one of the chairs, but he simply stood, waiting for her to be seated. Then, he knelt right in front of her, his hands falling over hers where they rested in her lap.

"You do not need to explain anything to me," she said, gazing down into his eyes. "It became clear to me when I first saw Lord Wortham in the same room with you and Lady Clayton that there must be some history there. The two of them wounded you deeply, didn't they?"

Sinclair nodded, his brow furrowed, lips pinched. "I first met Miles a few weeks after becoming the master of Buckton. He had just taken ownership of an estate not far from this one and had wished to make the acquaintance of Hertfordshire's infamous cherry farmer. By then, word of how I'd worked my way toward claiming Buckton had spread through the county. We became fast friends ... or so I thought. It did not take me long to notice the way Drucilla looked at him, the way she seemed to purposely put herself in our path whenever he happened to visit the manor."

Lydia shook her head in disbelief, still unable to understand how any woman could set her eyes upon another with someone like Sinclair to call her own. He was her heart's one true desire, and having him would be the manifestation of her sweetest dreams. She could not imagine allowing her head to be turned should she be fortunate to call him truly hers.

"I thought nothing of it in the beginning," he went on. "Drucilla had always been flirtatious. It was part of what made her charming, part of what drew people to her. But I was so sure of our love for each other, of her devotion to me. She'd waited for me to earn my way into her father's good graces, to win her hand. She loved me, and I did not think her glances and smiles would grow to become anything more than harmless flirtation.

"The changes happened so slowly, her demeanor toward me shifting as she became more and more familiar with Miles. She began spurning my affection, turning me away from her bed, often using her fragile health as a shield to bar me from getting too close. Yet, I began to notice her sending off notes in the hands of servants, her frequent carriage rides to visit 'friends' throughout the county … visits that would last entire days, and once even an entire week for a house party. By then, I'd spread my efforts over Buckton and my other estates, as well as a handful of burgeoning investments. I worked often, *too* often, perhaps, to watch her vigilantly. Looking back now, I see things so clearly … but back then, the moment I realized she had been unfaithful to me with him … I felt as if the rug had been pulled out from beneath my feet. As if my entire world had been destroyed. Perhaps because at that time, she *was* my entire world. I had built my existence around Drucilla, only for her to betray me with a man I counted as a friend."

Leaning forward, she reached out to run her fingers through his hair, a tight fist of pity wrapped around her heart and causing an ache deep within her chest. "How did you find them out?"

He scoffed. "I quite literally walked in on the two of them in bed together."

She gasped, her free hand coming up over her mouth as his words sank in. He'd said them in such a matter-of-fact manner, but she heard the years' worth of hurt underneath them, saw it in the harsh lines marring his face as he seemed to struggle to keep his composure.

"Drucilla did not expect me home from London for another fortnight. Otherwise, she'd have never been so indiscreet. I had thought to surprise her, to return home early so that I might make up for so much time spent away. When I came upon them together, the shock of it … I cannot explain how it overtook every other emotion—the anger, the sadness, the pain. It numbed me, and all I could do was turn around and leave the room without a word to either of them. It did not quite settle in until hours later, and by then, Miles, coward that he is, had tucked tail to run off to his own estate."

"Did you ever confront him?" she prodded, intrigued by the story now that she was being given all the little pieces she'd been missing.

"Not right away," he replied. "But I did demand an explanation of her. It was all my fault, she claimed. I was never at home, did not give her enough of my time and attention. I was no longer the fun-loving young man she'd married. I'd become too serious, too invested in protecting our assets. I had changed since we'd married, and she no longer felt the same way about me as she once had."

Lydia snorted derisively, unable to believe what she was hearing. "You became a man, like any other who finds so much responsibility thrust upon them. You grew up, Sinclair."

He nodded in agreement. "Yes. But Drucilla did not. She wanted parties and to be constantly surrounded by people so she could be admired. She wanted the sort of life I found to be filled with shallow pursuits, while I wanted nothing more than a home and a family … children."

Her gut twisted at the broken way that last word fell from his lips. She thought of Henry, the boy he had claimed as his own, but who had clearly been sired by someone else.

"I had hoped Dru and I would have several of them by now," he confessed. "It was my dream. Buckton, Drucilla, and the children who would fill this place with so much life. When she sent a letter to Essex to inform me that she was with child several weeks later, I began to grow hopeful. I thought that perhaps this would be the thing to bring us back together—a child, our child. Becoming a mother would change her, soften her, and … I do not know what I was thinking."

She stroked his hair again, inclining her head and giving him a small smile. "Perhaps you thought that your dreams hadn't been destroyed, after all. You were willing to forgive her, if there was even the slightest chance you could be a family again."

He nodded. "Yes. Yes, that is it exactly. Those months spent waiting for Henry's arrival were good. We decorated the nursery, interviewed nannies, spoke of names for both boys and girls. Miles had become like a ghost between us—there, but never spoken of. We were having a baby, and we were happy, and … I thought things could only get better from there. All that changed the night of Henry's birth."

Lydia held her breath, sitting as still as possible as she waited for him to confirm what she already knew to be true.

"I sat outside her chamber for hours, waiting for him to be born," he said with a little laugh. "I was nervous, excited, a bit afraid for Drucilla. Her health has always been a fragile thing, and I would have been devastated to lose her in childbirth. Yet, late in the night, a maid emerged from the room to tell me my son had been born and his mother had gotten through it well. I waited while they prepared the babe for me, for Drucilla to be made presentable, because even after our long years together, she'd never allow me to see her any way other than perfectly polished. Then, at last, I was ushered inside, where Drucilla lay abed with the boy in her arms. I approached the bed, took one look into her eyes, and I knew … I just *knew*."

Her shoulders sagged, her gaze dropping to the hand she held in her lap. "You knew that you hadn't fathered him."

"It was not just Henry's face," he replied. "It was *her* face, its expressions I had come to know so well in all my years of loving her. Her face told me everything I needed to know, but, I could not be content with that. I had to be absolutely certain, so I asked her. I held the babe in my arms and glanced from him, to her, then back again, and asked, 'Is he mine, or is he Wortham's?' She simply said to me, 'What does it matter, Sin?'. Just like that. And I always wondered whether she said it out of spite, because she knew I'd be forced to raise him regardless of who his father happened to be, or because she truly did not know which of us had sired Henry. I left for London the very next day."

Her eyes widened. "Where you met me."

He nodded. "I went to London to escape her, to escape the truth of what awaited me here. A wife who did not love me, who perhaps never did. I went to gather my bearings and prepare myself to return and raise a child that I hadn't had a hand in creating. I hate London … I hate the parties, the people, the false veneer laid over the hypocritical corruption of people who call themselves my 'betters.' I was just as miserable there as I'd been here, but at least there, I did not have to face Dru, or the babe, or any of it. And then …"

He shifted closer, until her knees were forced apart to accommodate him, her gown hitching up a bit. Kneeling between her legs, he reached up to cup her face with both hands.

"Then a shoe fell out of the sky and struck my shoulder," he murmured with a little smile. "And my life was forever changed. I saw all the things I'd striven for and realized how meaningless they'd become without someone I could truly call my own to share them with. Without *you*."

Her eyes stung with unshed tears, her hands shaking as she brought them up over his. Knowing what he'd suffered before the night they had met, understanding what had driven him from Hertfordshire to London and right into her arms, Lydia felt like the worst sort of person for the things she'd accused him of.

"I was so wrong," she whispered, a tear slipping free and splashing her cheek, wetting his fingers. "Sinclair, I am sorry."

Shaking his head, he swiped the tear away, then kissed her cheek. "There is nothing for you to be sorry about. You could not have known. I wanted to tell you everything, even having just met you. But, the way you looked at me, the way you felt in my arms, and the way you tasted … I did not want to spoil it. Even for that short time sitting up in that tree, I wanted a moment, something sweet, and pure, and mine. Something I could bring back to Buckton with me to get me through the days and years ahead.

"So, I returned home and went into Henry's nursery. I sat and held my son and looked at him—really looked at him in a way I had not on the night of his birth. And even though he was not mine by blood, there was one thing tying us together from the beginning—the distinction of having been born in sin, under circumstances outside our control. I knew then that I would love him, I *chose* to love him, because I knew what it was to live in a home where I felt out of place and unwelcome. I would never let another child feel that way … not when I stood in a position to give him the best of everything life had to offer."

She smiled at him, turning her head to kiss his palm. "Henry could not ask for a better man to care for him, Sinclair. It does not matter what part Wortham played in his conception. In all the ways that count, *you* are Henry's father."

With a heavy sigh, he leaned forward, resting his head against her breast. She clung to him, holding him there while stroking his hair, lowering her head to nuzzle his crown, to inhale his scent … the sorts of things she'd wanted to do for so long but had not allowed herself to. But, no more. She'd come to realize that she loved him, that she could no longer deny him or herself.

"This party, this night, all of it, made me realize that I cannot live like this any longer," he said, his breath warming her skin through the thin layer of her nightgown.

"I know," she whispered, still steadily caressing his hair, kissing him, holding him close. "Neither can I."

Then, sitting up straight, she tipped his head back and urged him to look up at her.

"I have walked about in a state of half-death for so long," she murmured. "I survive, and I move about life from day to day, but I have not *lived*. I cannot go on that way for another day. Not another hour, or another minute. Perhaps, the future is a bit uncertain, and there is nothing we can do about our circumstances … but, we do not have to allow them to rule us, Sinclair. We do not have to allow them to keep us apart."

His gaze dropped to where her hand rested, just over the button holding her nightgown closed at the throat. "Lydia …"

"I've changed my mind," she whispered, her voice hoarse as she opened that first button, then skimmed her fingertip to the one below it. "I no longer wish to fight this. I have tried—*we* have tried. And for what? So that we might both suffer for wanting each other so badly? I am tired of suffering, Sinclair, tired of wanting and yearning, dying a little inside each day. So, I have changed my mind. I will no longer fight this. I am giving in."

He made a low sound, a growl that rumbled from deep in his chest as she loosened button after button, revealing the patch of skin between her breasts. His expression of turmoil melted away, replaced by one of pure desire, his gaze fixated upon the skin she revealed inch by slow inch. Her hands shook, but she did not stop, working the buttons free of the holes until she'd opened the garment to the waist, a swath of skin visible from her throat to her navel.

Sinclair lifted one hand, hesitating for only a moment before turning it so that his bruised knuckles kissed the skin laid over her breastbone. They released a breath in unison—her a breathy sigh; him a low, tortured groan. His touch skimmed downward, his knuckles tickling between her breasts, then over her belly, pausing at her navel, which he circled gently with the tip of his first finger. Then, he moved back up, caressing his way toward her throat, finding her pulse at the juncture of her neck and shoulder. He leaned in to kiss her there, making her heart flutter and her blood rush. Then, he was moving toward the open edge of her nightgown, his finger hooking in the fabric and slowly moving it to bare one shoulder, then farther until it fell to uncover her breast. She shivered, the movement of the gown like a caress of its own, causing goose bumps to ripple over the surface of her skin and the exposed nipple to pebble under his hungry gaze.

"I need to know you are certain," he said, his gaze once again finding hers, his hand pausing on the other side of the garment still hanging from one shoulder. "If you tell me to stop right now, I will cover you and leave this room. I'll never touch you again."

Sitting up a bit straighter, she brought her own hand to the nightgown and pulled it off her shoulder, allowing the entire thing to fall to her waist, baring herself to him. A heady rush of pride flooded her as she took in his reaction to her state of half-nudity, his lips parting, breath growing harsher, pupils dilating to turn his eyes nearly black. Taking both his hands in hers, she placed them over her breasts, arching her back to settle the weight of them in his palms. Her nipples tightened at the brush of his hands, the sensation of the light touch sending little shivers of pleasure straight down between her legs. Gasping, she closed her eyes, reveling in the sensations, in the little burst of pleasure it sent through her, causing her to shift restlessly in her chair.

"I've never been more sure about anything," she assured him. "Now, kiss me, Sinclair. Touch me. Make love to me."

Her words seemed to free him, and he was on her in an instant, all lips and hands, kissing her, touching her, everywhere all at once. He claimed her mouth with his own, dipping his tongue inside while leaning her against the back of the chair. His hands kneaded her breasts, cupping and squeezing, his fingers plucking at her nipples, gently at first, and then with building urgency.

She melted, her body growing boneless and weightless as he brought one arm beneath her, his hand pressed tight against the curve in her back, his head lowering so that he could taste her throat, her shoulders, her breasts. She cried out when he captured a nipple, the ravenous pulls of his mouth and urgent lash of his tongue setting her on fire. Liquid heat gathered between her thighs when he sank his teeth in, the slight sting melting into molten heat as he lapped at the teeth marks he'd left behind with his tongue. She thrashed beneath him, lightning strikes of pure ecstasy striking deep in her core with each pull of his lips on her breast, each nip of his teeth, each swipe of his circling tongue.

He kissed his way down her body while working her nightgown over her hips and legs, yanking it free and tossing it across the room. Then, he straightened, his gaze drinking her in, traveling over every inch of her exposed skin, following his gaze with his hands. There was no room for fear or worry over the parts of her body she wished she could change. Not when he was staring at her as if she were the embodiment of his every fantasy, his gaze and his touch so reverent that they made her feel like the most beautiful creature ever created.

"I've imagined you so many times," he whispered, his palms skimming her thighs, hands tightening around her knees, then spreading her legs wider, pulling her so that her bottom rested on the very edge of the chair, her body slouching. "So many times and in so many different ways. But I never imagined you could be so perfect."

He released her just long enough to snatch open the belt of his dressing gown, letting the garment fall off his shoulders to the floor. Then, he was gripping her thighs again, spreading them wide. She gasped, her face heating with equal parts desire and embarrassment as he opened her, revealing her most secret of places. This was not the same as him touching her in the woods, his hands slipping into her clothing. This was exposure, no barriers or secrets between them from this moment on, every part of her open to his view.

With a tortured moan, he laid his head against the inside of one thigh, his rushing breath tickling the damp curls blanketing her mons. He kissed her there, a day's worth of stubble stinging the tender skin in juxtaposition to his soft, plush lips and warm tongue. Her back bowed, hips rising up off the chair as he slid his hands beneath her, cupping her buttocks and holding her up as he found her with his mouth.

She pressed the back of her hand against her mouth to quiet the moan he forced from her with the first touch of his lips, soft and searching, nibbling on the swollen flesh hidden within the seam of her mons. Then, his hot tongue followed, dragging over her slick folds to then press against her clit.

"Sinclair!" she exclaimed, her thighs trembling on either side of his body, her belly clenching as the pleasure of his mouth upon her stole her very breath away.

It was too much, yet not enough. She wanted him to stop, but needed for him to go on, to drive her back to those heights of ecstasy she'd reached when he had brought her to spend with only the touch of his hand. He moaned in response, the sound vibrating through her entire body from where they were connected, his mouth to her quim. His hands kneaded her buttocks, the strength of his grip keeping her held at the angle he desired. He left no part of her unexplored, dragging his tongue over the inner folds of her cunt, then pressing it against her clit until she saw stars. Then he was lapping at her entrance and tickling the sensitive expanse of skin between it and her rear passage, before going back to that sensitive little nub, sucking at it with gentle pulls between swift lashes of his tongue that chased away the last of her thoughts and reservations until only his mouth on her quim existed.

She had known such things were possible, her very illuminating education on carnal matters having prepared her for all the things she would experience this night. Still, nothing could have prepared her for this feeling, as if she were falling and flying all at once, shattering into pieces and being put back together.

Gripping the arms of her chair, fingernails rasping the fabric, she rode the waves of a thunderous climax. Legs quivering, back arching as she went tense from scalp to toes, she bit back an ecstatic cry, swallowing the sounds of her rapturous pleasure while he went on licking her, sucking her, heightening her finish with soft touches of his lips and laps of his tongue. As the pounding spasms in her core began to die away, she relaxed in the chair with a sigh. She felt boneless, weightless, as if she would sink to the floor and simply cease to maintain a solid form.

Only Sinclair's touch kept her grounded while her head swam, his hands tight at her waist while he kissed his way back up her body. She whimpered when he reached her lips, her inner channel clenching at the heady scent and taste of her own arousal. It was so wrong, so wicked, yet so right. Wrapping her arms around him, she allowed him to help her to her feet, clinging tight to him as he went on kissing her, exploring her body with his hands. The urgency of his erection pressed against her belly served as a grave reminder that he was not nearly finished with her.

Without preamble, he swept her off her feet and began to cross the room with long strides, carrying her to the waiting bed.

CHAPTER 14

*S*inclair stood beside Lydia's bed, hands shaking as he worked to unbutton his shirt while kicking off his slippers. The soul-deep trembling that seemed to wrack him from the inside out wouldn't abate, not until he had finally sated his most acute desire —sinking into her as deep as he could go. It had been four long years since he'd been inside a woman, and he was aware that any experience after such starvation would be an explosive one. However, he also knew that it was this particular woman who added an additional degree of ecstasy to the encounter, making it difficult to breath as he considered all the ways he'd like to take her.

His dreams had been filled with so many possibilities that he could hardly decide on a single one. Did he want her beneath him, arching into each of his thrusts, hands clutching the sheets? Or did he want her sitting astride, hips and waist undulating as she rode him with wild abandon? His cock positively throbbed at the notion of arranging her on all fours and driving into her from behind, hands gripping tight to the plump cheeks of her arse as he pulled her back into each of his strokes.

Tearing his shirt off over his head, he took a deep, slow breath and reminded himself of reality. Even the tentative probing of his fingers at her entrance had been enough to tell him that she was still a virgin. The weight of that, the responsibility of being the one to initiate her into carnal pleasure, fell upon his shoulders while also sending a heady rush of pride straight to his head. Had she been waiting for him all this time? Had she gone untouched, unloved, for so long for want of him, need of him? On one hand, it made him incredibly sad to know someone as passionate as Lydia was still a maiden at the age of two and twenty. Yet, there seemed to be a touch of destiny about the entire thing, the years they'd spent apart in suffering bringing them full circle, to this moment where they would finish what had been started the night they'd kissed in that garden.

Lydia sat up, her breasts high and tempting, her nipples pink and tightened by desire as she watched him undress. He tossed the shirt aside and swiftly opened his trousers. His lack of drawers allowed his cock to spring free, the hungry organ hard and straining toward her with a mind of its own, as if sensing she would be the one to sate it. He heard her sharp intake of breath and glanced up to find her gazing upon him with wonder, eyes wide and shining in the meager light of the fire, lips parted.

He'd imagined this moment often, thought of her looking upon him just like this so many times. It could not have prepared him for the exhilarating feeling of having her gaze at him as if entranced, the desire that shone from her eyes emanating brightly.

She came up onto her knees as he climbed onto the bed, and they knelt facing one another. His every muscle seemed to tense when she reached out toward him, a tentative hand aimed toward his chest. He held his breath while waiting for the first touch against his bare skin, something else he had not been nearly prepared for. Her fingertips scorched him, producing a sharp gasp as she traced the outline of one pectoral muscle before flattening her palm against it.

Placing a hand over hers, he kept it there, gazing up and into her eyes. He hid nothing from her, needing her to see what this meant to him, that he took not a moment of what she was giving him for granted. Taking her other hand, he placed it upon his chest, as well, closing his eyes and reveling in the feel of her palms upon him.

Taking the lead, she began moving those hands of her own accord, smoothing them up to his shoulders, where she kneaded and explored before moving back downward, tickling the springy dark hair sprinkled over his chest and down his abdomen toward his cock.

"Sinclair," she whispered, her breath teasing his neck as she leaned close—so close that his cock brushed against the downy blonde curls between her legs. "Sin ..."

He groaned, letting his head fall back as she began kissing his neck, her hands tracing over his ribs and onto his back, holding him as she tasted of his flesh. She had never called him by the shortened version of his name before, and he liked it. Sin. It made him feel wicked, liked some dark, dirty creature sullying this innocent angel with his kiss and his touch. Instinct seemed to drive her as she kissed him, her tongue finding the sensitive places on his neck, his shoulder, his chest. She seemed to know what he wanted without being told, and while he would have been delighted to tutor her, the experience was made all the better by simply being allowed to feel, to exult in her attention and lust.

His gut clenched when she reached his stomach, nuzzling and kissing her way down toward his groin. He let out a hoarse groan when she gripped his cock, her fist a gentle squeeze around hard, throbbing flesh.

"Lydia," he panted, chest heaving as he fought not to spend in her hand. "Yes, love. Touch me ... just like that."

She grew bolder with his encouragement, crouching before him, her golden head bowed as she watched herself pump him, her hand now a tight fist around his shaft. He leaned back, bracing himself on his elbows as she worked him, kissing the ridges of his stomach, then flicking her hot tongue at one nipple, then the other.

He bit his lip, hips thrusting into her strokes with a wildness he could not control. It had been too long since he'd been touched or kissed, and that it was his angel, his beautiful Lydia, made it all the harder to keep from spewing his seed within seconds like some untried lad.

"Lydia … God … that feels …"

His mindless mutterings choked off on a ragged gasp when she enveloped the tip of him with her mouth. The wet, warm slide of her tongue against his slit was his undoing, and he could no longer fight back a release that had been four years coming. Keeping himself braced with one hand, he gripped her hair with the other, bucking into her mouth as she took up a steady rhythm, sucking him to the finish. He threw his head back and let go, his bollocks drawing up tight against his body as his seed shot from him in hot spurts.

She made a little sound of surprise, but didn't release him, her lips tugging at him with gentle pulls, her throat convulsing as she swallowed down every drop. He shuddered and panted as she drained him dry, the tension in his body easing a bit.

Lydia released him from her mouth, then sat up on her haunches, staring at him with eyes gone heavy-lidded. Her breasts heaved with every breath, and the insides of her spread thighs showed the evidence of her need, wet and glistening. Reaching for her, he drew her flush against his body, his cock already stirring again at the feel of her against him, warm and lush and his.

"Just when I think you could not be more intriguing, more magnetic, you find some way to prove me wrong," he murmured, nuzzling her crown. "I want to know how you are so knowledgeable in carnal matters … but at the same time worry that the answer will make me want to murder someone."

She giggled, wrapping her arms and legs around him, and he lifted her, turning to deposit her against the pillows.

"It isn't what you think. Someone was very frank in explaining intercourse to me. Perhaps, too frank."

He chuckled, lying down atop her, his cock lengthening even more as his hips fit into the cradle of hers, pressing him up against wet, warm flesh. "Ah. The sister-in-law, I presume. The one who wears breeches and shoots rifles."

"The very one," she replied. "But you will be the only man I've ever … I mean, I haven't …"

He kissed her, softly, swiftly, tangling his hands in her hair to begin unpinning it, spreading the golden strands over the pillow. "You are still a virgin. How, Lydia? I know that you had a difficult time on the Marriage Mart, but a woman as beautiful and passionate as you … I just cannot imagine you going untouched for so long."

She stilled beneath him, closing her eyes with a heavy sigh. He frowned, plucking the last pin free, leaving it scattered over the bed sheet amongst the others. Stroking her hair, he kissed her forehead, then the bridge of her nose.

"What is it, Lydia?" he urged. "What's wrong?"

Shaking her head, she opened her eyes and reluctantly met his gaze. "The truth is, I have had several opportunities to dispense with my maidenhead. I've had my share of salacious offers, and … well, I was not quite honest with you about the marriage issue. While it was difficult for me to make a match, there were certain men who did not seem to mind my eccentricities. I could have had them if I'd wanted. But I didn't."

He smiled, smoothing his thumb over the arch of one eyebrow. "Why not?"

Biting her lower lip, she averted her gaze again, her face flushing. "Because you ruined me with a kiss. After that night in the garden, I spent weeks looking for you, searching for your face in the crowd everywhere I went. When I began to realize I would never see you again, it hurt … perhaps more than it should have. From there, any man to cross my path held no allure for me. I have felt attraction and wondered if I should not simply force myself to go through with it with someone—anyone. But, I never did, and after a while, my status as a spinster governess did the job of keeping any such prospects at bay."

Sinclair kissed one lowered eyelid, then the other, then nuzzled her nose with his own. "Look at me, angel."

She hesitated only a moment before raising her eyes and looking into his. He smiled at her, absently toying with a lock of hair.

"It makes me sad to think of you alone and yearning, especially when I spent just as much time pining after you," he murmured. "And I wish I could say that you should have found pleasure wherever you could, with whomever you could. However, I find it difficult to say or think any of that, when I can't help feeling so damned proud that you did not. I have no right to assume that you were waiting for me—"

"But I was," she interjected, reaching up to caress his face. "I did not realize it, of course, but lying here with you, tonight, I understand that my heart knew something my mind did not. I have waited all this time for you, Sin. I could not have had this with anyone but you."

Her words sent a surge of sudden tenderness through him, and he wrapped his arms around her, holding her closer, tighter, pressing little kisses against her temple, her cheek, her lips, her chin.

"It is a gift I do not deserve," he whispered.

"I am giving it to you anyway," she replied, returning his kisses with equal fervor. "Take it, Sin. Take *me*."

Reaching down between them, he palmed his cock, wincing at the tenderness of his freshly-sprung erection, the ache that had built and built for four endless years. Even sating himself in her mouth had not been enough. Only finding his way inside the warm haven between her thighs would satisfy him, and even then, it would only do until he could find his way into her again, and then again.

"I will not let you down," he promised, urging his head toward her tight, slick opening. The kiss of the sensitive flesh to that wet, slick passage sent a shudder through him, anticipation making his mouth go dry.

Stroking his hair, she opened her legs wider, letting him in. "You could never."

He paused, primed to enter her, her wetness coating his tip and slicking the way inside. One dainty, soft hand gripped his buttocks, urging him on with a squeeze. He groaned, responding to her silent command by thrusting his hips, easing his way into her.

She gasped, the hand on his arse tightening, her other grasping his neck and holding fast. He grit his teeth and forced his way in with excruciating slowness, opening her tight channel, exploring the untouched. He braced a hand upon the pillow beside her head, his other seeking out the little bud of her pleasure, needing to do whatever he could to make this first invasion easier for her, more pleasurable than painful.

"Sin," she whispered when he found her clit. "Oh … *Sin*."

He buried his face in the curve of her neck, steadily strumming the little bundle of nerves as he paused halfway into her. He stroked and stroked as she grew wetter, moaning and writhing beneath him. He waited until she was positively mindless from the pleasure before he withdrew a few inches and then plunged, opening her the rest of the way and seating himself fully inside of her. She screamed against his shoulder, her hips bucking against his, her arms tightening around him.

The tight squeeze of her virgin passage around him nearly unmanned him, forcing him to pause within her, afraid that if he moved, it would end before they'd even begun. His balls drew up tight against his body, his spine tingling as climax hovered just within his reach. It had been far too long, and it took every ounce of his will to keep from spilling into her right then and there.

Once he felt certain he could move without embarrassing himself, he circled his hips, digging deeper, searching for the hidden places inside that would drive her mad for him. She groaned, her body undulating beneath his, her legs coming around him and holding him deep.

He braced himself over her, hands tangled in her hair, his hips working in a timeless rhythm that even four years of starvation could not have made him forget. Dipping his head, he sought every inch of available skin he could find, nibbling at her collarbone, her neck, her chest. She arched, offering him her breasts, and he took them, lavishing them with kisses and flicks of his tongue while he drilled his cock into her, slowly at first, then with mounting speed as her channel began to ease open for him, accommodating his length and girth.

Wrapping his arms around her, he turned so that they lay on their sides facing one another, his cock still buried deep. Hooking one arm beneath her bent leg, he lifted it, draping it over his hip and opening her even more. She gasped, squirming in his arms as he drove into her, no longer able to control himself now that he'd found this deep, swift rhythm inside her. He needed to possess her, touch the parts of her that had never been touched, mark her and stake his claim. She clung to him, seeking out his mouth for a kiss. He obliged her, thrusting his tongue into her mouth much the way he thrust into her cunt, tangling with her, tasting her. The little sounds of pleasure she made from deep in her throat drove him, urged him on as he took her, his hold on her hip brutal enough to leave fingerprints. Perhaps he would feel guilty later about having been so rough with her this first time, but just now, he could not stop, would not stop until he'd driven them over the edge and into the depths of rapture together.

He felt her oncoming climax, the delicious tremors of her inner walls around him pushing him closer to his own. It only spurred him on, harder, faster.

"That's it, angel," he murmured against her lips, his hips battering her in a rhythm that forced each of her breaths out on a rough pant, his hold tight on her thigh. "You're so close. Let go … let go and come for me."

He dipped his head to latch on to one nipple, clenching it in his teeth and lashing it with his tongue. It sent her over the edge, and she stiffened for a moment before falling apart, wailing her pleasure and clawing at him, her nails digging into his back, her channel clenching tight around him as the pounding spasms of climax rippled through her.

A rough growl tore from him as he fought for more time, the nearly unbearable squeeze of her cunt pushing him toward his end far too fast. Inevitably, he was forced to pull away from her, turning so his seed spilled on the sheets instead of inside her. He buried his face in the pillow and groaned as an alarming amount of mettle poured from him—what felt like four years' worth of tortuous need forced out of him in a matter of seconds. Even after spending in her mouth a moment ago, it felt as if he still contained so much. It took his breath away, and for a moment, he could only lie there on his side, eyes closed, his breathing harsh while he attempted to slow his pounding heart.

His body began to unwind when Lydia's hand came against his back, resting between his shoulder blades. A moment later, she lay against him, her chest pressed to his back, one arm wrapped around his waist. She kissed the back of his neck, then his ear, her breath on the sensitive skin both a comfort and torment at once.

Finally, he found the strength to move, turning over and keeping her away from the mess he'd made on his side of the bed. He pulled the counterpane up around them and held her, letting her legs tangle with his, burying his face against the wildly tousled locks of hair splayed over the pillow.

He studied her face, marking the changes that making love had put there—the flushed cheeks, the sparkle in her eye, the wondrous expression as she gazed back at him. He grinned, elated to have been the cause.

"How do you feel?" he asked, running a hand up and down her back. "I was not as gentle as I should have been."

She giggled, nestling even closer to him. "Nonsense. I wouldn't have wanted it any other way. As for how I feel … I suppose I feel … like myself."

He furrowed his brow. "That is certainly something a man likes to hear."

She laughed again, the sound all the sweeter for its pitch and unfettered abandon. He'd never heard her laugh too loudly or so freely and found that he'd have happily remained in this bed with her for the rest of his life, listening to that sound again and again.

"I suppose I should explain myself," she said. "You see, becoming a governess has forced me to stifle certain parts of my personality so that I can be as unassuming as possible. Otherwise, no family would ever hire me. I keep my voice low, I try not to laugh, I dress plainly and do my best not to appear too attractive or too young, or too …"

"Something," he filled in for her when she trailed off.

She grinned and nodded. "Yes, that is it exactly. Living at Oakmoor became difficult as I grew into a spinster and my brothers went on to create their families … it is why I left, why I have not gone back. It hurt too much, watching them fall so in love with their wives and live the sorts of lives I'd always wanted."

Her statement sank into his heart like a dagger as he realized that all he wanted was to give her those things. It ate him alive to realize it was not within his power to give them to her. For certain, he could buy her a home of her own, pay for her to have any material thing she could ask for. He could even sire children upon her. But he could not give her the things he wished to give: his surname, his ring upon her finger, his promise to love and cherish her for life. He held her tighter.

"I'm sorry," he whispered, hoping she understood.

She seemed to, as she rewarded him with a gentle kiss upon his brow. "It is no fault of yours. Fate has put us where we are for a reason. I suppose in time, we will understand why. But, as I was saying … the thing I miss most about Oakmoor is the freedom I had there. To be able to ride and shoot and wear breeches … to laugh and let it echo down the corridors. I am not always myself when I act as a governess to someone else's children, because to fill such a role, one must become an idea, a position, not a person. But, this, here with you, tonight … it made me feel more like myself than I have in years, and I want you to know that I will never forget it."

Sinclair rolled onto his back, taking her with him so she lay draped over him, one elbow propping her up, her hair enclosing them in a golden curtain. He reached up to cup her face, his thumb brushing her lower lip.

"There are things I want to say to you," he murmured. "But I do not think it wise to do so. You must know by now that I …"

She nodded, a tear wetting her cheek and falling into his palm. Her voice came out rough and tortured when she replied.

"I know, Sin. I do, too."

He pulled her down to him for a kiss, swiping away the remnants of the shed tear. Their bodies came together once more, her curves fitting perfectly against his planes, his cock having sprung to life yet again, insatiable after its four-year period of denial. She parted her legs for him without hesitation, letting him impale her, his hands maintaining a hold on her hips as he moved her in the rhythm he wanted, showing her how to ride him.

Closing his eyes, he surrendered to the ecstasy of the moment and tried not to think overmuch about the words he so desperately wanted to say to her. But, if he said them, how could he ever prove it to her while married to someone else? His words would ring hollow, becoming meaningless with each passing day, week, month, and year in which he was incapable of giving her everything she deserved.

He did not regret what they had just done, and had a feeling they would be unable to cease after this one encounter. Yet, in the back of his mind, Sinclair could not help but wonder if they had just damned themselves by surrendering to a love that would eventually tear them apart.

CHAPTER 15

$\mathcal{S}$inclair remained in Lydia's room for as much of the night as he was able, taking as much pleasure as he could derive from having her in his arms. He held her and slept, awakening to find his body already straining toward her, his cock hard and pulsing. Despite knowing she must be sore after their first joining and the one that had followed, he'd taken her again, then again by the time the first rays of dawn had appeared on the horizon. Each time, he'd forced himself to pull away from her to spill his seed, aware of what planting a child inside of her could mean for her future. While he owed his own existence to such a circumstance, he could not do that to Lydia. As badly as he wanted more children—with the woman he loved, at that—he could never be so selfish. If she noticed that he did this, she did not remark upon it.

As a bedmate, Lydia turned out to be far more than he'd ever expected. But, he should not have been surprised to discover how eager she was to please, to explore her own wants and needs and learn his. It made sense that she was as vivacious in bed as she was out of it, coming alive in his hands.

He had not wanted to leave the warm haven beneath the counterpane with her, but he'd understood the sense in leaving before servants began to stir. As well, he had not yet spoken with Doctor Tunstall, who he'd left with his wife without asking any questions about her condition. He'd been too angry, rubbed raw after the incident with Wortham. Now, he felt as if he could face the world with a level head, the usual turbulence plaguing him going to complete stillness.

Rising from the bed, he quickly donned his clothing, then bent over the bed to kiss her one last time.

"You are to remain abed for as long as you wish," he urged. "Henry will be too worried about his mother to focus upon his studies, so I'm giving you both a day of respite."

She smiled. "I should feel guilty about it, but thanks to you, I am so bloody tired."

He laughed, smoothing her hair back from her face. "As am I. If I could stay and rest with you, I would."

He would climb back into that bed with her and never leave.

"You have matters to attend," she said with a yawn that had no right to be so endearing but still made him smile. "I understand."

She promptly fell asleep then, her eyes sliding closed, head burrowing beneath her pillow to block out the light of the rising sun. He reluctantly took his leave, hastening to his chamber. He did not bother ringing for his valet, seeing to his own toilette using the water that had been set out for him last night but had now grown cold. He washed, shuddering and shivering, then dried and dressed, donning comfortable half-dress since he had no intention of leaving the house today.

By the time he made his way to his wife's room, Doctor Tunstall had roused from his vigil beside the chair and was waiting for him. Based upon the man's expression, the diagnosis would be far more dire than croup.

"Doctor," he said, shaking the physician's offered hand. "Thank you for staying with her through the night. Her little spell last evening took us all quite by surprise."

He glanced over to where Drucilla lay sleeping, her emaciated body nearly swallowed by the bedclothes. She lay with her back to them, as well as the windows allowing in the light of the sun. Even from where Sinclair stood, he could hear her breathing, the sound shallow, with a slight rattle to it, as if she'd swallowed a handful of nails.

Removing a pair of round spectacles, Doctor Tunstall ran a hand over his weathered face. "Do you remember when I first came to Buckton to meet and examine your wife, Mr. Clayton?"

He remembered distinctly. They'd only been married a few months at the time, and while Sinclair had known Drucilla to be prone to such illnesses, she'd become sicker than he had ever seen her. He'd been frightened to death when he'd sent for Tunstall, afraid his wife would die before they ever had the chance to begin a real life together.

It was ironic now, that the man had become such a part of their lives, as much as the bitterness and scorn they felt toward each other.

"Yes, of course," he replied. "That was some time ago."

"And do you remember what I told you about your wife's condition?" the doctor prodded. "Do you remember me telling you that it was a miracle Lady Clayton had even lived to become a woman grown, and that her days might be numbered?"

Despite recalling the words, Sinclair was still taken aback by their sudden resurgence. "Yes, but … that was ten years ago. You and I both know that Drucilla is a force of nature. She has survived every illness that has befallen her over the past decade, and the ones that afflicted her as a child. Are you now telling me that something has changed?"

Tunstall sighed, crossing his arms over his chest and giving him a measured look. "Nothing has changed. Your wife was born ill, and has been ill her entire life. The defect of her lungs cannot be healed by medicine. She has survived a long time, yes, but … I am afraid she will not last much longer. She will survive as long as a month if she is fortunate, mere days if she is not. The coughing up of blood is a sign I have been watching and waiting for—one I've seen in others with her same affliction, and the outcome is always the same. We are near the end, Mr. Clayton."

Sinclair blinked, his vision beginning to swim. His head spun as the doctor's words sank in, penetrating deep. His conflicting emotions did war with one another, leaving him uncertain how to feel or even what to say.

Tunstall, seeming to mistake his confusion and numbness for grief, placed a gentle hand on his shoulder. "I am sorry, Mr. Clayton, but I have tried to prepare you for this over the years. You can only keep her comfortable … she may eat whatever she wishes if her stomach will allow it. Broth or tea will soothe a sore throat. I daresay she'd welcome laudanum or spirits for the pain. I can remain for as long as you need me."

He cleared his throat, forcing a swallow past the lump that had formed there. "I understand, Doctor. Thank you. I think that we can manage things from here. I am certain you're anxious to return home and rest."

The man nodded, going to one of Drucilla's bedside tables to begin collecting his belongings. "I will return in a few days to look in on her, if you do not mind. Lady Clayton has been one of my favorite patients over the years … a more resilient woman than any I've ever treated."

Typically, some sarcastic remark would dance on the tip of his tongue when someone said something complimentary about his wife. But, this time, Sinclair had to agree with the man. Drucilla had proved many wrong by living as long as she had, and he supposed that was to be respected and admired. It was all he could conjure beyond this sick feeling, this conflicting mixture of reactions roiling in his middle.

The doctor quickly took his leave, so Sinclair approached the bed, finding that Drucilla's breathing had quieted a bit, changing, becoming more shallow. She still lay with her back to him, her hair hanging in a single braid across the pillow. It made him think of Lydia, whose unbound hair had been darker, richer against the sheets he'd laid her on, her face a warm peaches and cream in contrast to Drucilla's porcelain.

This was the bed he'd first made love to Drucilla in, the bed she'd borne Henry in, and now, he supposed it was where she would die. He pressed a hand against his middle, trying to tame this toxic mingling of emotions making him feel as if he would be sick. Lowering himself into the chair Tunstall had just occupied, he leaned forward, resting his elbows upon his knees, his chin atop his folded hands.

"I know you are awake, Dru," he said. "I heard it the moment your breathing changed."

Drucilla released a heavy sigh, then slowly rolled over onto her back. After she'd turned her head to look at him, her eyes narrowed with the usual malevolence and spite. He winced at the sight of the bloodstained handkerchief held in one hand, as well as a few droplets staining her pillow.

"Why are you here?" she spat, her voice tortured from constant coughing.

"You are my wife, and you happen to be dying."

She snorted, but the sound turned into a wheeze before a coughing fit seized her. Sinclair got to his feet, helping her to sit up and reaching for a fresh handkerchief from the stack of them resting on the bedside table. He propped her up while she coughed, pity lancing through him as he felt the way it tore through her, shaking her willowy frame. The handkerchief came away stained with more blood, and he took it away as well as the one she'd been holding in her sleep, dropping them into a basket on the floor filled with other stained squares of linen.

"Do not come to me still smelling of the governess and pretend as if you aren't relieved," she muttered, falling back onto her pillows with a sigh.

He inclined his head and pursed his lips, wondering how he'd gone so long being fooled by her outward appearance. Now, when he gazed upon her, the petulance that was such a part of her personality overshadowed all the beauty that had once captivated him.

"You misjudge me," he replied. "Of course I am not relieved. No matter what has happened between us, I would never have wished for you to die."

She folded her arms over her chest and rolled her eyes. "You will not even deny that you have been with her."

He sighed, running a hand through his hair. "Why would I, Dru? One thing I have never done is lie to you."

"Have you no respect for me at all?" she spat. "That you would crawl into her bed while I lay here languishing—"

"And where has your respect for me been all these years?" he snapped, his patience badly frayed by fatigue.

His knuckles still ached from pummeling Wortham, and his sleepless night with Lydia, while blissful, had left him unprepared to deal with Drucilla.

"Where was your consideration for me when you invited your lover into our home, flaunting him before me knowing I could do nothing lest I risk making us the laughingstocks of Hertfordshire?"

He paused and chuckled, the irony of it all too damn good to ignore.

"Yet, we are probably on the tips of everyone's tongues this morning," he grumbled. "Or rather, we will be once our guests leave and word of last night's events spread. If you did not care what it would do to me, did you not at least consider what the gossip might mean for Henry? How it would feel for the other families to decide their pedigreed children should not play with the son of the bastard and his whore of a wife who flaunts her lover with no care for discretion?"

"No one told you to act like some sort of ill-bred commoner," she groused, turning her head to avoid looking at him. "Though, I am hardly—"

"Surprised that a bastard like me would behave in such a way?" he finished for her, raising his eyebrows. "That is what you were going to say, wasn't it? You are, as always, so predictable, Dru. What did you think would happen when you invited him here, as if to rub my nose in your little affair? Did you expect me to stand back and do nothing as I have all these years, protecting your reputation and claiming

Henry, going about life as if you did not stab me in the heart? Then, you think to bring him here and force me to host him under my own roof, eat with him at my table, *look* at the face that shows me what my son will look like when he is grown?"

Drucilla moved as if to leave the bed, but Sinclair rose from his chair, towering over her and preventing it.

"No," he ground out from between clenched teeth, hands balled into fists at his sides. "You will not leave this room. You will lie there and listen to what I have to say."

Seemingly shocked by his sudden forcefulness, she shrank back against the pillows and stared up at him with wide eyes.

"I've spent years allowing you to treat me as if I am a dog not good enough to eat the scraps from your table," he went on, unable to stop the words he'd held in for so long. "I have held my tongue, and done my best to keep the peace for Henry's sake. I have ignored your many affairs—yes, I know Wortham was not the only one, simply the man whose seed took root. And even then, I provided for you, I denied you nothing … I kept my breeches buttoned, because a part of me would not let go of the girl I loved, the one I built my entire life around, the one I would have moved mountains for. And you may as well have spat in my face for all the love and respect you denied me. Why? I want to know what I ever did to deserve to be lied to, cuckolded, and altogether trampled on for the past ten years!"

For a long moment, she simply stared at him, lips pinched, face white as a sheet. Sinclair began to think she would not answer him, and had almost made up his mind to quit the room, when she finally opened her mouth.

"You were never what I wanted for myself, Sin," she said, her voice a hoarse whisper as tears filled her eyes. "Not for my future, anyway. Oh, you were handsome and charming, and I'll admit the fact that you were a bastard thrilled me. You were forbidden, the sort of man I should never wed. But then, my father could not seem to get enough of your company, always speaking of Sinclair, the brilliant young man with a head for investments. He wanted you for me, and I ... I had always wanted so desperately to please him, to gain his notice."

Sinclair frowned, thinking back to their past and the first years he'd spent visiting Buckton. Yes, he'd come with Drucilla's brother, mostly to escape the tension in his own household. But over time, his trips to Hertfordshire had become more about the girl with the secretive smile and white blonde hair than about her father. He remembered how the earl had doted upon him, as well as his own son ... then recalled the aloofness with which he'd treated his daughter. A sickly thing, who could not make a good match for marriage because no man wanted an ailing wife he had to worry would die before birthing him an heir.

None of that had mattered to Sinclair, of course, him being a bastard and in need of no heir. He'd only wanted Drucilla and Buckton. Was that why the earl had so readily handed his only daughter over to him? Had he decided it made no difference if she died before giving Sinclair a son?

"You did not have to accept me," he said quietly, a bit of the tension easing out of his body, his hands uncurling at his sides. "If you did not love me, you should have simply said so. It would have hurt, but I could have recovered."

I could have gone on to meet Lydia, free and unattached.

She snorted. "And risk upsetting Papa, who was so determined for you to become the master of Buckton? He always believed you'd do it ... you were so bloody brilliant, and everyone knew it. Besides, we both know no other man in the country would have me. Not with my ... disease."

Sinclair studied his wife, wondering how he'd never seen this insecurity in her. A woman so beautiful she had men trailing in her wake everywhere she went, even after she'd wed. She was wrong. She could have had any man she'd wanted, he was certain. But, perhaps she had not known that. Maybe, he thought suddenly, she'd been told otherwise. For all the love he bore the earl, he cursed the man in this moment for what he'd done to Drucilla, and by proxy, Sinclair himself.

"We are quite a pair, aren't we?" he said with a little laugh. "A bastard and sickly shrew."

She met his gaze again, her lips quivering with mirth. "It is fodder worthy of one of those illicit novels."

He smirked, leaning against one of the bedposts, staring down at her. "I tried, Dru. I did try to love you, to make you love me. Even if you never loved me back, I would have been content if you'd simply tried, as well. We could have been something better than this … something … I do not know. Friends, perhaps."

"Perhaps," she hedged, glancing down at the counterpane. "But, after Henry was born, I didn't think you would ever forgive me. When you returned from London, you were so cold, so distant …"

"You never asked," he told her. "I might have forgiven you if you'd asked, if you had explained why you and Miles had betrayed me. It would have been difficult, but I was already prepared to claim Henry. I could have brought myself to forgive you."

Drucilla squeezed her eyes shut and sighed, leaning back against her pillows. "God, what a mess we've made."

"Yes," he agreed. "But that is over now. You should … you should rest."

She laughed, the sound a rough bark. "I've been resting in beds since I was a girl. I am sick to death of resting. I want Henry. I want to hold him and talk to him and … will you send him to me?"

Pity lanced through him, for her as well as for his son. This would be hell for her, knowing she did not have much time, and hell for his son after she was gone. The days ahead of them would be dark ones, and he had no notion how to navigate them.

But, he nodded, deciding that even after all the pain she'd caused him, in her last days, Drucilla would have everything she wanted.

"Of course," he replied. "I'll have Mrs. Beecham bring him as soon as he has had breakfast."

She nodded and closed her eyes again, a tear tracking down one hollowed cheek. "Sin … I'm afraid."

He perched on the edge of the bed and reached for her hand—the first time he'd touched her with any sort of tenderness in years. Raising it to his lips, he kissed her knuckles. Her eyes opened in shock, and she gazed up at him as he patted her hand.

"I know," he murmured. "But we are all here, for whatever you need."

She sighed. "Henry will do for now."

He patted her hand again and stood to leave once more, but her voice drew him up short at the door.

"Sin?"

He turned, one hand braced upon the doorknob. "Yes?"

"Miss Darling. I do not like her."

He shrugged one shoulder. "That does not surprise me at all."

"She is brash and common," Drucilla went on, her voice taking on its haughty tone once again. "She's a hoyden who enjoys men's pursuits, and it is no wonder she's gone unmarried for so long."

Leaning against the door, he smiled, a laugh simmering in his chest. "Yes. All those things are true … they also happen to be all the reasons I love her."

Drucilla nodded, as if she'd suspected as much. "Yes, well. She is quite perfect for you, you know. Be sure you do a better job of making her happy than you did me."

He raised an eyebrow and fought not to laugh again, knowing that this was as close to a blessing or any sort of well-wishes he was likely to get from Drucilla. "I will certainly try."

"That is, if she will even have you," she added. "After all, she might be a brash hoyden, but she does have some sense."

"That, she does," he added before finally taking his leave.

In the corridor, he encountered Alice, Drucilla's lady's maid, and instructed her to see to her mistress' every need, keeping her as comfortable as possible and send for him if he was needed. He then returned to the third floor, bypassing Lydia's closed door to go to the nursery, where he spent a few moments with his son before directing him and Mrs. Beecham to Drucilla's room.

Then, he trudged to his study, grateful that he did not encounter any of his guests. It was still quite early, and most would not rise for another hour or so before setting out for home. Outside, carriages and horses were already being prepared for their journeys.

Through the open door connecting his study to Charles', he saw that his friend and steward had arrived, despite having been given the day off.

"I told you to remain at home today," he said when he entered the little space to find Charles rearranging some items on his desk.

His friend looked as if he'd slept better than Sinclair last night, dressed in his usual stark black attire. "Yes, but after the events of last night, I thought it prudent to come anyway. What do you need, Sin?"

Sinclair sighed, once again raking a hand through his hair. His weariness had sunk bone deep, his emotionally-draining encounter with Drucilla taking what little strength he'd had left.

"There are still guests here and I … I cannot … I don't have the forbearance to put on a mask for them, Charles. Not today."

His friend nodded, seeming to understand, even though Sinclair had not told him all of it. "I will take care of it. Everyone will be gone by noon, and I will see to it that they have a decent breakfast beforehand."

Sinclair sighed, relief sagging his shoulders. "Thank you."

"Of course," Charles said with a little smile. "Now, I suppose you have not been to bed yet?"

Thinking of Lydia sleeping in the bed they'd shared through the night, he fought back a smile. He would not betray her by spilling their secret, not even to his best friend.

"Not exactly," he hedged.

Charles sighed. "Go, then. I believe I can manage things until you awaken. You look like hell."

Sinclair laughed, but took himself off to do what he was told, too tired to argue. He managed to reach his chamber before he heard the stir of guests farther down the corridor. Leaning against his door with a relieved sigh, he paused for a moment, taking and releasing a deep breath.

He stripped off his clothing on the way to the bed, leaving a trail of garments along the way. His valet would grumble over having to pick them up, but he could not find it in him to care at the moment. He fell facedown onto the bed with a groan of satisfaction.

But then, sleep eluded him for a long while. He turned onto his back, one hand braced under his head as he stared at the ceiling. The feelings he had compressed while in Drucilla's chambers came rushing back at him now, unfurling in his gut. They seized him so quickly, he could hardly grapple with what was happening before the pressure in his chest released, burning in his throat.

And as he turned onto his side, burying his face into the pillow, he allowed every bit of it to claim him—the anger, the sadness, the grief, and yes, the relief. A sob burned his tongue, and tears sprang to his eyes for the first time in years. Doing his best to muffle the sounds, he allowed himself to weep.

CHAPTER 16

$\mathcal{L}$ady Drucilla Clayton languished for three weeks before finally succumbing to her disease. Lydia had been in the schoolroom, just beginning the day's lessons, when Sinclair appeared in the doorway, brow furrowed, lips tight. She had paused in the midst of writing on the slate board and put her chalk aside, her throat constricting and her chest beginning to ache as he'd entered the room and approached Henry.

The news of Lady Clayton's imminent death had shocked her when it had first been delivered, but Sinclair had hardly seemed surprised. She supposed, given how long the woman had suffered, it must have been inevitable. He had shared with her his conflicting feelings in regards to the news, the grief and sadness mingling with his hurt and anger over her years of neglect and mistreatment. He had come to her on the evening following the one they'd spent together, climbing into her bed and taking her into his arms. They hadn't made love, simply lying together while she allowed Sinclair to unburden himself to her, finding in her a resting place for his pain. She'd listened, stroking his hair and kissing his brow as he'd talked, her own emotions torn in so many directions, she could hardly register it all.

As she stood back, one hand pressed over her mouth while she watched Sinclair go down on one knee before his son and gravely inform him that his mother had died, Lydia felt it all over again. Grief for the now motherless boy. Sadness for Sinclair, who was left grappling with his own grief while also doing his best to help Henry through his. Confusion over the relief that stole through her that it was over, and guilt that she would even think to be relieved. Her eyes stung when Henry began to wail, falling into his father's arm, his little body shaken by sobs.

Sinclair had done his best to prepare the lad for his mother's death, informing him weeks ago that his mama was ill and might not get better. Lydia had kept their daily lessons short, so that Henry could spend as much time with Lady Clayton as possible. Yet, she could remember being a young girl while her father had suffered from pneumonia, being told much the same thing, and still being unprepared to hear that her father had died.

Her chest ached as Sinclair looked at her over Henry's shoulder, his own eyes watery and unfocused, as if he wrestled with himself. Lydia went to them, placing one hand upon Sinclair's back, and another atop Henry's head. The boy wept against his father's shoulder while the father gazed up at her, pleadingly, mournfully.

She moved her hand up from his shoulder into his hair, and he sighed, leaning his head against her thigh and closing his eyes.

"I am so sorry," she whispered, for lack of anything better to say. "When?"

"This morning," he said, his voice low as he rubbed Henry's back, the large hand strong and sure. "Alice found her ... she simply fell asleep and never woke."

That should have been comforting, but Lydia had heard the servants whisper about how Lady Clayton had suffered in her last days, the coughing so violent, even the potion she'd once relied upon had had no effect. The woman had wasted away before the eyes of her husband and lady's maid.

"What can I do?" she asked, needing to be able to help in some way, even as guilt continued to assail her with every breath she took.

He shook his head, closing his eyes again with a sigh. "You are already doing it. Just … stand here."

She obliged him, remaining still and silent while Sinclair murmured words of comfort to his son. Eventually the boy quieted, sniffing and swiping at his watery eyes. He asked if he could see his mother, and of course, Sinclair did not deny him. Rising to his feet, he lifted Henry into the crook of one arm, holding him tight against his chest. The boy buried his face in Sinclair's neck and did not come out, his shoulders still shuddering with the aftershocks of his cries.

Sinclair cupped her face with his free hand, then lowered his head to kiss her brow. "Thank you."

Taking his hand, she kissed his knuckles, the bruises having almost completely faded, the swelling gone. "Anything, Sinclair … anything you need."

"Later," he murmured, his knuckles now stroking her cheek in a tender caress. "Tonight. For now, I have to—"

"You do not need to explain," she said swiftly, wanting him to know she did not begrudge him the time he needed, the space required for him to lay his wife to rest. "I am here, always."

With a nod, he turned away, both arms now around Henry as he left the room. Lydia moved slowly back to her desk, sinking into the chair behind it and burying her face in her hands. She wept for Sinclair and Henry, and yes, even for Lady Clayton. The woman had hurt Sinclair, almost beyond repair, but Lydia would not have wished death on her.

After she had calmed, left the schoolroom. The rest of the day passed with a speed that left her breathless, as if time had decided to move forward at a breakneck pace after the insufferable days and weeks it had dragged on leading up to this. Sinclair set Charles to work making preparations for Lady Clayton's body to be taken to Belcourt, the family seat of her family, the Strattons. Her brother would want her buried there, and Sinclair wished to honor that. Word would be sent ahead that he and Henry would soon arrive with Drucilla's body in tow. Lydia supposed that they would spend some time at Belcourt, as they should after the loss of a family member.

They would set out the following day, which would leave her here at Buckton with Charles and the other servants to await their return. Yet, as she left her room that evening, her thoughts were not of how much she would miss them, or what might happen once they returned. Her thoughts were only of Sinclair as she approached his chamber, finding the door hanging open.

She found him inside, sitting in the dark upon the bed, head in his hands. He looked as if he'd been there for hours without moving, the rise and fall of his shoulders the only indication that he even breathed.

Without hesitation, she crossed to his bedside table and found a lamp there. She quickly lit it, then closed the door, closeting them from the rest of the house. He glanced up as she approached, blinking as if just coming out of a daze. Kneeling between his parted legs, she reached for him, taking his face into her hands and bringing him to her for a kiss.

He released a sigh against her lips, giving himself over to her, leaning forward to let her loop her arms around his neck as she kissed him—soft, tender kisses that spoke to him of her sadness on his behalf, her grief for Henry's sake. She released his lips, peppering his face with more affection, her lips touching his eyelids, his brow, his cheeks, the line of his jaw.

He reached for her, hands tight on her shoulders as he held her close. "Lydia ... my angel."

She kissed his lips again, then pulled back to stare into his eyes. "I'm here. Let me take care of you."

His haggard appearance spoke of his exhaustion, the dark smudges under his eyes and lines around his mouth making her heart ache for him. Nodding in response, he submitted to her, dropping his hands and waiting quietly, patiently.

She rose to her feet, glancing about for the bell cord. "Your valet. If I send for him, will he ..."

"He will be discreet," he said.

Satisfied with that, she rang and waited for the man to arrive.

"Send for a hot bath for Mr. Clayton," she said once the valet entered, eyes going wide at finding her in the room of his master. "And a light supper, as well … whatever can be scrounged from the kitchen will do. As quickly as you can, please."

When the valet cast a nervous glance to his master, Sinclair nodded. "Do whatever she says, all of you."

He nodded. "Right away, Mr. Clayton … Miss Darling."

She did not have time to worry over the valet's reaction, or whether or not he might gossip to the other servants about what went on in the master's chamber. She only knew that Sinclair needed her and that he had gone so long without having a person to care for him like this, to worry over him and soothe his hurts. The time had come for him to have that, and she would be the one to give it to him.

While they waited for the bath, she busied herself about the chamber, lighting another lamp and a few tapers, as well as stoking the fire in the hearth. By the time the valet returned with several footmen carting a large copper tub, she'd set the room alight with a yellow glow, drawn the curtains, and coaxed him to the table near the fire so that she could turn down his bed. She persuaded him to attempt to eat the light meal that had been sent from the kitchen while she helped to prepare his bath.

He ate in silence, his gaze blank and unfocused as he mechanically placed the food into his mouth and chewed, hardly looking as if he even registered the taste of it. Once the tub was filled, she dismissed the servants and then urged him up from his place at the table, noticing he had finished eating.

Her hands moved swiftly and deftly as she began undressing him—untying his cravat, then pulling his coat off his shoulders before attacking the buttons of his waistcoat. She knelt to remove his boots and peel off his stockings, leaving his breeches for last.

Her gaze moved over his body, beautiful in its masculinity and hardness. She had missed the sight of him, as they had not been together since their first night—at least not physically. He'd come to her many evenings to simply lie in her arms, and even that she had reveled in, having dreamt of being with him in such a way for so long.

She paused for a moment to place a kiss against his chest, his soft hairs tickling her lips. Then, she took his hand and led him to the tub. He climbed inside at her prompting and sank into the water with a sigh. She tended him deliberately, slowly, soaping her hands and using them to wash him. She scrubbed his arms and chest, working the suds into his skin with efficiency as well as love, caressing every inch of him and attempting to massage away as much of the hurt as she could. She had him stand so she could reach the parts of him hidden by the water, then once he sank back into the depths again, she cupped her hands and gathered water to wet his hair before cleaning it, using her nails to soothe his scalp. By the time she'd finished, he lay there with his head resting against the tub, eyes closed. She left him there for a moment, allowing him to relax, but rousing him once she realized he'd begun to fall asleep.

Urging him from the tub, she dried him herself. Then, she led him to the bed, coaxing him down onto the sheets. While he lay there, naked, watching her, she began to undress. His dark eyes glittered in the lamplight as he watched her open her gown and drop it to her feet, then swiftly remove her stays, petticoat, and chemise, leaving them all in a pile on the floor.

He opened his arms to her when she climbed naked into bed, gathering her close as she pulled the counterpane over them. They lay facing one another, legs intertwined, eyes locked. He reached up to move a stray lock of hair from her face, his touch agonizing and tender all at once. It had not seemed right to be with him physically with Lady Clayton ailing in the same house, and it still felt wrong, lying in bed with him next to the room in which she had just died that morning. Yet, she could not have left him for anything just then, her need to be here for him when he most needed it overwhelming any guilt she might feel.

"I must leave tomorrow," he murmured, resting his hand at the curve of her waist and leaving it there.

"I know," she replied. "I will miss you, but it's what must be done."

"Yes. But, I've been thinking … perhaps now might be a good time for you to visit your family."

She frowned. "As much as I would like that, my place is in Buckton. I want to be here when you return."

His lips curved into a slight smile. "I would like nothing more than to return to you waiting for me. But, I cannot know how long we will remain at Belcourt, and I hate the thought of you left here alone with nothing to do. At least, if you return to Norfolk for a time you will be surrounded by your family. I know they must miss you terribly."

And she missed them. Another letter had come from Oakmoor, filled with news. Visiting was a good idea and would help occupy her while Sinclair and Henry were gone. Still …

"I am not certain I will know what to do without you," she told him. "Occupying a space that you do not fill."

"Neither do I," he admitted. "But, perhaps it is for the best, just for now. I will send word when we are prepared to return home, as well as a coach to retrieve you."

She nestled closer to him, resting her head against his chest. "Very well. I shall miss you terribly, and Henry. How is he?"

He sighed, his grip on her tightening. "He finally fell asleep just before I came here. I think the strain and exhaustion claimed him. He slept like the dead, but I told Mrs. Beecham to send for me should he awaken in the night."

"The poor love," she murmured. "I can remember losing my father and feeling as if my entire world had been shattered. But I was older than Henry then. I cannot imagine how he must feel."

"Neither can I," he said. "I was not so young as Henry either when my own mother died. I do not know how I will ever manage to get him through this."

"It will be difficult, but I believe that no one could do a better job of caring for him during this time than you. The two of you will get through this together, Sin. You'll rely on each other. It will take time, but Henry will be all right someday."

Kissing her forehead, he gathered her even closer, until their bodies mashed together from shoulder to hip. "You are a godsend, angel. Do you know that? I do not think I could weather this without you. And I know it may be too soon to speak of this, but … whatever the future holds from here, I need you to know that I want you in it."

Tears stung her eyes once again, but she tried to hold them in, wanting to maintain at least an outward strength for his sake. "I want that, too. Even when I feel like the worst sort of person for wanting it."

"I understand the sentiment," he assured her. "I know that I must first finish burying the past, closing the door on past chapters before beginning a new one. I just needed you to know. I love you, Lydia, and when all this has ended, that will not have changed. When I return home, it will be with every intention of showing you every day just how much you mean to me."

She could not hold the tears back any longer, her elation at finally hearing those words from his lips making her weep.

"I love you, too, Sin," she whispered. "And I want that, too. All of it, with you."

He captured her mouth, engaging her in a melding of lips and tongues and souls. She felt the kiss deep, its warmth suffusing her from the inside out, the surface of her skin tingling as she became more and more aware of his nudity, his cock beginning to stir between them.

"Lydia," he murmured. "We have waited because it felt right to do so, but tonight, I need you. I need you now."

She turned him so that he lay on his back, then came over him, all her most intimate places pressed against his. Bracing her hands against his chest, she kissed him again, deeper this time, slipping her tongue into his mouth and writhing against him, creating friction and heat between their bodies. She needed him, too. She needed to have him this one time before they were separated for weeks, perhaps even months. Parting did not worry her, for she knew his love for her was as real now as it had ever been, perhaps even more so after all they had weathered to be able to look one another in the eye and confess their adoration. But, she could not leave him tomorrow without this, the joining of their bodies and solidification of all the things they felt for one another.

"Yes, Sin," she murmured against his mouth, reaching between them to palm his cock. "Yes."

He groaned, surging his hips to thrust the hard, pulsating length into the circle of her fist, a bead of moisture wetting her fingers. She kissed his neck, his shoulder, working her way down his body while steadily teasing him to full hardness, marveling at the way the organ in her hand grew in reaction to the stimuli. Even being told all there was to know about intercourse could not have prepared her for the real thing … for being with Sin and finding out for herself how it could be with the man she loved.

His hands tangled in her hair, holding tight as she crouched between his legs, her tongue circling slowly around his engorged head. Another drop of his mettle found her tongue, and she moaned at the taste of him, primal and masculine. She sucked him into her mouth with more relish and less timidity than she had the first time, knowing now how he would react, the things that would drive him mad with lust.

His hips undulated in rhythm with the strokes of her mouth, each upward movement timed with her downward ones. He went slowly at first, then quickened when she found his desired pace, relaxing her jaw and surrendering to him, allowing him to fuck her mouth the way he wanted. Despite being the one giving pleasure, her body reacted to each of his groans and sharp breaths, her breasts tingling, the tips going tight, and her core pulsing with every beat of her heart, wetness already beginning to gather there. She felt as if each sound from him were a caress, stroking down her spine, filling the spaces within her that hungered for him.

She opened her eyes, glancing up to watch him, captivated by the sight he made. Chest and stomach tight and strained as he seemed to fight against climaxing while still seeking the pleasure, thrusting into the open cavern of her mouth. Sweat had begun gathering along his brow, his eyes squeezed shut, lips parted as guttural groans of pure ecstasy spilled from him in time with the pulls of her mouth. She tentatively brought her fingers to the swollen sac below the root of his cock, eyes widening when he responded with a hoarse shout. Realizing it increased his pleasure, she went on fondling him there, exploring him as she had not done before, gently squeezing and caressing him while working him with her lips and tongue.

"God, Lydia," he groaned, his hold on her hair becoming downright painful, his thrusts into her mouth less precise. "You have to stop, or I'll … damn it, stop … no, don't …"

She smirked as she released him from her mouth, responding to the pull of his hands in her hair. He breathed heavily, shuddering as he seemed to try to bring himself back under control. She would have been happy to continue, having quite enjoyed the heady pleasure of making him spend in her mouth as she had their first night together. Sinclair had other ideas, however, reaching for her with insistent hands to urge her back over his body.

He stole a swift kiss, but continued moving her up his body, up and up until she was straddling his head. Her cheeks burned as he grasped her hips, positioning her so that her quim hovered within his line of sight.

"Sin," she protested, slightly embarrassed, but also curious as he pried her thighs farther apart, then opened her lower lips, staring up at the hidden pink flesh. "What—"

His tongue lashing against her clit stole the air from her lungs, and her words broke off on a startled gasp. She had to grasp the headboard in order to steady herself, her hips bucking as he licked her again and again, making little sounds in the back of his throat as if responding to the taste of her.

She forgot her reticence in an instant, unable to think past the feel of his lips and tongue against her. He squeezed her thighs, then gripped her buttocks, urging her even closer, deeper into his mouth. He suckled at her, torturing the little bud of her pleasure, drawing sharp cries of bliss from her. Her hips moved of their own accord, and she rode his mouth much the way he had done hers, her grip so tight on the headboard, she was surprised her fingernails did not gouge the wood.

He managed to slip a finger between his face and her groin, seeking her opening. Her head fell back, another cry lodging in her chest as he slid one finger, then another into her, taking up a steady rhythm inside as his tongue went on working at her clit, coaxing so much moisture from her, it was a wonder he did not drown in it. She lost herself to it, to the explosive pleasure of his tongue on her while his fingers filled her, twisting to find a place inside her that made her toes curl and her entire body tremble with the force of an impending climax.

"Sin," she moaned, reaching down to grasp his hair, holding on for purchase as it swept over her too swiftly to be controlled. "*Sinclair!*"

He refused to let up, his fingers moving even faster inside her, his other hand coming up to pinch a nipple and adding another surge of heat and ecstasy spiraling straight to her core. She shuddered and groaned atop him, her hips bucking against his face as her climax crested and swelled, then slowly abated, turning from pounding spasms into light flutters drawn out by his gentle kisses and softening caresses.

When she went limp, he took hold of her hips and threw her onto the bed beside him. She had hardly recovered before he was on her, swiftly snatching her legs apart and hooking his arms beneath her knees to draw her up against him. He knocked the wind from her, slamming into her with a swift, brutal thrust. The invasion stung after so many weeks without having had him inside her, but the way was eased by her wetness, letting him fall into her to the hilt. He lifted her until her hips came up off the bed, his grip on her legs keeping her from moving, putting her at his mercy. Then, he began driving into her, swift, hard thrusts that dragged each breath from her on a whimper, the impact of them resounding through her entire body.

Gripping the bedclothes, she held on for dear life as he closed his eyes and pounded her relentlessly, his tortured expression melting away into something else. She let him, laid there and opened her body to him, accepting his pain and his loss, letting him give it all to her. His eyes flew open, and he was gazing down at her, his fingers digging into her hips possessively, the cords in his neck tensing and straining as he seemed to hover on the edge of rapture, intent on holding it back.

"My Lydia," he rasped, his voice strained and gruff, breathless from his exertions. "You will be mine when I come back for you … all mine … mine alone."

"Yes," she moaned, another climax looming close, her body going taut in anticipation. "Yes, Sinclair."

She cried out, her back arching and lifting her farther off the bed as he rode the waves of her rapture, his hips surging harder, faster, heightening every ripple of the orgasm as it tore through her like a hurricane. He let her hips drop back to the bed, palming her thighs and spreading them wide, pushing them up toward her shoulders to open her up more.

Modesty had long ago left her, and she delighted in the way he looked at her, staring down at the place where their bodies were joined as if enthralled, unable to look away. He fucked her like a man possessed, thick veins appearing along his arms, the strain of his muscles causing them to bulge, the grooves between them becoming more prominent. She could hardly look away from him, not wanting to miss the exquisite moment when he finally spent.

"Christ," he growled, his movements becoming less controlled, tremors beginning to wrack him from head to toe. "Lydia … Lydia … *Lydia.*"

He pulled from her abruptly, one hand fumbling to grip his cock as his head fell back, his lips parting on a rough groan as he spent, his seed spilling from him and wetting her thighs, her belly, her mons. It seemed to go on and on, spurts of his hot mettle staining her, marking her.

When it had finished, he went back on his haunches, struggling to calm his breathing. She could not even think of moving, her limbs like jelly and her mind floating in some blissful place, her vision swimming dizzily. She faintly registered the dip of the mattress as Sinclair began to move, his weight going away. She heard him rifling about across the room for a moment before he came back, appearing above her. Something warm and wet touched her, and she realized it was a damp cloth, which he used to clean her of his seed.

"I'm sorry," he said, gently abrading her skin with the linen until he'd removed the evidence of what they'd just done. "If there's one thing I desire most, it is to stay buried deep inside when you when I come, so I can fill you. Pulling out at the end is torture."

She gathered the strength to move, resting a hand over his and bringing it over her belly, where a child might grow if he allowed himself to spend inside of her. "You do not have to explain. I understand that we cannot risk it."

Rising to dispose of the cloth, he returned quickly, climbing back into bed with her, gathering her close before covering them both with the counterpane. "No, not now, but … someday, Lydia. If it is what you want, I will give you as many children as you wish."

She grinned at that, thinking of the things he'd confided in her, his dreams of a Buckton overrun with children, filled with laughter and pounding feet. It was exactly the same dream she'd had for herself when considering her future. That she would now get to have it with Sinclair only made it all the sweeter, all the more real.

Kissing his neck, she closed her eyes and began drifting to sleep, nestled close to his side.

"Someday," she murmured, a smile remaining on her lips even as fatigue finally began to drag her under.

CHAPTER 17

*L*ydia pulled the curtain back so she could peer through the coach window at the passing scenery. A soft smile curved her lips at the familiar sights that made up home. They'd just arrived on Oakmoor lands, a few short days after setting out from Buckton. Before leaving with Henry for Belcourt, Sinclair had seen to it that a coach was prepared for her journey, as well as two footmen to act as her escorts. The morning of his departure, he'd pulled her into his chamber for a private goodbye, taking her into his arms.

"I know we decided this was best, but I cannot tell you how difficult this is for me," he'd murmured against the top of her head. "After being away from you for so many years, I hate the thought of being without you, even for a few weeks."

"I feel the same way," she had assured him. "But this time, we will part ways knowing this is not the end. I will wait for you, Sin, and when you send the word, I will come back to you."

He'd kissed her thoroughly then, his hands tight and possessive at her back, his tongue invading her mouth and imprinting his taste into her memory. "You had better."

She had visited Henry, as well, finding him in his chambers

waiting for his things to be taken down to the waiting coach. He'd clung to her with tears in his eyes, stating that he did not understand why she could not come with them to Belcourt. Her heart had broken at those tear-filled eyes, so young, yet so filled with pain and confusion.

"Because, after the death of a loved one, families need one another," she told him, stroking his hair as she held him close against her side. "And as much as I adore you, and as fond as we are of each other, we are not family, Henry. You and your father must go and visit your Uncle Milton and help him to lay your mama to rest. But I will be here when you return, I swear it."

He'd simply held her tighter, his tears wetting her bodice. "I wish you were our family, Miss Darling. Then you could come with us."

So do I, little love, she had thought. *With all my heart.*

She had stood on the front steps beside Charles and Amberly, waving as the coach disappeared down the lane with them, a wagon carrying Lady Clayton's coffin trailing behind it.

The following day, she'd departed on her own journey, her heart heavy in her chest with each mile that separated her from Buckton.

However, as the coach now rolled into a stop before the grand mansion she had grown up in, the heart of Oakmoor, her spirits began to lift. If she must be away from Sinclair and Henry, then this was the only place she would wish to be.

She thanked the footman who opened the door for her, accepting his assistance in alighting from the coach. Her steps were light as she approached the house, only making it halfway up the stairs before one of the massive double doors swung open to reveal Shaw, the man who had served as butler of Oakmoor for as long as she could remember.

His eyes widened at the sight of her, his mouth dropping open in shock. "Miss Lydia, is that you?"

Removing her hat, she beamed up at him. "So it is, Shaw."

He held his arms open as she approached, chuckling as she graced him with a hug. He smelled like tobacco and the polish he used upon the silver, just as he always had. The memories that scent brought up made her want to weep. She had not realized how much she'd missed home until she stood on its threshold.

"Come in, come in," Shaw urged, releasing her and stepping back to let her inside. "We were not expecting you. Your mother will be so elated."

"There was not time to send word," she told him, allowing him to take her hat and gazing about the familiar vestibule. "I have been given a short holiday and decided to come home for a visit."

Shaw opened his mouth as if to reply, when a familiar voice came booming at her from the corridor stretching farther into the house.

"Lydia!"

She glanced up to find her eldest brother, Michael, descending upon her, a wide grin stretched across his face. Tears filled her eyes at the sight of him, perhaps her favorite person in the world, second only to Sinclair. He reminded her so much of their father, tall and broad, his bulky farmer's frame wrapped up in deceptive finery—the doing of his valet, no doubt. Long, blond hair was clubbed back from his face, his merry blue eyes twinkling like sapphires in a handsome but friendly visage.

Lydia threw herself at him with a sound that was half a laugh, half a sob, her elation at coming home overwhelming her along with guilt for having stayed away for so long. Michael caught her up easily, holding her against him with massive arms that were surprisingly gentle. That was her brother … a gentle giant a person could not help but love. The tenants of Oakmoor adored him, and with good reason.

The two of them had always been close, Michael having filled the shoes of her father in so many ways after Phillip Darling's untimely death.

"Well, now," he murmured, setting her back on her feet. "To what do we owe the sudden visit?"

Taking his hand, she sighed. "It is a long story. One I think I could only tell once. Where is everyone?"

"Amelia is in the garden with the children," he told her, already leading her in that direction. "Mother is in her drawing room—

making candles, you know how she loves it. We'll send for her from the garden. You will be a nice surprise for her. Archie and Hesper have taken their children off visiting neighbors and will not be back until later."

"That is quite all right," she said, following Michael through winding corridors leading toward a set of doors opening onto the terrace, which overlooked the gardens. "You, Amelia, and Mama are the ones I really wish to speak of this to. No offense to Archie."

"Much offense to Archie, always," Michael joked, tousling her hair. "I will be sure to let him know you did not think him important enough to await his return before telling us your news."

She scowled at him, knowing he was only jesting. "Brute."

"Imp," he fired back as they stepped onto the terrace.

Her response died on her tongue at the sight that greeted her. On the stretch of grass separating them from the walled-in garden was Amelia and Lydia's niece and nephew. They were quite a sight, Amelia tall and slender, still svelte even after birthing children, in her usual attire of men's breeches and boots, hair unbound and flying about her face as she chased the two children. Their son, Phillip, took after Amelia, and at four years old, already stood taller than most boys his age. His hair was dark, nearly black like his mother's, his face made in Amelia's image, complete with a dimple in the left cheek and the too-wide, mischievous smile.

Their daughter, Diana, had just passed her second birthday, her little legs much shorter than her brother's as she toddled after him and her mother, struggling to keep pace with them. She looked as if Michael had created her himself—all blonde curls, big, blue eyes, and a cherub's face. As a babe, she'd even displayed Michael's sunny disposition, smiling more than she cried, and generally wrapping every person who encountered her right around her chubby little fingers.

"Oh, Michael," she whispered as she stood at the stone railing surrounding the terrace. "How they've grown."

He draped an arm over her shoulders and smiled, his gaze heavy with affection as he watched his wife run about with their children, the evidence of the one now growing inside her already showing against the front of her breeches and shirt.

"Perhaps it would not come as such a surprise if you visited more often," he said.

While his voice was light and carried not a hint of accusation, Lydia still felt wretched. It had been so long since her last visit.

"I know," she murmured. "I haven't wanted to stay away, but … Michael, it has been so hard. I've missed home, I've missed you all."

He leaned down from his substantial height to kiss the top of her head. "Well, you are here now, and that is all that matters. Go to them. I will send for Mama."

She did as he said, leaving the terrace to approach her sister-in-law. Amelia happened to glance up, halting in her tracks at the sight of Lydia coming across the slightly sloping lawn. A shocked huff of laughter left her, and she bent to lift Diana into her arms and rush forward to greet her, Phillip hot on her heels.

"Lydia!" she exclaimed, her silvery eyes twinkling with mirth and mischief. "What are you doing here? Not that I am not glad to see you, but …"

Lydia smiled. "It is a long story. Michael is fetching Mama so that I can tell you all about it."

Little Diana began reaching for Lydia, so Amelia handed her over, while Phillip wrapped himself around her leg, chattering excitedly about the pony his father had begun teaching him to ride. As the four of them began making their way toward the terrace, the burden resting heavily upon her shoulders began to ease a little. For the first time in years, coming home did not feel so daunting, after all.

Hours later, Lydia sat in her mother's favorite drawing room, where tea had been ordered, the children sent off with their nurse. Her mother had wept at the sight of her, making her feel even worse about staying away for as long as she had. Once she had calmed, she had ushered Lydia and the others inside, insisting they have tea while they took the time to catch up.

She had been too anxious to eat much of anything, but had taken sips of tea as she told them of Lady Clayton's illness and demise, which had led to her unexpected holiday and reappearance at Oakmoor. That part had been easy. Yet, she could feel both her mother and Amelia watching her, then trading glances with one another, as if communicating silently. The two had grown close, and she could see that they both understood there was more going on here … something Lydia was not telling them.

They waited until Michael had left them, declaring he had some affairs to tend to, before joining them this evening for dinner. Pausing to kiss both their mother and his wife, he tousled Lydia's hair again, before tugging on her earlobe in a way he knew set her teeth on edge.

"Welcome home, imp," he teased before leaving the room and closing the door behind him.

"Now that he is gone," Amelia declared, turning to face Lydia's mother. "Perdita, shall I ask her, or will you?"

Lydia frowned, her hands breaking out into a sweat. They knew something.

"Ask me what?" she hedged.

Her mother gave her a stern expression, before reaching for the teapot. "You were never any good at playing coy, Lydia."

"It is true," Amelia declared, polishing off her biscuit and reaching for another while rubbing her swelling belly. "One of the few things I tried to teach you that you couldn't quite master. Pistols, you excelled at … playing coy and keeping your feelings out of your eyes, you failed at time and time again."

She scowled, uncertain whether to be insulted or relieved that they'd broached the subject. "It wouldn't be a proper homecoming without your tactlessness, Amelia."

Shrugging, Amelia took a bite of her biscuit while her mother stirred milk into her tea.

"Something has happened," her mother declared. "I can see it all over your face. A mother is rarely wrong about such things. What is it, Lydia?"

Sighing, she arranged herself more comfortably on the loveseat she occupied, kicking off her slippers and folding her legs beneath her. "This is difficult. I have wanted to tell you about this so often … but worried you would not understand."

Her mother eyed her over the rim of her teacup, her gaze far too knowing. She'd always been that way, able to look at one of her children and decipher just what they needed. She'd been told she was Perdita's image, with the same blonde hair and face. Though, on Lydia, the features could often appear downright girlish, while her mother had grown into those same traits with age, the silver in her hair and lines around her eyes marking her with wisdom and grace.

"My dear, I am your mother, and Amelia is your sister. Even when we may not completely understand you, we will always love you."

She'd known that, but the reminder of her mother's unconditional love gave her the courage she needed to tell them everything. And Amelia, who had indulged in her share of affairs before marrying Michael at the age of thirty, might even know something of what Lydia had been through.

"Four years ago, at a ball in London, I met a man," she began. "We … we were only together for a short time. No more than an hour, if that. I cannot explain what happened, but I do believe I fell quite madly in love with him."

Amelia choked on her tea, eyes wide with disbelief, while her mother raised her eyebrows.

"I see," Perdita said, clearing her throat and setting her cup aside. "Did you … were you compromised?"

She wanted to tell them that, yes, Sinclair had ruined her. A single kiss from him had been enough to ruin her for any man who came after him.

"No," she said instead. "But my time with him left an impression. So much so that I was miserable the rest of the Season for want of him."

Amelia wiped her mouth with a napkin, setting her teacup and saucer aside. "Is that why you were so miserable? I had wondered what it could be, but thought you simply had a difficult time adjusting. London can be daunting for a young girl fresh from the country."

Lydia nodded. "That was part of it. I will admit that I did not feel I belonged. I missed home. But more than anything else, I missed *him*. A man whose name I did not even know."

Perdita moved to sit beside Lydia, concern wrinkling her brow as she reached out to take her hand. "Oh, Lydia. I had no idea it had been so difficult for you."

She offered her mother a little smile. "I did not want you to worry for me. You already seemed concerned about my marriage prospects."

"Because I wanted you to find happiness," her mother insisted. "But if remaining unwed would have made you happier, you could have stayed here with me. I would never have pushed you into a Season."

"You didn't," Lydia assured her. "It was what I thought I wanted. After realizing none of it was enough to stop me from thinking of this man ... I did not believe I could ever make a match. The idea of marriage no longer pleased me, and no matter how many men I allowed to court me, none of them could keep my interest. Living at Oakmoor had become difficult for me. Seeing Michael and Archie so happy with their families ... it just made me mourn the things I thought I'd never have."

Amelia rose and came to sit on the floor near Lydia's feet, taking her other hand and giving it a squeeze. "I wish you would have come to me, Lydia. We were always close, you and I."

A lone tear streaked down Lydia's face, and she sniffled, trying to keep the rest at bay. "I wanted to, but you and Michael were so happy, and I know how difficult it was for the two of you in the beginning. I did not want to burden you. So, I left. Becoming a governess seemed like the best way to escape living at Oakmoor while making my own way in the world. Living here as an unwed spinster would make me feel like a burden before long, and I wanted to feel useful."

"I would insist that you could never be a burden," her mother said. "But I know you. You will insist otherwise, even now."

"I would," Lydia agreed. "It was what I felt I needed to do. But then, I was hired by Lady Clayton. Things were going so well at first … until I discovered that Mr. Clayton was none other than the man from that ball in London."

Her mother gasped, while Amelia grinned, shifting to a more comfortable position on the floor.

"Oh, this is like something out of a novel," she murmured, earning herself a withering glare from Perdita.

"Lydia," her mother said, her voice stern but uncertain. "Please tell me you did not … with your employer?"

Lydia bit her lip, trying to determine where to go from here. She did not want to lie to her mother, but some parts of her relationship with Sinclair felt too close to her heart to share.

"It isn't what you may think," she said quickly, her hands beginning to shake. "His marriage was a loveless one, but even still, he was determined to honor his vows. We tried … we resisted, but our feelings for one another were always there, stronger than ever."

Amelia laid her chin on Lydia's knee and sighed. "An honorable sort. I like him already."

Perdita's mouth grew tight at the corners as she stared off across the room, seeming unable to meet Lydia's gaze.

"Mother, please, look at me," she urged. "I know you must think me horrible for loving a married man, but I could not help it any more than I could having blue eyes."

Perdita turned to her, looking as if she might weep. "Tell me you have not become his mistress, Lydia. Tell me you have not allowed this man to turn you into something … something your father and I, and Michael, raised you not to be. Even for love, there are certain things a lady should never allow herself to fall to. Not when she has a loving family to come home to."

"I am not his mistress," she said. "But I will not lie to you, Mama. We could only resist one another for so long."

Amelia sighed. "It is not ideal, but one can hardly fault you for your feelings. Besides, I've met Lady Drucilla Clayton and have heard some less than favorable rumors about her ... habits. It's no wonder Mr. Clayton was miserable with her."

"Amelia!" Perdita exclaimed. "Honestly. The woman has just died."

Amelia shrugged. "That does not negate the truth about her, Perdie. Besides, her death means that he and Lydia can now be together."

Lydia's mother probed her with a pensive gaze, her chin quivering. "Is that what will happen now, Lydia? Will you return to Buckton to become his wife?"

"Th-that has not been decided officially," she hedged, choosing her words very carefully. "Sinclair has made it clear he wants a future with me. But we are both aware that it may not happen as quickly as we might want. There is Henry to consider, after all. We would not want him to think we are trying to replace his mother."

Perdita lowered her head, taking in a deep breath and releasing it on a sigh before looking back at Lydia. "You are two and twenty years old, and have always known your own mind. If you tell me you love this man, and that he loves you, I believe you. But I cannot pretend I do not have reservations concerning the circumstances that brought you together. I must also say this ... I have concerns that this man's supposed ardor for you will cool once this part of his life has passed. Perhaps he thought you a pleasant diversion, someone to find succor in during his loveless marriage. I do not wish to frighten or worry you, but you must prepare yourself for the possibility that things might change now."

She shook her head, her heart sinking at the thought of her mother coming to dislike Sinclair before she'd ever met him. It would break her heart if her family could not accept the man she loved.

"I understand why you feel that way, Mama," she said, turning her hand over and fitting her palm against her mother's. "But when you meet Sinclair, and come to know him, you will see. You will love him, as I do, I am sure of it."

Raising her chin, Perdita nodded. "Very well. I will reserve my opinions for after I have met this Mr. Clayton. When will that be, exactly?"

She glanced to Amelia, who gave her a little smile of encouragement. Lydia knew if she could count on anyone in this, it would be her sister-in-law. She would help bring her mother around.

"A few weeks at the least, a few months at most," she said. "Lady Clayton's body needed to be transported to Belcourt so she could be buried among her family. Sinclair thought some time spent there with the Strattons would be good for Henry. He will write to me when he intends to return home, and we will determine how things will happen from here. You'll see, Mama. Everything will be all right."

With another sigh, Perdita nodded. "Very well. I am glad you are home, and will enjoy your company in the meantime. Now, there is only one last issue at hand, and we are not leaving this room until it has been dealt with."

Lydia furrowed her brow, confused. "What issue is that?"

Perdita looked to Amelia, who winced, averting her gaze.

"Which of us is going to tell Michael about this?" she asked.

CHAPTER 18

Sinclair's grip on his reins tightened as he rode into view of Oakmoor Manor, the sprawling mansion situated in a holding that spanned tens of thousands of acres. Despite the anxiety twisting his insides into knots, he found himself smiling. Somewhere within those walls, Lydia waited for him.

They'd been apart far longer than he had intended, his time at Belcourt with Drucilla's family having given way to an unexpected journey to Essex, where matters of his estate there demanded his attention. He'd put things to rights as quickly as he'd been able while spending all his spare time with Henry. The boy seemed more himself as the days went on, though he often fell into moments of melancholy. The evenings were especially hard, as he was accustomed to spending time with his mother just before bed. Henry had taken to sleeping with him, and Sinclair found it chased away his own loneliness, so he did not mind sharing his bed with the lad in the least.

He'd written to Lydia often, assuring her of his continued devotion and his intention to come to her as soon as possible. She'd sent letters of her own, telling him of her family's reservations concerning their relationship, but assuring him that the Darlings would love him once they'd met him.

So, here he was, setting out from the inn in Norfolk, where he had left Henry in the care of Mrs. Beecham. It was his intention to call upon Lydia, meet her family, and perhaps find some way to assure them that his intentions were honorable ones. He could not remain in Norfolk long, matters at Buckton requiring his return. However, it was his hope that when he left, he would have Lydia with him. And once he got her back home, he was never letting her out of his sight again.

As he drew near the house, he was forced to pull up on his reins at the sight of a figure racing toward him across the grounds. Squinting against the bright afternoon sun, he made out a person in a white shirt and breeches, a pair of braces holding them up over her shoulders. Her hair hung over one shoulder in a messy golden braid, stray strands falling around her face.

A wide grin split his face as he dismounted, abandoning his horse to set off in her direction. Leaving the lane, he dashed across the soft grass blanketing the well-manicured land surrounding the manor, his eyes fixated upon the woman growing closer by the second.

A little laugh escaped him, and he opened his arms as she came flying at him, her body colliding with him, arms and legs wrapping around him so tightly, he could hardly tell where she ended and he began. He buried his face in her hair and inhaled, flooding his senses with the scent of open air and Lydia.

She was laughing, the sound so joyous, his heart swelled as she clung to him, kissing his face, his neck, his lips. He kissed her back, keeping a firm grasp on her as he turned and began walking back toward his horse, refusing to put her back on her feet.

"Are all men welcomed to Oakmoor this way?" he quipped.

Lydia giggled, gracing him with another kiss, this one on the tip of his nose. "Yes. It is why we get so many visitors."

He scowled, giving her arse a little pinch through the indecent breeches. "Hmm. I do not know whether to be amused or jealous of all the men who have visited here in the past three months."

"Oh, you ought to be curious," she teased, her lips and tongue tickling his ear and sending a lightning strike of pure desire straight to his groin. "Don't you want to know what the most handsome of Oakmoor's visitors are treated to?"

He paused near his mount, which had remained docile, waiting for his return. This time, he gave her bottom a good slap before setting her on her feet.

"Behave yourself," he scolded. "I wish to make a good impression on your brother, and I cannot do that if he catches me carrying you off into the woods so that I can mount you."

Folding her hands behind her back, she rocked back and forth on her heels and gave him a coy smile. "I would rather it was the other way around."

Sinclair's mouth fell open, and he studied her again from head to toe, taking in the familiar as well as the changes that had come over her in their time apart. She looked like herself, only more beautiful and vibrant than he remembered. Her expression … he'd never seen her so happy, so free. The men's clothing suited her more than any gown he'd ever seen her in, the single braid hanging over her shoulder giving her an air of girlish innocence that only made her more endearing. She was no girl, however. The curves presenting themselves through the snug breeches belonged to a woman … one he knew the taste and feel of.

This what she had meant, when she told him she'd begun to feel more like herself. This laughing girl standing before him, her eyes twinkling and her skin flushed from the mad dash across the lawn … she was perfect, and beautiful. Now, she would be his.

He gestured toward the horse. "There will be time enough for that later. For now, get on the horse."

She gave him a sly glance as she passed him, but did his bidding, swinging herself up into the saddle and sliding forward to make room for him. He came up behind her, taking the reins again, which allowed him to keep her held between his arms. As they continued toward the house, she laid her head back against his shoulder with a sigh.

"I've missed you," she murmured.

He kissed her temple. "And I've missed you. Henry has, as well. He wanted to come with me to see you, but I wanted him to stay behind at the inn with Mrs. Beecham until I had gotten this part out of the way."

She laughed. "You might have done better to bring him. The fastest way to my mother's heart is with a child … the younger and more adorable, the better."

Sinclair chuckled. "I will remember that if she turns out to hate me after this first meeting."

He wanted to tell her more … about all the things he'd been dreaming of doing to her during their time apart, how he intended to make up for being away from her for so long. However, they had drawn close to the house, and at the top of the front steps stood a veritable giant of a man.

Sinclair's mouth fell open as he reined up his mount, staring up at the chap built like the trunk of a tree. Even from this distance, Sinclair could see this man stood at least a head taller than him. Hair the same shade of Lydia's fell around his face while a pair of indiscernible eyes bored into him from a hard, implacable face.

"Christ above," he murmured in Lydia's ear. "Is that your brother?"

Lydia snorted. "Yes, but do not allow him to intimidate you. He isn't nearly as fearsome as he looks."

Based on the massive arms straining the seams of the man's coat, Sinclair begged to differ. As he dismounted, then offered Lydia a hand down, he told himself that he could do this. He'd never had to work hard to impress Drucilla's family, as he'd gained their approval as a friend of Milton's first, eventually becoming a suitor to their daughter. This family knew only that he was Lydia's employer who had just been widowed three months prior.

While he admired that Lydia had been honest with her family about him, he also dreaded their opinions on the matter. He did not need their approval to wed Lydia, but he wanted it. He would prefer not to estrange her from her family if he could help it.

So, as he took Lydia's hand and allowed her to lead him up the front steps, leaving his horse in the care of a stable groom, he squared his shoulders and held his head high. This brother of hers had had a hand in raising her, and Sinclair respected that. He would take things from here, and he needed Mr. Darling to see him as a serious suitor for his sister's hand, not simply some rake who had duped her into an illicit affair.

Lydia grinned up at the giant once they reached the open front doors, flanked on either side by large, smooth, white pillars. "Michael, if you continue making that face, it will become stuck that way and you'll scare all the tenants' children."

The man's scowl deepened as he shot his sister a glare, though Sinclair immediately registered the clear affection between them.

"Amelia, Mama, and Hesper are in the rose drawing room with the children having tea," Michael declared. "Go and join them. Mr. Clayton and I have matters to attend to in my study, and will join you when we have finished."

Lydia stiffened, her hand tightening around his. She glanced up at him, but Sinclair smiled at her and nodded.

"It's all right," he murmured. "I will see you in a moment."

Lydia nodded, though she still seemed uncertain about leaving them alone. Eventually, she dropped his hand, reluctantly edging past Michael. Sinclair fought back a smirk at the warning glare she gave her brother before disappearing inside.

Tearing his gaze away from the sight of those enticing hips of hers swaying beneath those damned breeches, he glanced up at the man towering over him.

Extending a hand, he cleared his throat. "Sinclair Clayton. Lydia has told me quite a lot about you. She speaks of no one as highly as she does you."

Michael accepted his hand and shook it with an iron grip. "Michael Darling. Lydia tells us good things about you, as well. While she is beyond the age of needing a guardian, my father entrusted me to see to her happiness and well-being. So, I am certain you understand that I wish to have a word with you before anything else occurs between you and my sister."

He inclined his head at the man, looking past the gruff exterior and finding curiosity and concern in the depths of his eyes. This, he could understand. This, he could handle.

"Naturally," he replied. "I would expect nothing less."

"My study is right this way," Michael said, motioning for Sinclair to follow him.

He took stock of what little of the house he could see, finding it not so different from Buckton, though it was several times larger. The Darlings were a wealthy family, though lacking a title. Lydia had told him it had been Amelia's massive dowry which had saved Oakmoor from ruin five years ago when a series of unfortunate events had left them in dire straits. Things seemed to be on the mend now, the lands he'd passed through on his way in flourishing, the tenants' cottages a testament to the generosity of their landowner.

Once the two men were alone, Michael gestured toward two armchairs near the fire while crossing to the sideboard himself. "Drink?"

"Whisky, if you have it," Sinclair replied.

"Lydia's favorite," Michael said while filling two tumblers.

Sinclair grinned, remembering the first time he'd watched her take a sip of whisky and his shock over her enjoyment of the drink.

"Yes, I know."

Michael eyed him curiously. He offered Sinclair the tumbler, and the two sat facing one another.

The large man barely fit into his chair, resting his tumbler on one knee and slouching a bit. Sinclair crossed one leg over the other, his ankle rested on his thigh, and took a sip of the drink. It was a fine whisky, as good as the stuff he kept at Buckton.

"Lydia has told us a bit about how the two of you met," Michael began. "As well as the events that led to her becoming a governess in your home. Needless to say, we were quite concerned at the notion of Lydia becoming involved with a married man."

They were cutting right to the chase, then. Good. Sinclair appreciated that the man did not seem to want to dance around the issue at hand.

"The circumstances were not ideal," he replied. "But there are a great number of things you may not be aware of. Such as the fact that my marriage was no real marriage at all. Or that I never coerced Lydia into doing anything against her will, nor did I ever use my position as her employer to gain favors from her. Anything that happened between us occurred for one simple reason. We love each other. No matter how hard we fought not to give in to our feelings, some things just cannot be helped."

Michael studied him, taking a few sips of whisky while seeming to try to take his measure.

"I understand the intricacies of marriage as well as anyone else," he said after a while. "Not all unions are loving ones, and many wedded couples live separate lives. My concern, Mr. Clayton—and I can attest that my mother shares this sentiment—is that your attachment to Lydia might have been born out of discontent in your marriage … that perhaps it is not Lydia you love, but the idea of her, the notion that she could offer you something Lady Clayton could not."

Sinclair stiffened, his teeth clenching as the other man's words struck him like a blow to the face. He took a deep breath and fought not to lash out, to ask the man where he had been while Lydia had been living the life of a lonely, spinster governess, removed from her family. But, he needed this man to like him, to accept his union with Lydia. As well, he understood that Michael's concerns were valid only because he did not know Sinclair, did not understand the depth of his affection for Lydia.

"The first time I saw your sister, she was sitting in a tree," he said.

Michael's brow wrinkled, but his lips twitched as if he found that amusing. "A tree?"

"A tree," Sinclair confirmed. "I saw her and wondered what a lovely young woman, obviously one of good breeding, could be doing in such a position. I made it my business to find out, and what I discovered quite knocked me off my feet. I learned that Lydia is unlike any woman I have ever known. Then, when I found her again, I was shown just how true that is. I might not know her as well as you do, but I do know that she loves to walk and run outdoors, that she loves to ride. I know that she can hit a spoon dangling from a bit of twine with a rifle at twenty yards. I know that ham and eggs are her favorite breakfast and that she enjoys lemon in her tea. I know that she loves her family more than anything in the world, and her worst fear all these years has been disappointing you or making you worry. I know that she has shown my son so much love and affection that my heart aches when I see them together. I know that she loves whisky and hates sherry, that she prefers breeches to gowns, and that she is tone deaf."

Michael chuckled, the smile that split his lips transforming his face at once into an almost boyish visage. It reminded him of the girlish charm in Lydia's grin.

"Perhaps the worst singer in all of England and an even worse pianoforte player."

Sinclair smiled at that, but went on, needing this man to understand him. "I spent ten years married to a woman who spurned me, who made me feel as if I were alone in my own home every hour of every day. A woman who cuckolded me, and attempted to emasculate me at every turn. I have had my fair share of opportunities to conduct affairs, have come across many women who were willing to give me everything Drucilla denied me. I never professed love for any of them. I never longed for any of them. I never cared for any of them. So, you see, that is how I know that this is real. Because, it is not the idea of Lydia that I love … it is the woman who *is* Lydia that I love. I have promised her a future, and I intend to uphold that promise with or without your blessing. I would rather have it, as I know how close Lydia is with her family, you especially. I would never want to destroy what you have, or force her to choose between us."

Michael was silent again, the tumbler moving in a slow circle as he worried it with his hand. After what felt like an eternity, he finally softened, his expression melting away into something more approachable, the lines between his eyebrows disappearing.

"Well, Sinclair … I can confess you've caught me off guard," he said with a little laugh. "Here I've been thinking I would take you to task for taking advantage of my sister, and you come in here and say such wonderful things about her. I hardly know what to say to that."

"Say you'll give us your blessing to wed," Sinclair replied. "It is what I want, and it is what Lydia wants. Too many things have stood between us until now. We just want to be together."

Michael took another sip of his whisky, then smiled. "Amelia and I had a less than conventional beginning, so I can hardly begrudge you that. The circumstances aside, I can see that you truly do care for my sister. So, I will give you my blessing to wed her and help smooth the way with my mother … if you give me something in return."

The tension in Sinclair's spine eased a bit, and he released a little sigh of relief. "If it's within my power, you can have it."

Michael's expression grew serious again as he sat up straight, leveling Sinclair with a meaningful glance. "Nine months."

Sinclair frowned. "I beg your pardon?"

"I want you and Lydia to wait nine months before you marry. Hear me out," he said quickly, when Sinclair opened his mouth to protest. "I assume you intend to reside primarily in Hertfordshire with Lydia, at Buckton?"

Sinclair nodded, wondering what Michael could be getting at. "Of course."

"As I thought. You would take Lydia back to Buckton now and wed her, three short months after your wife's death, after Lydia has lived in your home as a governess for several months before that. Do you not see how this could pose a problem for you both?"

Sinclair's heart sank as he considered this. He hadn't thought of how things might appear to anyone else. He'd been so determined to make Lydia his, to end both their torment.

"I hadn't thought of it that way," he said, bringing his fingers up to one pulsating temple.

Nine months without Lydia? He had already gone so long deprived of her, and was not certain he could survive another nine long months. He would have been away from her for an entire year by then.

"You should come to visit her whenever you can," Michael went on. "She ought to remain here, so that a time of separation can offer her a bit of respectability. If rumors have begun circulating about the two of you, the time apart will help to squelch them. I will not keep you from her. Come as often as you wish. You will be welcomed here at Oakmoor, where we have dozens of guest chambers you may use."

"I suppose that makes sense. Though, I can tell you, Lydia will not be pleased with being made to wait."

Michael snorted. "You leave her to me. So long as you honor my request, and she does not turn up pregnant before the wedding, you have my most ardent blessing."

Rising to his feet, Michael set his glass aside and offered Sinclair his hand once more. "Do we have an agreement?"

Sinclair stood, as well, accepting Michael's hand. "We do. Thank you for hearing me out."

"I was willing to give you a chance simply because Lydia loved you. Now, I feel confident in my decision based off our conversation. May I be the first to welcome you to our family? We are loud, and our numbers are high, but there's always room for one more."

Sinclair couldn't help another smile at that as Michael took his shoulder and guided him toward the door, declaring it was time to join the rest of the family.

Family. It had always been the most uncertain part of his life. He'd lost his mother, only to learn his father had decided to take him in. Even then, his father's true family had shunned him, his half-siblings following their mother's lead in treating him as an outsider. The Strattons had been the closest thing he'd ever had to a family, and Drucilla had tainted that for him over the years. Henry was all he'd had, and had been enough for him thus far.

But, as he entered the drawing room to find the Darling brood with Lydia sitting in their midst, he realized that that part of his life had just come to an end. Lydia rose from where she'd sat on the floor playing with children he assumed to be her nieces and nephews and came to him, gaze searching, expectant. Grasping her shoulders, he kissed her cheek.

"Well?" she prodded.

"Nine months," he told her, his voice low so the others could not overhear. "Michael has asked we wait that long to wed, and we have his blessing."

She started as if he'd struck her, indignation rising swiftly in her expression. "Nine months?"

He kissed her on the lips this time, chastely—the most he dared to do with Lydia's mother looking on from the corner of the room. "It will help keep the gossip to a minimum over the swiftness of our union. When I bring you to Buckton as my wife, I would hate for our neighbors to shun you, spreading gossip over things they know nothing about. It will be better this way, you'll see."

Lydia sighed, seeming to relent, though she still did not look pleased. "I suppose you are right. But, nine months is such a long time when it feels as if we've already been kept apart so long."

Giving her a little smile, he stroked her cheek. "I feel as if I've been waiting for you my entire life. What is nine months in comparison to that? Besides, we will not be kept apart. I would never allow anything to keep me from you. We will be together, and it will be forever."

Lydia returned his smile, the last of her reticence melting away. "Have I told you how much I love you?"

He chuckled. "Yes, but I'll never grow tired of hearing it. Now, your family is starting to stare. Perhaps you might introduce me?"

"Oh!"

She blushed, taking his hand and pulling him farther into the room. Michael had perched on the arm of a sofa, one arm around the slender shoulders of a woman who could only be Amelia. She wore trousers and a well-tailored frock coat, the swell of her midsection showing against the fabric of her shirt. Beside her sat a slender, mousy woman, who must be Lydia's other sister-in-law, Hesper. Sharing a loveseat nearby was a man not quite as large as Michael, but with similar coloring who could only be Archie, and Lydia's mother, Perdita Darling.

Lydia had written about them so much, he felt as if he already knew them, so found it easy to be brought into their midst, settling into an armchair while Lydia pulled a matching one from across the room so she could sit beside him.

As he was introduced to Lydia's mother, the woman took his hand and gazed at him with eyes so open and wise that he nearly wept. He felt as if he was seeing Lydia in thirty more years, with grey strands turning her hair silver and smile lines enhancing her eyes.

"Welcome, Sinclair," she said with a warm smile he felt to his soul, easing the last of his trepidation. "Lydia thinks the world of you, so I am anxious to come to know you better. Oh, and you should leave whatever stuffy old inn you are occupying immediately and bring your precious son here. I will not have you staying anywhere else while you are in Norfolk. Our home is your home now."

Sinclair glanced to Lydia, who gave him a little nod and a reassuring smile. This would take some growing used to, this warmth and camaraderie that felt so foreign to him.

"I would be delighted, thank you," he managed.

Lydia made the rest of the introductions, and before long, Amelia had sent for champagne to toast to Sinclair and Lydia's engagement.

While they waited for it to arrive, Lydia reached out to take his hand, giving it a little squeeze. As he turned to look into her eyes, an overwhelming sense of rightness fell over him in that moment. And for the first time in his life, he realized why he'd never felt as if he belonged anywhere. It was because he hadn't found this yet, this woman, this family.

At last, Sinclair was home.

EPILOGUE

*L*ydia dashed down the opening between the trees, her skirts gathered in both hands, little giggles escaping from between her lips as she let the shadows claim her. The pounding of footsteps behind her warned of Sinclair's approach, which only made her heart pound faster, her breaths come more swiftly. The moon hung high over them in a cloudless summer sky, casting the shadows of the trees against the ground. It illuminated this year's cherries, ripe and red and nearly ready for harvesting.

Ducking between two of the trees, she dashed farther into the groves, leading Sinclair out of sight of the house and anyone who might happen to peer through one of the windows. She had spent her entire day being gawked at and fawned over, congratulated over champagne toasts and wedding cake. But now, tonight, she did not want any other eyes on her. She did not need well wishes or champagne. Just now, she only needed Sinclair, moonlight, and the rather sturdy-looking branches of the cherry tree nestled in a far-flung corner of the orchard.

Taking hold of the lowest limb, she hoisted herself up, doing her best not to ruin the custom-made gown her mother had insisted upon for this day. Lydia was her only daughter, after all, and Michael and Amelia had ruined her opportunity to plan a lavish wedding by procuring a special license and getting married in a London drawing room.

So, Lydia had married Sinclair in a church, though their own special license had allowed them to host the wedding in the evening instead of the morning, which they both preferred. Lydia had wanted moonlight shining down on her as she left the church, the exact lighting in which she'd first laid eyes on her husband.

As she climbed, holding the short train of her silver and pale blue gown over one arm, she thought back to the ceremony with fondness. It had been everything she'd ever wanted in a wedding—Amelia standing up with her, Michael giving her away, Sinclair's deep, solemn voice wrapping hypnotically around her as he said his vows, her mother looking on with tears in her eyes.

All the waiting, the wanting, the trials that had preceded this moment, had been worth it. As she settled on a limb halfway up the tree, her legs dangling over the side, the moonlight catching on the tiny clear gems embroidered into her gown, Lydia decided she would not have done any of it differently. Even the four years of longing and loneliness had been worth it.

The sudden appearance of Sinclair below sent her heart spiraling up into her throat. He was resplendent in black, much like on the night she'd met him—only now, his waistcoat was a robin's egg blue with a silvery sheen to match her gown.

A sudden thought occurred to her, a memory brought to life by the sight of him under her, head turning left and right as he searched for her.

Bracing her toes against the heel of her opposite foot, she pushed her slipper off, allowing it to dangle for a moment, before flicking her foot and allowing it to fall. It landed true, striking Sinclair's shoulder and drawing his attention upward.

His white teeth glowed in the dark when he smiled, his laughter floating toward her. That sound sent warmth suffusing through her from the depths of her belly out to the far reaches of her body. With each day, week, and month that had passed since Drucilla's death, she'd watched Sinclair transform. Still brooding at times, because it seemed such a part of his nature, but also less burdened, no longer sullen. He smiled often, he laughed with a freedom she'd never before noticed in him. If she'd thought she could not love him more, she'd been unprepared for this.

Retrieving her shoe, he tucked it into the breast pocket of his coat and began to climb. He reached her in no time at all, swinging one leg over the limb she perched on, leaning back against the trunk as he studied her, his dark eyes glittering with desire and love.

"Ah, a fallen angel right here in my own groves," he teased, reaching out to caress a curl that had fallen free of her coiffure. "May I keep you forever?"

She gave him a coy smirk. "That all depends, sir. You see, angels need certain things to thrive, and I must be sure that you can provide them before I promise to stay with you."

Leaning forward a bit, his lips curving into the most deliciously wicked smirk, he raised an eyebrow at her. "Whatever you need, I feel more than up to the task of providing it."

A little thrill went through her as he took her hand, tugging at her gloves to free her of them.

"Well, we need laughter and freedom," she told him, watching as he divested her of first one glove and then the other.

"I shall endeavor to keep laughter dancing on your lips," he murmured, kissing the back of her hand and working his way up her arm. "And you are free to be whomever you want to be with me, even if who you wish to be just now happens to be a wanton slut."

Lydia gasped, slapping playfully at his chest. "Sin!"

"What?" he countered with a shrug. "I have not seen you in weeks and haven't had you to myself all day. But, do go on. What else does my angel need?"

"Rifles and pistols," she declared as he went back to kissing her arm, intertwining his fingers with hers. "We angels enjoy our target practice, after all. And horses, and whisky, and cigars."

"You like cigars?"

She inclined her head. "Well, I do not know yet, as I've never tried one. But I would like the option."

He snorted, as if he found her both insufferable and adorable at the same time. "Your every wish is my command, angel. And what of kisses? Does my angel need to be kissed?"

She gasped when he took hold of her waist and urged her closer, his strength making her confident that she would not go falling out of the tree. "Yes … often."

He nuzzled her neck, placing a kiss there, then working his way up toward her mouth. "I shall drown you in kisses every day. What of caresses, my angel? Do you need my hands on you?"

Her only reply came on a whimper as he cupped her breast, his fingers seeking out her nipple and giving it a light tug. She was dizzy, the sky spinning about over her, the tree limb seeming to sway below, Sinclair's grip on her the only thing keeping her from floating away.

He was still kissing her, his hand busy at her bodice, dipping inside to cup her through her stays and chemise.

"What else, angel? Tell me what else you need, and it is yours."

Turning her body a bit, she threw her arms around him. "You, Sin. I only need you."

His lips claimed hers, his urgency stoking an answering need in her. She moaned against his mouth, her body coming to life at his touch and reminding her that six long weeks had stood between their last meeting and today's wedding. Now that she knew what it was to be loved by him, to feel him inside her, she could not believe she'd survived so long without it. She felt as if she would go up in flames from only the stroke of his tongue against hers, the nip of his teeth at her lower lip.

Then, he was grasping her legs, helping her to turn and face him, straddling the branch just as he did. Heat flared in his gaze at the sight of her, skirts now hitched up around her hips, legs bared, her other slipper having fallen to the ground below them. The rough bark abraded the insides of her thighs through her stockings, but Sinclair swiftly put an end to that, grasping her hips and pulling her until she straddled him.

The limb they sat on was quite sturdy, the ancient cherry tree more than strong enough to bear their combined weight. Taking her face in his hands, he kissed her again, deeper this time, slower, seeming to relish the sensations of their lips and tongues meeting and parting in a languid dance. He tasted of cake and champagne, and some other thing that seemed uniquely Sinclair.

His hands traveled, stroking her hair, smoothing over her back, grasping her buttocks to fit her closer to him, so she could feel the thick ridge of desire straining toward her through his breeches.

"Lydia," he murmured, sprinkling little kisses along her collarbone, then dipping his tongue into her bodice to find her nipple. "If we do not stop this, I am going to fulfill the promise I made to you on the night we met. Do you remember?"

She grinned at the reminder. Sinclair had urged her to climb out of the tree and leave before their kiss turned into something more. He had promised her that he'd want to free his cock and thrust inside her, not letting the fact that they were sitting in a tree stop him.

Her smile turned devilish as she reached down between them, finding his fall. "I've always been curious how you would have managed that."

His eyelids grew heavy as he gazed down to watch her deftly open his breeches. "This angel is definitely fallen. Thrown out of Heaven for being such a little wanton."

She giggled, taking hold of his cock and giving him a squeeze. He groaned, the organ pulsing in her fist. "Whatever will you do with me?"

Reaching down to help her free him completely, he finished

hitching up her skirts, ensuring she was free from the tangle of petticoats and chemise as he angled her over him. His knuckles brushed against the wet inner flesh as he urged his cock toward her opening, forcing a little gasp from her at the sudden contact.

"Hold on to me, angel," he told her, one hand holding tight to her hip and urging her down onto his erection. "You'll have to hold on tight unless you want to go tumbling out of this tree."

She did as he instructed, grasping his shoulders, her head falling back with a sigh as she sank onto him, his cock filling her inch by slow inch. His kisses and caresses had been enough to make her wet, their time apart making her desperate for him.

He groaned against her shoulder, kissing and lapping at her pulse with his tongue, one hand coming up to pull her bodice, chemise, and stays down to free her breasts. His other hand squeezed her arse, urging her to undulate against him, ride him to her satisfaction. The motion sent a ripple of ecstasy through her, her place on top of him allowing him in as deep as he could go, their closeness permitting each motion to stimulate her clit.

"Sin," she whispered, his name falling from her lips heavy with awe and wonder as well as love.

She was making love in a tree. Her husband had taken her astride his hips, and she was now riding him while straddling a tree limb. She would have laughed if it didn't feel so bloody good, each surge of her hips creating heat and friction in the place where their bodies were joined, Sinclair's tight grip on her arse and busy mouth on her breasts only adding to the pleasure.

He bit at her nipples with gentle pulls of his teeth, then showered her exposed skin with kisses, traveling up her throat to her lips, then back again, seeking her breasts once again. His breath raced against her skin, teasing the places left damp from his tongue.

"My wicked little angel," he murmured, kissing along the line of her jaw. "Letting me fuck you in a tree on your wedding day. What else will you let me do to you, I wonder?"

She moaned, his wicked words and their location out in the open where they could be seen should anyone decide to venture out for fresh air only adding fuel to her desire, urging her to shift against him faster, pressing down to create even more of the tortuous friction.

"Anything," she whimpered. "You could do anything to me, Sinclair … I am yours, your angel."

"Anything?" he murmured, just before his hand on one of her buttocks began to move, his fingers finding their way into the cleft between her cheeks.

She gasped, her face flaming hot with equal parts shame and shock. "Sinclair!"

His name crescendoed on a cry as his first finger probed her second passage, gently circling it at first, then breaching the tight hole. The foreign pleasure felt wrong and utterly filthy, but oh, so right in the pleasure it shot through her, combining with the slow slide of his cock inside her to send her spiraling toward climax. It shocked her how much she liked it, his invasion of a place that seemed so taboo, so off limits. For all the things she'd been taught about intercourse, this was the one thing that had been left out.

"More?" he asked, his own voice growing strained, as if he hurtled toward his end as quickly as she did.

"Yes!" she cried out, no longer caring to think about what might be right or wrong, or forbidden. Nothing could be forbidden with him, this man who loved her so well.

He obliged her, sinking his finger in deep, probing, finding a place that triggered the spasm of her core around him in climax. She went limp against him, her hoarse cries echoing through the night as the most powerful orgasm she'd ever experienced went through her, knocking the air from her lungs and causing the edges of her vision to grow hazy.

Sinclair followed her, and for the first time since the night she'd offered him her maidenhead, he did not pull away. He no longer needed to. With a guttural groan, he seated himself fully inside her and released, his seed bathing her insides in a warm rush.

She sighed at the feel of it, warm and slick in the place she wanted it most. Smiling against the fabric of his coat, she thought of his seed taking root, of their coupling eventually resulting in new life. It was her deepest desire now that the thing she'd most wanted had been given to her. She had Sinclair for her husband, and now, she wanted more. She wanted the family they'd both dreamt of, wanted to be the one to give him the children he'd longed for.

After, they simply sat there for a time, catching their breaths. Sinclair withdrew both his finger and his cock from inside her, letting her skirts fall over her as much as possible. He swiftly buttoned his fall, then leaned back against the trunk of the tree, satisfaction relaxing his features and making his eyelids heavy.

"That … was everything I always knew it would be," he said with a little laugh. "I fantasized about it often, you know … pulling up your skirts in that tree and having my way with you."

"Yes, well, I hardly thought it would be possible," she admitted. "So, thank you for a most thorough demonstration."

He lifted his sleepy eyes to hers and grinned. "Oh, I look forward to demonstrating plenty of things to you now that we are wed."

A little shiver ran down her spine as she thought of the way he'd just breached her back passage with his finger, that delicious feeling of both embarrassment and lust making her cunt throb for him again.

After a short time for Sinclair to finish gathering his bearings, they descended from the tree, Lydia first, then him. Once on the ground, he helped her back into her slippers, then took her hand to lead her back to the house.

"It has been nice, seeing Buckton so full of people," he remarked as they walked, taking their time along the path leading away from the groves. "People I actually like, anyway."

She smiled, giving his hand a squeeze. "They like you, too. Michael, especially. I think he's been waiting for the day I find a suitable husband so that there can be more men in the family. Mother is quite fond of you. Oh, and it is nice to see Henry getting on so well with my nieces and nephews. He's seemed so happy since they arrived."

"Yes, they get on well, and I am glad," he agreed. "I feel as if I've gained so much by marrying you. You've not only given me yourself, but also an entire family. I hardly feel as if I've given you enough in return."

She halted, her grip on his hand drawing him up short. "What a thing for you to say! Of course you've given me as much as I have you. Perhaps even more so."

He faced her with a sheepish smile and a shrug. "Have I upset you already? Wed less than a day, and I am already in trouble."

She scoffed. "Don't be silly. Of course I am not upset. I only want you to understand that I feel as if I've gained the entire world by marrying you. Do not diminish that ever again."

Inclining his head, he acquiesced. "Yes, of course, my dear. Did I say that well enough? Michael insisted it was the best way to keep you happy with me. 'Yes, of course, my dear.'"

Lydia made a face at him, wrinkling her nose. "Oh, I am going to have a word with him first thing—"

Sinclair drew her to him abruptly, silencing her with a kiss. He kept a hand firm at the small of her back, bending her over a bit until she felt off balance and dizzy as she had in the tree. By the time he'd finished with her, she could hardly think, having forgotten what she'd been about to take him to task over already.

"Hm, I did not think that would work, but Michael was right about that, too," Sinclair quipped. "Quite effective in silencing a wife."

Lydia stamped one foot, hands braced upon her hips. "Is it a silent wife you want, then?"

He took her in his arms again and kissed her, short and sweet. "Of course not, Mrs. Clayton. I quite love the sound of your sweet little voice, and your loud laughter, and your passionate moans most of all."

Her heart fluttered at the sound of her new name falling from his lips. "Call me that again. Mrs. Clayton … I quite liked it."

With a grin, he bent his head to kiss her cheek. "Mrs. Clayton. Yes, it does have a nice ring to it. Shall we go to bed now, Mrs. Clayton? I can think of a few more things I'd like to … show you."

"The last one there must stoke the fire," she declared before taking off at a run toward the house.

Sinclair's shout of dismay rang out through the night, followed by his laughter as he gave chase. Buckton loomed before her, growing closer by the second, her home. And just then, the pounding of her heart had little to do with how swiftly she ran, laughter spilling from her lips. It had everything to do with the thrill of a new adventure, of the life spread out before her with Sinclair.

And so, Lydia decided that dreams were not so foolish, after all. They were not to be shoved aside and forgotten. They were to be cherished and nurtured … because, eventually, somehow, they found a way to come true.

Start the Scandalous Ballroom Encounters Series from the beginning with TWO free books!

Click here to download Masquerade from your favorite ebook retailer!

Continue Camden and Maggie's story with free copy of A Honeymoon Masquerade when you sign up for Victoria's newsletter. Click here to get your freebie!

inheritance, she decides to investigate rumors of a secret London agency which provides the services of male courtesans. Someone to teach her the secrets of the bedchamber and do away with the nuisance of her maidenhead is all Evelyn anticipates from such an arrangement.

The Honourable Hugh Radcliffe is in dire financial straits after being disowned by his family for pursuing a career as a portraitist. When he's asked to go into business to form The Gentleman Courtesans, he agrees, needing the income until his work is accepted into the Royal Academy of the Arts' annual Summer Exhibition—an event that could earn him the exposure needed to launch him to fame.

The arrangement with Evelyn is only supposed to be temporary, and Hugh is determined for her to be his last paramour. But when physical attraction evolves into a deeper connection, she becomes the muse for his greatest work of art yet. With their affair coming to an end, Hugh will be forced to acknowledge that Evelyn is the key to his success as well as his joy.

Will their newfound happiness end when their arrangement does, or will what began as a matter of lust and convenience lead to true and lasting love?

ABOUT THE AUTHOR

Sexy heroes ... sassy heroines ... electrifying erotic romance.
Victoria Vale has written over two dozen Romance and Young Adult
novels under various pseudonyms. As a lover of erotic romance, she
enjoys nothing more than a sexy hero paired with a sassy heroine,
flavored with a dash of spice and lots of heat. A wife and mother of
three, she enjoys reading (of course), cooking, sewing ... and other
activities that aren't appropriate for inclusion in a biography.